2/07

W9-CKI-708

OFFICIALLY NOTED

China Dolls

THOMAS DUNNE BOOKS ≋ ST. MARTIN'S PRESS
New York

China Dolls

**MICHELLE YU
AND BLOSSOM KAN**

This is a work of fiction. All of the characters, organizations, and events portrayed in this novel are either products of the authors' imagination or are used fictitiously.

THOMAS DUNNE BOOKS.
An imprint of St. Martin's Press.

www.thomasdunnebooks.com
www.stmartins.com

Library of Congress Cataloging-in-Publication Data

Yu, Michelle.
    China dolls / Michelle Yu and Blossom Kan.—1st ed.
       p. cm.
    Thomas Dunne Books
    ISBN-13: 978-0-312-36280-5
    ISBN-10: 0-312-36280-3
    1. Asian American women—Fiction.   2. New York (N.Y.)—Fiction.

PS3625.U16 C45 2007
813'.6—dc22   2006050572

First Edition: February 2007

10 9 8 7 6 5 4 3 2 1

for our parents

Acknowledgments

We owe many thanks to too many people to include here. Most particularly, we thank our agent, Natasha Kern, for being the perfect advisor, motivator, and den mother; our editor, Diana Szu, for all her patience and all those lunchtime phone calls and after-work, above-and-beyond-the-call-of-duty coffee breaks; and, of course, our friends and family who believed and supported us all the way, including Kirsten, Patrick, Jaymie, Jerry, and Ken Karp.

Special thanks also to our friends at Ling Skincare Spa, Sean Kelly Gallery, Chelsea Wine Vault, the White Rabbit, and Rickshaw Dumpling Bar.

China Dolls

Prologue

THERE WAS no turning back. Standing at the corner of Canal and Mott, Alex Kwan checked her watch and gazed into the sea of strange faces. It was noon, and the sidewalks of Chinatown were already filled with bustling Asian grandmothers and wandering tourists, drawn by the barks of merchants peddling everything from underwear to baby snapping turtles. A petite young woman with long jet hair and steely charcoal eyes, Alex stood out from the crowd in her crisply tailored black linen suit. She shivered a little as she wondered how she had let her friends talk her into ditching work for this latest unexplained adventure.

"Alex!" a familiar voice called. "Over here!"

Alex turned around to see her two best friends, Lin Cho and M. J. Wyn, hurrying toward her. They were quite the odd couple: Lin, with her perfectly coiffed hair, pashmina wrap, and expensive silk sheath—and M.J., with her ponytail, layered Billabong T-shirts, and cargo pants. A stockbroker and a sportswriter, respectively, they occupied opposite ends of the spectrum in both appearance and personality. Alex was so busy grinning at the contrast that she almost didn't notice their companion: Lin's diminutive mother, Kim.

"Oh, hi, Mrs. Cho, nice to see you. . . ." Alex was completely befuddled at the sight of Lin's frowning, force-of-nature mother. Lin and M.J. had never mentioned they were bringing her along.

"Hello, Alex-ah," Kim greeted her in her usual grave manner.

"You look thin—too thin. You eating? You lawyer—you need to eat more so you can use your brain."

Lin groaned, but Alex couldn't help smiling. She'd known Kim since she was a child; Mrs. Cho was close friends with Alex's mom, and the girls' mothers had all become friends after shuttling their daughters to the same Chinese school for years. For some strange reason, Alex was never as bothered by Kim as Lin was, perhaps because she understood Mrs. Cho's mother-bear instinct all too well.

"*A yi*," Alex said, politely addressing Lin's mom as Auntie, "if I had known you were coming, I would have invited my mother—"

"Actually," Lin interrupted, "Mom is here to take us to *Tai-Sheung*."

Alex blinked. "Tai-what?"

"She means we're going to get our fortunes told," M.J. explained.

"It's not as simple as fortune-telling." Lin paused, momentarily distracted by a display of knockoff Prada handbags. "A lot of Chinese people believe that a person's destiny is determined by the relative yin and yang properties of their face. The woman who we're going to visit—Auntie Lee—is supposed to be really uncanny in reading people's features. She's done this for every one of my aunts and most of their kids, too."

Alex frowned. "But . . . why are we doing this?"

"Because," Lin said, "it's tradition in my family to go have your face read when you have a birthday. And since I just celebrated mine, what better time for all of us to get our fortunes told?" She lowered her voice. "Plus, my mother won't leave me alone . . . I could really use the company!"

"It could be kind of fun." M.J. elbowed Alex. "Don't you want to know if you'll live happily ever after?"

"I don't know." Alex hesitated. "What if she tells me I'm going to end up a crack whore in Times Square?"

"Don't be silly!" Lin interjected. "Would M.J. and I steer you wrong?"

Alex smiled and rolled her eyes. The three women had been friends for years, longer than she could remember. They had been mere munchkins when they were first brought together at their families' holiday gatherings. They had their differences, of course; M.J.'s hip-hop sportswriter lingo often seemed like a foreign language, and Alex and Lin had conflicting views on just about everything. Plus, Alex was a few years older than Lin, who had just turned twenty-seven, and M.J., who was twenty-six. And yet, despite all that, there was an unshakable bond between them that had shielded their friendship from all assailing forces through the years.

"It time for appointment, Alex-ah," Kim said briskly, "we go see Auntie Lee now."

And that was that.

Auntie Lee was nothing like what Alex imagined her to be. She had envisioned some mysterious, gypsylike creature swathed in scarves, predicting death and doom in some dank, dark cave. But Auntie Lee's parlor was a bright, incense-filled little room with red silk lanterns and black lacquered wall coverings, and Auntie Lee herself was a tiny grandmotherly woman in a plain black *meen-nap*, a Chinese quilted jacket, who looked downright . . . sensible.

Still, Alex hung back as they all entered the room. Sensing her hesitation, M.J. gave her a comforting smile and nudged her toward the fortune-teller, who took Alex's hand in hers.

"Don't look so scared, child. Sit down, and let me look at you."

Alex gingerly lowered herself onto the chair across from the old woman. She held her breath as Auntie Lee gently touched her face.

"You have a wide mouth and a broad chin," she announced.

Alex bit her lip. "Is that bad?"

"No, no." Auntie Lee shook her head emphatically. "It means that you have a good and prosperous old age to look forward to."

Okay, Alex thought, at least she wasn't going to end up selling herself on Forty-second Street.

"Tell me," the old woman said, "what do you want, child?"

Alex shrugged. "Nothing. Well, not really."

Auntie Lee looked at her keenly. "We all want something, even if we don't know it . . . or reveal it."

Alex didn't know how to respond to that—so she said nothing.

"There's a lot of conflict going on right now," the fortune-teller continued. "It will take a while before you will be able to find peace. But change is coming and coming soon—you may be surprised when things start happening suddenly."

"What kind of things?" Alex furrowed her brow, not quite sure she liked the sound of that.

"Life-changing things, things you do not expect from people you do not expect," Auntie Lee said very seriously. "But in the end, it will all lead to happiness, if . . ."

"If what?" Alex demanded.

"If you open yourself to new possibilities."

Alex stared at her blankly, wondering what possibilities Auntie Lee could be talking about. Meanwhile, Kim pushed Lin forward.

"My daughter Lin," she said, "when she find good Asian boy and marry?"

Lin clutched her head. "Ma!"

"Lin broker, work all the time. Soon she too old to give me grandchildren."

Lin started to protest but stopped as Auntie Lee caught her face in her hands. They all fell silent as the fortune-teller traced Lin's heart-shaped face.

"You have luck and that will help you find love," she said finally in Cantonese, "but not with who you think."

There was a moment of silence. Then Kim erupted.

"What that mean? Lin marry poor man? Or *bok gwai*, some stupid white guy? *Huck gwai*, a black guy?" Kim looked positively horrified.

"Ma!" Lin yelled. "Stop that—"

As Lin and her mother bickered, M.J. and Alex exchanged wide-eyed looks. M.J. was so busy grinning that she was utterly unprepared for when Auntie Lee turned toward her.

"And you, child? What is it you wish to know?"

M.J. swallowed and took a deep breath. "Auntie Lee, will I achieve my dream of becoming an on-air sportscaster?"

Auntie Lee squinted at her thoughtfully, then ran her fingertips across M.J.'s face.

"You will get what you dream of," she said, "but then you will find that you do not want it anymore."

M.J. frowned. "That would never happen," she muttered. There was no way she was giving up her lifelong dream.

Meanwhile, Auntie Lee sat back, apparently done. M.J. chewed her lip, trying to figure out what her fortune meant. Next to her, Alex looked just as perplexed, no doubt because she wasn't used to not having all the answers.

There was no such confusion for Mama Kim, however. She pushed her way over.

"How soon these things come true?" she demanded, hands on hips. "How soon before my daughter marry some dumb white guy and ruin her life?"

Auntie Lee seemed unfazed by Kim's outbursts. She just stared forward, as though looking at something none of them could see. "By the next Lunar New Year Festival, you will all know your fates." She gazed at each of them slowly, sending a shiver up M.J.'s spine.

Since it appeared Auntie Lee had no further insights for them, they got up to leave. After paying the fortune-teller and promising to come back in the new year, Kim quickly hustled them out, all the while expressing her pet peeves about fortune-tellers who had nothing good to say.

"That was weird," M.J. said once they were in the car and headed toward home.

"You said it." Lin gave a mock shudder, cheerfully oblivious to her mother's mutterings in the backseat.

Alex nodded. "I agree." She pushed her foot down harder on the pedal, eager to get Mama Kim home before she had a stroke.

Mrs. Cho was still carrying on a half hour later as they pulled up at Kim's doorstep. "These fortune-tellers. What do they know? White guy my foot!"

The three women sighed and exchanged looks. But inwardly, they were all beset with the same questions. What had Auntie Lee's fortunes meant? And how could they make her prophecies come true?

m. j.

Thoughts to Wyn

BY M. J. WYN

My obsession began in high school. His name was Justin Howard, and we were both on the school's sports broadcasting team, SPORTV. To the girls in our class, he was a perfect 10 with his blond hair, blue eyes, and made-for-football body. To the guys, he was nothing short of a god.

And then there was me with my black hair, black almond-shaped eyes, and very non-*Baywatch* looks. Maybe I should have known that there never was a contest between us. What did it matter that he didn't know a deuce from an ace or that he couldn't get through two sentences on air without a stutter or a stammer? He was a man, and a white man at that. How could he not be chosen over me as SPORTV's "National High School Sports Correspondent" sophomore year? And yet, even though I knew all this, there I was, crying my eyes out in my room for four straight hours, reenacting a Nancy Kerrigan and screaming "Why? Why me!"

Nobody really understood my pain. They all thought I was in way over my head and a sore loser to boot. Never mind the fact that I was leagues and miles better than Justin Howard or that I'd nailed SPORTV's "entrance exam" while he'd barely mustered a passing mark. After all, what kind of sportscaster didn't know that the Chicago Cubs hadn't won a World Series since 1908 or that the only player in tennis history to win a Golden Slam was Steffi Graf? As I watched Justin high-fiving his buddies and regaling the cheerleaders about the gig he'd been handed on a silver platter, I decided then and there that I'd never feel that way again. But what was a girl to do?

Dyeing my hair blond was an option, but peroxide and I didn't quite go together. Besides, there was still that messy little Y-chromosome problem. So I did the only thing I could do. I studied tapes, obsessed over stats, and played as hard as I could—all in preparation for that one day when my moment would come. If sports has taught me anything, it's that we all need one chance, that one moment when the years of hard work come together in a perfect confluence of timing and events. It's that moment in 1980 when the U.S. Olympic Men's Ice Hockey team won their "Miracle" gold medal. In 2000 when Rulon Gardner beat the Russian Goliath of Greco-Roman wrestling. And in 2004 when the no-name, no-star Detroit Pistons crushed the razzle-dazzle glamour of the L.A. Lakers.

There's no real strategy to finding the right path to life and success. Anyone who's ever played to win knows that working hard is the best way. Not all of us get to land our dreams as quickly as Justin Howard did.

First Quarter

one

"IT'S BOGUS that the score's tied. I thought the Knicks would steamroll through the Clippers for sure." It was Thursday night, and M.J. was trying to shout above the din at the local sports bar, Ship of Fools.

"I don't know how you spend all day watching this stuff." Lin took a sip of her Carlo Rossi. "It's just a bunch of sweaty guys trying to get a ball into a basket. What's so exciting about that?"

M.J. chuckled as she watched Lin make her patented *ew-cheap-wine* face. Lin's taste certainly hadn't changed much since their first day of freshman year in college. She had sighed as she watched her childhood friend show up at the dorm with her twelve-piece, matching Louis Vuitton luggage. With her porcelain skin, silky black hair, and perfectly accessorized wardrobe, Lin was the epitome of sophistication and chic. Next to her, M.J. always felt like a pre–fairy godmother Cinderella, especially with her no-nonsense ponytail and no-name jeans. While she would occasionally make a halfhearted foray into the world of makeup, M.J. always ended up looking like a character fresh out of a Judy Collins song. Somewhere between Lin's amethyst purple cell phone and M.J.'s tennis rackets, however, the two had managed to find common ground.

Lin got up. "I need to see if they have anything better than cooking wine in this place." She wrinkled her nose. "Do you want anything?"

M.J. nodded. "Another Amstel Light would be great, thanks."

She took a look at her watch as Lin stepped away to order their drinks. The Heat–Rockets game was coming up soon on TNT, and she wanted to make sure she didn't miss the big showdown between Yao Ming and Shaquille O'Neal. Just as she gulped down the rest of her beer, the *Knight Rider* ring tone on her cell phone started playing.

"Hello?" M.J. said, putting down her glass.

"Hey, it's Ming. What's happening? What are you up to tonight?"

Ming Chan was a sportswriter with the *Big Apple Times*, as well as the son of a family friend of the Wyns. After meeting at several Lunar New Year parties and spending considerable time together covering games on the road, Ming and M.J. had become good friends. Picturing his round, boyish face and stocky, solid build, she couldn't help smiling.

M.J. cranked up the volume on her phone. "Hey, Ming, I'm good. Actually watching the Knicks game right now at Ship of Fools. You?"

"I'm just finishing up a story—calling to see if you wanted to hang with May and me. But it's Thursday night, so I'm guessing you're out with someone named Harry or William or Prescott."

M.J. rolled her eyes. Growing up in the predominantly Caucasian neighborhood of Riverdale up in the Bronx, she had inevitably dated some of her Abercrombie & Fitch–type classmates.

"You're such a moron, Ming. FYI, I'm not here with any white boys, just Lin. When will you stop with your stupid comments?"

"Whatever," he said, "you're always complaining to me about how you never meet the right guy."

M.J. sighed. "I don't have time for this. I don't know how May puts up with your bullshit."

Ming was undeterred. "That's because May knows about relationships—Asian relationships, that is."

She slapped her hand down on the table. "Ming!"

"Fine, fine. Just don't come crawling to me when your mom flips out the day you head to the altar. I can just imagine how upset she'll be when she sees that her new son-in-law is a white dude."

"Good-bye, Ming," M.J. said curtly. "I'll ring you later. Hopefully, we can do dinner next week."

As she flipped her phone closed, Lin came back with their drinks.

"Who was that on the phone?" she asked.

"Just Ming," M.J. muttered. "I told him to leave me alone."

"Oh, is he ragging on you about your boyfriends again? How are Ming and May, by the way? Still planning the traditional Asian wedding with the red *qipao*?"

"Yup." She nodded. "The two of them are so much in love that I sometimes can't stand hanging out with them. They even take me to Chinatown to scope out Asian men."

"Sounds like something my family would do." Lin rolled her eyes.

M.J. laughed at the thought of Lin's mother, Kim—she could picture her shaking her finger at them and saying, "You marry good Chinese man, you not have these problems."

Lin sipped her drink. "I guess Ming and May don't understand about your thing for preppy types."

M.J. shrugged and took a swig of her Amstel Light. "Yeah, whatever. Let's get back to the game." That was when she caught sight of a made-up blond woman batting her eyelashes at the seven guys milling around her.

"Ugh, J . . . do we really have to sit through another two hours of this?" Lin moaned at the television. "I don't know how you ever got into this basketball thing."

"Oh, come on, Lin, you know I've been a Michael Jordan fan since I was eight." M.J. had had her life mapped out the moment she watched the Chicago Bulls win their first NBA title in 1991. Her birthday was the day after, and when she blew out her eleven birthday candles, she closed her eyes and made a wish that she would one day become the first female Asian sportscaster on ESPN.

"Oh, and guess what? I'm meeting with the sports director of PlayBall Network next week to show him my demo reel."

"No way—that's great! I'm sure you're totally going to dazzle him." Lin looked up at the monitor. "You know, maybe if *you* were announcing these games, I'd be more interested in watching."

M.J. laughed as she glanced back over in the direction of the blond chick, who was making overly enthusiastic cheers every time the Knicks scored a point. It was scenarios like these she couldn't stand. "Looks like that girl's pretending to like sports to get those dudes to like her, and they're eating it all up. Every last one of them."

"Well, not everyone knows sports." Lin turned around to see what was going on. "Look at me—I only know money."

"Yeah, but at least you don't pretend. Some girls just put on this act so they can get a guy. But you know what bothers me most?" M.J. leaned forward. "Men say they like girls who like sports. That's a lie. What they really like are women who prance around in cute little tennis skirts and cheer."

Lin chuckled. "You're probably right. That girl seems pretty clueless."

M.J. finished her third Amstel Light and shoved aside the bowl of peanuts she'd been munching on. Feeling a buzz, she nodded at Lin and started walking toward the guys. Looking like she'd seen this scenario before, Lin trailed after her friend.

"What are you doing, J?" Lin hissed.

"I'm going to prove to you I'm right. Get ready to be entertained," M.J. whispered. She marched up to one of the guys—a typical corporate type—and tapped him on the shoulder. "Excuse me, hi!" M.J. batted her eyelashes. "Do you know how many points Jamaal Winston scored tonight?"

The wannabe Brooks Brothers model in the oxford shirt smiled. "He scored seventeen. Are you a Knicks fan?"

"Of course I am. I've been a fan all my life. My favorite player on the team is Patrick Ewing," she chirped.

The guy laughed as his buddies all turned to check the girls out. Meanwhile, the blonde tossed her hair and pranced away in a huff.

"Umm . . . Patrick Ewing retired." He raised an eyebrow. "He doesn't play for the Knicks anymore."

M.J. clapped a hand to her mouth. "Oops. I didn't know that. He's great, though."

"Yes, he is." One of the other guys smirked. "So, what's your name?

"Well, I'm M.J., and this is my friend, Lin." She smiled. "What about you boys?"

The wannabe Brooks Brothers model nodded toward his friends. "I'm Dan, and these are my buddies, John, Damon, Keith, Lucas, Gil, and Jeremy."

M.J. grinned as she exchanged greetings with the group. She lived for moments like this. There was nothing sweeter to her than toying with a bunch of Neanderthals.

"Nice to meet you all," she said as Lin just smiled.

"Did anyone ever tell you that you look like Lucy Liu?" Damon leered at M.J.

"She gets that sometimes," Lin piped up. "She could be a Charlie's Angel."

M.J. just smiled. "I can definitely kick some ass—when the situation calls for it. So . . . Dan, what other teams do you like?"

"Well, I was a big Bulls fan back in the days of Jordan and Pippen."

"Really? Me, too! I know everything about them."

This was really too easy. Anyone who knew M.J. knew better than to get her started on the Chicago Bulls and Michael Jordan. After all, it had to be fate that she had the same initials as Michael Jordan, right?

"Everything?" Dan chuckled. "You're funny."

"What do you mean?" M.J. opened her eyes wide.

"Well, it's just a bold statement, that's all."

M.J.'s innocent smile turned sly. "You don't believe me, do you?"

"Well . . ." He shrugged. "You did think Ewing still played for the Knicks."

"Try me. Just one question. Loser buys the other a beer. In fact," M.J. paused, "I'll buy all your buddies a round of beer if I'm wrong."

That was enough to make all of Dan's friends turn and cheer him on.

"Sounds good to me." He grinned. "Here's a teaser. Who scored the game-winning shot in the last game of the Bulls' fifth championship title?"

M.J. scratched her head very slowly. "Uh-oh." Then she turned and winked at Lin, who laughed.

"I'm sorry," Dan smirked, "but I guess you owe me and my buddies a round of Bass."

She flashed him her biggest smile. "Not so fast. I believe that the individual you're talking about was a Second Team All-American senior at Arizona in 1988 by the name of Steve Kerr. The current TNT analyst scored with .2 seconds left in the game with an assist by Michael Jeffrey Jordan to lift the Bulls to a 1997 title."

The guys' jaws dropped.

M.J. smiled. "That would be a round of beer for me and my friend, I believe. But since I can't bear being around people who don't know sports, I think I'm gonna pass."

She glanced over at Lin and signaled her to go.

"She's a sportswriter," Lin called out as she ran off with M.J., leaving the boys shaking their heads behind them.

"Told you I'm right." M.J. grinned. "Now do you believe that men don't really like women who know sports?"

Lin just laughed.

two

M.J. OFTEN wished she felt half as confident about life as she did about sports. After all, life would be so much easier if nerve came in a nice prepackaged can. Brides would stroll down the aisle with nary a worry. Serena Williams would never miss a forehand. And come Monday morning, M.J. would not be sweating her first big one-on-one interview with New York Knicks guard, Jamaal Winston.

Sporting Adidas shell tops, hip-hugger jeans, a blue button-down blouse, and a black blazer, M.J. walked through the press room at Madison Square Garden with her *Sporting Life* magazine credentials. Ah, Madison Square Garden—in M.J.'s mind, there was no question that this was the greatest arena in the world. Every time she set foot in those hallowed halls, it felt like the first time. The great domed ceiling, the seemingly endless tiers of seats, the rafters drenched with championship banners and all the attendant history . . . it was a heady feeling that she never tired of.

Before she got to the interview, though, she had to hang out in a raucous pressroom filled with smoke and testosterone. Most of the other reporters were twice her age, but they all had one thing in common—they were glaring daggers at M.J.

At twenty-six, M.J. was still considered an outsider, a newbie in the world of sports. In an industry dominated by fifty-year-old men, no woman was really taken seriously, and this was even more true for a young Asian-American female.

"So you'll never guess who I ran into last week!" Ming plopped down next to M.J. on one of the benches. As the Knicks beat writer for the *Big Apple Times*, Ming practically lived in the Garden.

"Who?" M.J. asked. "Chow Yun Fat?"

"Shut up, you dork." Ming laughed. "I saw Susan Huang at my uncle's dinner party last week, and she asked about you."

"Susan from our Chinese school classes?" M.J. yelped. "She hated me! She was such a teacher's pet. She even told on me once when she saw me playing Game Boy in class. As punishment, I had to write my name in Chinese on the board a thousand times."

"Yup." He nodded. "I mentioned that we see each other at games a lot, and she told me to say hi to you when I saw you at practice."

Chinese school was just one of the many parent-induced burdens that M.J. had been subjected to during her childhood. It was the most tedious thing to her—she still remembered how jealous she'd been when the kids next door got to play hopscotch on Sunday mornings while she would trudge by them, mushroom-cut head bowed, carrying her Pochacco bookbag and ink brush set to Chinese school.

"Ugh." M.J. made a face. "Susan's one of those girls that I'd be happy to forget. She was always so full of herself, not to mention the biggest tattletale in the world."

"Don't worry, darling." Ming grinned gleefully. "I got her back for you. I told her that not only were you doing great but that you were the president of the Chinese School Scholarship Foundation and that you were teaching Chinese reading and writing to kids. That just killed her."

M.J. cracked up. "Thanks! I bet she flipped when she heard that. Her dream, even when she was twelve, was to be head of that foundation."

Ming started laughing, too, then stopped as a shadow fell over them.

"M.J.? Is that really you?" a voice called out from behind her.

She turned around. Her face lit up when she saw who it was. "Kevin? What are you doing here? How the hell are you?" She broke into a grin as the newcomer reached over to give her a hug.

Beside her, Ming was craning his neck in curiosity.

"I'm good. I write for *Dunk* magazine now, which is why I'm here. But look at you—you look great!" Kevin exclaimed as he gave her a once-over.

"Don't sound so surprised," she teased. "You're not looking so bad yourself."

Kevin laughed modestly.

That laugh wasn't new to M.J. She'd heard it so many times— the pseudo-humble chuckle with the underlying "Yeah, I know I'm hot" tone.

"There it is. The 'let me be a stud but play dumb' act. Some things never change," she said lightly.

Trying to look as composed as she sounded, M.J. took a quick sip from her water bottle. She still couldn't believe it. Talk about a blast from the past. She hadn't seen Kevin Taylor since high school. With his chestnut hair, olive skin, green eyes, and formidable forehand, Kevin had been the school's premier tennis player—and premier catch. They had been hitting partners who had shared the same aspiring sportswriting dreams, as well as most of their free time during senior year. In fact, she really was once head over heels for him, and he . . . well, M.J. never was quite sure exactly how Kevin felt.

Meanwhile, Ming was giving Kevin a disapproving look. He'd clearly made up his mind within minutes of seeing M.J. chatting with him.

"Ming, this is Kevin," she said finally, caving in to the inevitable. "He went to high school with me. Kevin, this is my friend Ming."

"How are you?" Kevin extended his hand.

"Good, what's up?" Ming forced a smile. "So, you and M.J. are old high school pals, huh?"

"Yeah." Kevin looked M.J. in the eye with a glimmer of mischief. "She was quite a tennis player back in high school. Not only was she a great hitting partner, but she always kept up with my strokes."

Ming raised his eyebrows. Catching his reaction, M.J. knew that it was time to break this little party up. Three was definitely a crowd here.

Ming was one of her closest friends, and she knew that he wanted the best for her. Still, sometimes he protected her too much. Her entire life, all the Asian men she knew had told her what to do. Her father was in the military and he lived to lecture M.J. on the dos and don'ts of life. Ditto for her male cousins and other assorted relatives. M.J. hated it all.

"You know, Ming," she said as casually as she could, "I ran into one of the PR guys before and they mentioned your name. You might want to check to see if they needed you for something."

Ming was no dummy. "All right," he said, "I guess I should. It was nice meeting you, Kevin. I'll catch you later."

As Ming strolled off, M.J. breathed a deep sigh of relief. Now that Ming was taken care of, she could finally concentrate on Kevin . . . and that was when she felt a tap on her shoulder.

"M.J.!" a voice called out.

"Jagger?" She whirled around. With her mouth open, M.J. exclaimed, "What are you doing here?"

"Did you think just because you cool *Sporting Life* people could do a cover on Jamaal Winston that other sportswriters couldn't?" Jagger Quinn responded in his typical smart-alecky manner.

Beside her, M.J. could tell that Kevin was staring at Jagger like he was some strange alien insect. And why wouldn't he be? In his cargo pants, Vans, and bright blue T-shirt with the words DONUTS GOOD on it, he cut quite the contrasting figure from Kevin. Jagger was a producer for RealSports, a cable sports network in the same building as *Sporting Life*. Since he was not only friendly with a number of her colleagues but was also a frequent guest columnist for *Sporting Life*, he could routinely be found strolling around the offices chatting up the employees there—especially M.J. Scruffy and spiky-haired, Jagger looked like a skater boy in an Avril Lavigne video, so much so that she had nicknamed him "Ratboy" for his grungy attire.

"So," Jagger swiveled toward Kevin with interest, "who do we have here?"

"Ummm . . . Jagger, this is Kevin. We went to high school together. He writes for *Dunk* magazine." M.J. cleared her throat. "Kevin, this is my friend . . . I mean Jagger. He's the producing guru for RealSports."

"Aww, M.J." Jagger flashed an amused smile. "You're too kind, calling me a guru."

As M.J. made a face, he turned toward Kevin. "So, man, how's it shakin'?"

Kevin looked a little confused. "Um, it's shaking fine. . . ."

"So you knew M.J. back in high school, huh?" Jagger shot her a mischievous look. "Bet you've got lots of good stories. . . ."

M.J. cringed. Was it a full moon out? Crazy enough that she had run into Kevin here, but to throw Ming and Jagger in the mix, too? Ming had his own set of problems with his instant disapproval for all things Caucasian. But here was Jagger, looking at Kevin in that he's-a-wanker way. And Kevin—well, he was probably wondering what she was doing hanging out with someone who looked like he lived out of the Salvation Army.

M.J. took a deep breath. She had to put an end to this before Jagger said anything embarrassing—now.

"So, Jagger, don't you have to check in and see when they're letting the writers into the locker room?" she said quickly.

Jagger shot M.J. an I'm-onto-you look, but he obediently turned and shook Kevin's hand politely.

"Bye!" She waved, trying to hide her relief. Jagger just shook his head as he left.

M.J. exhaled and turned back to Kevin, all smiles. "So who are you here to interview?" he asked.

"Jamaal Winston. *Sporting Life* is doing a cover story on him and his chump change contract. You?"

"We're doing an Isaac Thomas story. Typical that *Dunk* magazine would do something like that. Still dreaming of interviewing his Airness one day, though."

"That makes two of us." M.J. smiled. "At least you're doing a real story and not some crazy pretend-sports piece. Some guy in our office is doing an article about this new dating service called sportsdating.com, where fans can all come together and find their soul mates while rooting for the same teams."

"Hmm . . . sounds interesting," Kevin said. "I guess you never know what people will think of next."

"I know." M.J. shook her head. "Um, listen, I have to get going. Jamaal's waiting for me in there. It was great to see you, though!"

Kevin rifled through his bag. "I'm glad I bumped into you. Here's my card. Maybe we can catch up some time."

"Okay, here's mine." Her hand touched his for a brief instant. "We'll definitely have to catch up soon."

AS SHE entered the long gray concrete hallway to the Knicks locker room, M.J. was besieged by a torrent of emotions. Her heart was pounding a mile a minute, her head was a jumble of racing thoughts, and her stomach was all twisted up into knots. She couldn't believe the timing—wasn't it just like fate to drop Kevin back into her life five minutes before her first locker room interview? After all, what were the odds of seeing Kevin Taylor again? It had been almost ten years since she'd last laid eyes on him. He was the first boy she'd kissed, the first boy she'd shared her dreams and hopes with, the first boy she'd ever fallen in love with. Just seeing him now for a few fleeting minutes was enough to bring all the old emotions back.

But she didn't have time to analyze Kevin Taylor right then and there. A moment later, she walked into the Knicks locker room and found a room full of naked NBA players. It was M.J.'s first time in an NBA locker room, and while she had been ready for the whooping and the hollering, the steam from the showers and the smell of sweat, she was most certainly not ready for the wall of naked muscular flesh. While most of the players wore itty-bitty towels, the others looked like they were auditioning for *The Full Monty*. Trying her hardest to maintain her composure, she finally spotted Jamaal Winston waiting by his locker for her.

M.J. was fully prepared to do the story on number 20 of the Knicks, but as she approached, her knuckles went white from holding her tape recorder too tightly. Feeling her fingers shake, she could just imagine the headline—FEMALE REPORTER DROPS RECORDER, FINDS KNICKS PLAYER'S JEWELS.

With an effort, she snapped out of her reverie.

"Hey, Jamaal." She smiled as she shook his hand. "What's up? Ready to talk some ball?"

"Sure thing," he said warmly. For such a tall, massively sculpted man with a smooth-shaven head, Jamaal had a surprisingly soft voice.

"So, you're going to be in your first All-Star game next week," M.J. began. "Are you looking forward to it?"

"You bet." Jamaal beamed. "I've been dreaming about this all my life. Now that it's finally here, I almost can't believe it's happening."

"What are you looking forward to the most?" M.J. asked.

Jamaal rubbed his chin. "Hmm. That's a tough question. I would have to say . . . watching Beyoncé boogie at the halftime show."

M.J. chuckled. "Right on. So, switching gears a little, any vacations planned?"

"Well, every summer, my buddies and I take this fishing trip to Alaska. Even though it's a long ways off, I can't wait. We had such a blast last summer."

"Really?" M.J. said. "What happened?"

"It was absolutely amazing," he began. "We caught all these huge fish. Plus, it was so beautiful that I could have just stared at the mountains the whole time." He smiled at the memory. "In fact, everything was pretty much perfect until I fell in the lake one day trying to hold on to this king salmon I was reeling in. It took three of my buddies to pull me out of the water, but it was all worth it because I had that damn fish—even though I had to stuff it into my pants to hold on to it!"

M.J. and Jamaal both howled, catching the attention of the other media and personnel in the locker room.

"Wow!" she exclaimed. "So you and the salmon got to know each other pretty well, huh?"

Jamaal laughed. "You can say that, all right."

"I hear you." M.J. chuckled. "So are you glad to be back on the hardwood?"

"Hey—" He shook his head. "—after handling that fish, I'm pretty sure I'm not going to be making turnovers anytime soon!"

M.J. and Jamaal broke out into laughter again. A moment later, one of the Knicks' spokesmen came over.

"Excuse me, I'm Roy Davidson with the Knicks." The balding, middle-aged man looked at M.J. pointedly. "May I speak to you for a second?"

"Sure." She got up, confused. She quickly thanked Jamaal for his time and followed Roy to a corner of the locker room.

"Um, it's nice to meet you. I'm M. J. Wyn, by the way," she said, still trying to figure out what was going on. "What's—?"

"What publication are you from?" he asked sternly.

"I'm from *Sporting Life*," she answered, still puzzled. "Is there a problem?"

"Can I see some ID, please?" he demanded.

M.J. was stunned. Did this guy think she was impersonating a journalist just to talk to an NBA player? Glaring at him, she whipped out her driver's license.

"This is fine, Ms. Wyn—" Roy glanced at her license. "—but in the future, I'd appreciate it if you could act more appropriate."

"Excuse me?" Her jaw dropped.

"You heard me." He handed her back the license. "These interviews are strictly for business. We don't want people to think these are flirt sessions with NBA players."

M.J. couldn't believe her ears. If she were in a bar instead of the Knicks locker room, she would have slapped this dude right across the face.

"First of all," she said as calmly as possible, "Mr. Winston and I were not flirting. We were having a conversation, which is what reporters are supposed to do with their interviewees. There was absolutely nothing inappropriate about our interview."

"Ms. Wyn," Roy said dismissively, "there's no need for explanations. I'm just trying to help you out, kid. Flirting isn't the best way to get into this gig."

M.J. knew she had to walk away from this conversation before she lost her cool.

"Thank you for such inspiring words," she managed despite the lump in her throat. "Now, if you don't mind, I have to get back to work."

As she stormed off, her face flushed and her head pounding, M.J. couldn't help but think that if she were a man, this incident with Roy the asshole would never have happened. The worst thing was that it had completely marred a great interview with Jamaal.

Holding back tears, she strode out of the locker room. Which was when, of course, she ran into Jagger.

"M.J." Jagger looked at her with concern. "How did it go? Why do you look like you're going to cry?"

"I don't want to talk about it," she snapped, the humiliation threatening to engulf her. The last person she wanted to see right now was someone of the male persuasion. "It's nothing."

"Are you sure?" He frowned. "You don't look so good."

Suddenly Kevin walked up behind the both of them. "Hey, guys," he said brightly, "how's everything going?"

"Fine." She forced a smile. "How about you?"

"Good," Kevin replied. "My interview was great. Isaac Thomas and I really hit it off. In fact, he was telling me that he golfs at my country club."

Jagger narrowed his eyes. "That's awesome, man, but I don't think M.J. wants to hear about your interview right now."

Her eyes widened. How could Jagger do this to her? There was no need for him to open his big mouth and tell the world that she had just been totally humiliated her first time out with a player. Especially in front of Kevin.

"What happened?" Kevin asked.

"Oh, nothing." M.J. tried to shake it off.

Looking at Kevin, she could tell he was relieved. She knew he hated dealing with other people's problems. Kevin's attention usually waned when it came to other people. Somehow, though, M.J. could never bring herself to hold that against him. Kevin had a way of making her forgive his worst flaws—just looking into his green eyes was always enough to make her forget his latest transgression.

"Oh, okay." Kevin shrugged. "Well, anyway, I gotta run, but M.J., let's try to keep in touch."

M.J. pasted on a smile, determined not to let him see how upset she was. "Of course. Bye!" She gave him a hug and a kiss goodbye and watched as he strolled off. Then, she immediately whirled around and confronted Jagger.

"Why did you do that?" she demanded furiously. It was bad enough she'd been humiliated by Roy in front of an entire locker room. Now she'd just been embarrassed again in front of the one guy she wanted to impress. "It's not your place to be all up in my business then try to spread it to the world."

"Look," Jagger retorted, "I just thought you deserved a little support. If you don't want my help, forget it."

He stalked off angrily, but not before she'd seen the hurt in his eyes.

HOURS LATER, as she was speeding down south on I-95, M.J. wondered why she'd had to be such a bitch to Jagger. Really, what did he do that was so wrong other than be in the absolutely wrong place at the wrong time? He couldn't help it that he'd walked in on her once-unimaginable reunion with the one man who could make her resolve weaken—the one man who never failed to turn her into a shaky-kneed schoolgirl.

M.J. and Kevin were seventeen when they started dating the summer before their senior year. He'd invited her to his family's country club for the summer so that they could both work on their tennis game. The Taylors were exactly as M.J. expected them to be: Kevin's father, Edward, was CEO of a JPMorgan branch while his wife, Meredith, was the perfect manicured hostess and mother. Kevin's brother was a star quarterback at Stanford. And his little sister, Amanda, was a precocious ten-year-old, perpetually decked out in cute little frilly dresses and blond pigtails.

Sitting at the club's Fourth of July party, M.J. had looked at the Taylor family with envy. They were beautiful in their designer outfits and expensive white-shoe accessories, playing tennis in the morning and having tea and cocktails in the afternoon. Most important, they were a family with no troubles or problems. M.J. had never seen any of them raise their voices or show even the slightest hint of discontent. So different from her own family . . .

Now that Kevin had reentered her life, M.J. wasn't sure what she'd expected; after all, just because they exchanged cards didn't mean that he was interested in rekindling anything. For all she knew, Kevin could be married, engaged, dating, or simply not interested. And M.J. herself wasn't sure how she felt about him; it wasn't easy reconciling her hurt back when he dumped her with the fluttery feeling in her stomach when she saw him that morning. In the end, though, she couldn't help wondering why he would suggest getting together if there wasn't some interest there. Which was why, as she drove to her PlayBall interview, it was all she could do to concentrate on the task at hand instead of the memory of Kevin's voice.

three

BECOMING AN on-air sportscaster had been M.J.'s own Holy Grail for as long as she could recall. She still remembered prancing around her bedroom doing her best Al Michaels/Miracle on Ice impersonation with her hairbrush. But having arrived at PlayBall's cavernous gray steel-and-concrete offices, she couldn't help feeling a twinge of doubt about her long-cherished aspirations ever coming true.

"It's very nice to meet you." M.J. beamed at Ben Fowler, the PlayBall sports director, as he ushered her to a seat in his office. Having changed into an understated black pin-striped suit, M.J. was ready to work her charm.

"So, tell me about your reel before I watch it," he began. A grizzled man in his fifties, Ben Fowler was a classic sports guy in his beat-up sweater and coffee-stained tie.

"Well, I did a few features," she explained. "One of them focuses on an upcoming high school player, Karim Livingston from Brooklyn, who's being touted as the next big NYC point guard. I also have a hockey and a tennis piece."

Ben nodded as he pushed the VHS tape into the VCR. As her montage began playing, she stared at him, trying to decipher his facial expressions. Three minutes later, she had her answer.

"Well," Ben swiveled around in his chair, "you've obviously got the look, but I'm sorry. I just don't think that these pieces have that extra special something we're looking for. They're generally good but a little ordinary, and unfortunately, that means we see a lot of pieces that come through here like that. We're hoping to find something with a fresh, unique voice."

M.J.'s heart sank. She'd been working on these feature packages for months now with a production crew. In a matter of minutes, Ben had ripped it apart. Somehow though, she managed to keep smiling.

"You may want to sit down and rethink your approach," he went on. "You need to think about what will set you apart from the crowd. Because right now, you're just vanilla, kind of boring, one of the herd."

"Thank you." She forced another smile. "I appreciate the feedback."

"Good luck to you, Miss Wyn." Ben shook her hand.

M.J. quickly dumped the tape into her bag and all but ran out of the office. She felt her eyes welling up as she rushed into the elevator. As the doors closed, she collapsed against the cool steel walls and wiped her tears away on her sleeve. So much for Auntie Lee's prophecy—she wasn't even going to get the chance to give up her dream. She couldn't believe how bad she felt—worse than being dumped by a boyfriend, worse than losing her favorite Michael Jordan highlight DVD, even worse than when all the girls laughed at her Mickey Mouse underwear in the locker room after gym class.

M.J. quickly grabbed her phone from her bag. She needed her girls.

. . .

A TYPICAL Friday night for M.J. consisted of beers, her girlfriends Alex and Lin, and some harmless flirting with boys. She had a particular affinity for mellow dives with jukebox music. This week, they all congregated at Buster's Garage in TriBeCa.

"And here's a toast, ladies." Lin raised her glass. "To a night of fun and to meeting gorgeous men."

M.J. and Alex raised their drinks. "Cheers."

As they clinked glasses, M.J. couldn't help but think back to that afternoon's PlayBall interview. "Vanilla, kind of boring, one of the herd." Just thinking about Ben's words now made her feel like banging her head against a wall. How could this have happened? She'd worked so hard on that tape, had sweated over shots, lost sleep over the scripts. The worst thing was that Ben's complaints weren't neat little technical things that could easily be fixed. How did you fix the fact that someone thought you were boring? Especially when M.J. thought she was the furthest thing from dull. It was all enough to make her want to storm back into Fowler's office, let out a primal, ear-piercing scream, and demand if he still thought she was "vanilla."

Stop it, she told herself. *You're going to drive yourself insane.*

She tried to concentrate on something frivolous. "So did you guys watch *The Set-Up* last night? Can you believe Bill dumped Dana for that Melissa chick?"

"I know—it was all everyone at the office could talk about," Lin exclaimed. "What I can't believe is how there are so many gorgeous women out there who are willing to jump through hoops to get this one guy. I've always wondered what would possess these women to do those shows."

"Well, not everyone gets to meet their boyfriend on the job," Alex drawled.

The girls *ooh*ed as Lin turned bright red. They all knew that Lin had a history of falling for her coworkers.

"Look, Alex," Lin retorted, "not all of us can be automatons at work. Some of us actually have feelings. Emotions. Needs."

M.J. gaped. Despite her petite stature and deceptively delicate features, Alex was a spitfire in sheep's clothing. Once angered, she was all flashing eyes and sharp wit, and M.J. had seen men twice her size cower under her fury. Fortunately, she herself rarely had occasion to clash with Alex, but she also knew better than to do so purposely. Lin knew better, too, but that didn't stop her from starting with their friend.

Alex scowled. "This is not about having 'emotions.' This is about being professional. You're a professional, and that means no flirting with your colleagues at work, no commenting on each other's posterior, and most definitely no playing footsie underneath the conference room table."

Uh-oh. M.J. bit her lip as Lin inhaled sharply. This was getting a little too testy. M.J. loved both her girls, but she also knew their faults. Lin was impetuous and careless. Alex, on the other hand, had never met an unpopular opinion she was afraid to voice. Bringing these two personalities together meant there would be the inevitable clash.

M.J. decided that it was time to intercede. "So, guess what? I ran into this guy Kevin I dated. Remember the tennis player I told you about? It was such a shock—not bad or even a big deal, just kind of crazy."

"You mean Kevin Taylor?" Alex asked. "The one you went out with in high school?"

"Yep." M.J. nodded. "I ran into him at MSG the other day. We exchanged cards."

"Look at your face, J," Lin teased. "You're glowing. You're really excited about him, huh?"

"It's not that I'm excited about him—it's just that it was a shock to see him again. I mean we had something once, but that was years ago." M.J. tried to play it down. "We were young then."

"So, are you going to meet up with him?" Alex asked.

"We'll see if he calls, but even if he doesn't, it's really not a big deal. I mean, it's not like I'm expecting anything." M.J. took a long swig of her beer.

. . .

M.J. KEPT telling herself she didn't care if Kevin never called her. After all, she'd survived all these years without him—why would she need him now? And yet, as Tuesday morning rolled around, she found herself spending an inordinate amount of time checking her messages. . . .

Fortunately, she didn't have too much free time to dwell on Kevin. Determined not to let the PlayBall interview crush her, she peppered every contact she had at every broadcasting station she could find with her tape. Ben Fowler was an idiot, she told herself, and she was going to prove him wrong.

The first few days, M.J. floated along on her conviction that the phone would be ringing off the hook the minute people got a peek at her tape. A week later, her optimism began to flag as not a single call came through about her reel. By the end of the next week, disappointment started to sink in, dragging M.J. inexorably down from her cloud of hope.

And then the rejection letters came.

It was devastating to open her mailbox every night and see yet another thin white envelope lying there, mocking her. It got to the point where M.J. dreaded checking her mail. After all, every trip to the mailbox in her six-story East Village walk-up just brought yet another crushing let-down, another "Thank you, but we don't think this is right for our show." It took every bit of her innate optimism not to let the simmering bitterness within her well up and engulf her.

But, as the days went by and the rejection letters dribbled in, M.J. found herself doubting Auntie Lee's prophecy even more. It was all she could do to keep her head above water and ignore the vicious little voice that told her she just wasn't good enough—not for sportscasting or anything else.

BETWEEN KEVIN'S reentry into her life, the disaster of the PlayBall interview, and the never-ending stream of rejection letters, M.J.'s once orderly life had been thrown into turmoil. Which was why a nice, quiet meal with the family Wednesday night seemed like a welcome respite to M.J., who was all too happy to escape to her family's little brick row house in Flushing for their annual pre-spring feast.

According to Chinese tradition, a Thanksgiving-esque meal was cooked to celebrate every change of season. M.J.'s grandfather Kam could be counted on to whip up a mouthwatering, calorie-inducing, diet-busting meal come every one of these occasions. Salted chicken with lemon, dried shrimp with vermicelli, and sea cucumbers with mushrooms and scallions were omnipresent decorations on the Wyn family table during these meals. They would eat voraciously, while "catching up."

"Meilin," M.J.'s mother, Esther, said, calling her daughter by her Chinese name, "so can you go to your cousin's wedding banquet on Sunday night?"

"Oh, is it Sunday?" M.J. shook her head as she shoveled some bok choy onto her plate. "Sorry, I have a game to cover that night."

Esther frowned, looking none too pleased. "Again? You couldn't go to dim sum with the family last Sunday, and now you can't go to wedding banquet?"

"There's nothing I can do about it, Mom. It's work. You know that has to come first."

Her mother pursed her lips. M.J. knew that in any other situation, her mother would have badgered her into going. But work was the one area no Chinese parent would dare wage war over, and Esther was no exception.

"Fine," she grumbled. "So how is everything going? How is sending out tapes for TV job?"

"Okay." M.J. took a bite of her tofu delight. "I got a couple of rejections from a few small networks, but it's no big deal. I'm sure someone will think differently soon—no matter what that jerk at PlayBall says."

Esther gave M.J. a puzzled look. "What do you mean?"

"I met this sports director, and he said my tape was terrible and that no one would ever like it." She sighed, her shoulders slumped. "I'm over it."

"Well, don't you think he is an expert? Maybe this is a sign that you should give up on this dream of yours. Sometimes you have to be realistic. Dreams don't always come true."

"Your mom is right," M.J.'s dad, Michael, interjected. "Maybe you should think about being a real estate broker or going into business like Lin."

M.J.'s nostrils began to flare. She hated it when her parents ganged up on her, and there was no worse topic than her career. "I don't want to start with you guys." Her voice rose. "I'm just here to enjoy a nice evening with Grandpa and everyone."

That was absolutely the wrong thing for M.J. to say. Her father, who had a notoriously quick temper, immediately launched into a familiar rant.

"Don't talk to us like that." Michael pointed his chopsticks at M.J. "We are your parents and love you very much. We just want to see you do well. We're not some stupid American family trying to tell their kids to reach for their dreams, and then when they are thirty, have no money and nothing to live for."

M.J. flinched. "Look, I know you're concerned about me, but I'm twenty-six and a big girl," she snapped, her appetite gone. "I know what I'm doing."

And with that, she stormed out of her parents' house.

Second
Quarter

four

FIGHTING WITH her parents always left M.J. feeling like she had a perpetual black cloud hanging over her. Sure, these kinds of dust-ups with her folks were nothing new. They were, in fact, par for the course for their family. She knew that things would blow over in a few days, and soon, the Wyns would be back having dinner and bickering over some other issue like nothing had ever happened. Until then, M.J. had only one refuge: work.

As she got off the phone with the Devils' spokesman the next day, Jagger plopped himself down in her office and started shooting hoops into her mini-basket. Today, he was wearing a bright red T-shirt with a lightbulb on it. M.J. hadn't seen him since the de-bacle with Kevin, and she was hoping Jagger wouldn't bring the whole episode up.

"So, Wyn, what are you working on now?" Jagger bounced the small foam basketball against the wall.

"None of your business," she said airily. "Don't they have enough work over at RealSports to keep you guys busy?"

"Oh, don't you worry about me. Can't I just come and chat with you? You should be nice to me since I always use your mate-rial for our shows. Besides, there ain't no hottie at RealSports for me to flirt with." Jagger gave her his most winning smile.

M.J. snorted. But before she could retort, someone knocked on the door. Looking up, she saw that it was Gary Martin and Anthony Doherty, sports geeks from the marketing department. They came carrying a camera and tripod.

"Hey there, Michelle Kwan." Gary smiled. "How are ya? Ready to take your photo for the Web site?"

"I think M.J.'s definitely more of a Michelle Wie," Anthony said. "What's cooking?"

M.J. and Jagger exchanged looks that screamed one word—"Weirdos!"

"Um . . . hi," she muttered. "Are you guys only saying that because those two are the most famous female Asian athletes out there, or do I really look like them?"

The guys paused momentarily but quickly rebounded.

"No, you're as cute as Michelle Wie," Gary replied.

"Right," M.J. said, "so let me get this straight. First, a little teenager looks really hot, and second, I look underage? Are you two perverts or what?"

Jagger broke into laughter. "Good one, Wyn."

"Funny how we Asians all look alike," she continued. "Next thing you know people will be mistaking Elizabeth Vargas for J. Lo."

"Well," Jagger said slyly, "I got to say, you do got some nice junk in that trunk, Jenny from the Block."

Despite herself, M.J. chuckled. She smacked him on the arm. "You are such a fool, Quinn."

Meanwhile, Gary and Anthony just looked confused.

"Uh, so are you ready to take your picture?" Gary lined up the tripod.

"Sure." M.J. rolled her eyes. "Ready as I'll ever be."

The guys quickly snapped the photo and then stood there awkwardly. She and Jagger glanced at each other.

"So, was there anything else you needed?" she asked.

The guys shook their heads in unison.

"Well, all of this has been fun, boys," Jagger interrupted, "but

M.J. and I have to discuss some editorial content for the next Real-Sports show."

"Okay." Gary edged toward the door with Anthony following behind him. "Later, M.J. Hopefully, we'll see you at the cafeteria around lunchtime."

Jagger closed the door firmly behind them.

"Well, I sure didn't expect that." M.J. raised an eyebrow.

"You're welcome, babycakes." Jagger flexed his bicep. "Quinn to the rescue. Now I have you all to myself so I can annoy you in peace."

M.J. crinkled her nose. "You are so ridiculous!" But she laughed as she said it.

"Look, would you rather be bothered by dorks like them, or would you rather have a stud like me to chat with?" He grinned.

"Neither." She tossed her head. "Now, if you don't mind, I'm very busy—"

Someone knocked on the door again. M.J. sighed. "Come in."

It was Cindy Sweeney, the office secretary. With her big hair, liberal use of eye shadow, nasal New Jersey accent, and gaudy, pseudo–white trash outfits, Cindy was pure bridge-and-tunnel. Still, it wasn't the makeup or the attitude that irritated M.J.—it was Cindy's propensity for hitting on every man within a mile of her with the intensity of a Mack truck. Like the way she had immediately latched on to this guy Mike that M.J. had been dating. Ultimately, she realized that Cindy had done her a favor by taking the jerk off her hands. Nevertheless, it didn't exactly make her a fan of the office seductress.

"Hey, guys, what's up?" Cindy giggled when she saw Jagger. "Here's a letter for you, M.J. It's from this writer at the L.A. Times. Apparently he likes you for some reason and wants to give you tickets to an NFL game."

M.J. glared at her. "Thanks for checking my mail, Cindy."

Cindy ignored her. "So, Jagger, whatcha up to tonight?"

"I don't know." He frowned at a loose thread on his sleeve.

M.J. began typing away on her computer. "If you guys are going to play love connection, please do it elsewhere."

"Lighten up," Cindy said. "You're always grumpy. All you think about is work, work, work. Maybe you need to get laid."

With that, she sashayed out of the office. M.J. scowled after her. Jagger, however, made no move to leave her office.

"Hey, Wyn." He looked at M.J. intently. "Would you be jealous if I went out with her?"

M.J. turned back to her computer, laughing. "Quinn, I wouldn't care if you became a Mormon and had five wives. Maybe you and Cindy *should* go out. She would probably cook for you and let you do whatever the heck you wanted."

Jagger frowned, as if disappointed. "I don't need anyone to cook for me. Believe it or not, I happen to be an excellent chef," he retorted. "Maybe I'll cook you dinner one day."

M.J. giggled at the thought. "You? A chef? That's a good one, Quinn."

"Oh, you don't believe me?" he challenged. "Wyn, when are you going to realize that people aren't always what they seem to be?"

She rolled her eyes. "And sometimes they're exactly what they seem to be."

Jagger shook his head. "Just wait, Wyn. You might be surprised one day." He stood up. "In the meantime, I'm out to get some food and make some phone calls. I think Jennie Finch is supposed to call me back. Take a message, okay?"

"Good-bye forever!" she sang out loudly.

"What's this?" Jagger picked up a tape on M.J.'s desk. "Watching porn again in the office?"

"Give that back to me!" she yelled as she tried to snatch the tape from him.

The two wrestled for a minute, but ultimately, she lost the fight. Jagger grabbed the tape and popped it into her VCR. M.J. covered her face, not looking forward to hearing whatever commentary he had in store for her.

Jagger smiled as he heard the words. "And that's all for now. I'm M. J. Wyn."

"I didn't know you wanted to be an on-air anchor."

"Whatever," she snapped. "Apparently, no one in America likes it."

"What are you talking about?" he asked. "That piece was solid."

M.J. blinked. Was Jagger being nice to her for the third time in the last few days? And did he really think her piece was solid? She had thought so, too—back when Auntie Lee had told her she would achieve her dreams. And before the onslaught of rejection letters.

"Now is not the time to pretend to be nice to me," she scowled.

"Look—" He touched her shoulder. "—I'm just trying to give you a compliment here."

"You wouldn't understand," M.J. mumbled. She buried her head in her arms.

"Understand what?" Jagger persisted.

"You really want to know?" she said finally, feeling her stomach tie up in knots.

"Only if you want to tell me." He folded his arms and looked at her expectantly, his expression surprisingly understanding.

"Well, PlayBall Network said it sucked. They said that my features were too vanilla and boring and that I needed a more original, creative reel." M.J. sighed and slumped back in her chair, resigned to the prospect of more criticism.

Jagger studied her for a moment. Then he hopped off her desk.

"Wyn, if you're going to let people talk smack about your stuff and eat it, you're not the person I think you are. You've got good potential. If they want 'creative,' then give them 'creative.' But don't try to use that as an excuse to quit." He paused. "If you want some suggestions, I've got a couple of ideas." Then without another word, he turned heel and walked out of the office.

Puzzled, M.J. stared after him.

There was something about Jagger Quinn that always seemed to irk the hell out of her. Without a doubt, the twenty-seven-year-old RealSports producer was one of the most unusual people M.J. had ever met. He didn't care about money or looks or any of the usual material possessions that preoccupied most people their age. Sometimes, M.J. didn't know what she found more annoying: Jagger himself or the fact that he made her question everything she believed in.

. . .

FORTUNATELY, M.J. didn't need to worry about anything happening with Jagger—or anyone else, for that matter. Because come Friday night, Kevin still hadn't called, and she was spending the evening with her most reliable dates: her girls, Lin and Alex.

Well, Lin and Alex and the rest of M.J.'s family, that is, including her parents, her grandparents, her aunts, her uncles, and her umpteen cousins. It was her grandmother's eightieth birthday, and as was the way with Chinese families, the occasion was celebrated with massive amounts of food. The Jade Palace Restaurant in Flushing boasted a mouthwatering prix fixe that included steamed sea bass, giant prawns, salted chicken with ginger garnish, and barbecued spareribs.

After paying their respects to M.J.'s smiling grandmother, who was all decked out in an ornate velvet *meen-nap* that complemented her halo of stone-white hair, the girls sneaked off to the ladies' room.

"I can't wait," M.J. announced as she fixed her ponytail. "I didn't eat all day, because I wanted to make sure I had enough room for tonight."

Alex laughed. "When I tell people how much food there is at these things, no one ever believes it. They don't quite grasp the concept of having, like, nine courses."

"You mean ten courses," Lin corrected her. "Or eight. There has to be an even number of courses or else it's bad luck."

"Yeah, yeah," M.J. said, "I'm just glad you guys are here, because I don't think I could take a whole evening with my entire family by myself."

Alex frowned. "Oh come on, what are they going to do? Make you eat until you burst?"

M.J. thought back to some of her past family gatherings. "Just wait, Alex. You'll see."

Sure enough, her family didn't disappoint. The minute they walked out of the ladies' room, M.J.'s mother accosted her.

"Meilin!" Esther scolded. "I told you this Grandma's eightieth birthday! You show respect and not look like beggar! This nice banquet—what you wearing? I told you wear dress!" She jabbed a finger toward the front of her daughter's Bob Dylan T-shirt. "Who this Bob person?"

M.J. shrugged. Being Esther's only child, she was used to her mother's scrutiny and even more used to her expectations. Growing up, she wore cute little *qipaos*—traditional, quilted Oriental dresses—took violin lessons, and learned Mandarin in Sunday school—all to fulfill her mother's quest of making her little Meilin the next Doogie Howser. While M.J. was attractive, smart, and, most important, possessed the confidence and charisma that her parents were sure would lead them to *sic woo*—a Chinese expression that meant "right-on-the-money successful"—in no time, it wasn't long before the Asian princess started ditching her violin lessons for dodgeball games and smashball tennis.

"Sorry, Ma," she said. "I came from work and didn't have time to change."

Esther calmed down, the invocation of work having its usual magic elixir effect.

"Okay, you girls go sit at adult table tonight. Too many children at children table."

M.J. flashed a grin at her friends as they made their way to the "adult" table.

"Wow," Alex murmured, "I feel honored—like I just graduated."

"You should feel honored," M.J. said, "this is the first time I've ever gotten to sit at the adult table!"

"Well, I'm just glad that we're not with the kiddies," Lin remarked. "Some of them can be really vicious about getting their food!"

M.J. laughed. "Don't be too excited. The adult table has its own problems."

Sure enough, within fifteen minutes of sitting down, the conversation among the aunts and uncles turned to the inevitable: the grandchildren.

"John graduated first in his class!" M.J.'s aunt Lily announced proudly. "He going to start MIT next year!"

"So?" Aunt Mary scoffed. "MIT no Harvard. Everyone knows Harvard number one. That's why Sue now a doctor."

"Doctor who don't make money," Uncle Jim retorted. "Why she work in hospital? She need to open office and start making some money. Peter make half million last year at Morgan Stanley. How much Sue make?"

M.J. turned and gave her friends a see-what-I-mean look. The Wyns were the classic Chinese immigrant family: they'd come to America with little money but high hopes in the Great American Dream. Even though they were far from being the Rockefellers, they had done relatively well for themselves. Indeed, they'd taken quickly to their new country's capitalistic ideals, and there was no more valuable currency than education and its attendant benefits. Sometimes M.J. thought they had been a little too overzealous in their adaptation. The only things her family ever seemed to care about were who went to what school, who was in what career, and who made how much money. In the first category, it was all about the Ivy Leagues. In the second category, there were the doctors, the lawyers, and maybe a stockbroker or two. As for the last category, the answer was obvious.

"This is awful," Lin whispered to M.J.

"I've actually started to find this entertaining," M.J. whispered back. "When you're never actually the topic of conversation, it's much easier to detach yourself and pretend you're just watching a bunch of strangers."

Lin and Alex looked at her quizzically. M.J. smiled as a cassette recorder started playing in the background, and the whole family began clapping and singing a heavily accented rendition of "Happy Birthday." Her friends didn't understand, of course, but then M.J. hadn't expected them to. As a lawyer and a trader respectively, Alex and Lin had probably never had the experience of being an outsider. They were, after all, the perfect Asian grandchildren, with family-approved professions and six-figure salaries.

. . .

"WOW, THAT was brutal," Alex declared as she plopped down on one of the couches at the Back Page Bar on the Upper East Side.

It was an hour after dinner, and the girls had taken the 7 train back to Manhattan for some alcohol to take the edge off the evening.

M.J. just smiled at Alex's words—clearly, her friend had no idea what her life was like. Dinners like this were par for the course in her family, and M.J. had long come to accept the bickering and one-upmanship as a way of life.

"Don't get me wrong," Alex said. "The food was amazing, and I'm really glad your family invited us. But could they talk about anything but schools and money?"

"Nope." M.J. took a swig of her beer. "They can't."

"Does it bother you, J?" Lin said slowly. "How they talk about every grandchild except you?"

M.J. shook her head. "Not anymore. Maybe before, when I was still in school. But now that I'm doing what I want . . . well, I couldn't care less. Truth is, if there's anyone who it does bother, it's probably my mother." Okay, well, maybe that wasn't the complete truth. Much as M.J. didn't want to care what her relatives said about her, it was inevitable that being treated like a nonentity by them would dredge up all her childhood insecurities.

"Well, I think it's bullshit," Alex declared, "and I don't think we should spend another minute dwelling on this crap."

M.J. raised her beer. "I second that."

"Okay, well, then, let's talk about the fact that we have three wonderful women here tonight, and there isn't a single decent guy in sight. Can someone explain this to me?" Lin lamented over her watermelon martini. "There must be a reason why none of us have boyfriends. Well, except for M.J.—we all know why she doesn't, don't we?"

M.J. chugged her beer. "Why? Because I'm a girl and I like sports and I can talk ball?"

Lin and Alex both laughed. They knew their friend had scared off many a man with her encyclopedic knowledge of sports—not to mention her killer forehand.

As M.J. took a sip of her fourth Amstel Light, her phone rang. She flipped the phone open carelessly. "Hello?"

"Hey. It's Kevin. What's going on?"

M.J. stifled a gasp. Both Lin and Alex stopped talking and perked up their ears.

"Hi, Kevin. Whatcha doing?" M.J. said as casually as she could.

"Not much. Just wanted to see what you were up to and if you wanted to get together soon. *Dunk* is having a party on Thursday night at 40/40, and a lot of NBA players are going to be there. I was thinking we could grab some dinner beforehand, then go to the party."

M.J. smiled and winked at the girls. "Oh, that sounds sweet. Sure, I'd love to go," she said, trying hard to sound nonchalant.

"Great! It's a date then. Pick you up at . . . ?"

"Seven is great," she laughed.

Kevin chuckled. "After all these years, you still know that seven is my 'date time.' "

M.J. got off the phone and took a deep breath. She didn't know what to think. On one hand, she couldn't help feeling triumphant about Kevin seeking her out after he'd tossed her aside back in high school. It was a second chance out of nowhere, an opportunity to rewrite the past. On the other hand, being with Kevin dredged up all her old, hurt feelings from that time when her world had come crashing down around her—when Kevin had told her she had no place in his life anymore.

"I can't believe Kevin just called me," M.J. burst out.

"What did he want?" Alex asked.

"I don't know. Well, I mean, I do know, sort of. He said he wanted to invite me to this party. But what he really wanted? Who knows?"

"So you haven't talked to him since you guys broke up?" Lin asked.

M.J. nodded. "Not since I was eighteen. Until I saw him at the Garden, I didn't even know if he was alive or dead. It's crazy."

"Well, since he was a jerk to you, maybe it's not such a bad thing," Alex said.

M.J. and Lin both turned to stare at her.

Alex licked her lips. "I mean, it's just that after the way he dumped you in high school, I don't want to see him hurt you again."

M.J. smiled. "Don't worry, Alex. I'm a long way from being seventeen. It's just—am I allowed to feel happy and mad at the same time?"

"Sure you are," Lin said.

M.J. shook her head. Maybe good things really did come to those who wait. Or perhaps this was Auntie Lee's prophecy coming true. . . .

"I don't know, guys." M.J. sighed. "This seems too good to be true. Not only am I going out with Kevin, but I'm also going to an NBA party with him. I don't know if you've heard much about them, but they can get pretty crazy!" She drained her beer. "You know, the problem with Kevin is that he would make me the happiest girl in the world, but in the back of my mind, I'd always felt that I wasn't good enough for him."

"Don't be ridiculous," Alex exclaimed. "Of course you're good enough! The real question is whether he's good enough for you."

"I know, I know," M.J. said. "I always have this fear that I'm going to have the rug pulled out from under me when I'm with Kevin."

"You're just being cautious," Lin observed. "It's okay for a girl to be cautious. Just go have fun with him, and if you don't, find yourself an NBA sugar daddy!"

five

WHEN M.J. was a child, her mother used to tell her that all she had to do was work hard and be good and everyone would love her. But if there was one thing that junior high taught her, it was that image really was everything.

M.J. remembered being twelve, and a tomboy, and surrounded by all the things that Esther Wyn had deemed part of evil America. She had never been a girlie girl; she could barely remember to pocket her lip gloss in the morning. For a long time, that didn't matter. But then sixth grade came, and suddenly all the girls were obsessing about clothes, endlessly fixing their hair, and speaking a foreign language called makeup. And then there was M.J. in her ponytail, high tops, and high-collared shirt that her mother made sure was buttoned to the very top button every morning. Add to that the fact that she could beat all the boys in gym class, and all the girls were convinced that she was a lesbian.

So while people always said that looks didn't matter, M.J. couldn't help being self-conscious about her appearance Thursday night on her way to dinner with Kevin. Decked out in a black wrap, teal halter dress with crystal chandelier earrings and a Shanghai Tang clutch, she cursed her heels after tripping twice before reaching the pricey Gotham Bar and Grill by Union Square. Like a giddy schoolgirl going to her first prom, M.J. was a mass of nerves as she entered the restaurant. As she spotted Kevin in the far corner of the bar, she did a quick hair-and-makeup check.

"Hey, there." M.J. smiled as she leaned in to give him a hug.

"What's going on? You look great." Kevin grinned at her.

"You, too," she said, trying to appear cool and confident.

Of course, Kevin looked like he'd spent the whole day in front of the mirror. He wore a button-down shirt and Banana Republic chinos, and his hair was immaculately gelled. In short, he looked exactly as M.J. remembered him from high school—perfect.

"So, would you like a drink?" Kevin asked. "Let me guess. Mandarin, Sprite, splash of cranberry?"

M.J. broke into a smile. "Very good. My turn. You want a Grey Goose on the rocks."

"Wow!" Kevin looked impressed. "I didn't think you'd remember the Grey Goose."

M.J. laughed. "Remember? How could I forget? You stole a whole bottle from your parents so we could play stupid games like duck duck goose, drink some Grey Goose in my house."

"That was a great night." He smiled. "I taught you how to dance the alphabet."

"You were so crazy then." She chuckled at the memory. "But now you're all Kevin Schmooze. You're quite the snazzy one these days with your NBA parties, Mr. Tennis Star."

Kevin smiled. "The sarcasm. You haven't changed, M.J., but I like it, always did."

She blushed, not having a comeback this time. For the rest of the dinner, she couldn't stop thinking about how great it all felt. There was something about Kevin that always made her feel like they were the only two people in the room. Even after ten years, M.J. still felt like that gangly teenager who couldn't believe the school's golden boy would give her a second glance. So while her dinner was delicious, she could only pick at it for fear of staining her new dress or worse, ending up with food stuck between her teeth.

"So tell me, are you happy with your life right now?" Kevin asked.

"I am." The moment the words left her lips, M.J. inwardly cringed at the lie. Who was she fooling? "Well, mostly. My career is something that's always been important and to be where I am right now means a lot to me. But recently I've been sending out these resumé reels, and so far no luck."

M.J. hesitated, the specter of all those rejection letters suddenly coming back to haunt her. With an effort, she wrenched her thoughts away from that morass. *Stop it,* she told herself firmly, *you're ruining a perfectly wonderful night.*

"Not that I'm complaining. I mean, my life isn't perfect, but . . ."

He finished her sentence as they said in unison, "It's not too shabby."

The two laughed, then stopped as their eyes met.

"That's good to hear." Kevin finally broke the silence. "I'm glad. I feel the same way. You know what's funny? We had this exact same conversation about eight years ago. I remember we were at the park sitting on one of those cruddy benches, and we had this intense conversation about what we wanted in life."

"Yeah, I remember. Then you started throwing tennis balls at me." She laughed.

"Was that before or after I kissed you?"

That stopped M.J. She met Kevin's gaze as the silence descended upon them. Then she looked away.

"I think that was before," she said, still not looking at him.

"You know, that was one of my favorite memories. If there's one thing I remember about high school, it's that day." Kevin took her hand, and M.J. felt her heart begin to melt.

"Yeah, it was nice," she admitted. M.J. cleared her throat. "You know, it's so weird that we ran into each other."

"I was just thinking that!" he said, releasing her hand. "I'm glad we did, though. Tonight made me realize how much I've missed M. J. Wyn."

"Well, everyone does love her." M.J. grinned. "After all, Ray Madden did ask her out. And I just might get a few marriage proposals at this *Dunk* party tonight."

Kevin laughed. "Oh, yeah? So you have men flocking to you now, huh? Including NBA stars?"

She smiled in what she hoped was a suitably mysterious way.

"So, Sporty Spice, are you seeing anyone?" he said, finally taking the bait.

At that moment, M.J. felt her heart skip a beat.

She shrugged as coolly as she could. "You know me. I'm not really seeing anyone serious right now . . . are you?"

"No . . . I guess I just haven't found the right person." Kevin looked her in the eye.

"I know what you mean," M.J. whispered.

Afterward, as they stepped out of the restaurant into the chilly March evening, M.J. barely felt a breeze. So far, the evening had been perfect. And now came her favorite part of every date—the post-dinner period. Tonight, they decided to take a stroll through Union Square Park en route to the 40/40 party.

"You know, M.J.," Kevin said slowly, "I had a really good time at dinner. It made me feel like—"

"Old times?"

"Stop reading my mind," he teased.

M.J. laughed. She stopped as Kevin caught her arm and turned her to face him.

"This was really special," he said softly. "I forgot how much fun we used to have together."

They both smiled as they leaned in for the kiss. M.J. closed her eyes, not believing what was happening even as their lips met. Her heart was beating double-time, her hands were trembling, and her head was suddenly awash in a swirl of unaccustomed emotions.

"Feels like we're back in high school again," he whispered when they finally pulled apart.

M.J. smiled. "Yeah, it kind of does."

MOVIE STARS had their high-profile soirees in Hollywood. Paris Hilton and Donald Trump had their socialite outings. In the world of sports, professional athletes partied until the wee hours of the night at the city hot spots. Members of the New York Knicks and the New Jersey Nets were both on hand at *Dunk* magazine's twenty-fifth anniversary party at the 40/40 Club in Manhattan.

For M.J., this was the perfect end to an already perfect evening. Going out with Kevin and feeling that old magic between them was heaven in itself. But gaining entry to one of Manhattan's hottest fetes and having access to the crème de la crème of the NBA—well, there was nothing like a little professional advancement to make personal triumphs even sweeter.

"This is so amazing." She beamed as she walked arm in arm with Kevin into the club's gold-plated, velvet-curtained VIP room. "I can't wait to try the five-hundred-dollar bottle of Grey Goose."

As they glided into the room, M.J. caught a glimpse of their reflection in a passing mirror. They looked beautiful—not quite Ken and Barbie, but at least Ken and Suzie Wong. Walking next to Kevin, M.J. felt like she was born to frequent such places.

"It's pretty cool, isn't it?" Kevin smiled. "Let me go get you a drink."

"Sounds like a plan. I'll have my usual."

M.J. did a quick survey of the room as Kevin walked away. Two seconds later, she spotted the entire Knicks and Nets teams in the corner. She had interviewed a lot of athletes in her career, but for some reason being at a party with them felt totally different. She decided a quick mirror check was definitely needed as she dug into her purse for her Vera Wang compact. As she took it out, someone accidentally bumped into her and knocked it out of her hand. Without even looking to see who it was, she quickly bent down to pick it up. But as she leaned down, a tall, familiar man dressed in a snazzy gray Armani suit already had it in his hand.

"I'm so sorry," Jamaal Winston apologized. "I'm the biggest klutz in the world. I'll buy you a new one."

M.J. immediately forgot all about the compact.

"Jamaal?" She smiled. "Hey, it's M.J. We met the other day."

"Of course . . . I remember you. M.J. Wyn! *Sporting Life.* It's good to see you again. So sorry about your . . ."

"No big deal. I have a dozen of these. It's good to see you, too. Great party tonight, huh?"

"Yeah." Jamaal nodded. "The place is pretty cool. Some of the guys and I are just chillin'. Wanna come hang with us?"

Hang with the team? Did she? M.J. could still remember how

consumed with envy she'd been when she was nine and obsessively watching Summer Sanders hang out with the basketball players on *NBA Inside Stuff*. With a shiver of anticipation, she grabbed her compact and stuffed it inside her purse.

"I'd love to." She smiled. "I'm just waiting for my friend, who is . . . wait! He's coming back right now."

With two drinks in hand, Kevin came over to M.J. and Jamaal.

"Thanks for the drink, Kevin," M.J. said quickly. "Kevin, this is Jamaal. Jamaal, this is Kevin."

Jamaal extended a hand. "Nice to meet you, man."

"Same here, Jamaal." Kevin grinned. "I work with *Dunk* magazine, so I guess it's my duty to ask if you're enjoying the party."

"It's a good time," Jamaal said earnestly. "In fact, I was telling M.J. to come over and hang out with the team."

"That sounds like a great idea." Kevin sipped his drink. "Lead the way."

They headed to the back corner. But before Jamaal even made any sort of introduction, all eyes were quickly on M.J.

"Hey, guys," Jamaal called above the music, "this is M.J. She writes for *Sporting Life*, and this is her friend Kevin. He's with *Dunk*."

M.J. waved. "Nice to meet you all."

Everyone waved back with ear-to-ear grins. Then, to her utter shock, Richard Robinson from the New Jersey Nets stood up to shake her hand. Wearing a tight muscle shirt and flaunting the Chinese character for "luck" on his right arm, he grinned at M.J.

"Haven't we met before?" he said in such a charming way that M.J. didn't even notice the hackneyed line.

The rest of the guys burst out laughing. She stole a glance at Kevin, who was watching all this and looking a little in shock. For once, it was M.J. who was at ease.

"We might have." She grinned at Richard. "I did a team interview with you guys two years ago on a freelance project, although we didn't really speak."

"That's right!" He snapped his fingers. "Before the Eastern Conference championship. See, I knew I'd remember a sweet china doll like you. There ain't that many in the business, ya know?"

"No, there aren't. And I can't say that I've met that many Wild-cats either. I would love to hear about the Final Four."

Out of the corner of her eye, M.J. was faintly aware of Kevin standing on the sidelines, watching. She wasn't sure if the expression on his face was amusement at watching a herd of NBA players hit on M.J. or jealousy. And if the latter, M.J. wasn't sure whether it was jealousy about these guys hitting on his date or jealousy that nobody was paying attention to him. Whatever it was, he apparently tried to edge closer to chat up some of the players, but before he could strike up a conversation, Eric Davis—*Dunk* magazine's managing editor and Kevin's boss—walked over to him. Nodding at whatever Richard was saying, M.J. tried to listen to Kevin and Eric's conversation.

"Hey, Kevin," Eric said urgently, "I need to talk to you for a second."

"Sure." Kevin frowned. "What's wrong?"

"Well, there's this situation," he sighed. "We're on deadline and one of the editors was rushed to the hospital with appendicitis. We need someone to go back to the office immediately to fill in for him."

"Right now?" Kevin took a deep breath. "Uh . . . sure, of course. Just let me tell my friend."

"Thanks, Kevin." Eric smiled. "You're the best."

As Kevin approached, M.J. turned toward him. "What's up, Kevin?" she said cheerily.

"I have to go. There's an emergency at work," he complained. "One of the editors has appendicitis and had to go to the hospital. Since they're closing the magazine tonight, I have to go back to the office to help out."

"Oh," she said, feeling a stab of disappointment. "That's too bad."

"Why don't I call you a cab?" Kevin asked, pulling out his cell phone.

"Well," M.J. hesitated, "Richard was just going to introduce me to some of the other players. . . ."

"Oh. So you want to stay?" Kevin looked taken aback.

M.J. bit her lip. She could tell that Kevin wasn't pleased about this turn of events. At the same time, it wasn't like she had anywhere she had to be. This was a great opportunity for her to make some important connections—of all people, Kevin should understand this.

"Well," she said slowly, "this is a great networking opportunity. I would love to stay, but if you would rather I didn't—"

"Did I say that?" he snapped. "You can stay if you want—I don't care."

M.J. stepped back, startled at his tone. Kevin must have sensed her reaction because he quickly touched her arm.

"I'm sorry," he said. "I didn't mean that. I'm just pissed I have to go to work. You should definitely stay. It's a great chance to meet some of the players."

"No, no." She hesitated. "Are you sure? I feel bad that you have to go back to work, while I have a good time here."

"Trust me, M.J., it's okay. I had fun tonight." He smiled at her then and all of M.J.'s misgivings evaporated.

"I really enjoyed myself, too." She smiled. "Especially our walk in the park."

Kevin leaned in to give her a kiss. "Yeah, that was just like old times, wasn't it? So, we'll talk tomorrow?"

"We better." M.J. kissed him back. "Well, as long as some NBA player and I don't elope to Vegas tonight."

Kevin laughed. "Oh, is that how it's going to be? Well, you behave yourself. I see these guys flirting with you and it's making me a little jealous."

Hearing Kevin say that he was jealous was almost as good as a bowl of butter pecan Häagen-Dazs with whipped cream. In all the time that M.J. and Kevin dated in high school, M.J. was the one who would get peeved when she saw some cheerleader chat up Kevin after a tennis match. And yet, here they were, years later, with the tables turned.

M.J. couldn't repress a little shiver of glee. Who would have thought that she'd be presented with this chance to rewrite the past? Who would have thought she'd have Kevin Taylor, the elite high school tennis star, jealous over her? Then again, she never imagined partying with a bunch of NBA millionaires either. It was almost too much to take in all at once.

"Jealous, huh?" she whispered. "There's nothing to be jealous about. Promise."

"Okay." Kevin kissed her again as he took off. "Talk to you tomorrow!"

One hour and six martinis later, M.J. was pretty giddy—and drunk. She was talking a mile a minute when Richard Robinson sat down beside her and handed her the seventh drink of the night. As she took the martini glass, Justin Timberlake's "Rock Your Body" started blasting.

"So, M.J." Richard grinned at her. "Do you dance?"

"You don't want to dance with me." She sipped her martini. "Asian chicks are the worst dancers ever."

"Come on." Richard took her hand. "Show me how horrible you are."

Suddenly, all the other players started chanting. "Dance! Dance! Dance!" They clapped and pounded the floor.

"Oh, okay . . . shush!" M.J. laughed as she took Richard's hand and started grooving with him on the dance floor.

The rest of the night was a blur. All M.J. knew was that she was moving on the dance floor, people were cheering her on, and she was having a fabulous time. Richard was a great dancer and taught her quite a few moves, one of which was grabbing M.J.'s waist from behind and twirling her around twice under the hot disco lights. Thankfully, Kevin wasn't there to see her.

Third
Quarter

six

THE NEXT morning was a no-Wyn situation. Not only was M.J. extremely hungover, but her phone started ringing the moment she walked into her office. She didn't even have time to eat the McGriddles sandwich or drink the coffee she'd picked up on the way to work.

"M.J. Wyn," she mumbled into the phone as she dropped her food, mail, and stack of newspapers on her desk. She paused as she noticed two suspiciously thin envelopes among her mail. *Great, some more rejection letters.*

"*Ahh-ya!*" M.J.'s mom, Esther, screamed so loudly that M.J. almost dropped the phone. "Explain to me about the newspaper, M.J.! What are you doing with that black man? Is he your boyfriend?"

M.J. crinkled her nose. "What are you talking about, Mom? And stop screaming in my ear. I just got to work."

"Look at page six of the newspaper today," Esther shouted. "There is a picture of you dancing with some black man named Richard Robinson. Who is he? Your new boyfriend? Your grandma saw this picture and she is very upset with you! She may not know how to read or speak English, but she keep on pointing at him and calling him *huck gwai*! She thinks you're a disgrace!"

M.J. rummaged through her mail to get to the newspaper and

turned to the gossip column, "Page Six." She dropped her hash brown on her desk.

"Shit!"

The photo caption under the picture of her and Richard Robinson dancing read "Dribblin' and Nibblin': New Jersey Nets star Richard Robinson gets down and dirty with new flame, *Sporting Life* writer M.J. Wyn, at *Dunk* magazine's 25th anniversary last night at 40/40."

"Mom—" M.J. took a deep breath. "—you got it all wrong. I went to this basketball party last night, and I was dancing with Richard Robinson from the New Jersey Nets. He's an NBA player. You know I would never date a ball player. I'm a sportswriter, and it would be completely unprofessional. I was just having some fun."

"Fun?" Esther continued to scream. "Do you know what's fun? You playing mah-jong with your aunties and uncles is what's fun. Not you dancing with a black man and being photographed in the newspaper for the whole world to see. *Ahh-ya!*"

M.J. groaned, wondering what she had done to deserve this. So what if M.J. really was dating Richard Robinson? The man was rich, famous, an amazing ball player, and gorgeous to boot. Who wouldn't want to date him? Of course, her mother wouldn't understand any of this. The problem was that M.J. knew this wouldn't stop. Now that the picture was plastered over the newspaper, she was going to be besieged with questions from all fronts.

"Look, Mom." M.J. was losing her patience. "I don't know what to tell you. I'm sorry if I've disgraced you, but nothing happened. Richard is one of the nicest guys in the NBA, and we were just having a good time. If you can't accept that I have friends like Richard, then I can't explain anything more to you. And Grandma is ninety years old. She's going to think horribly of me as long as I marry anyone who's not Chinese."

"I know that you love your job." Esther was calming down a bit. "I just want you to be careful and not do anything stupid. I worry."

"I understand, Mom." She sighed. "I have to go to a meeting now. I'll talk to you later."

As M.J. hung up the phone, she took a swig of her coffee to fortify herself. Two seconds later, her phone rang again.

"Yes?" she answered warily.

"You're, like, famous!" Lin screamed. "I told everyone at work how my cool friend, J, was getting jiggy with an NBA player!"

"Lin—" M.J. shook her head. "My mother just called to lecture me. I can't deal with this right now. Everyone is freaking out."

"Wait," Lin said, "are you okay? How was your date with Kevin?"

Kevin. Shockingly, M.J. had forgotten all about him. She flashed back to her kiss that seemed like an eternity ago. Thinking about him, she had a sudden moment of panic. What if Kevin saw the picture of her and Richard Robinson in the paper? What if he actually believed that there was something going on between her and Richard? Kevin hadn't exactly been thrilled about M.J. staying at the party, and she knew it.

"It was amazing," M.J. gushed, her voice changing at the mere mention of him. "He was so sweet, and we had such a great time."

"That's wonderful!" Lin exclaimed. "I want details!"

"I would love to give them to you"—M.J. frowned at the persistent ringing on her other line—"but I've got another call. It's probably the *Enquirer*. I'll call you later. Bye, hon."

She quickly took a bite out of her sandwich before she answered her next phone call. It was Kevin.

"Hey!" M.J. quickly swallowed her food. "How are you?"

"You tell me how you are," Kevin said. "Looks like you forgot about me and ran off to Vegas with Richie Rich last night, huh?"

M.J. pulled at her hair in frustration. "Kevin, I can explain. He asked me to dance, and I guess these photographers started snapping pictures. I had no idea they were going to appear on 'Page Six.' "

There was a long pause. Then Kevin laughed. "It's okay. Really. I didn't call you to give you a hard time. I called to tell you that I'm glad you had a good time last night, and I hope you had an even better time before the party."

M.J.'s face cleared. "Of course I did," she said, a slow smile creeping across her face. "I'm sorry you had to work. Did everything pan out with the magazine?"

"Everything was fine," he assured her. "I mean, it sucked to be at the office instead of the party. Especially since it took a lot of hard work for me to score an invite. It's not easy getting a chance to talk to these players, especially in an informal setting. I guess I should be glad that one of us put my hard work to good use."

M.J. frowned, not sure how to respond. This was crazy. She couldn't actually be put in a position to have to choose between her career and her crush, could she?

"Anyway," Kevin cleared his throat, "I just called to say hi. I actually have to go because we have a meeting in a few about the close. I'll call you later?"

"Okay." She smiled hesitantly. "Bye."

The morning couldn't have been more bizarre for M.J. First, she had to deal with a hangover and her mother's tongue-lashing, but now Kevin had just made it all better. Or had he?

That was when her phone rang for the fourth time in the past fifteen minutes.

"Hello?" she answered.

"This is exactly what I'm talking about!" a familiar male voice started ranting. "This is exactly how women lose credibility in the business. I thought I'd taught you enough for you to know better, M.J."

"Good morning to you, too, Ming," she said as lightly as possible.

"You know what? I'm not even going to say anything. You're a smart and attractive girl. If you want to trash your career by partying away your rep, go ahead, but don't come to me when you have no job. How many times have I told you that Asian girls need to maintain a professional reputation and not do things like this!"

"I hear you, Ming," M.J. said, "and maybe I was a little stupid. But I'm allowed to have fun, you know . . . even if my eyes are slanted."

Ming was furious. "You are unbelievable, M.J. You never learn, do you?"

"I'm just speaking the truth," she snapped. "You need to quit it with your Asian dos and don'ts. People are allowed to do whatever they want now. Different races can even get it on if they like."

"Oh, so you're saying you did get it on with Richard Robinson?"

"No!" she screamed. "Ugh . . . think what you want. I can't have this conversation with you right now."

M.J. couldn't believe it. Who would guess that dancing with someone would and could become such a big deal? She had barely hung up on Ming when there was a knock on her door. A moment later, in barged Jagger. He was dressed in his typical "ratboy" fashion—baseball cap, Taco Bell T-shirt, battered jeans, Skechers. Looking at him, she couldn't help contrasting him with the ever-polished and immaculately attired Kevin.

"What's up, man?" Jagger popped a Munchkin into his mouth. "Why the long face?"

"Shut up, Quinn," M.J. growled. "I don't need this from you right now."

"Need what? Some loving from me early in the morning? Everyone does."

M.J. was confused. Could Jagger really be that clueless?

"Earth to Quinn—do you have any idea what I've been through this morning? It's spelled *H-E-L-L!*"

"Really? What's going on? Do you need a hug?" He grinned.

"You really don't know, do you? Hello! 'Page Six,' me, Robinson?"

"Oh, that." He shrugged. "That's no biggie. Why do you care what people think of you?"

"What?"

"You heard me," he said. "What happens in your life is nobody's business but yours."

M.J. stopped. Sitting in her chair, she suddenly felt tremendously calmer. In a way, Jagger was right. She was just having some fun—drinking and dancing. Everyone did it, so why should she be penalized for it? It wasn't like she'd committed a crime. For once, Jagger was making sense, a lot of sense.

"You know, Quinn," she said slowly, "you're completely right. Who cares about those pictures?"

"Now you're catching on, Wyn." Jagger winked as he stood up. "Anyway, I'm out—I've got a phoner with that hot tennis player Daniela Hantuchova. I'll catch you later."

"Later, Quinn." M.J. smiled and watched him walk out the door. Who would have thought that of everyone she knew, Jagger would turn out to be the coolest about this whole episode?

AFTER THE drama with the 40/40 Club and the "Page Six" debacle, all M.J. wanted was to get far away from the glitz and the glamour that she usually loved so much. Which is how M.J. and Alex ended up at McCormack's Friday night. It was one of M.J.'s favorite haunts, even though it was the kind of place that Lin would turn her nose up at. But when it came to a low-key establishment offering a good pint of Bass and unrestricted views of the basketball game du jour, McCormack's was the place to be.

Fortunately, Alex had that hard-nosed lawyer's affinity for no-frills sports bars and anything smacking of competition. While on first glance, the sportswriter and the lawyer didn't seem to have much in common, time had shown otherwise. In fact, M.J. often thought that she and Alex had more in common than she and Lin did. Like M.J., Alex didn't care about designer labels or girly beauty products or sleazy brokers on the make.

"Okay," Alex said, plopping down on the barstool beside M.J., "so how was this fancy party of yours that your fancy ex-boyfriend took you to?"

M.J. decided to ignore the not-so-subtle dig. "The party was great. The after-party—not so great."

"Yeah," Alex said dryly, "Lin filled me in on 'Page Six.' "

"Who would think that a little dance could cause such a ruckus? Anyway, I don't want to talk or think about it anymore."

Alex shrugged. "Fine by me. So when's the Texas–UConn game on?"

"In ten minutes. Why? You got money on the game?"

"Damn straight." Alex took a swig of her beer. "I need this game to win the office pool—"

"What's this about the office pool?" A well-dressed, strikingly handsome guy in his thirties eased into the seat beside Alex.

M.J. regarded the newcomer with interest, her journalistic antennae perking up immediately. Alex, on the other hand, looked ready to have a stroke.

"Brady—what are you doing here?"

"I'm stalking you, of course." Their new barmate appeared undeterred as he turned to M.J. with a gleaming smile. "Why hello there, I'm Brady. I work with Alex. And you would be . . . ?"

"M.J. A friend." M.J. smiled and shook the hand he extended.

"Pleasure to meet you," Brady said. "What brings you two gals to McCormack's?"

M.J. opened her mouth to answer, but Alex beat her to the punch.

"Nothing," she replied quickly. "M.J. and I are just getting a few drinks at our favorite bar."

"Actually," M.J. pointed up to the TV screen, "we were planning to catch the Texas–UConn game."

"Really?" Brady exclaimed. "What do you know? So was I!"

"You were not, Brady." Alex rolled her eyes.

"I beg your pardon," he said. "You know I'm a big Huskies fan."

"No way." M.J. broke into a smile. "I'm actually a Husky myself—I went to UConn."

"Well, then." Brady grinned. "I guess we'll have ourselves a little rooting section here." He slung an easy arm on the back of Alex's chair and hissed to M.J. in a stage whisper. "Good thing I don't give up easily, huh?"

M.J. chuckled. In a way, Brady reminded her of Jagger. Especially when Jagger was doing his pseudo-antagonistic-flirtation bit.

Stop it. M.J. shook herself. Why was she giving Jagger a second's thought when she should be concentrating on Kevin? Quickly pulling her cell phone out of her bag, she punched in Kevin's number. A moment later, he answered. "Hello?"

"Hey," M.J. said, "I was just thinking about you. . . ."

seven

BY MONDAY morning, M.J. was feeling immeasurably calmer. Her mother was no longer convinced that she was having an affair with Richard Robinson, she had gotten only one rejection letter all week long, Ming was talking to her again, and Kevin seemed to have gotten over whatever resentment he harbored over the 40/40 party. In fact, they had a lovely picnic on the Great Lawn on Saturday, and M.J. was finally feeling like everything was under control again. Or so she thought.

"Wyn, I want a story on Roger Clemens's perfect game by Friday," M.J.'s editor Walt barked on the phone.

"You got it, Walt." M.J. nodded, mentally counting off the hundred other things she had on her plate. It had been an insane morning with the phone ringing off the hook and e-mails popping up every two seconds. Her mother had called to harangue her about missing their weekly family dinner for a feature in Pittsburgh. She had barely been able to get her story on Asian-American athletes in by the deadline. And, now, on top of all that, she had her editor harassing her.

As if sensing the bad timing, Jagger barged into M.J.'s office just as she got off the phone with Walt.

"So, Wyn, you going to give me some competition this year for the Ed Press Award? I'm getting a little tired of winning every year."

"Actually, I just might give you a run for your money," she smirked. "I just submitted a kick-ass article this morning on Asian-American athletes."

"Asian-American athletes, huh? Interesting. Guess those geeks Gary and Anthony inspired you."

M.J. rolled her eyes. "Yeah, right."

"Well, we're doing a feature on Clemens's three hundred for our special baseball edition," Jagger said. "It's no 'Asian-American athlete' story, but it's still pretty cool."

"A feature, huh?" M.J. felt a stab of envy as she suddenly flashed back to her PlayBall nightmare. What she wouldn't give to be working on a "feature" . . .

"Yup. Jealous?" Jagger joked.

Suddenly, M.J. lost it. Perhaps it was the stress of her deadlines, or maybe it was the whole PlayBall incident coming back to mock her on-air aspirations. Most likely it was because Jagger had struck too close to home.

"My story is going to be so hot that it's going to make your piece look like a kiddie book," she snapped, "even though you think you're all that because you've won the Ed Press Award. My story is going to blow yours out of the stands!"

Jagger stepped back. "Whoa! Where's this coming from?"

"I don't need this!" she yelled, feeling ready to tear her hair out. "Don't come barging into my office like we're 'buds' anymore!"

The minute the words left M.J.'s lips, she regretted them. But it had been a tough morning, and she just couldn't handle it anymore.

Jagger stared at her, a stunned look on his face. For the first time since she had known him, he didn't have a comeback—and for Jagger Quinn, that was something big. M.J. swallowed, not sure how she could retract her words.

She opened her mouth to say something just as Cindy walked in, wearing a typically trashy, office-inappropriate outfit consisting of a ruffled blouse with a plunging neckline and a miniskirt. "Is everything okay in here? You two are always fighting. You're like an old married couple."

"Now's not a good time, Cindy," M.J. snapped.

"What's the matter, Wyn?" Jagger demanded, an undercurrent of hurt and anger tingeing his voice. "Afraid that I'll say something?"

M.J. groaned. She didn't know what ancient Chinese gods she'd offended to deserve a horrible day like this. Add Cindy to the mix, and M.J. was close to heading to her grandmother's Chinese witch doctor.

"Please"—M.J. threw her hands up in total exasperation—"can everyone please just leave?"

"Why are you always so mean to Jagger?" Cindy asked.

Great, M.J. thought, now she was being a bitch on top of it all. All she wanted to do was go home, take a long, hot bath, and forget about this entire day. Too bad she still had a deadline to meet. When Cindy wasn't around, she decided, she would apologize to Jagger, explain the pressure she was under.

"Jagger, I'll talk to you later, and Cindy, I'm going to say this nicely one more time," M.J. said coolly, "please leave my office."

AFTERWARD, AFTER M.J. had calmed down, she wondered why she had lost it with Jagger. Yes, he had been a wiseass, but no more so than usual. What it boiled down to was that he'd had the bad timing to come in just when she was at her most strung out. With all that was going on in her life with her continuing on-air job search, the rejection letters, and Kevin, M.J. was feeling a little stretched thin, and it didn't help that her editor was now piling on the work.

Still, that was no excuse for taking her frustrations out on Jagger. Feeling guilty, M.J. vowed to apologize to him the next time she saw him.

"Here, have a drink." Lin handed her a glass of wine.

M.J. gave her a grateful smile. "Thanks. Believe me, I need this."

After a long day at work, M.J. and Lin had stopped by a recruiting event hosted by Alex's law firm at the Sean Kelly Gallery in Chelsea. A sleek, ultramodern space with white walls and gleaming concrete floors, the art gallery featured a series of black-and-white photographs that converged in a striking, windowlike grid.

"Pretty cool." M.J. strolled up to read the label next to one of the pictures. "Lorna Simpson. Can't say I've heard of her, but then again this is the first gallery I've ever been to."

"You're kidding me," Alex exclaimed. "Didn't you ever take an art class? School trip?"

M.J. shook her head. "Actually . . . no."

Alex sighed. "Well, then, I guess you've never heard of this gallery."

"Nope." M.J. shrugged. "But you know what's funny? This place does look kind of familiar."

"Probably because you saw it on *Sex and the City*," Lin said. "This is the gallery where Carrie and Charlotte saw that performance artist—you know, the one who spent twelve days living here."

"Ohhh, that's right!" M.J.'s eyes lit up. "This is the place where Carrie met Mikhail Baryshnikov!"

"Exactly." Lin smiled.

Alex took a sip of her drink. "Well, at least you recognized something."

M.J. dropped her shoulders and stared at her glass as several of Alex's colleagues came over to talk to Alex and Lin began chatting up one of the lawyers. It was times like these when she felt like there was a gulf between her and her friends that could never be bridged. She would never be smart and cultured like Alex, or the belle of every ball like Lin. Standing alone in her battered Levi's and Skechers, M.J. wondered if she would always be that awkward loser in seventh grade.

In junior high, M.J. had always stood out—she remembered being taller than the tallest boy in class and slouching through the hallways with jeans that were never the right shade of stonewash, an ugly bowl haircut, and the Hello Kitty sweater that no self-respecting girl over the age of ten would ever don. She couldn't forget the giggles—the titters at her Kmart clothing, the gagging noises at the pungent rice-and-lotus-leaf-and-preserved-egg combinations that her mother concocted for her every day for lunch. Back then, the only place she found solace from the whispers was out on the tennis court, where the only sound was the steady thump of yellow felt on hot green asphalt and the only tears were from the sweat on her brow.

M.J. wished she were there now. She noticed Brady waving at her from across the room, but she was afraid he'd try to engage her in some high-brow discourse on art. Quickly waving back, she slunk around the corner and ran straight into—Stephen Xiang.

"Stephen? Is that you?" M.J. almost didn't recognize him in his funky square glasses and vintage shirt. Lin's ex-boyfriend of five years, Stephen had dated her friend through her senior year of college, all the way up until about a year ago when Lin decided she and Stephen weren't meant to be.

"M.J.?" Stephen said, giving her a hug. "Wow, this is a surprise. I haven't seen you since your birthday party last year." He smiled at the memory. "How are you doing?"

"I'm good," M.J. said. "You?"

"Can't complain," he replied. "I have to say—I would never have expected to see you here."

M.J. chuckled. "That makes two of us. I'm here for some event that Alex's firm is hosting. What about you? Just taking in some art?"

"That I am," he said. "The gallery is sponsoring a 'New Visions' exhibition of unknown artists, and I was thinking about submitting some of my pictures."

M.J.'s mouth dropped. "That's great! That would be so cool if you got to show your stuff here."

"I know," he said. "I'm keeping my fingers crossed. The competition's pretty fierce."

"Yeah," M.J. nodded, "I can see that. I have to admit though, I don't know much about art."

"There's nothing wrong with that," Stephen said. "I didn't used to know anything either. Hey, after tonight, I bet you'll know who Lorna Simpson is, right?"

M.J. laughed. "I guess so."

Feeling better, she smiled at Stephen and glanced back at the other end of the room. "Uh, Lin is actually over there if you want to talk to her."

Stephen followed M.J.'s gaze to where Lin was tossing her hair and laughing with some blond guy from Alex's firm. His smile faded.

"She looks a little busy," he murmured. "And I really have to get going, too. Can you just tell her hello from me?"

M.J. nodded. As she watched him leave, she found herself thinking that maybe Mama Kim wasn't so crazy after all . . .

"There you are!" Lin appeared at M.J.'s elbow. "I've been looking for you everywhere. You missed it—I was talking to this really cute guy at Alex's firm—"

"I saw," M.J. interrupted. "Actually, guess who I just ran into? Stephen!"

Lin blinked. "Stephen? My Stephen? What was he doing here?"

"He's trying to get his pictures into this exhibit the gallery is having. Isn't that cool?" It was funny, M.J. thought. Who knew that Stephen had this artsy, creative side?

Lin frowned. "Since when did Stephen take up photography?"

"I don't know," M.J. replied, "but he was looking kind of cool tonight. He was wearing these funky square glasses and had this whole hipster thing going on."

"Really?" Lin said. "That's weird. Anyway, do you still want to grab a bite to eat?"

M.J. nodded. As she followed her friend out of the gallery, she suddenly felt grateful that she had reconnected with Kevin. Otherwise, she might have been like Stephen now—still pining after an old flame who couldn't care less about him.

"I THINK J is falling in love," Lin teased half an hour later as she buttered her bread at Serafina. A trendy Italian restaurant in the Village, the popular weekend hot spot boasted its very own DJ and dance floor.

"Am not." M.J. blushed. "Yes, we've been seeing a lot of each other, but it's not like we're ready to run off and get married. I mean, I like Kevin. And I like us, but I don't want to jinx it. I just feel like this is all too good to be true."

"Sometimes—" Lin took a bite of her bread. "—you have to let go. You may think it sounds too good to be true, but who knows? Maybe it really is as good as it seems."

M.J. smiled at her friend gratefully. At times like these, she forgave Lin for all her girly-girl antics and was just glad to have Lin on her side. Even if Lin had dumped a great guy like Stephen. Yes, Lin was a little boy-crazy, and yes, her taste was a little suspect when it came to guys. Give her a smooth talker with a silver tongue and an Armani wardrobe, and Lin was sold. M.J. had never understood that part of Lin, had always chalked it up to another example of how they were polar opposites of each other—but now, for the first time, she was beginning to think they weren't so different after all.

"I know. I just think that—" M.J. stopped as she caught sight of Jagger walking into the restaurant with Cindy and his buddies. All her frustration from the morning came rushing back. She had left work thinking that she had to apologize to Jagger, that she didn't give him enough credit sometimes. As she watched Cindy, M.J. decided that she gave Jagger exactly the amount of credit he deserved.

Lin shook her arm. "What's going on, J?"

"Brace yourself," M.J. whispered as Jagger and Cindy walked over.

"What's up, Wyn?" Jagger grinned. "You're looking good tonight. What are you doing in this part of town?"

"Just getting some food after a party. I had no idea that you and Cindy would be here, too," M.J. said, feeling an unexpected stab of jealousy.

"Isn't it a small world, M.J.? I ran into Jagger at the gym, and he told me he was going out, so I decided to join him," Cindy said cheerfully. Per her usual attire, she was all decked out in fishnet stockings, stiletto heels, and midriff-baring top.

M.J. hated the situation for about a million reasons. It was bad enough that she had to see Cindy and Jagger after work hours, but somehow, seeing them both together made her—what? There was that word again. Jealous.

Lin faked a cough, obviously wanting to be introduced.

"Guys, I want you to meet my friend, Lin," M.J. said, smiling lightly. "Lin, this is Jagger and Cindy."

Jagger and Cindy took turns shaking Lin's hand.

Lin smiled as she quickly shot M.J. an omigosh-this-is-Jagger look. M.J. suppressed a grin. Jagger was the antithesis of Lin's kind of guy—laid-back, messy, had never walked into a Kenneth Cole store in his life.

"And these are my friends Danny, Brian, and Justin," Jagger said.

"Nice to meet you," the guys said in unison.

"Would you care to join us?" Lin asked politely.

M.J. kicked Lin, who smiled mischievously.

"Sure, but I'm going to sit next to Wyn. She'll keep me warm." Jagger waved his buddies to sit down.

"Ugh!" M.J. made a face at Jagger. "You're so . . . so . . ."

"It's okay, Wyn. I know you like me," he said airily.

The table roared with laughter as everyone watched the M.J. and Jagger show.

That is except for Cindy, who looked disgusted as she changed the topic. "So, Jagger and I were thinking of going clubbing later on. Anyone want to join us?"

M.J. shook her head. "I'll pass. I have work tomorrow."

"Come on, Wyn. It could be like a date," Jagger teased.

"I'd rather relace my tennis shoes," she shot back.

"That's right, I forgot. You only go for Ken dolls who shop at Banana Republic." Jagger looked her straight in the eye. "When are you going to realize that there's more to a person than their appearance?"

"Guys, guys, let's simmer down," Danny said, trying to play peacemaker.

M.J. rubbed her temples, not wanting Jagger to see how close to home he'd hit. All her life, she had felt like an outsider looking in, whether it was at work, at school, or at the Sean Kelly Gallery. She had always wanted to be with someone beautiful, someone socially acceptable, someone who might bring her into the inner circle where all her hopes and dreams seemed to live. Even Kevin had been someone who fulfilled her criteria for looks, attire, and country club background. Someone who could make her forget about being the tall girl with the Kmart clothes and the weird Chinese lunches, the girl who never got a passing glance from any of the boys except when they were facing off against her in gym class.

"Just admit it, M.J. You don't think I'm good enough for you." Jagger stared at her, refusing to let her avoid the issue.

"You two should just do it and get it over with," Brian suddenly interrupted, breaking the tension of the moment and causing a smattering of laughter among the relieved crew.

M.J.'s face flushed. "Screw all of you."

M.J. STALKED toward the door, completely and utterly furious. But more than that—hurt. Who did Jagger think he was, embarrassing her like that? And his friends—what jerks! Jagger deserved to be with Cindy. In fact, they could live happily ever after and move into a trailer park and have wretched trailer trash kids.

"J!" Lin chased after her friend. "Will you wait up?"

M.J. was still fuming, but she forced herself to stop. Lin trotted up, a little out of breath. "Okay, that was annoying," Lin acknowledged.

M.J. whirled around. "Who is he to make judgments about me? I could just wring his skinny little neck!"

"Forget about him," Lin said soothingly. "Why don't we call it a night and head home? You look like you could use some rest."

M.J. fought back tears, her thoughts still on Jagger. "You know, Lin—I think you're right."

But as she headed home, M.J.'s thoughts were in turmoil. Not only had she felt like an ignoramus and a wallflower at the art gallery, but now she was angry at Jagger, angry at Cindy, and angry at herself for being angry at all. So what if she wanted to be with someone who represented everything she had always wanted but could never quite attain in her life? Was being with someone rich and handsome so different from the way her family had come to America trying to better themselves?

And yet, despite all this, she couldn't help feeling like a hypocrite. Somehow, her weakness for Kevin made M.J. betray her girl-power bar challenges, her tirades about females playing dumb, and everything she had ever said about being a strong, independent woman.

Fourth Quarter

eight

AS TERRIBLE as her evening was, the morning after brought unexpected bliss. For M.J., writing a piece that made the cover story was something akin to winning an Oscar. Which was why she was ecstatic today. Not only was her story on aspiring Asian-American athletes in the U.S. on the front cover of the March issue of *SL*, but it had also been nominated for the Ed Press Journalism Award. It might not be as good as getting her dream of an on-air gig, but it did take some of the sting out of all her rejection letters.

M.J. strolled into the conference room in her power suit to see that all the bigwigs of the company were present to discuss the upcoming anniversary issue. Edward Tucci, the senior executive vice president of *SL*, walked over to her.

"Congratulations, M.J. That was a great story. I've heard a lot of good things about it, and we're doing our best to get you this award."

"Thanks," she said, blushing.

She took a look around the crowded conference room and spotted an empty seat next to Jagger, who was wearing a *Dukes of Hazzard* T-shirt. As M.J. met his gaze, he flashed her a flirtatious smile and wagged his finger for her to sit down next to him, as if nothing had happened between them last night.

Reluctantly, she plopped down beside him. She was still peeved

with Jagger, but had calmed down enough to see that maybe she'd
overreacted about the whole thing. In retrospect, she didn't know
why she was so bothered by it. After all, she should be used to spar-
ring with him by now, given their daily jabfests. So what if he wanted
to spend his time trolling around with women like Cindy? He was
free to do as he wished—and M.J. had absolutely no say in any of it.

"So you're invading our private editorial meetings now? Doesn't
RealSports have its own 'gatherings'?" she quipped.

"No, but thanks for your concern," Jagger said blithely. "You
know," he said in a more serious tone, "that was a really good piece
you wrote. You did a great job and got a lot of first-rate material.
Nice work, Wyn."

M.J. was shocked but touched by his compliment. Jagger was a
winner of several journalism awards, so his opinion definitely
counted.

"Thanks, Jagger," she said, shifting awkwardly in her seat.

"Why don't we go celebrate tonight?" he suggested. "Tequila
shots on me."

"Thanks." Her voice softened. "I appreciate the invite, but I already have other plans."

Surprisingly, M.J. felt a stab of regret as the words left her lips.
She knew he was trying to make amends, and she didn't want him
to think that she really *did* think she was too good for him. Fortunately, if that was what Jagger thought, he hid it well.

"Come on, what better plans could you possibly have besides
hanging out with me?" he teased. "Are you going to break my heart,
M.J., and tell me that you have another man?"

That caught her off guard. *Did* she have a "man"? She and
Kevin had been seeing each other for a while now, but they hadn't
come close to having "the talk." Still, they had a lot of fun together,
and M.J. was feeling more and more sure about their relationship.
She was confident that it would only be a matter of time before
they became a "real" couple.

"You never can tell," she replied mysteriously. "Sorry, but
maybe I'll call you later."

As she watched Jagger's face fall, M.J. felt a twinge of regret. To her surprise, he looked truly disappointed. But then he shrugged it off and smiled at her as if to say it was all okay.

HOURS LATER, M.J. was still mulling over Jagger's new attitude as she braved the rain to meet Kevin downtown. It was with an effort that she wrenched her thoughts away from him as she greeted Kevin with a kiss.

"So, are you ready to retire now that your story might win an Ed Press Award?" Kevin playfully nudged M.J. as they strolled together under his umbrella.

"Maybe. I mean, my house is waiting for me now on Park Avenue, and I'll be hobnobbing with my new neighbor Katie Couric on Saturday," M.J. joked.

"You're such a wiseass." Kevin laughed as he leaned into her. "Maybe it's a good thing we broke up. Otherwise, we'd be married now, and I'd have to support your expensive habits!"

M.J. frowned, not quite sure how to take the remark, but she quickly forgot about it as Kevin kissed her.

After a long moment, they finally came up for air.

"So, do you want to come over to my place tonight?" he whispered.

"Your place, huh?" M.J. smiled.

EVEN THOUGH they'd been going out for several weeks now, M.J. had yet to make it back to Kevin's apartment. Now that she was finally there, she was more than a little surprised at the immaculate condition. In fact, she was completely floored by the antiseptic cleanliness of the place.

"Your place is a lot neater than mine," M.J. observed.

"I can't stand a messy room." Kevin wrinkled his nose as he stamped his shoes dry on the doormat. "Do you want something to drink?"

"Sure, I'll have whatever you're having."

M.J. carefully sat down on the leather couch, amazed by its perfectly flawless exterior. It wasn't just that, though. Everything was cold, impersonal, sterile. There were no picture frames or posters, nothing with even a hint of personality. Sure, the furniture was expensive, but the room could have been lifted straight out of the show window of Macy's.

Kevin walked over to the coffee table with a bottle of merlot in hand.

"So, how's your job going?" M.J. asked as she took a sip of her wine.

"It's going well," he replied. "It's tough sometimes. I always thought that this was what I wanted to do, but now I'm not so sure. The travel can be grueling. But I'm young. We'll see what happens."

"Well, if you weren't going to be doing this, what would you be doing?"

"To be honest, I don't know. I just want to be on ESPN and have a beautiful wife." Kevin drained his wineglass.

"A beautiful wife, huh?" M.J. grinned. "Sounds like you have your whole life planned out."

Kevin chuckled. "Well, you don't grow up being a Taylor without mapping your future."

M.J. paused. "What do you mean?"

"Oh, you know." He made a vague wave. "My family has all these expectations about everything I do—where I go to school, where I work, who I marry."

M.J.'s grip on her wineglass suddenly stiffened. She flashed him her brightest smile. "So do you have an arranged marriage somewhere in your future?"

He laughed but didn't answer her. Instead, he drew her to him and started to kiss her. M.J. sat on the couch, still tense, as he nuzzled her neck. Fortunately—or unfortunately—Kevin didn't appear to notice.

"This is perfect," he murmured into her hair. "So much better than high school."

High school? M.J. blinked. So this was Kevin's memory of their senior year? She had too many memories of their short-lived courtship, and the last memory involved her staring at her tear-streaked face in the girls' bathroom mirror.

Kevin kissed her neck as he started unbuttoning her blouse. "You know, because we don't have to worry about where all this is going."

M.J. froze. She couldn't help thinking about the "Taylor marriage plan." Jerking away abruptly, she almost pushed Kevin off the couch.

"What do you mean by that?" she demanded.

"Nothing," Kevin said quickly, "I just meant that it's great that we can have an adult relationship now. Not like in high school, where we had to worry about things like going steady and promise rings and all that."

M.J. pursed her lips. "Is that what we have now? An adult relationship? What exactly does that mean? Hooking up?"

"No. I mean, I don't know. These past couple weeks have been amazing." Kevin ran a hand through his hair nervously. "But I'm not ready for a commitment. I mean, I know you really well, and I . . ."

"You want what, Kevin? You want me in your life, but you don't want 'us'?" M.J. was fast losing her cool, her perfect night slowly becoming a perfect nightmare.

"Exactly," Kevin took her hand, "so you understand! You and I are such great friends, and we have this connection. I don't want to lose you, but I'm not ready to tie myself down to one woman."

There was nothing more that M.J. wanted at that moment than to run away and not have to deal with the situation, to escape to the refuge of the tennis courts, just like in high school. But she wasn't seventeen anymore, and she wasn't going to settle for being somebody else's training wheels.

"I'm not going to lie to you, Kevin. I think we're great together, but you need to figure out exactly what you want out of this relationship."

Kevin frowned. "I don't know what the problem is, M.J. I mean,

I thought you were enjoying our time together. We go to dinner, I take you to fancy parties like the 40/40 Club. You would never have gotten to hang out with those NBA players if it wasn't for me. Believe me, I had to work really hard just to get an invite to that party. If it wasn't for the magazine closing, I would have been the one making the contacts."

"I see," she said slowly, "so you *were* pissed that I stayed and hung out with those players. Why? Because for the first time ever, I was actually better at something than you?"

"Don't be ridiculous," Kevin snapped, "we both know that Richard Robinson would rather be hanging out with some cute Asian girl than me. That's not the point—"

"But it is," she cut in. "You're mad because I outscooped you. Shouldn't you be happy that at least one of us got something out of the night since you couldn't? I was always your biggest cheerleader at your matches. Why can't you be mine?"

"You're blowing this out of proportion," Kevin declared, obviously deciding it was time to backtrack.

"I don't think so," M.J. said quietly. "Maybe you always have to be better than me. The better tennis player, the better reporter. Is that why you're afraid to commit to this relationship? Because you think I'm not good enough for you?"

"M.J.—" Kevin shook his head. "This has nothing to do with any of that. Look, I want you in my life, but I don't know if I can handle a relationship right now. Maybe if we could just see each other once in a while . . ."

Crying wasn't something that M.J. did very often. In fact, it had happened only a few times before: once when she lost the state tennis championship, once when she got her job at *Sporting Life*, once when the PlayBall director told her she was too "vanilla," and once when she got in a fight with her parents. Make that five now.

Tears welling up in her eyes, M.J. mumbled, "I'm sorry you feel that way, but I won't and can't just be someone you call when you feel lonely. Obviously, I was being naïve to think we really had something again."

"You have it all wrong, M.J. You've been one of the most important people in my life. I just don't want to promise you something I can't give you."

And there it was. He had finally come right out and said it—he would never be able to give her what she wanted, would never be able to make her a member of that inner circle. . . .

Kevin looked at M.J.'s expression and sighed. "I guess I can't make you understand how I feel."

"No, you can't." M.J. grabbed her bag. "And I can't make you understand how I feel."

"M.J., please don't go," Kevin yelled as she fled down the hallway. But this time, she didn't look back.

A MONTH *before they broke up in high school, Kevin had invited M.J. to the Christmas party at the country club.*

M.J. was thrilled. Parties at the country club were always extravagant affairs, and she had no doubt that the Christmas party would exceed even her expectations. Listening to Kevin's family discuss the party only served to heighten her anticipation.

"I hear Jimmy Carter is going to play Santa Claus this year," Kevin's mother said over dinner one night.

M.J.'s eyes widened as she paused in the middle of cutting her steak. The Jimmy Carter?

"Really?" Kevin said. "How did the club swing that?"

"Apparently, he went to school with the club president," his mother replied. "Now that he has some extra time on his hands, he was more than happy to accept the invitation."

"That's great," Kevin's brother, Tom, announced. "Mom, can Lizzie's family come to the party, too? I'm sure they would love to meet Jimmy Carter."

Lizzie was Tom's girlfriend of two months. M.J. had met her briefly over dinner at Kevin's house one night. While no brain surgeon, Lizzie was sweet enough that M.J. didn't mind the occasional double date with the Taylor brothers.

"Of course, Lizzie's family can come, dear." Mrs. Taylor smiled indulgently.

M.J. turned and looked expectantly at Kevin, waiting for the impending invitation. Except that . . . it never came. Kevin studiously ate his meat loaf, completely avoiding M.J. Confused, she glanced around the table, only to find the entire Taylor family fixated on the dishes before them, each and every one of them evading eye contact with her.

It was then that M.J. knew that she and Kevin were doomed. While she may have been an acceptable invitee at the country club, it was clear that the Wyn family was not. And if the Wyn family wasn't accepted at the club, how could they ever be accepted by the Taylor family?

The rest of dinner was pure, unmitigated torture. M.J. focused on chewing her food, which suddenly tasted like sea-drenched sand in her mouth. She knew she should have spoken out, should have called them on their hypocrisy, should have confronted Kevin about his spinelessness. But the minute she did that, this would all come to an end—the refined conversations, the gourmet dinners at the Taylor home, the invitations to the country club. The feeling, for the first time in her life, that she belonged, an outsider no more. And she wasn't ready for that.

So instead she stayed silent, hated herself for her cowardice, and waited for that inevitable moment when Kevin would break her heart.

"IT'S SO hard," M.J. sobbed to Lin and Alex on the phone. "How could he say all those things?"

After leaving Kevin's apartment, M.J. had stumbled home blindly in the rain, not even caring that she was wet and freezing because she'd left her umbrella behind at Kevin's. Tears flowing freely, she'd stomped back to her apartment, furious at herself. She couldn't believe this had happened to her—again. Why did the world seem intent on yanking away any glimmer of happiness she had? All she could think about was how she was fated never to get the things she wanted so desperately: she would never get her dream job, she would never get the man of her dreams, and she would never be good enough for anyone or anything.

In that moment of desperation, M.J. knew exactly what she had to do. Picking up the phone, she three-way-dialed Alex and Lin.

"Deep down, J, I think he's confused. He probably loves you more than he's ever loved anyone else," Lin consoled her.

Grabbing a spoon and a pint of Ben & Jerry's Sweet Cream & Cookies from her fridge, M.J. collapsed onto the couch. Not even caring that she was completely ruining her one-scoop-a-week rule, she dug in.

"I don't know," M.J. lamented through a mouthful of ice cream. "I've always felt like Kevin was biding time with me. Once he had other options in college, it was sayonara, M.J. And now, he's pulling the same stunt. Like he doesn't want to commit to me because he thinks he can find someone better out there, but in the meantime, he can hook up with me."

"M.J.! Stop that!" Alex admonished. "You are so much better than this guy and you know it."

"I know," M.J. sniffled. "I guess there was a part of me that hoped that things would be different, that I could change the way things turned out in high school. I wanted to make him see how great I was. I wanted him to want to be with me."

"I know it really hurts right now," Alex said soothingly, "but maybe this is for the best. Maybe Kevin isn't the right guy for you after all."

"I guess so. Some things are just harder than others to let go."

Lin agreed. "I know Kevin was your first love, but I really believe there's someone better for you out there."

"Totally," Alex added. "M.J., you deserve to have someone who treats you like the amazing person you are."

"Thanks, guys." M.J. smiled. "What would I do without you?"

"Exactly what you have been doing," Alex said, "being a great reporter. Who needs Kevin?"

"Besides, you're too busy hanging with Jagger these days to worry about Kevin," Lin joked. "Speaking of, how is Jagger? Still demented as usual?"

M.J. broke into a laugh. "He's not so bad." She pictured his smart-aleck smile, his goofy T-shirts, the way she could always count on him to liven up the workday.

Lin gasped in horror. "You've got to be kidding me, J. That guy is such a slob! He dresses horribly—I mean, isn't he a little old to be wearing T-shirts and sneakers to work?"

M.J. sighed. "Look, Lin, I know this may come as a shock to you, but not every guy out there is Brad Pitt. Besides, that's Jagger's style."

"Let's not talk about Brad Pitt," Lin said. "Jagger isn't even Jack Black. J, please don't tell me you're falling for this guy just because you're on the rebound. You can do so much better than Jagger—even if you hate wearing heels!"

M.J. shoved another bite of ice cream in her mouth. Lin was her best friend, but she could never see past the designer labels and expensive aftershave.

"Look," M.J. said, "I'm not falling for Jagger. I just don't think he's as bad as you make him out to be. He's smart and funny and a really creative producer. Plus, he's honest and he tells it like it is. Besides, I kind of like his T-shirts."

Alex agreed. "There's nothing wrong with T-shirts."

"Whatever," Lin said. "He'll never be the kind of guy you'll want to bring as a date to your high school reunion."

M.J. started to say something then stopped. It occurred to her at that moment that if Jagger wasn't the kind of date to bring to a high school reunion, she had definitely not been the kind of date to spend Christmas with Kevin's family and Jimmy Carter. Why hadn't she seen that she was just as bad as they were?

"I know what will make you feel better," Lin told M.J. "I'm going to book us a spa day. You'll look so beautiful, you'll have the boys flocking to you and it'll be 'Kevin who?'"

M.J. laughed despite herself. "Sounds great. Thanks again, guys. I'll talk to you soon."

As she hung up, M.J. couldn't help but chuckle. It was pretty funny how Lin was so worked up about the prospect of Jagger—probably because she liked to think of guys as matching accessories to her designer wardrobe. M.J. had to admit that she'd been susceptible to that kind of thinking as well, but she was beginning to question the importance of clothes and looks and labels. After all, Kevin had all that, and where had that gotten her? What good was the fancy attire and white-shoe background to her when she was never going to be good enough for him? Or for that world?

Regardless, M.J. wanted to tell Lin that she had nothing to worry about. She and Jagger—the mere idea was ludicrous. All they ever did was argue and all he ever did was provoke her, although the truth was that she was just as bad about antagonizing him. Sometimes M.J. wondered what things would be like if they both stopped needling each other long enough to get to know each other. She shook her head. *Stop it*, M.J. told herself, *the last thing you need in your life is Jagger Quinn.*

THERE WAS nothing like work to take her mind off boys, and for once, M.J. welcomed going to the office the next day. Still, after a morning of long meetings, she was exhausted when she returned back to her *SL* office—only to find Jagger in a PIZZA TALKS T-shirt, sitting at her desk and reading a magazine.

"Ugh." M.J. sighed as she took off her cropped navy jacket. "Why can't maintenance get rid of the life-size rodents in my office?"

"Cute, M.J.," Jagger replied. "Actually, that's a nice jacket. Hot date or something?"

"Yeah!" She perched on the corner of her desk. "Me and Rick and Ed were having an orgy in the editing room."

There was a pause. Then Jagger started laughing and M.J. followed suit—both doubled over at the image of her with their two portly, balding editors. M.J. hadn't laughed like this since the night Kevin broke up with her. It was a surprisingly nice feeling.

"Anyhow"—Jagger put the magazine aside—"I gotta jet. I need to head over to MSG to talk to the Rangers people."

"Ahh . . . hockey," M.J. drawled, "sounds like a puck of joy."

"Tell me about it." He shook his head. "I'm not a hockey fan either."

At that moment, their eyes met briefly but M.J. quickly turned away.

"Well, have fun," she said, all businesslike.

"I will." Jagger paused. "Oh, before I forget—I was wondering if you would shoot some footage for us about your Asian-American athlete story. We might be able to use some of the material as a voice-over for one of our shows."

"Oh!" M.J. was startled that he was requesting some footage from her—as if he actually liked her work. Never mind the fact that she hadn't even come close to making Auntie Lee's prophecy a reality. "Uh, sure. At this point, a voice-over may be the closest I'll ever get to being on-air."

"Great!" Jagger beamed. "Hey . . . don't forget I owe you a shot, so if you feel like one this weekend, let me know."

M.J. didn't know what to say. In the past, Jagger had always been a pain, but this time, he had actually sounded sincere about hanging out.

"Okay." M.J. smiled.

LIN'S FAVORITE remedy for getting over heartbreak was a little pampering and primping—which was why M.J. and Lin found themselves at the Ling Skincare Spa in Union Square on Saturday morning.

"Now, don't you feel about a million times better?" Lin exclaimed as they strolled out from their treatments into the tranquil, bamboo-planted lobby. "I always treat myself to one of these ginseng facials when I'm feeling blue. Things somehow seem better after that." She touched her face. "And even if they aren't, well, at least my skin looks great."

M.J. grinned. She couldn't help being amused at her friend's unique "logic." "I have to admit, you have a point. I really enjoyed that jade massage treatment." She rubbed her cheek. "And I am feeling better—even if this place is kind of girly for me."

"M. J. Wyn," Lin said with mock seriousness, "are you saying that you actually like this spa stuff?" She burst into a gleeful smile. "Too bad Alex isn't here to see this . . . maybe we should get her a little something." Lin picked up a bright pink lotus candle. "What do you think of this, J? It's very Zen. I think it would look great in Alex's bedroom."

M.J. chuckled. "It's pretty. Somehow, I never thought of Alex as being a very Zen person though."

"You never know with Alex," Lin said. "I sometimes think that she could use a little serenity in her life."

M.J. considered this for a moment then nodded in agreement. "It is hard to tell what's going on in her head. She's not big on talking about how she feels. Or about guys she likes or even guys she thinks are cute." She chewed her lip. "Then again, maybe she has good reason to be careful about falling in love. I've been thinking how I could have been a little more careful myself."

Lin stopped fiddling with the candles. "Oh, M.J.!" She reached over to hug her friend. "How are you holding up?"

"Fine." M.J. tried to smile. "Most of the time. I know Kevin and I aren't meant to be, but still, there are times when I can't help thinking how close we were . . ."

"To having something again?" Lin asked.

"Yeah." She took a deep breath. "And now I've used up my allotment of Kevin discussion time. Change of subject?"

"Absolutely," Lin said. "Hey, look at these cute little bottle warmers!" She pointed to a display on the wall. "They're in the shape of a cheongsam! I've always wanted one of those dresses . . . maybe we should go shopping for some after lunch."

M.J. studied the miniature red silk dress with the coquettish slit up the side. No doubt Lin would look adorable in it, but M.J.? Just looking at the dress was enough to make her inner tomboy scream out for her tennis shoes.

"Excuse me."

Lin and M.J. both turned to see a Wall Street young Turk–type grinning at them. He was a typical broker, decked out in an expensive Hugo Boss suit, silk tie, and gleaming Rolex. In short, he was everything Lin loved in a guy.

Sure enough, Lin went straight into flirt mode.

"Why, hello there," she said brightly. "Were you talking to us?"

"I most certainly was." He flashed a gleaming smile at her. "I was wondering if you could help translate some Chinese characters on these soaps for me."

"Oh, of course." Lin batted her eyelashes at him. "I'd love to."

"Great!" He extended a hand. "I'm Will, by the way."

Lin shook his hand. "I'm Lin." Then, as if remembering M.J., she quickly gestured toward her friend. "And this is M.J."

M.J. waved. Will smiled at her politely, but he clearly wasn't interested in the jeans-wearing, ponytailed Asian girl in T-shirt and sneakers. Apparently, she wasn't the kind of Chinese ware he was shopping for. To her surprise, M.J. realized that the feeling was mutual.

BEING A finalist for the Ed Press Award did have its perks. Even though it wasn't as good as having Auntie Lee's prophecy about an on-air position come true, it did get M.J. nice little benefits like a ticket to the ESPY Awards. Unfortunately, M.J.'s mother didn't feel the same way.

"What? You mean you're not coming home tonight?" Esther exclaimed. It was Thursday, several days after the Ed Press announcement, and M.J. had just arrived at work when her mom called.

"I told you," M.J. said patiently as she rifled through her mail, "I'm going to the ESPY Awards tonight. I can't come home. What's the big deal about tonight anyway?"

"You mean you forgot?" her mother gasped.

M.J. chewed her lip and thought furiously. What had she forgotten?

"Um," she hesitated then decided to give up. "I guess I did. What's tonight?"

"It's your grandfather's birthday!" Esther's voice pierced through the phone shrilly.

M.J. winced. It was true—she *had* forgotten.

"I . . ." She groped around for an excuse and found absolutely nothing.

"Of course," her mother said slowly, "if you really have to work, your grandfather will understand."

M.J. blinked. Could it be? Was her mother actually giving her an out here?

"Really?" she asked.

"Yes," her mother said sadly, "work come first."

M.J. hesitated. She glanced down at her desk and fingered the glossy ESPY ticket. She'd always wanted to go to the show, but had previously been relegated to watching it on her couch. And here was her first chance to go . . . versus her grandfather's birthday.

In the end, it was really no contest. If there was anything M.J. had learned these past few months, it was how fleeting some things were and how enduring other things could be.

"I'll be at grandfather's birthday tonight," she said.

"Really?" Esther's voice changed, suddenly tinged with surprise and hope.

M.J. tossed the ESPY ticket to the side without a second glance.

"Really," she said firmly.

M.J. USUALLY hated change, but even she had to admit that change could be a beautiful thing. It opened new doors and shut the ones that she didn't ever want to enter again.

She was walking in Central Park several days later when her phone rang.

She answered the call. "This is M.J."

"Yo, firecracker," Jagger said, "what's the good word?"

M.J. broke out into a reluctant smile. "What's up?"

"Can we meet in an hour? We need to talk."

"Uh—what's this about?" she asked, sidestepping one of the joggers headed in her direction.

"Meet me at the Westside Tavern. Just do it," he said, and hung up the phone before she could protest.

M.J. slammed her phone shut. Who did Jagger think he was? But that was men for you—just plain weird.

Ten minutes later, she marched into the bar where he sat on a stool in a T-shirt that read I LOVE FRIES. "This better be good."

"How are you?" Jagger smiled as he took her hand in his.

M.J. stared at him, befuddled. What was with the hand-holding?

"You made me rush here on a Saturday night to meet you," she said, pulling away her hand, "and—" She stopped when she saw the sideways grin he was flashing her.

Jagger laughed. "Relax. I'm getting you a beer."

M.J. gave up and sat down next to him. She stared at him pointedly, determined to not let him sidetrack her anymore.

"All right. All right. There is a reason I phoned you. A buddy of mine at ESPN called and said he wanted a writer to make weekly appearances on their *Sports Analysis* show and write a weekly column on their Web site. When he told me about it, I went into your office, stole your reel, and added all that stuff you contributed to us on the Asian-American athletes story." He looked up to catch M.J.'s reaction. "After I added some visuals, I sent it to him to show him the different kinds of things you could contribute to their show. I figured my thievery could help you jump-start your broadcasting career. And guess what? He loved the tape."

M.J. gasped. "What? Stop messing with me! My tape sucked!"

"Wow, I'm surprised you're not yelling at me for going into your office and stealing your stuff. Anyway," Jagger said, his eyes never leaving hers, "I said you had good potential. You just needed to jazz it up, be a little creative in the production. I took the liberty of doing a little splicing and editing here and there. It may not be a Picasso, but it was enough to convince them that you have something. So, congrats, M.J.! You'll get a phone call from them soon. I think they want to try you out on this weekend's show."

"I can't believe it!" Completely swept up in the moment, M.J. hugged Jagger, who was clearly startled. He hugged her back. For a moment, they stood there in each other's arms. Then they both let go as they realized what had just happened.

"Thanks, Jagger. I can't believe you did this for me and didn't tell me. I must say, you got me pretty good. I was ready to put my dreams on hiatus for a bit." M.J. smiled awkwardly at Jagger, her head a whirlpool of emotions.

She couldn't believe it. Her with an on-air gig? These things didn't happen to her—this had to be a dream, another vicious mirage to taunt her. But no—apparently Auntie Lee had been right—she was getting what she dreamed of. Feeling thrilled, excited, and stunned at the same time, M.J. sat down on a stool, her knees suddenly weak.

"Now, I don't want to hear you dissing yourself again," Jagger said.

M.J. reddened. "And here I thought my tape was the worst thing ever."

"You only need one person in this lifetime to like your stuff, M.J." Jagger squeezed her shoulder. "You know what they say—one is the magic number."

M.J. laughed, feeling good for the first time in days. Maybe this wasn't a dream—maybe, just maybe, she was actually wide awake for a change.

"So, I think we should celebrate," Jagger declared. "How 'bout we go back to my place, and I show you what a great chef I am?"

The mere thought of Jagger cooking was enough to make M.J. chortle with laughter.

"I'm in," she said. "Let's go."

As they headed out, M.J. couldn't help thinking about this strange twist of fate. Her going to Jagger's apartment for dinner? It was almost as unthinkable as . . . well, as M.J. becoming an on-air sportscaster.

nine

LIKE A child with her first cricket cage, M.J. was intrigued and curious about seeing Jagger's apartment. She pictured some dark, dingy hole, complete with graffiti on the walls, empty beer cans and pizza boxes, and dirty underwear strewn everywhere.

Which was why she was utterly unprepared for the hip interior of Jagger's Hell's Kitchen apartment. Not only was the apartment clean and tidy, but it was also warmly lit with retro neon lamps and decorated with cute little touches, like a Scooby-Doo clock on the wall and a Betty Boop bean bag chair in the corner. The couch was snazzy, seventies black leather, and the carpet was vintage orange shag. It was like something out of a design museum, except cooler.

"Well," M.J. cleared her throat, "if I had some advance warning, I would have brought some almond cakes over."

Jagger frowned. "Almond cakes?"

"It's an old Chinese tradition. My grandmother always says that when you visit someone's home, it's good manners to bring some kind of gift, like almond cakes."

"Huh," Jagger pondered this, "I guess you're lucky I'm not exactly Miss Manners myself. Tell you what, you can make it up to me and bring me some of these almond cakes tomorrow."

M.J. rolled her eyes. "Gee, thanks."

Jagger chuckled. "Make yourself at home," he said, heading into the kitchen. "Dinner will be ready in a bit."

"Take your time," M.J. responded as she wandered over to gaze at the row of black-and-white photographs on one wall. They were fascinating studies of what appeared to be random people on the street: a homeless man, a construction worker, two elderly men hunched over a chess game in Washington Square Park. What struck M.J. the most, though, was how beautiful and unique the portraits were in their depictions of the ordinary.

"These pictures are great," M.J. called to Jagger as he strolled up behind her. "Did you take them?"

Jagger wiped his hands on a dishrag. "Yeah, it's kind of a hobby of mine."

"They're really amazing," she remarked, "even though they're pictures of . . ."

"Ordinary people? You'd be surprised at what you find if you look below the surface."

M.J. bit her lip. Jagger was right; she'd tried looking below the surface with Kevin—and found nothing there. She cleared her throat. "Do you have anything to drink?"

"Beer okay?" Jagger asked as he headed toward the kitchen.

"Sure." M.J. wandered toward his bedroom. What she saw made her freeze in her tracks. A moment later, Jagger came over with a beer in each hand.

"Hope you're a Heineken girl," he said as he held out a bottle toward her.

"Jagger," M.J. said slowly, "is that a . . . sewing machine in the corner?"

"Um . . . yeah. It's nothing," he said quickly. "Dinner is actually ready. Why don't we go—"

But M.J. was already at the sewing machine. She touched the various swatches of fabric then noticed the batch of T-shirts lying to one side. Picking through them, she saw that they were all embroidered with various unique designs and witty sayings, much like the T-shirts that Jagger sported to work every day.

"Do you make your own T-shirts?" she asked.

"Uh, yeah, kind of . . ."

"There are a lot of shirts here," M.J. remarked as she noticed an entire box of T-shirts nearby. "These can't all be for you. Are you selling them or something?"

Jagger didn't answer immediately—which of course set off M.J.'s journalistic radar right away.

"You are, aren't you?" she gasped.

Jagger sighed and ran a hand through his platinum tips. "Okay, you busted me. I just started selling this line of T-shirts on the Internet. It's small fries, but there's apparently a market out there for these kinds of shirts."

M.J. picked up a decal with the word WWW.JAGGERSEDGE. COM and waved it at him. "I take it this is your site?"

"Um, yeah," he muttered. Jagger hesitated then picked up a T-shirt lying to one side. "Actually, I have a T-shirt for you. I was going to give it to you later, but now's as good a time as any, I guess."

He handed the shirt to M.J., who unfurled the bright blue fabric to reveal the words PLAY TO WYN emblazoned on it. M.J. burst into delighted laughter.

"This is great!" she exclaimed. "Thank you! I love it!"

Jagger grinned, looking like a pleased little boy. "So I guess you won't be suing me for using your name, huh?"

She shook her head and smiled at him. "What are you going to surprise me with next?"

He paused. "Are you hungry?"

JAGGER HAD prepared an Italian feast. Fettuccini carbonara, prosciutto and mozzarella appetizer, and fried calamari for dinner, followed by tiramisu and cappuccinos for dessert. By the end of the meal, M.J. was stuffed. And she didn't even think once about whether she looked like she was pigging out.

"That was unbelievable." She shook her head happily. "You really can cook, Quinn."

"Hey, I paid attention to what my grandmother was doing in the kitchen," Jagger said as he finished his glass of Chianti. "There's nothing like Old World cooking to really satisfy your stomach."

M.J. rolled her eyes. "Don't tell me you're going to get all Emeril on me now."

"Well, hey, there's nothing wrong with that—what do you say we kick it up a notch!" He slammed the table in mock imitation of the TV chef.

Despite herself, M.J. laughed. She was feeling happy, relaxed, comfortable—something that didn't seem possible after Kevin had stomped on her heart for the second time. Jagger was funny and entertaining and made her feel like she didn't have a worry in the world. When he smiled at her, she couldn't help but smile back. . . .

She cleared her throat. "Well, I must say I never would have figured you for a family person."

"Hey, when it comes right down to it, your family is your family. Don't get me wrong. We yell; we scream. Sometimes my mom will even throw things. But then it's over, we sit down, and we break bread." Jagger leaned close toward M.J. to pour her some more wine. "I think it's healthy. It's the families that repress everything who end up going berserk and pulling a gun out one day. In my family, if there's a problem, we deal with it right away."

"Hmm." M.J. pondered this. "I never thought of it that way, but I guess you're right." She smiled suddenly. "I bet your family would get along with my family."

Jagger grinned. "Is that an invitation?"

Seeing his hazel eyes glimmer with interest, M.J. tried to think of something funny to say, but her sense of humor had apparently decided to abandon her. Deciding that silence was the best course, she got up and strolled toward the window. She took a deep breath as she climbed out onto the fire escape. A moment later, Jagger joined her.

"What are you thinking about?" he asked.

"Oh," she shrugged, "just that I can't believe I finally have all the things I've dreamed of. I'm going to be on-air! Do you know what that means? All those years of trying to make everyone see that I could succeed. My family, all the men in the sports world who thought I was chasing a pipe dream." She shook her head. "It got to a point where I thought they were right and I'd never break in."

Jagger looked at her curiously. "Why do you care so much about what other people think about you?"

She sighed. "I guess I never felt like I really belonged anywhere. Not with my family, who thinks I should be a good little Asian daughter and get a real job that pays real money. Not at the country club, where they let me play tennis but won't let me into the membership. And certainly not in the sports world, where being a woman and Chinese means that I couldn't possibly know anything about sports."

There was a long pause. Then Jagger stepped forward and touched her hand. "You don't need to be like them, M.J.," he said quietly. "You're funny and unique and original, and you shouldn't have to pretend to be someone you're not. You're you, and you're amazing as you are. I hope you finally see that."

M.J. looked at Jagger, really looked at him for the first time. And suddenly, she felt her heart flutter. Who would believe it? She'd known Jagger for years now and had felt only annoyance, irritation, and amused tolerance toward him. And yet, here he was, inches from her, and her stomach was doing backflips.

Jagger looked down at her and whispered huskily, "So, would it be okay if I kissed you right now?"

M.J. smiled. "Okay," she said as she leaned in to kiss him gently.

The kiss was tender, everything Jagger seemed not to be. Suddenly, it was like all the hard edges had disappeared, and in their place was this gentle guy with the soft hands and even softer eyes. After a moment, the kiss deepened. M.J. ran her fingers through his hair and forgot about everything but Jagger.

IN THE end, M.J. decided that moving on didn't mean forgetting about the past. She couldn't erase the fact that her heart had been broken by Kevin any more than she could change the fact that she didn't go to an Ivy League school or that her grandmother had seen a picture of her and Richard Robinson on "Page Six." But she could look forward to her future—as an analyst on ESPN.

"What's up, firecracker?" Jagger strolled into her office, closing the door behind him. "Winding down the days here, huh? Ready for ESPN?"

She turned around in her chair. "Sure am."

There was an awkward silence. M.J. tried to think of something light and breezy to say, but her mind drew a complete blank. Even though she would never admit it, she was having trouble concentrating around Jagger.

Finally, he broke the ice.

"So, you were all over me the other night." Jagger grinned, his eyes glinting mischievously.

M.J. threw her mini-basketball at him. "You wish. You took advantage of me."

"Yeah, and you loved it." He smiled. "I have to say, that night was pretty amazing."

He was gazing intently at M.J., and while that in itself wasn't unusual, there was something different this time, a certain softness in the way he looked at her that made her heart skip a beat.

"It was all right," she blushed. "But keep it on the DL."

"Ditto, M.J." Jagger smiled. "So what are you up to tonight?"

"Oh, it's my cousin's birthday," she said. "We're going to Flushing for one of those ten-course Chinese banquets."

"Wow, that sounds good. I think it's cool how your family has these big food fests. I wish my family would do that."

M.J. frowned and stared at him. Was Jagger making fun of her? But no, he seemed earnest about the whole thing.

"Maybe you'll invite me to one of these family get-togethers someday," he said lightly.

That took M.J. completely by surprise. Jagger at one of her family dinners? She could just see him sitting amid her bickering aunts and uncles in one of his outlandish T-shirts. . . .

She blinked. "Um, yeah."

"Well," Jagger got up. "We'll chat later. I got some things to do."

"Yeah, see you around," she said as she watched Jagger walk out the door.

ten

M.J. HAD no illusions about the episode with Jagger. She'd long ago stopped believing in fairy tales—especially after Kevin. No, she was a big girl now and she didn't have any regrets, but she also wasn't going to let Jagger—or anyone else, for that matter—derail her express train to broadcast television.

So she forgot about Kevin and she forgot about Jagger. Instead, she poured all of her energy into preparing for her new job: diction lessons, learning to shoot with a camera, even having Lin teach her the finer points of hair and makeup. And when the time finally

came for her big on-air debut, M.J. stood in front of the camera—
and felt, for the first time she could remember, that she was where
she belonged.

One month later, *Sporting Life* magazine seemed like a century
ago for M.J. She was having the time of her life at ESPN, attaining
that long-coveted on-air broadcasting job. Sure, the traveling was
grueling—she was spending at least three nights a week covering
games in some remote Midwestern city, and she was racking up frequent flyer points by the bushel. But that was a small price to
pay—especially when her parents had finally come to the realiza-
tion that this was what their daughter truly loved and had given her
their blessing. But the best was yet to come. Just a month into her
new job, M.J. had been handed the plum assignment of covering
her very first NBA Finals.

"We're live at the Staples Center as the L.A. Lakers set their
sights on a fourth NBA title in six years," M.J. rehearsed to herself
as she frowned down at her notes. As she continued jotting down a
possible script for the night's game, her phone rang.

"This is M.J.," she answered.

"Hey, M.J." It was Devon Fairweather, M.J.'s senior producer.
"We're doing a new angle tonight. We want to get some analysis
from a couple of the NBA experts in the media. I've lined up a few
senior writers from different media outlets that I'd like you to talk
to before the game so we can do a pretaped segment that'll air during halftime. They should be in the locker room now. One of our
production assistants will have the names of everyone for you."

"Sounds great. I'm on it. I'll head to the locker room right away."

Sporting her now trademark leather jacket, M.J. took out her
compact to check on her makeup as she walked toward the locker
room. As she reapplied a thin layer of lip gloss, she felt someone
staring at her. When she looked up, her mouth opened slightly.

"Well, if it isn't the hottest chick that put the *B* in *babyface*."
Jagger smiled as he walked over to give her a hug. "How are ya?"

It was unbelievable. It had been a month since she'd seen Jagger
at her good-bye party. Oh, he'd called her and left her a message

after that, but she was just about to leave for an assignment in Phoenix, and in the rush, she hadn't been able to call him. Afterward, it seemed like so much time had passed that M.J. didn't know what there was to say to him. It wasn't like they were dating, and with her commuting around the country and him back in New York—well, what was the point? She and Jagger had never spoken about any kind of commitment, and after what happened with Kevin, she was certainly not going to be the one to bring the subject up.

Still, there were times, especially when she was spending yet another lonely night on the road, that M.J. wished she could pick up the phone and hear Jagger's voice. He had a knack for making her laugh, whether it was because of the latest RealSports gossip or because of some new T-shirt scheme he had. More than anything, she missed the way he supported her unconditionally and made her feel like she could face anything.

M.J. shook her head and laughed. "I'm great, but I can see you're still as obnoxious as ever, Quinn."

"You better believe it." Jagger leaned up against one of the lockers. "So, covering the NBA Finals, huh? How's life treating you now that you're a big-time superstar? I think I saw a herd of Asian people with signs wanting to get your autograph."

"I'm no superstar." She laughed. "But life is pretty sweet. This gig is amazing. There are so many things that I never dreamed of doing that I'm finally allowed to do."

"That's awesome," Jagger said sincerely. "I hear everyone at *SL* misses ya, you know. They lost a really great writer."

He was smiling at her, not his trademark smirk but a real, genuine smile. And the look in his eye—if M.J. didn't know better, she'd think that there was actual emotion there. Which, of course, brought her right back to that night at his apartment. . . .

As if he sensed her thoughts, he winked at her. M.J. blushed. This was so surreal. She hadn't seen Jagger in weeks, but somehow it seemed like she'd just seen him yesterday. As he stood in front of her now, all she could think about was kissing him.

"Since when did you start handing out compliments?" She tried to play it off. "And just for your—"

"Hey, M.J.," John, M.J.'s production assistant, interrupted, "I'm glad you met Jagger. He's the first writer we're going to talk to."

M.J. looked at John, then back at Jagger, who sported a big smirk on his face.

"Thanks, John," she said coolly. "Can you go get the camera guy?"

"Sure." He nodded as he walked away.

"What's the matter, M.J.?" Jagger teased. "Shocked that this day has finally come? I'm ready for you. Grill me. You can ask me anything."

"Oh, shut up." M.J. crinkled her nose. "You love this. You love that I have to interview you."

"What's not to love?" he countered. "Maybe I can do a tell-all interview."

M.J.'s eyes widened in horror.

"Lower your voice." She slapped his arm. "This is not the time or the place. Besides, that was ages ago, and it was just a stupid moment of insanity."

"Come on, M.J." Jagger leaned forward, his tone suddenly serious. "You wanted me. We both know it. In fact, I think a part of you still wants me." He paused, and when he spoke again, his voice was husky. "And I want you."

M.J. was speechless for a moment. Of all the men that she had ever met, Jagger was the only one who had ever kept it real with her. She'd met all these wishy-washy guys who didn't know what they wanted—especially in their relationship with her. No guy had ever straight up asked her what the deal was—until now.

"I don't know what you're talking about." M.J. looked away, trying to avoid the subject. "Where's that camera guy anyway?"

"You know what your problem is?" Jagger continued, apparently determined not to let it go. "Your inability to face new challenges. I always thought that you could do anything. I guess I was wrong."

"And what challenges might those be?" she retorted. "Dating Jagger Quinn?"

"Maybe," Jagger snapped. "You never returned any of my calls after you left. That was shitty."

M.J. blinked, taken aback by the sudden anger in his voice. She hadn't been prepared to see Jagger—and she certainly wasn't prepared for this straight-up moment of honesty between them. So she did what she'd always done—and retreated behind the old war of words.

"Like you even cared, Mr. Journalism. You were busy with your own rodent fan club, Cindy."

Ten minutes had passed, and there was still no sign of the camera guy or John. M.J. looked around nervously. She couldn't believe she was having this conversation with Jagger—here, of all places.

"This isn't about Cindy," he retorted. "It's about you. You think that everything and everyone you meet in life has to be perfect, but life isn't perfect."

"M.J.!" John shouted across the room. "We're ready to roll."

"Great!" she said quickly. "Jagger, are you ready?"

"I've been ready all my life," he said, still staring at her pointedly.

M.J. took a deep breath, turned away, and swung into action as she faced the camera. "And we're here with RealSports' Jagger Quinn. Jagger, what do you think will be the key for the Lakers to win their fourth title in six years?"

"It depends on how healthy Kobe is. If his toe continues to bother him, his team will have to step up. And Kobe will also have to look deep within himself because the ball's in his court now and it's his game to lose. But this situation isn't new for the Lakers. They've got depth and most importantly, heart. They'll pull out this series in five."

Jagger stared straight at M.J. as he uttered the words, and for a moment, she lost track of time, still caught up in what he had just said. It took a discreet cough from her cameraman to jolt her back to reality.

"Thank you, Jagger," she said as the camera faded off.

As John and the camera guy walked away to disassemble the equipment, Jagger turned to walk off without a word. M.J. stared after him. She suddenly flashed back to Auntie Lee's words: "You will get what you dream of, but then you will find that you do not want it anymore." What if the "dream" that Auntie Lee had referred to wasn't her job, but Kevin? Thinking about him now, M.J. realized she really didn't want him anymore. . . .

"Quinn," she shouted across the room.

"What?" he said coldly as he turned around.

"So, do you think maybe I can have that shot you owe me?"

"Maybe." Jagger broke into a smile. "How 'bout we go over to Jay-Z's new West Coast joint? Maybe we can find you some Lakers to dance with."

M.J. smiled as she caught up with Jagger, a new spring in her step. "You got it."

AS M.J. curled up in her chair at the ESPN office to do her weekly column, she began to write.

So why does the world love sports? The answer is simple. Every day, we all play a sport. It's called life. You can come up big on day one but lose the advantage on day two. It doesn't matter how many times you've pictured yourself draining that three in the championship game or how you've fantasized about nailing that triple salchow to win the gold. What matters is what happens during game time—real-life moments that result in real-life decisions. It's inevitable that not all of our hopes and dreams play out. There's no way to foresee the box scores of our lives. The only thing we can do is prepare and practice and train. We're the ones who'll ultimately decide whether we win or lose even if we can't predict by how much. Like sports, things aren't always perfect, but all life asks of you is that you live to play. . . .

alex

UNITED STATES DISTRICT COURT
SOUTHERN DISTRICT OF NEW YORK

....

WOMEN OF NEW YORK CITY,

        PLAINTIFFS.

  —against—

THE MALE GENDER,

        DEFENDANTS.

01CIV3452(LUV)

....

COMPLAINT

Plaintiffs Women of New York City (the "Women"), through their under-signed counsel, hereby submit this complaint against Defendants The Male Gender (the "Men").

THE PARTIES

1. Plaintiffs are the attractive, successful, and very personable women of New York who are unable to meet a single normal man for fun, a relationship, or possibly love.
2. Defendants are the psychotic, commitment-phobic, and macho men who are terrified of women who want a relationship, women who don't want a relationship, women who don't need men, and women who have a mind of their own.

NATURE OF THE ACTION

3. Plaintiffs bring this action against Defendants for running away from commitment; for being intimidated by women who have it all; for chasing anything in a skirt; for being cheating, unfaithful dogs; for being sexist, chauvinist pigs; for being in love with themselves; for always putting their buddies first; and for their inability to stop playing mind games.

Opening
Statement

eleven

"LOOK, WE'LL give you 360 for the release and that's our final offer."

Cradling the phone in her neck, Alex Kwan flipped through a manila folder, took a sip of her black coffee, and scribbled a note on her legal pad. It was Monday morning, and she was already steeped in an intense settlement negotiation. Checking her mail, she noticed a cream-colored invitation on her desk. She picked it up and realized it was for her law firm's anniversary party—and that it was addressed to ALEX KWAN AND GUEST. Great, she thought, just what she needed.

"So that's your final offer?" her opposing counsel barked. A lawyer from a Death Star–like law firm notorious for its bulldog litigators, Richard Evans wasn't exactly one for tact. "Maybe you should consult your superiors before you start making statements like that."

Clenching her jaw, Alex drummed her nails against her mahogany desk clock.

"I appreciate the suggestion, but the offer still stands," she replied coolly, thinking how nice it would be if she could hurl the clock at the other attorney. "Perhaps you should consult with your client before you turn down any more offers."

"I don't need your advice, Miss Kwan. I've been practicing long before you ever saw the inside of a law school."

Alex shook her head. *Keep your cool,* she told herself, *you are not going to let this jerk steamroll you.*

"With all due respect, Mr. Evans, you're wasting my time. Do we have a deal or not?" she snapped. Tapping her invitation against the desk, Alex waited for an answer. She tried to think of her next move if he turned this offer down. . . .

"Fine," Evans said coldly, much to Alex's surprise, "let's just get this done."

Clearing her throat, Alex tossed the invitation aside and readjusted her grip on the phone.

"Good, I'm glad to hear that," she responded tersely. "I'll draft up the agreement and send it over to you today. Talk to you later, Richard."

Flipping the receiver back into its cradle, she carefully moved the clock back to its perfect ninety-degree angle from her pencil holder and stapler.

Typical asshole lawyer, she thought. After all this time, she still had these jackasses questioning her judgment every step of the way.

Alex glanced at her watch. It was time for her client meeting. Smoothing the lines of her sleek crepe suit, she quickly grabbed her brief and started power-walking down the hallway to the conference room.

"Do you ever stop, Ally?"

Alex looked up to see her colleague, Brady Jameson, watching her from the doorway of the conference room. Slouched against its frame, he looked the part of the legal shark with his sharply tailored suit, thick, dark blond hair, and startling, ice-blue eyes. Brushing back the loose hairs of her tightly wound chignon, Alex sighed.

"Stop what?" she said archly. "Working? You should try it sometime."

Brady chuckled. "Can I help it that some of us take twice as long to accomplish the same task?"

"I know it's hard to understand," she said as she rifled through the papers in her hand, "but some of us aspire to do more than a half-assed job."

"That hurts, Lex," he sighed, "but I guess we only hurt the ones we love, huh?"

Alex rolled her eyes. There were times when she found it hard to believe that there could be someone as incredibly cocky and arrogant as Brady Jameson.

"What planet are you from?" she asked.

Brady just laughed and strolled off with a wave. "Catch you later, sweetheart."

Alex shook her head and strode away in the opposite direction.

AS A seasoned lawyer, Alex knew all about Brady's kind: legal eagles with a god complex and the soul of an assassin. She'd seen the way he was—how he was uniformly superior to everyone, whether it was to a partner or the most junior associate. She'd even seen him checking his reflection in the conference room window in the middle of a deposition. If that wasn't bad enough, Brady was also a snake charmer of women; there was not a single female, from the receptionist to the most senior female partner, who was immune to his charm.

Despite all that, Alex had to admit he wasn't the worst kind of lawyer out there. She'd encountered more than her share of jerks in the legal profession, whether it was some swaggering, loud-mouthed blowhard or some condescending graybeard who still hadn't come around to the idea of women lawyers. But while Alex was well prepared for encounters-of-the-asshole kind, there was still one area of men she would be the first to admit she knew nothing about: what it was like to have a real, honest-to-goodness, I'm-crazy-about-you boyfriend.

"—so after two days of this crap, the asshole finally signed the damn settlement agreement. I'm telling you," Alex said, "after the week I've had so far, I'll need five drinks to get me through the rest of it." She hailed a passing waitress. "I think I'll start with one of those lychee apple martinis."

Catching her breath, Alex looked around the sleek, Lower East

Side lounge. The White Rabbit was packed for a Wednesday night as the girls convened for an after-work drink on an unseasonably warm spring evening.

"That sounds great," M.J. licked her lips as the waitress came over with her order, "but I'm sticking with my paradise martini and lumpia."

"Lump-what?" Lin cringed. "Didn't you have a slice of pizza an hour ago? Don't tell me you're hungry already!"

M.J. took a bite of her Filipino egg roll. "Mmm," she said, savoring the flavor, "can't wait to order some more."

Alex turned back to the girls after giving her order to the waitress. "With the way you eat, J, I bet you could write a book on every bar menu in every city you've traveled to."

M.J. chuckled. "Close."

"I'm just going to get my usual ginger spice martini," Lin said as she collapsed on the white leather couch. "I'm beat."

"What happened?" M.J. asked. "Hard day on Wall Street?"

"You know, the usual . . . people yelling at me. I lost half a mil today. Unlike Alex, I don't handle those situations well."

Alex frowned. "What is *that* supposed to mean?"

"Nothing," Lin said. "You just don't let anyone bother you."

M.J. laughed, taking a gulp of her martini. "And if they do, you just run right over them." She made a steamrolling gesture with her fist.

"Oh, please," Alex said, "I've never been mean for no reason." Looking at M.J. and Lin, she noticed neither spoke a word.

"Well, screw the both of you," Alex declared. But she couldn't hide the flicker of a smile that formed on her lips.

Her friends laughed and high-fived each other. They were able to joke about this, knowing Alex the way that they did. She was their great defender, the ever-vigilant protector of her friends, the one they could always count on to come through for them in a pinch—and they all knew it.

Despite herself, Alex chuckled, too.

"So, Alex," M.J. reached for another egg roll, "what are we doing for your birthday?"

Alex sighed. The last thing she wanted was a party to remind her that she was turning thirty. Just thinking about her birthday brought up all sorts of questions about the things she had yet to accomplish in her life—and she found the list much too long for her liking.

So she just shrugged. "I'm not a big birthday person."

"How can you say that?" Lin gasped. "Birthdays are huge!"

"Why? Because I'm a year closer to being old and decrepit?" Alex rolled her eyes.

"No, because it's the beginning of the newest and best chapter of your life. Which is why," Lin announced, "I'm going to throw you a party."

"Party?" Alex frowned.

"Yeah." M.J. grinned. "The biggest, baddest birthday party ever."

A birthday party . . . well, maybe getting trashed wasn't such a bad idea. She could stand to forget about everything for a night.

"And if you give me a hard time about it," Lin continued, "I'm going to invite your wealthy broker friend."

Alex groaned. She should have known Lin would bring this up. Despite her solo status, she wasn't actually short of prospects. Lin used to joke that if she had a dollar for every love interest of Alex's that popped up, she'd own her own Fortune 500 company by now. And yet, somehow, here she was—wondering how her entire twenties had gone by without a single serious long-term relationship. What had she spent the past decade doing?

The answer was easy: she'd spent the last ten years chasing career success—racking up the billables at her firm and slaving through all-nighters. Being Asian and a woman in the predominantly white, male world of law meant having to go the extra mile and having to outwork everyone else just to keep pace. Under these circumstances, dates were the first offering to go on the sacrificial altar—after all, who had time for frivolous small talk when there were briefs to file and trials to prepare for?

"Is this the blind date you went on last week?" M.J. perked up. "How'd that go?"

"It was hideous!" Alex burst out. "He was all power-suity and cocky. He kept babbling on about margins and what a killing he made in the market. Like I'd be impressed with all that crap."

Lin made a face. "My mom would probably like him—if he was Chinese."

Alex and M.J. both laughed. More than once, they had heard Lin's mother Kim say, "Lin-ah! You marry good Chinese boy and I die happy woman." To which, Lin would roll her eyes, wait until her mother was gone, and turn around and flirt with the next non-Asian boy she laid eyes on.

"The best was when he went to pay the tab. He pulled out this roll of bills and a twenty fell on the floor. So I told him, and what does he say?" Alex struck a blasé pose. " 'Oh, that's okay. It's only a twenty.' And he wouldn't pick it up!"

The girls broke into laughter.

"What the hell was he thinking?" M.J. asked.

"Was he drunk?" Lin said at the same time.

Alex shook her head. "Completely sober. This was his schtick. Throw some bills around, make the girl think you're a big shot, and dazzle her straight into bed."

"That's pathetic," Lin remarked.

"It's sickening," Alex corrected. "I was thinking, I make just as much as you do, maybe more when the market's dropping. Flashing the cash isn't going to get you anywhere with me."

The girls nodded in agreement. It was almost tradition by now—the inevitable story about how yet another one of Alex's dates had turned out to be a disaster.

"Well, he sure picked the wrong girl," M.J. said, popping an olive into her mouth.

"Yeah," Alex agreed, studying the rim of her glass reflectively. "I guess that's why I'm always the wrong girl."

TO MOST women, Alex seemed to have it all: a successful career as a high-powered attorney, a cozy brownstone on a tree-lined street in NoHo, and the financial wherewithal to live her life the way she wanted to. Add to that a supportive family and a couple of very close and very loyal friends, and there weren't many other things that a girl could really want. Except for, perhaps, someone to share it all with.

Not that Alex would ever admit this to anyone else. She always said that she had everything she needed and that she wasn't one of those pathetic, sad-sack women who sat around pining for their Prince Charming. Then she'd happen to catch sight of some happy couple and wonder what it would be like to have someone around who cared, who felt what she felt.

Of course, great guys didn't exactly grow on trees. After all, here she was: a certified failure when it came to men. Alex tried to be patient; she really did. After all, if there was one thing her mother had taught her, it was the Chinese virtue of patience.

Alex remembered being thirteen and distraught because her archrival, Sara Harrington, had been named valedictorian of their class. She'd run home in tears and spent the next three hours crying to her mother about how utterly unfair it all was when she had studied more than anyone else, had obsessed over her grades, had pinned her hopes and dreams on that coveted title.

Her mother, Margaret, had listened quietly to all this, and when Alex had finally exhausted herself, she drew her daughter to her.

"Alex," she said, "you must learn to be patient."

"Patient!" Alex exclaimed. "What is that going to do?"

"Listen to me, Alex. You are Chinese. Not one of these American kids who want everything now, now, now. When we Chinese suffer disappointment, we don't scream and cry and fall apart. We remember how we feel, we let the disappointment make us stronger, and we work even harder to achieve our goals. In time, everything will fall into place—we just have to be patient. That is the Chinese way."

"But does that really work?" Alex asked.

Margaret nodded. "When I first came to this country, I had a neighbor named Mrs. Woo. One day, she won the lottery. Suddenly, she had beautiful clothes, a Rolls-Royce, a house in New Jersey. I was so envious of her. But I told myself that my time would come and that I just had to work harder."

Alex frowned. "But you never won the lottery."

"But I did." Her mother smiled. "I have a beautiful, smart daughter who will make me proud with her success. Mrs. Woo? Her son is a lazy boy who spends her money and only comes home to her when he needs more."

Years later, Alex would remember that story. Her mother had been right about her being a success. Well, at least with her career. She wasn't quite so successful when it came to love.

twelve

"SO, JUST sign on the dotted line and we'll be done," Alex said.

It was Friday afternoon, and Alex and Brady were closing a deal in their law firm conference room. Simon Sinclair, the debonair, silver fox CEO of Synergy Corporation, leaned down and signed the agreement with a flourish. Immediately, Brady stepped forward to shake his hand, before Simon had even put his pen down. Alex rolled her eyes at Brady's typical brownnosing.

"Congratulations, Simon. You just added another winner to your portfolio."

"Thanks for your help, Brady," Simon said sincerely. "A bottle of Dom will be in your name when we open for business." He turned to Alex. "And you, my dear, will receive an invitation to be my escort for that evening."

Great, she thought, *yet another man trying to cultivate me as his own oriental delicacy.* Behind Simon, Brady wagged his eyebrows at Alex.

She pasted on a smile. "Let me walk you out." As she turned to leave, Simon caught her wrist.

"Actually," he said, "why wait? Let's have dinner tonight to celebrate. I can have the chef at Per Se prepare a private meal for us."

Alex pursed her lips and glared at Brady, who was pretending to play the violin. She looked away from him to smile brightly at Simon.

"Sorry, Simon. I already have plans."

"Of course you do," he replied. "I wouldn't expect anything else of such a lovely lady. Tomorrow night?"

"Oh, well." Alex licked her lips, thinking hard for an excuse, "I . . ."

"We have to prepare a witness," Brady interjected. "He's going on trial this Friday."

Alex tried to repress her surprise. "Uh, yes," she said quickly, "duty calls."

"I understand." Simon leaned over to kiss her cheek. "I'll call you next week, and we'll schedule a rendezvous then." He headed toward the door. "See you later, Brady."

Alex shook her head once Simon was out of earshot. "That guy is too much."

"I don't get it," Brady said. "Why didn't you go out with him? He's loaded, and has been married twice so he obviously has nothing against getting hitched."

"I know this might be hard for you to believe," Alex sighed, "but not all women are obsessed with money and marriage."

Brady frowned. "Really?"

Alex started to say "of course" but then something stopped her. It was true that she didn't care about the money, but what about getting married? There were times when she couldn't help thinking how nice it would be to have someone around to share a bowl of microwave popcorn with. . . .

Suddenly, Alex realized that Brady was staring at her.

She cleared her throat. "You're hopeless." Alex started to walk away, then paused. "If you're such a big Simon supporter, why did you just bail me out there?"

He shrugged. "Couldn't let you get a leg up on me with the client just because you're hitting it off with him. Now could I, Alexie?"

Alex sighed. "Don't worry," she said as she strolled off, "you can be Simon's date at the opening."

BY THE time the weekend came around, Alex was all too happy to hear about the men who were in her friends' lives—and not her own.

"So my mother called Stephen again," Lin complained. She brushed her stylishly cut, ebony hair back with a sigh. With her perfectly accessorized jewelry, immaculately manicured nails, and straight-out-of-Barneys wardrobe, Lin always managed to cut a so-phisticated figure, even when they were sitting in the middle of a crowded Flushing restaurant filled with screaming Chinese women pushing metal carts.

It was Sunday, or as M.J. liked to call it, dim sum day. While there were the occasional forays with their families, M.J., Alex, and Lin had made dim sum their own special get-together, where they would enthusiastically dig into beef tripe and marinated chicken feet.

"Ugh," Alex shuddered, "there's nothing worse than the parents calling the ex."

"I know." Lin sipped some hot chrysanthemum tea. "I can just imagine what ridiculous schemes she has in store for him."

M.J. took a bite of her fried turnip cake. "Doesn't she get the fact that you guys are over? Maybe you should try telling her that." In her ponytail, jeans, and T-shirt, M.J. fit right into the casual fam-ily lunch scene. A dash of lip gloss, a flick of the comb, and a quick powder check were usually the extent of her daily cosmetic rou-tine.

"I've tried." Lin exhaled in frustration. "Only about a gazillion times. It's getting so bad that I've even thought about calling Stephen up to apologize. That, or telling him to change his number."

Alex raised her eyebrow. "Did you?"

"No," Lin said. "What would I say? I'm sorry that my mother thinks I'm an idiot for breaking up with you?"

The girls all shuddered and made faces in silent concurrence that this would not be a good course of action.

"You don't know how good you have it, J," Lin said. "Now that you have a boyfriend, you don't have to worry about finding a guy anymore."

M.J. chuckled. "I don't know about that. . . . Jagger and I are still figuring out this whole relationship thing. But yeah—I guess you could say I don't have to 'find a guy' anymore."

"Well," Lin sighed, "I think I got to keep looking. Alex, didn't the fortune-teller say you had to try something new to find love?"

Alex paused in mid-bite of her shrimp shumai. She hadn't thought about Auntie Lee in a while. "Oh, that." She shrugged. "Yeah, there was something about opening myself up to new possibilities. Whatever."

"Now, don't scoff at Auntie Lee," Lin chided. "She's always been right. And I think she's right about this, too."

Alex frowned. "What do you mean?"

"I mean—" Lin grinned mischievously. "—that I think you and I should take up speed-dating!"

The girls all laughed.

"Oh, please!" Alex rolled her eyes. "Okay, so maybe I do need to get out more, but speed-dating? I'm not *that* desperate."

"Lin, you know that Alex would never go with you!" M.J. exclaimed.

"Oh yeah, J, what was I thinking? Alex is afraid of stuff like that."

Lin and M.J. chuckled, exchanging knowing glances. Alex tried to smile, but it felt forced, strained at the dimples.

It wasn't that her friends weren't right about her. They were— 100 percent. Alex would never do something like speed-dating, but that didn't mean she liked coming off as a loser. Especially to her friends.

All her life, Alex had been the responsible one. She always got good grades, didn't do drugs, never even broke curfew. Oh, she had her pranks, but to the outside world, she was perfect. And when it came to her friends, she was a rock. Whether it was holding Lin's hair while she worshipped the porcelain god after too much partying or picking M.J. up after her wisdom tooth appointment, Alex could always be counted on to be at the right place at the right time.

The flip side of all this was that she sometimes felt more like her friends' mother than their girlfriend. It seemed like she was always nagging Lin about her exorbitant spending habits or M.J. about registering to vote or some other ridiculous thing that only seemed to remember in her anal-retentive, photographic-memory way. It didn't help that she was a few years older than both Lin and M.J. and the first to approach that once seemingly ancient age of thirty. No wonder M.J. and Lin were always rolling their eyes, shaking their heads, and exchanging looks that screamed, "There Alex goes again." It was enough to make Alex feel like a third wheel sometimes.

"I'm not afraid of speed-dating," Alex retorted. "I just . . ."

"We know, we know." M.J. bit heartily into an egg roll. "You hate it when you don't know what to expect. But maybe if you weren't so concerned about being in control all the time, you might have some more fun."

Alex tossed her head. "There's nothing wrong with being in control. It's when you're not in control that things go bad."

ALEX MET *Josh the first week of Yale. They were standing in line at the dining hall. It was chicken Kiev night, and Alex had to fight back a gag reflex as she stared at the slab of lukewarm meat sitting in a pool of congealed grease.*

"Looks pretty gross, doesn't it?"

Alex looked up at the tall, broad-shouldered boy next to her. He was cute, a prototypical All-American boy with tousled, wavy chestnut hair, aquamarine eyes, and the kind of healthy golden tan that had seen a lot of California sun.

"Um, yeah," she said, "I already feel like puking, and I haven't even had a bite."

He chuckled. "So what do you say we blow this joint and go get us some wings?"

Alex chewed her lip. "It's ten-cent-wing night at Rudy's," she said slowly.

He clapped a hand to his chest. "I knew you were a goddess the minute my tray banged into yours."

Alex laughed, her first real laugh since she'd started college.

They had wings that night, and pizza the next night, and garlic bread the night after that. Chinese food was out because apparently no one in New Haven had heard of soy sauce. Being from San Francisco, Josh had food tastes rivaling Alex's New York snobbery, especially when it came to Chinese food. Now armed with an eating partner, they declared a boycott on all dining hall food with the exception of Cocoa Puffs and Rice Krispies. In between meals, they played pool, watched basketball, and managed to squeeze a few hours in to go to class.

It would have been easy for Alex to fall for Josh. They were kindred spirits with the same tastes, the same interests, and the same sense of humor. They could talk for hours about nothing and everything. There was just one problem, and her name was Christine.

Christine was Josh's high school girlfriend back in San Francisco. Alex met her when she came to visit one weekend. Alex had been expecting someone tall, blond, and sophisticated, but the girl who showed up with Josh at the dining hall that night was small and dark and . . . Asian.

Alex tried not to let it bother her. She really did. Josh was free to date and be friends with whoever he wanted. So what if the woman he was dating and the woman he was friends with both happened to be Asian? It didn't mean anything. It wasn't any different from Alex having white boyfriends and white boy friends. So why couldn't Alex stop obsessing about this?

The weird thing was that other than their ethnicity, Alex and Christine had absolutely nothing in common. After the initial shock, Alex had tried to befriend Christine, tried to understand her, tried to figure out what it was that Josh saw in her. But talking to Christine was like talking to an empty room. She wasn't mean or nasty or un-

friendly. She listened to everything Alex said, never disagreed with her, and was polite to a fault. But she also never expressed an opinion, never showed any flashes of personality, never gave any indication whatsoever as to what it was exactly that Josh saw in her.

And yet, what Christine did possess was the most amazing psychological grip over Josh that Alex had ever seen. The weird thing was that it wasn't even romantic. Josh never spoke or acted like he was madly in love with Christine. They had nothing in common and barely seemed to have anything to say to each other. The only thing that Alex could discern was that Christine really, deeply, truly needed Josh. She clung to him like an appendage, her arm always linked through his— her eyes constantly searching for potential threats.

What really drove Alex mad, though, was the way Christine completely deferred to and depended on Josh. It wasn't that Alex didn't agree with him—in fact, most of the time she did. But Christine's deference was more akin to slavish devotion. She never told Josh he was wrong, never expressed an opinion that could in any way conflict with his. She told him constantly how smart he was, baked him cookies with smiley faces, and followed him like a puppy dog panting after its master. She was the stereotypically perfect little Asian woman. In short, Christine was everything Alex most definitely was not.

It was almost enough to make Alex hate Josh. She couldn't reconcile this man and Christine with the guy she'd spent hours with playing foosball and arguing about the Knicks. How could he possibly like someone like Alex when he was with someone like Christine? Was there anything the girls had in common other than almond-shaped eyes and Chinese surnames? In the end, Alex wasn't sure of the answer.

So for a while, she pulled back. She racked up the phone bills complaining to Lin and M.J., hung out with her roommates, attended some dances, even went on a couple of dates. But three months later, she was back at Rudy's, watching a Knicks game over a plate of ten-cent chicken wings.

"Mind if I join you?"

Alex looked up to see Josh standing there. She hesitated. Then she nudged the plate of wings toward him. Josh sat down and they watched the game in silence.

They went on like that for the next three years—best friends and only friends. Alex had a couple of boyfriends, and Josh—well, Josh had Christine. It was status quo and it was the way things had to be. Alex had no expectations, so if there were moments when she wondered what could have been—well, they were no more real than her occasional fantasies of quitting school and becoming a tour guide on the Amazon.

And then it was graduation. Alex was returning to New York for law school, and Josh was headed back to California for business school. The world was bright, exciting, and waiting for them. So Alex and Josh celebrated the only way they could: by getting completely, totally, royally trashed.

"To the next Supreme Court Justice!" Josh yelled, half-hanging out the window of his dorm room, waving a bottle of Baileys in wild jubilation.

"Will you shut up and get back in here before you fall down!" she shouted. But she was laughing as she tried to drag him back into the room.

Finally, he tumbled backward, and they collapsed in one messy, hysterically laughing heap on the floor. They'd both been drinking since noon that day and had already moved beyond the wine and the beer to any alcohol they could scrounge up in the recesses of Josh's half-packed, half-in-disarray dorm room.

"You are such a nut," Alex said.

"Yeah, but that's why you love me," Josh responded unrepentantly.

Alex snorted but at the same time she pulled away from him. She started digging a little unsteadily through one of his cabinets.

"So do you have any food left in this dump?" she demanded, rifling through old T-shirts, books, and other crumpled items that were best left alone.

"Probably not," he said from his resting place on the floor. "I think I fed the dorm rat everything last night."

"When was the last time we ate today?" Alex couldn't remember eating anything but the Froot Loops that morning.

"Um, breakfast?"

Alex groaned. "I wish Rudy's would deliver."

"I really am going to miss those chicken wings," he sighed.

"Yeah, and to think it all started with chicken Kiev."

"Can you believe that was four years ago?" Josh shook his head. "God, I can't believe it's all over."

"Oh, stop that," Alex said, dropping down beside him and taking a swig of the Baileys. "You make it seem like it's the end of the world."

"That's because it is," he replied, sitting up suddenly. "It is the end of the world. The end of this world."

She rolled her eyes. "You're being so melodramatic. Things will just be a little . . . different. So we won't be eating wings at Rudy's anymore."

"And we won't be seeing each other anymore."

Alex stiffened. She looked up at him and saw that her laughing buddy was suddenly looking very serious.

"Well, maybe not every day," she said, trying to lighten the mood, "but we'll keep in touch. There's the phone and e-mail, and you're going to come to New York. We'll have real Chinese food and go to real-life Knicks games."

"It won't be the same." Josh shook his head. "Nothing is going to be the same."

Alex bit her lip. "Look, dude," she said, tugging at his arm, "you have to snap out of this. You are seriously bumming me out here."

He looked at her for a moment and then nodded. "You're right. I guess it was just about the right time for me to transition from crazy drunk guy to depressed drunk guy. I'm done with that." He lifted up the Baileys and took a long swig. Then he held out the bottle to Alex, who pondered it for a moment. She took a deep breath and followed suit.

She put the bottle carefully down on the floor. Looking slowly up at Josh, Alex found him staring at her, his gaze intense.

"I love you, Alex," Josh said.

Alex felt like she couldn't breathe. Her head was spinning, but she didn't know if it was from his words or the Baileys.

He leaned toward her and kissed her, a slow, tentative kiss, like baby steps on an icy pavement. Then he pulled away slightly to look at her. Alex stared back at him. That was the moment she was supposed *to pull back, tell him he was drunk, make sure that cooler heads would prevail so that they wouldn't be making this huge, colossal, terrible mistake. She knew all that and yet she couldn't move to save her life. And that was why, when he moved toward her, she wrapped her arms around him and gave in to the inevitable.*

thirteen

"SO—YOU must be Alex," George Vandenhauser boomed.

It was Tuesday afternoon, and Alex and Brady were at the offices of their opposing counsel. This time, the meeting was with George—a large, barrel-chested lawyer with salt-and-pepper hair.

Alex shook his hand. "Nice to meet you, George."

"Not as nice as it is to meet you, little lady."

Alex forced a smile. She'd met George's type so many times by now that she'd lost count.

"And you must be Brady," George said, turning aside and straightening his stance. "It's good to finally meet you." He shook Brady's hand firmly. "I'm looking forward to working with you."

"Same here," Brady responded. "I have every confidence that we'll be able to resolve this dispute amicably."

"I don't doubt it." George clapped a hand to Brady's shoulder, looking him squarely in the eye. "I already have a good feeling about you, Brady."

Alex shook her head. She knew she shouldn't let this bother her. After all, it wasn't the first time she'd witnessed the instant respect garnered by a tall fair-haired man.

As the two began walking and chatting, Alex trailed behind them into a plush mahogany-and-leather conference room. Once inside, George gestured toward a counter full of steaming food trays.

"I ordered us some lunch," he declared. "Alex, I made sure there was plenty of rice."

Brady coughed loudly.

"Thanks," she replied curtly. "I'm not really a rice eater, though."

"Oh, really?" George said. "I thought all orientals eat rice."

Alex gritted her teeth. She told herself he was just another patronizing graybeard who couldn't see past his own ignorance. . . .

"Hey, George," Brady quickly interjected, "do you have any potatoes? We Irish love those spuds."

She almost burst out laughing.

"LOOK," GEORGE bellowed, "this is ludicrous. Seven-point-three is the best you're going to get."

"No deal," Alex said coolly. "Eight-point-two and not a penny lower."

"Do you know what you're turning down here?" George glowered at her. "I've got a lot more years on you here, and I can tell you that seven-point-three is as high as you can expect for this kind of deal."

"And I said that we'll settle for eight-point-two," she snapped.

George turned to Brady, who lounged in a nearby armchair.

"Brady," he said, "are you guys really going to insist on this insanity?"

Brady looked at him languidly. "You heard my colleague."

George clenched his jaw. "This is pointless. I'm leaving." Picking up his briefcase, he stormed out of the room.

Alex and Brady turned to look at each other.

"Maybe I shouldn't have kept pushing," she groaned.

"Hey, no second-guessing," Brady said. "A good lawyer has to stand tough. That means playing with the hand you're dealt—even if you've got nothing."

She looked at him and then nodded. "I should have said something. I can't believe I let him get away with that 'oriental' crack."

Brady shook his head. "No, you did the right thing. You kept your cool and cut him off at the knees."

"I know you're right," Alex replied, "but I can't help feeling like I took the easy way out." And she couldn't help but be angry at herself for playing into George's passive-Asian-woman stereotype.

Brady leaned forward. "Alex," he said, "stop beating yourself up."

"You don't understand, Brady," she sighed. "It's so easy for you. You don't have to walk into every meeting feeling like you have to justify your presence."

He frowned. "What do you mean?"

"You saw what happened. George has never met either one of us. But the minute we walked in, he was practically falling at your feet. With me, he acted like I was your secretary."

"Oh, I don't know about that—"

"It's the truth," Alex said. "It happens all the time. It's not until I've proven myself or we've had some altercation that these lawyers actually take me seriously." She paused, catching sight of his confusion. "Anyway, thanks for jumping in there while I was battling Godzilla."

Brady shrugged. "I knew you could handle Vandenhauser."

"Well, he certainly didn't think so." Alex rubbed her temples. "I mean, you might have been a problem, but definitely not me."

"Well, of course not," Brady replied, "you're just the little rice-eating oriental."

Alex rolled her eyes.

"Besides," Brady grinned, "he doesn't know what a tiger you can be. But then again, who would guess there was a tiger under those angelic eyes?"

Alex just sighed.

"TIGER," HE'D called her. How ironic.

Later that afternoon, as Alex silently studied the passing cityscape on the train ride to her parents' house, she thought of Brady's words. Her stomach had been tied up in knots all afternoon, and she had to forcibly unclench her hands several times.

There had been a time, though, when she would have welcomed the confrontation with someone like George, a time when nothing scared her. . . .

As a little girl, Alex had been a holy terror hidden under the guise of an angel. With her innocent face and guileless eyes, she was the darling at all the family reunions and Chinese wedding banquets. After all, what Chinese parent wouldn't love the pretty girl who was the honor roll all-star, the school spelling bee champion, and the precocious piano player all wrapped up in one? But what the relatives and family friends didn't see was that same little girl stealthily putting salt in their teacups, mixing their hot sauce with soy sauce, and tripping unsuspecting waiters from beneath the tablecloths.

Of course, there was always a good reason for Alex's actions: the waiters were rude to her parents because their English wasn't perfect, the teacup drinkers were snooty to her family, and the soy sauce eaters had made some cruel comments about Alex's parents in flagrant disregard of their ever-vigilant, watchful daughter at the table. She'd seen how embarrassed her parents were after these episodes—especially her mother. . . .

"Alex, have some soup."

Alex put down the brief she was reading as her mother set a steaming bowl of pickled cabbage and preserved egg soup down on the table before her. After her trying day with George Vandenhauser, Alex had decided to make an impromptu trip to her parents' split-level on Long Island. Sometimes, a little home cooking was just the thing to combat an awful day at work. Fortunately, her mother was more than happy to feed her.

"Thanks, Ma." Alex took a happy sip of her soup.

Her mother frowned. "You skinny, Alex. Told you to eat more, work less."

"Can't help it," she replied, "work is insane. Dealing with some of the jerks there makes me lose my appetite."

"Ignore them," her mother advised. "They not important. You do your own work, and everything okay. Your father and I work hard when we come to America and that all we need. That all you need."

Alex smiled. She knew her parents had gone through a lot to give their little girl the perfect American life. They'd lost everything during the Cultural Revolution—their friends, their jobs, their home—and had come to this country with little more than a suitcase full of clothes and a fervent desire for a better life. Once in America, they'd scrimped and saved, determined to give their daughter every possible advantage to succeed. Not that it was easy; neither of them spoke English. Alex's father took on a job as a dishwasher, while Alex's mother toiled as a seamstress at one of Chinatown's infamous sweatshops. Living in a tiny, one-bedroom apartment on Canal Street, the Kwans somehow managed to hold their heads high, overcoming every hardship by dint of sheer pride and determination.

"This is the thing," Alex said, taking a bite of one of her mother's signature steamed mantou rolls. "These lawyers look down on me when we first meet because they think I'm just a little Chinese girl. I have to yell and argue and fight with them before they give me any respect."

Her mother knitted her brow. "Yell and fight no good. When I first came to America, the other workers laugh at me, call us FOB just because they here few more months than me. Waiters give us dirty face, say our tip too small. But I keep working, and now . . . I better than all of them." She looked into her daughter's eyes. "You do that, too, and you will be better than all of them."

"But, Mom . . . ," Alex groaned.

Her mother didn't understand—but then again, how could she? As long as Alex could remember, her mom had been a pillar of strength. No matter what anyone said, no matter what indignities she'd been subjected to, she held it all in. She was Chinese stoicism personified—aloof, impassive, impervious to insult. Caucasian histrionics were not for her—the tears, the screams, the naked emotion. Better to retain one's pride than be reduced to such petty behavior, she once told Alex. Better to work hard and have the last laugh in the end.

Margaret put a hand on her daughter's shoulder. "Alex," she said firmly, "listen to your mother. Your father and I know you will succeed. Even when you little girl and we come here with nothing, we know you one day succeed."

Alex nodded slowly. She knew she could never completely make up for everything her parents had sacrificed for her, but the least she could do was protect her mother and father from the small-minded people who tried to take advantage of them. Even as a child, she had a whole arsenal of tricks to draw upon, and she didn't hesitate to use them on the sad sap who thought to slight one of her own.

Still, that was nothing, a mere prelude to the devilry to come. It wasn't until Alex turned fourteen that she really hit her stride.

LIN HAD *just suffered the indignity of being dumped by the cutest boy at camp two days before the big end-of-the-summer dance. She went into immediate hiding, burying herself in her bunk bed with her Strawberry Shortcake comforter, Hello Kitty doll, and a box of tissues. Alex and M.J. made their daily visits to her, but all the mint chocolate chip ice cream and Girl Scout cookies in the world weren't going to budge Lin. Which was when Alex got her brilliant idea.*

"I don't know." M.J. chewed her lip. "What if he gets really mad?"

Alex tossed her head. "Who cares? He can't get away with what he did. If we're not going to stick up for Lin, who will? Now, are you with me or not?"

M.J. nodded, as Alex knew she would. If there was one thing that any fourteen-year-old girl knew, it was that there was no stronger call than the bonds of sisterhood—especially when one of their own was being threatened.

Which is how Alex ended up waiting outside the arts-and-crafts room for Todd to walk out.

"Hey, Todd." Alex batted her eyelashes at the tall boy with the Scott Baio haircut and the Matt Dillon smirk.

"Uh, hey, Alex." Todd stared at her a little blankly.

Alex and Todd had been in the same camp for years, but Todd had never spoken to her. The two of them didn't exactly travel in the same social circles; Todd hung with the jocks and the popular kids, while everyone knew Alex was Miss Brain.

"So where are you going?" Alex asked innocently. She licked her lips, which she had carefully plastered with strawberry lip gloss.

"Uh, I've got to get to shop class," Todd said uncomfortably.

Alex just looked at him and smiled.

"Well," he said, "I guess I'll see you later."

He started to move around her, but Alex stepped in his way.

"Have you seen the movie 9½ Weeks?"

Todd blinked. "Um, yeah," he said slowly.

"Me, too," Alex said. "Want to try some of that stuff out?"

Todd's jaw dropped. "What did you just say?"

She grinned at him and nodded toward the storage closet at the end of the hallway.

"Come on," she said. "I'll let you see me with my clothes off."

And with that, she started toward the closet. He gaped after her, as though still trying to process this unimaginable turn of events.

Alex stopped at the closet, turned, and smiled at him. Then she opened the door.

Todd stared at the door, his mouth open. He'd never even given Alex a second glance. She'd always been one of those geeky smart kids, Miss Honor Roll and Lin's best friend. Alex knew he was probably conjuring up fantasies of conquering both of them—juicy bait that few adolescent boys could resist.

Her lips twitched as she watched him look around the hallway to see if there was anyone around before following her in. For a moment, Alex felt a twinge of guilt. But then she thought of how devastated Lin had been and her resolve hardened.

The room was barely lit with a single bald lightbulb overhead. Alex stood before him, hands on her hips. She could almost see the wheels turning. It was obvious he thought she was pretty hot now. Quickly, she whipped out the blindfold.

"Shit—you're serious about that 9½ Weeks stuff?" Todd squeaked.

Alex stared back at him. "Well, of course, I am. Have you ever known me not to be serious?"

"So . . . what do we do now?" he said, sounding terrified.

She flashed him a grin. "We get naked. You first."

Todd gulped, but there was no backing out now. He started pulling off his clothes. She watched him solemnly then smiled when he yanked off his boxers.

"Wow," she said.

He turned bright red. "Uh, so I guess it's your turn now."

"Right." Alex started to unbutton her blouse then hesitated. He looked so hopeful, so guileless. . . .

Stop it, *she told herself sternly.* Remember Lin crying like there was no tomorrow. *She cleared her throat.*

"Wait, I have to tie you up first." She pulled out the rope.

"What?" Todd jumped back.

Alex frowned at him. "I thought you said you saw 9½ Weeks."

"I did!"

"Well, then you know I have to tie you up so you can watch me take my clothes off." She frowned at him, and he dropped his gaze, looking like he'd just flunked some math quiz.

"Oh, right." Todd swallowed.

She walked up to him and started tying his wrists to the coat hooks on the storage wall behind him. Finally done, she stepped back and paused.

He frowned at the delay, obviously annoyed. "Look, is this some weird chink thing or something?"

Alex froze. She stared at him, the anger hardening into resolve. Todd gulped, shivering slightly.

"Just kidding," he said, quickly backtracking. "I just wanted to know, like, are you going to take your clothes off or what?"

"Is that what you told Lin?" she asked.

He blinked. "What?"

"You heard me—is that why you dumped her? Because she wouldn't let you see her naked?"

Todd stiffened, his eyes wide. "What's going on here?" He started yanking at the rope, but Alex had done her Girl Scout best.

Alex headed over to the door. She flashed him a grin.

"Don't ever mess with one of my friends," she said. And she swung the door open to reveal—Lin and M.J.

Alex linked arms with her friends, who gave Todd smug smiles, as the three girls started to walk off.

"Hey, wait!" he called out desperately. "Are you just going to leave me here?"

Alex halted in midstride. "Yeah, I think I am. Don't worry, the rest of the camp will be up soon, so I'm sure someone will let you out."

She strolled off with her friends as Todd's cries of "No!" echoed behind them.

Once the girls were a safe distance away, they let out triumphant whoops as M.J. and Lin hugged Alex tightly.

"Omigosh, I can't believe you did that!" Lin exclaimed.

"That was so cool." M.J. shook her head, impressed. "I don't know if I would have had the guts to pull that off."

"Of course you would," Alex said. "Any of us would with a jerk like that."

"I definitely couldn't do that." Lin bit her lip. "And I can't believe I'm saying this, but I feel a little bad for Todd. He'll never live down having the whole camp see him naked!"

"Oh, don't worry," Alex said. "I'll tell one of the counselors to let him out. I just wanted him to sweat a little."

"Oh, he's sweating all right!" M.J. chuckled.

The girls all giggled at the thought.

Alex finally sobered up a little. "You know what really made me mad? The fact that he thought I would turn my back on Lin and hook up with him! Who does he think he is? Did he really think I would choose him over my friend?"

"Boys can be so stupid," M.J. remarked.

"Some girls would choose a boy over their girlfriends," Lin said hesitantly.

Alex tossed her head. "Well, that would never happen to us."

"That's right." M.J. held out her hand. "I promise never to choose a guy over you girls."

Alex reached out to clasp M.J.'s hand. "Let's all promise that we'll never let boys come between us."

"I'm in." Lin smiled as she joined hands with her friends.

And as they stood there, joined in their pledge, Alex knew that nothing—neither guys nor any other divisive force—would ever come between them.

"YOU WANT me to do what?" Alex asked.

"It's not me," Lin protested. "Do you think I want to go on this date? It's our parents!"

"That's ridiculous." Alex tossed her head. "My parents have never tried to set me up. They know better than to do that!"

"You mean they know better than to let you know that they did that."

Alex frowned and took a sip of her vanilla latte. It was after five on Friday—typical working time for Alex—but she had been lured out by the promise of caffeine and Lin's announcement of an emergency situation.

"I still don't understand. Why me?" Alex asked.

"Because," Lin explained, "J's covering that game in Miami this weekend. And even if she were here, she's taken, so that makes you the only single Asian girlfriend I've got. Besides," she grinned, "when my parents said they knew of two eligible Chinese guys, your mom suggested I bring you along."

Alex groaned. She probably should have known—their parents were neighbors, best friends, and apparently co-conspirators when it came to matchmaking their daughters. Alex and Lin had first met at one of those awkward gatherings where the adults would shoo the kids off into the other room to "play," while they retired to the mah-jong table. Although Alex had never been the type to make friends easily, there was something about Lin that was oddly endearing. While the other kids ran away from her, Lin stood her ground, eventually winning Alex over. She had been impressed by Lin's ballsiness—which was probably why Lin remained one of her best friends all these years later.

"Look," Lin continued, "I don't want to do this any more than you do. But my cousin June has already set the whole thing up. We're meeting her and her boyfriend John, and John's friends

Grant and Alan, at the Peking Duck House in Chinatown for dinner tomorrow night."

Alex sighed. The prospect of a triple date with June and John
was not a particularly appealing one, but then again, it wasn't like
she had that many romantic options. Besides, with Lin there, how
bad could it be?

"Do I have to break out the Cantonese when I meet them?" she
finally said.

Lin shook her head. "Haven't you ever gone out with an Asian
guy before?"

"Oh, yeah," Alex replied, "in college. Mike Tang. He was a nice
guy. He told me he loved me five minutes after we sat down for
dinner."

"Really?" Lin gaped. "What did you say?"

Alex took a sip of her coffee. "I told him I thought the bru-
schetta appetizer looked really good. I don't think that was the response he was looking for—I hear he's in a seminary now."

Lin groaned. "I have a bad feeling about tomorrow night."

"OKAY," LIN said, "remember what we agreed on? That you're not
going to say anything crazy?"

Alex rolled her eyes. It was Saturday night, and Lin had been a
complete stress case the whole evening. Alex didn't understand
how Lin could get so worked up about some stupid setup date. Or
put so much effort into it. Beautifully attired in a silk floral Prada
dress and Manolo slingbacks, Lin cut quite the contrast with Alex,
who wore a no-nonsense black skirt and knee-length boots.

"Yeah, yeah," Alex said, drumming her fingers on the table,
"where are these guys anyway? They're ten minutes late." She
rolled her eyes. "Typical Asian time."

As if on cue, the door to the Peking Duck House swung open
and Lin's cousin June walked in, arms entwined with her boyfriend, John. June was twenty-two, cute, ridiculously thin, and very
giggly. She was a perfect counterpart for John, who always looked

like a Chinatown gang member with his gaudy gold chains, baggy, barely-on-his-ass jeans, and platinum tips. Behind June and John trailed two strikingly opposite-looking Asian guys.

Alex studied their dates surreptitiously as the introductions were made. On first glance, they seemed okay—even slightly cute. Alan sported a typical, clean-cut look. He was a little J. Crew, but at least he wasn't Target. Grant, on the other hand, was pure Asian machismo. He strutted in wearing an expensive silk shirt and a sneer. Alex knew his type well. With his carefully slicked-back hair, meticulously groomed goatee, and arrogant good looks, Grant was the clear leader of the pack and he knew it.

"So," Lin said as they arrived at the table, "Alan, what do you do?"

"I'm a dermatologist," he replied, "at Columbia Presbyterian."

June slapped Lin. "Did you hear that?" she exclaimed. "He's a doctor!"

"I think we all heard that," Alex said, reaching for a menu.

Grant looked at Alex. "So you like doctors, huh?"

She didn't turn around. "They're fine."

"Oh, come on, doesn't every Chinese girl want a doctor for a husband?"

Lin swallowed. Alex turned around to look at Grant very slowly. "Oh, is that what you think?"

Grant shrugged. "It's what I know."

Alex stared at him, taken aback. Who did this guy think he was? One glance at Lin's warning face, however, quelled any potential snide remark. Alex took a deep breath.

"So"—she smiled brightly—"what do you do, Grant?"

"I work at Smith Barney," he replied. "What about you?"

"I'm a lawyer," Alex said, taking a sip of her tea.

"Nice. What's that like?"

She shrugged. "It's got its ups and downs—" She was about to go on about the trials and tribulations of a lawyer's life, when Alan suddenly shouted from the other side of the table.

"Hey, Grant! You wanna go to A.C. this weekend?"

Grant flashed a thumbs-up gesture.

"Atlantic City, huh?" Alex said. "What's your game?"

"Poker." Grant craned his head toward the other end of the table.

"Oh, yeah?" She tapped her nails on her glass. "I'm kind of partial to—"

"Hey, Alan." Grant got out of his chair. "What do you say we head up Friday night—?"

Without a backward glance, Grant was gone to the other end of the table. Alex drained her teacup and turned to give Lin her I'm-about-ready-to-give-up look.

Suddenly, John and Alan broke out into loud laughter.

Quickly seizing upon the possibility of a diversion, Lin leaned toward them and asked, "What are you guys laughing about?"

"Oh, nothing," John said. "We were just talking about playing craps."

"Yeah," Alan added, "we were talking about Vegas. Nothing you girls would be interested in."

"Why?" Alex asked. "Because girls don't gamble?"

"Alex is a great craps player," Lin volunteered.

John looked at Alex skeptically. "You know how to play craps?"

"I like to shoot some dice. Haven't you seen the busloads of Asian women heading to Atlantic City every day?"

The boys shrugged and exchanged grins that screamed "This girl *thinks* she knows how to gamble." The look was not lost on Alex, who scowled ominously.

"Hey, look," Lin quickly interrupted, "the food's here! Time to eat!"

She promptly began chattering away to Alan and Grant as the waiters set down the steaming plates of food. Alex frowned but didn't say anything as she joined the others at digging into their dishes. So was this what she had to look forward to with dating? Alex was beginning to remember why it was she didn't have a boyfriend.

In fact, she was so busy concentrating on her food that she almost missed what happened next. Just as everyone was eating and Lin was exhaling in relief, June started feeding John. First, she picked up the choicest slices of chicken and deposited them on his plate with a none-too-discreet "Here's a good piece, honey." Then, as John shook his head, she brought a morsel to his mouth with her chopsticks and started coaxing him to take a bite. Finally, John gave in and ate the chicken, for which he was rewarded with a spate of cooing baby talk from June. Lin and Alex watched this entire display, openmouthed and appalled.

"What are you doing?" Alex broke out, unable to take it anymore. Next to her, Alex could feel Lin nudging her, but she ignored her friend completely.

"What are you talking about?" John asked as June stopped to stare at Alex.

"I'm just curious," Alex said, "did you hurt your arm?"

John wrinkled his forehead. "No . . . why do you ask?"

"Then why is she feeding you?" Alex demanded.

An uncomfortable silence descended upon them. Then Grant stirred.

"June's a good girlfriend," he jumped in. "She wants to take care of her man. Maybe you should take a few pointers from her."

"Oh, is that what that's called?" Alex snorted with laughter. "I bet you think that a good girl should also sit at home, do laundry, and have a hot meal waiting for her man."

Grant smirked. "Nothing wrong with that."

"So I guess your wife won't really be working since she'll be so busy cooking and cleaning for you." Alex rolled her eyes.

"She's better off not working," Grant declared. "It's not like she'll be making that much money anyway. And if she is, well, she probably won't be for very long."

Alex stared at him. She couldn't believe the words coming out of this guy's mouth.

"What are you talking about?" she asked. "I know plenty of women who work at investment banks."

Grant held up his hands. "I see the girls in my office. Sure they make a lot of money now, but they're all going to quit eventually. Investment banks are no place for a woman."

"You have got to be kidding me!" Alex exclaimed. "Lin works at Merrill Lynch and she handles her job just fine. I billed three hundred fifty hours last month. You want to talk about pressure with me?"

Grant shrugged. "Whatever. Everyone knows that a woman is only going to work until she gets pregnant, and then it's sayonara. Look—how old are you?"

"I'm going to be thirty," Alex snapped, "and I have no intention of quitting my job anytime soon."

"Thirty!" Grant grimaced. "You better start thinking about quitting, or soon you'll be too old to have kids."

"I—I—" Alex sputtered, infuriated by Grant's comment. "For your information, women are not just baby-producing machines. I know it's hard for your Neanderthal mind to comprehend this, but we actually do have careers and other things we care about besides popping out kids."

Grant looked at Alex and folded his arms. "You're never going to get married with that attitude."

Alex stared at him, stunned. "Okay, that's it!" she yelled, shaking her chopsticks at him. "Who the hell do you think you are? You think that just because you make a couple bucks, you can go around spouting crap like that? You're obviously completely insecure and threatened by any woman who has a mind of her own. The only woman who would marry you would only be after your money, because you sure as heck won't be able to satisfy her in any other way!"

Deafening silence. Alex realized only then, as the red haze of fury slowly dissipated from her vision, that she was on her feet, still brandishing her chopsticks at Grant's throat. As she looked around, she saw that the entire restaurant was staring at her, all activity by the waitstaff and the other diners having ceased. June and her boyfriend looked stunned and a little afraid. Lin looked mortified and resigned, as if she should have known this would happen. And as for Grant—well, he looked plain terrified, and possibly for the first time in his life, shocked into complete silence.

Alex took a deep breath and slowly put down the chopsticks.

"And now," she said, "I'm going to leave." Picking up her bag, Alex walked out with as much dignity as she could muster.

"YOU DID what?" M.J. gasped. "And the dude said what!"

"He pretty much said no one would marry me because I had a big mouth," Alex said grimly as she sipped her tea.

It was the day after the fiasco, and the girls were at the Imperial Palace Restaurant in Chinatown for the *Moon-Yut* party of Lin's cousin Renee. It was Chinese tradition to have a banquet thirty days after the birth of a child to celebrate a thriving, healthy baby. Along with the usual ten-course feast, guests were expected to consume red eggs, red being the Chinese color of good luck and good health.

It wasn't Alex's first choice in ways to spend a beautiful Sunday afternoon, but Lin had begged her to come, and M.J. went on and on about the deliciousness of the crystal rice and seasoned prawns until she had given in. Not that Alex was against *Moon-Yut* parties per se. It was just that she was getting to the age where being at a party like this and all it symbolized just made her think about kids, having kids, and how the odds of her having kids weren't looking very good. Grant's insults about her age and her waning chances of motherhood didn't exactly help. Unfortunately, he wasn't the only one who thought this way.

Within minutes of her arrival, Alex had been besieged by a gaggle of her mother's friends, all of whom cooed over her and demanded to know when she was going to be having a *Moon-Yut* party of her own.

"Alex-ah." Mrs. Wong, her parents' next-door neighbor, grabbed her hand. "Such a smart girl—I hear you make lots of money. When you get married?"

"Yes," Mrs. Lee, another neighbor, jumped in, "you work too

hard. Girls don't need to earn so much money. You find yourself rich husband and he take care of you."

Alex did her best not to cringe as Mrs. Lee patted her on the shoulder.

"Don't you want to give your mother grandchildren?" Mrs. Yip, her mother's mah-jong partner, demanded. "She's been waiting for a very long time already."

Alex glanced over at her mom. She stood in the background, silent as always. While she had never tried to pressure her daughter about having children, Alex knew she thought about it—how could she not when all her friends kept wondering when her smart, accomplished daughter was going to settle down and give her grandkids?

Mercifully, her mother's friends eventually drifted away. M.J., meanwhile, was still absorbed with the Grant saga.

She whirled toward Lin. "So this is the guy your parents set you up with?"

"Well," Lin said, "I don't think they really knew—"

"That he was an ass?" Alex finished. "Well, they know now. Or at least my parents do. I called them as soon as I got home and told them they better never think about pulling a stunt like that again."

M.J. laughed. "I bet you did. Now do you see why Asian guys aren't my thing?"

"I've got to say," Alex admitted, "I don't care if they're Asian or not, but I do care if they're assholes. And these guys definitely fit the bill. They seemed shocked that a girl would dare disagree with them."

"That's exactly my problem with Asian guys!" M.J. said triumphantly. "They just want some quiet, meek little woman who will stay at home and slave away for them."

"That's not true for all Asian men!" Lin exclaimed.

"Well, maybe not," M.J. conceded, "but it's true for a lot of them. Asian men look at me and think that I am going to sit on them!"

Alex chuckled. "She's got a point there."

"Just look at Ming." M.J. gestured in the direction of her friend, whose mother was chatting with their parents. "He thinks the white guys are stealing all the Asian women away."

"Did someone say my name?" Ming asked. He dropped down beside M.J.

"Yeah," Alex said, taking a bite of her salt-baked chicken, "we were just talking about how great you are about protecting Asian women from the Big Bad White Menace."

"Let me guess," Ming speared a shrimp, "is M.J. talking about her whitey boyfriend?"

"As a matter of fact, I was," M.J. said. "You won't even meet Jagger—"

"Look, what I think Ming is saying is that dating outside of your race is kind of like turning your back on your culture," Lin said, "which, in a way, is true. It's like saying that you think guys of your own kind aren't good enough for you."

Ming raised his chopsticks. "Exactly!"

"Well, any guy who thinks I have a bad attitude just because I speak my mind isn't good enough for me, because I am *not* putting up with this chauvinistic crap from the Dark Ages," Alex announced. "And if the guy is Asian, well, I don't care if that's seen as turning my back on my culture."

M.J. clapped her hands. "Amen to that!"

Ming sighed and got up. "A little too much estrogen here. Catch you guys later."

"Bye, Asian Warrior Man," M.J. called out after Ming's retreating back.

Lin sighed. "I think things will eventually change. It just takes time—maybe the next generation will be different."

"You mean like that kid over there?" M.J. jabbed her fork toward a little boy who was chasing a screaming little girl around the restaurant.

"Why is it that boys always seem to be so much more trouble than girls?" Lin asked.

"It's because they're spoiled," Alex said. "Their mothers let them do whatever they want."

"True," M.J. agreed, "Chinese families always spoil the boys. Why is it that little girls are taught to cook and clean, while little boys are taught to give orders?"

"You're right," Lin said. "My brother gets away with everything. He's twenty-seven and still has never had a real job. Right now, he's hanging out with his friends in Hong Kong, supposedly 'learning about his heritage.'"

Just then, a cry rang out. As the little boy let go of the girl's hair, the kids' grandmother toddled over and shushed the girl. Lin looked over at M.J. and Alex and shrugged.

"I would love to see you with a baby," Lin said playfully to Alex.

Alex groaned inwardly. So much for getting through this party without any more baby talk. "Uh, yeah . . . ," she said. "I have to say, I don't know how I feel about having kids."

"Don't say that too loud!" Lin whispered. "We're at a *Moon-Yut* party, remember?"

Alex sighed. She knew she'd never escape the question, just like she knew she would get this reaction. "I didn't say I hated babies. I just can't handle one right now. . . . Anyway, it's a moot point. I mean, do you see any potential fathers anywhere?"

"Well," M.J. said, "You might've found one if you had come speed-dating with us."

"You guys went?" Alex exclaimed. She couldn't believe her friends had gone—and without telling her anything about it.

"Yeah," Lin said, sipping her tea slowly, "last week."

"Oh." Alex fiddled with her teacup. "I didn't know that."

"I told you about it." Lin speared a shrimp with her chopsticks.

"Yeah," M.J. added. "You were like 'ew, gross.' Which is why I had to step up to the plate and go with her."

"And?" Lin prompted.

"Okay," M.J. rolled her eyes, "it wasn't that bad. If I didn't have a boyfriend, maybe I'd do it for real. It was kind of funny even—remember the guy in the plaid plants?"

"Oh, he loved you!" Lin exclaimed. "They had to pry him away from your table."

"That's because I'm the only girl he's ever met who's watched a Ping-Pong match." M.J. took a bite of her red egg. "But I'm not the one who walked away with a date."

Alex's jaw dropped. "You actually went on a date with one of these guys, Lin?"

"Just coffee," she said casually. "I know what you're going to say, but it was perfectly innocent. We met at Starbucks, in full view of tons of people."

Alex licked her lips. "I wasn't going to lecture you."

"Of course you were," M.J. said, "but that's all right. Hey, Lin, remember that guy with the purple hair who asked you for your number—?"

As her friends chattered on, Alex couldn't help but feel a little twinge of jealousy. She told herself not to be stupid—just because they were all friends didn't mean the three of them had to do everything together. Truthfully, it wasn't so much that she envied their speed-dating expedition, but she did envy the laughs, the shared jokes, the boy stories they could now tell ad nauseam. . . . When was the last time she had a real boy story? Alex couldn't remember. As she studied her red egg dubiously, she couldn't help wondering when she stopped being fun and started being a wet blanket.

THE MORNING *of graduation was a blur. After she left Josh's room, Alex had to go back to her room, get ready, meet her parents for breakfast, and be at the graduate congregation area by ten. Suffice it to say, she wasn't even close to being on time. Which is why she didn't see Christine until it was too late.*

"Alex!" Christine cried, descending upon Alex like a dark cloud.

"Oh, Christine." Alex swallowed hard as she took a quick step back. Of all the people for her to run into this morning . . .

"Alex, have you seen Josh?" she asked frantically. "I've been looking for him everywhere."

"Um, no. I have no idea where Josh is right now," Alex replied truthfully.

"*Hmm, this is so strange.*" Christine looked around with a frown. "*He didn't answer the phone this morning, and he wasn't in his room when I knocked.*"

"*Huh, that is strange,*" Alex said, looking around frantically for any potential avenue of escape.

"*This is so unlike him,*" Christine remarked. "*I mean—Josh!*"

Alex whirled around. Josh stood before them, looking positively panicked.

Christine threw her arms around him. "*Josh! Sweetie, I was so worried about you. I couldn't find you.*"

"*Yeah,*" he mumbled, "*I was kind of busy.*"

"*Well, of course you were.*" Christine smiled. "*This is your big day—*"

As Christine babbled on, Alex looked up and her eyes met Josh's. He gazed at her helplessly then turned away. It was in that moment that Alex had her answer. She knew then that Josh would never leave Christine, would never have the guts to own up to his feelings, would never be the guy she so desperately wanted him to be.

"*I better get going,*" she interrupted. "*I'll see you guys later.*"

"*Oh, okay,*" Christine said brightly. Josh mumbled something, but when Alex turned back to look at him, he was already engrossed in a conversation with Christine.

Alex stormed off, so angry that she could barely speak. There was a part of her that wanted to yell at Josh, to hit him, to tell Christine exactly what had happened the night before. But then she thought of her mother and how she would have been strong, how she wouldn't have let him see how upset he'd made her.

Somehow, she made her way to the graduation site. Made her way onto the podium, accepted her diploma, smiled for the pictures. Somehow, she made it through the afternoon, managing to seal off the swirling emotions that threatened to engulf her at any moment.

It was only later, when she had returned to her room and dragged her last bag onto the quad, that she allowed herself to think about him. Looking out onto the campus, she saw the tree they'd spent hours sprawled under, the post office they raced each other to, the steps on *which they'd spent many a late evening. She remembered the mischievous glint in his eyes, his long, loping gait, the way he always smelled of fresh leaves. And then she remembered the way she felt watching him with Christine that morning—like her heart had been shredded to confetti that was being scattered to the four winds.*

JUST LIKE always, Alex's friends were there to help her pick up the pieces after Josh. After insisting that she come directly to Lin's house, Lin and M.J. hosted a sleepover reminiscent of the ones from their childhood. As Alex ranted about how spineless and whipped and unbelievable Josh was, Lin painted her nails and M.J. baked Alex's favorite chocolate chip cookies. And in the background, Lin's mother hovered and offered her own brand of advice: "Alex-ah, I fix you some *gung-pao* chicken soup. You stick with me. I find you a good Asian boy. No more fool around with white boys." Then she patted Alex's hand while Lin rolled her eyes.

Looking back, Alex didn't know how she would have gotten through those dark days without the constant phone calls and handholding from M.J. and Lin. Fortunately, with her friends' help, she did—and slowly but surely, Alex returned to a semblance of her old self. But no matter how hard she tried, she would never be the same again.

Because a little part of Alex died that morning of graduation.

$Direct$
$Examination$

fourteen

IN THE three months that had passed since her trip to the fortune-teller, Alex hadn't given Auntie Lee's prophecy much thought. After all, she still had no idea what the old woman had meant about the "new possibilities" helping her to find "happiness." Was she supposed to open herself up to new possibilities . . . at work?

It was the night of the firm's anniversary party—several days after the *Moon-Yut* celebration—and Alex was in hell. She was surrounded by couples: old partners and their wives, young junior associate couples, even support staff couples. And Alex? Well, she had the pleasure of being seated next to her partner David, David's wife, her junior associate Jenny, and Jenny's fiancé, Charlie.

"You're going to have a wonderful time at Martha's Vineyard, Jenny," David's wife was saying.

"I could really use some rest," Jenny said. "I had no idea picking out china patterns could be so exhausting!"

The two of them laughed. Meanwhile, David and Charlie were comparing golf scores. As Jenny and Mrs. Randall launched into a discussion of floral arrangements, Alex quickly escaped to the bar.

"Vodka straight," she ordered.

She leaned back against the bar in her black Vera Wang cocktail dress and surveyed the room. Apparently, everyone at her firm but her had brought an "And Guest" with them. Shaking her head, she took a long swig of her drink.

"Do you want to dance?"

Alex turned to see James Heine, a nasally tax lawyer with an unfortunate penchant for bow ties.

"James, I don't think—" she began automatically and then stopped. Hadn't the fortune-teller told her that the only way she would find happiness was if she opened herself up to new possibilities? Hadn't she promised herself that she was going to turn over a new leaf and start giving people a chance? Even if they wore bow ties and suspenders.

She took a deep breath. "Sure."

One song later, Alex was seriously regretting her decision. James not only had zero rhythm, but he also managed to step on her feet three times during one dance. Then, when she suggested that they get a drink at the bar, he spilled half his drink on himself and the other half on Alex.

"No, no," she said as James started apologizing profusely, "it's okay. Really. It's not a party until someone's wearing the vodka. Now, if you'll excuse me, I'm just going to get some club soda from the bar."

She was dabbing furiously at her dress with a napkin when she felt a tap on her shoulder. Turning around, she saw that it was Max "Fingers" Caldwell, a lawyer in corporate who gave new meaning to the word *sleazy*.

"Alex," he declared, "you look stunning."

"Oh, yeah?" Alex said. "So I guess you're into the big napkin stain on the dress thing, huh?"

Max laughed. "Har-har, Alex, you are a riot. You want to dance?"

"Oh," Alex hesitated, "I don't know—"

"Come on, Alex," Max threw his hand into the air, "why don't you live a little? Do something a little crazy?"

Alex sighed. There it was again—the whole "take a chance, stop being a dud, Alex" bit. Did someone send out a memo on this?

"Fine," she said reluctantly.

It didn't take very long for Alex to decide that this whole "being open to possibilities" thing was a crock. There was a reason why Max was nicknamed Fingers, and Alex had a front-row seat.

"Okay, Max," she said with gritted teeth as she forcibly relocated the hand he'd clamped onto her posterior. "What did I just tell you? Hands above the waist."

Max just leered at her. "I love it when you get frisky, Alex."

Alex's jaw dropped. "Why you haven't been brought up on sexual harassment charges, I have no idea—"

"Mind if I cut in?"

Alex and Max both looked up to see Brady standing there. As usual, he was immaculately attired in an expensive Savile Row suit and a silver tie that accentuated his ice-blue eyes.

"Oh," Max faltered, "well, I, uh—"

"Thanks, man," Brady grinned as he smoothly disengaged Alex from Max, "catch you later."

He swept Alex away swiftly with the very same confidence he wielded in the courtroom. Once out on the dance floor, Brady was a surprisingly good dancer—moving with a firm grip and a certain silkiness that said he knew what he was doing.

"Okay," she said, "I have to admit, that was pretty smooth. Presumptuous, but smooth."

"Presumptuous?" Brady raised an eyebrow. "You're telling me that you actually wanted to keep dancing with Max?"

Alex blinked as he twirled her. "You know I didn't."

"I got to say, Al, I was really surprised to see you dancing with Caldwell. Didn't think you enjoyed being groped in full view of the whole firm."

She sighed. "I don't. It's just that someone told me that I needed to open myself up to possibilities."

Brady looked skeptical. "What kind of possibilities?"

Alex shook her head. "It doesn't matter. It's stupid."

"All right," he said as he dipped her toward the floor. "So tell me, Lexa, am I sweeping you off your feet yet? Because the two-minute mark is usually when women start falling for me."

Alex just laughed.

. . .

AFTER HER evening with James Heine and "Fingers" Caldwell, Alex decided that being a loner might not be such an unattractive option after all.

And yet, she couldn't get Auntie Lee's prophecy out of her head. There had been something in her voice that had made even Alex, ever the skeptic, a believer. Which was why she was willing to do the unthinkable.

"I'm so happy you reconsidered!" Lin squealed.

"I still can't believe I'm doing this."

"I already paid your fifty-dollar admission, so there's no turning back now."

"I'd be happy to pay you back." Alex squirmed. "Consider it a . . . charitable donation."

Lin rolled her eyes. "There's no getting out of this, Alex. We're here for speed-dating, and that's exactly what we're going to do!"

Alex sighed and looked heavenward, where a large, cringe-worthy sign read: WELCOME, LONELY SINGLES. The speed-dating event that Lin had been so keen on trying—"Fast Lane"—was being held on the corporate meeting room floor of the Marriott Marquis in Times Square. That part was fine—after all, Alex had been there a number of times herself for work meetings. What had her ready to bolt, though, was "Fast Lane" itself. For the event, the spacious and sterile corporate meeting room had been transformed into a gaudy explosion of pink curtains, red sashes, and gigantic cardboard hearts. It was like someone had gone wild at a post–Valentine's Day sale and emptied a store of its entire inventory. Meanwhile, a crowd of women fluttered about on one side of the room, fluffing their hair and checking their makeup. A group of men fidgeted on the other side of the room, their hands shoved deep into their pockets.

"I'm having flashbacks to every school dance I've ever been to," Alex muttered to Lin as she tugged at her gray pencil skirt.

Lin, however, was preoccupied with other things. "The ad said there was going to be a one-to-one male-to-female ratio, but I see twice as many girls here as guys!"

"It's terrible." Alex shook her head. "Do you smell what I smell?"

Lin frowned. "Smell what?"

"This place positively reeks of desperation." Alex turned and started to head toward the door. "I have to get out of here!"

Lin grabbed Alex's wrist in a death grip. "Alex, stop! Look, you said you were willing to give this a shot, so why not try it? You always say you don't have time to spend more than a few minutes with the losers of the world. Here, we don't have to spend more than seven minutes with anyone if we don't want to." Lin let go of Alex's arm. "That means no endless evening trying to avoid being groped, no bad date being bored out of your mind, and no trying to get through an hour with some space cadet freak. Isn't that what you want?"

Alex considered that. "You have a point," she finally admitted. "Fine, let's do this."

TAKING A deep breath, Alex sat down heavily in her chair. All around the room, women sat at little "stations" like her own, a stack of profiles and a shiny, scary bell on each of the tables before them. Alex studied the gleaming object in front of her as if it were some strange, frightening insect. She sure hoped Auntie Lee knew what she was talking about.

"Alex!"

She glanced up to see Lin motioning to her from the next station.

"Remember, if you don't like the guy, just ring the bell and he has to leave pronto!"

Alex nodded. "Oh, don't you worry, I've got that covered!"

And she did—until the first "date" sat down across from her. On first glance, he seemed perfectly acceptable—a little frat-boyish, but generically good-looking.

"Hello." She smiled as she held out her hand. "I'm Alex."

He shook her hand. "Brad."

"So I'm kind of new to this," Alex began.

"All right, well, we only have seven minutes, so let's get right down to it," Brad interrupted, "I'm thirty-three, I'm a trader on Wall Street, I own my own place, and I've got a six-figure income."

Alex blinked. "Oh, well, that's . . . very nice for you."

"That's it? In case you haven't realized, I'm a hell of a catch."

"You also seem to have a hell of an ego," Alex said dryly.

His expression darkened. "Did I mention I went to Brown?"

Alex resisted the urge to roll her eyes. "Lovely."

"Where did you go to school?" Brad demanded.

Oh great, Alex thought, *here we go with the "battle of the schools."* She sighed. "Yale."

There was a moment's silence. Then Brad got up abruptly. "I got to go."

And just like that, he was gone. Alex looked over at Lin, who shot her a what-happened look. Alex just shrugged.

She checked her watch. "Wow," she muttered, "that didn't even break the three-minute mark. At this rate, I'll be out of here before the hour's up."

Four minutes later, Alex's next "date" showed up. On paper, Eric Weinstein had sounded pretty good: thirty-seven, never married, graduate of MIT, currently a physicist teaching at Columbia. In real life, Eric was shorter than her, scrawny, balding, and sported an actual, honest-to-goodness pocket protector.

Alex forced a smile. "So," she said, looking down at her carefully prepared list of questions, "tell me about your last date."

"Um." Eric wiped his brow. "I've never actually been on a date."

"Oh," she said, glancing down at her questions, "well, then, let's move on—" Looking up at him, she couldn't help but ask, "What do you mean you've never been on a date?"

Eric turned bright red. "Well, it—it's just that I'm always, um, really busy. You know, with school and research and, um, experiments. . . ."

Looking at him, Alex's expression softened. "I know how it is. Sometimes, you forget about things like dating."

He leaned forward. "Exactly! I know I should care about dating and finding someone, but—" He cast a bleak look around the room. "—I just don't think this is right for me."

"Let me guess, you would much rather meet someone in the—" Alex hesitated. "—lab?"

Eric's face lit up. "Yes! In fact, there's this wonderful young lady there. She's absolutely brilliant at quantum physics, but of course she would never be interested in me—"

"Don't say that!" Alex admonished. "Eric, you are a great . . . catch. What you need to do now is go back to the lab and ask her out—on your very first date!"

Eric's eyes widened. "Do you really think she would say yes?"

"Absolutely." Alex nodded. "Now go and do it!"

"Okay, I will!" he said, springing to his feet. Before she could react, Eric ran over to the other side of the table and gave her a quick hug before racing out of the room.

Alex watched his retreating back. "This place should pay me to help these people find true love."

"Did you say something about true love?"

Looking up, Alex saw a handsome man sporting a dashing blue suit and a picture-perfect tan.

She took a deep breath. "Hello, I'm Alex."

"Pleasure to meet you, Alex." He shook her hand. "I'm James Maxwell." Sitting down across from her, James flashed her a perfect Pepsodent smile.

"Now tell me," he said, "what is a looker like you doing in a place like this?"

Alex cleared her throat. "Oh, thank you. I could ask you the same thing."

"Easy—I work a lot, so I don't really have the time to meet people. Seven dates in an hour sounded like a pretty good way to maximize my time. The only thing that worried me was that I would end up in a room of, well," he leaned forward and whispered, "some not very attractive people."

Alex nodded solemnly. "I can see that."

"Look," James continued, "I'll freely admit that I can be pretty shallow. Kind of goes with the plastic surgeon territory. Fortunately," he said, "I can't find anything wrong with you."

"Oh," she paused, "thanks, I guess—"

"Of course, one of the benefits of being with me is the availability of free cosmetic procedures."

Alex was sure she heard wrong. Did he just say free cosmetic procedures?

"I know, it does seem a little extravagant, but look, I can't have any woman of mine looking less than perfect, can I?"

She gaped at him, for once at a loss for words.

"For example, you have very youthful skin," James went on, "so I don't think you need any Botox. Plus, you have a wonderful figure, so the liposuction's out. No," he said as he scanned her from head to toe, "I don't see any flaws—well, except for your breasts."

Alex's head snapped up. "What about my breasts?"

"You could just use a couple of extra cup sizes. It's the curse of Asian women—no wrinkles, skinny as a rail, but flat as a board." James leaned forward. "But don't you worry, we can take care of that easily."

Her jaw dropped. "Now, just wait a minute! I am not flat as a—"

"Time!" the organizer yelled.

James got up, making a call-me gesture with his hand. Alex glared after him as she crumpled his profile up. Of all the nerve!

"Hello?"

Alex looked up. What she saw was a solid, middle-aged man who was neither gorgeous nor a dork. Finally, she thought, someone normal.

He extended an arm. "I'm Martin."

Alex shook his hand. "Nice to meet you."

"Thank you," Martin said, sitting down stiffly. "I, uh, don't really know how to do this."

"Well, that makes two of us." Alex smiled.

"Call me a little old-fashioned, but this isn't how I expected to meet my future spouse."

Alex shook her head. "Me neither."

"But then I started thinking about how people used to have arranged marriages, and how statistics show that those marriages actually had a great success rate. Do you know why that is?"

She frowned. "Because divorce was still taboo?"

"No," he said, "it's because people married people not based on these new-fangled notions about chemistry and passion, but because they made a suitable spouse."

"I'm not sure I understand." Alex wrinkled her forehead.

"Well, take you, for example. You're a lawyer. Clearly, you're smart. And you're obviously attractive." Martin sat back in his chair. "Now, I just have to sample your culinary skills."

"My what?" She blinked. The only cooking she ever did was of the microwave-takeout variety.

"It's very important for a wife to have a good, hot meal waiting for me when I come home from work. Not to mention a clean house," he said. "I'm not springing for one of those cleaning ladies that everyone's throwing their money away on."

Alex couldn't believe she was actually hearing this. "Are you serious?" she asked.

"Well, of course," Martin said. "You should understand. One thing I've always admired about the Asian culture is how the wife makes her family her number-one priority . . . especially since I want to have at least a half dozen kids."

Alex slammed her hand down on the bell so hard, it almost fell off the table. Martin jumped up in shock.

"I really don't think this is going to work out, Martin."

"That's fine," he sneered. "You seem to be lacking in maternal instinct anyway."

Alex scowled and picked up the bell to launch at him, but he was already out of throwing range. Overflowing with indignation, she jumped to her feet. Who did he think he was?

Pushing past her next befuddled "date," she ran over to Lin, who was in the midst of a tête-à-tête with some guy with a goatee.

"I can't take this anymore," Alex yelled. "I'm out of here!"

She started to walk away, then stopped and came back over to

Lin. "Go for James Maxwell. He'll give you a free collagen injection."

Without waiting to see Lin's reaction, she jetted out the doors.

As she stormed out of the conference room, Alex shook her head. What had she been thinking? She must have been crazy to think that something as inane as speed-dating could bring her happiness. . . .

"Alex?" a familiar voice said.

She looked up—and almost fell over in shock. "Brady?" she squeaked. "What are you doing here?"

"I'm here for that client development reception, remember?"

"Oh, right," she said, her mind racing. How could she have forgotten?

Brady was looking at her strangely. "Are you okay, Alexandra?"

"Oh." She tried to look casual. "Of course I am."

Of all the people in the world who she could have run into, Brady was, without a doubt, the last person on earth she would want to run into here. If he actually knew what she was doing here . . .

"So what brings you here?" Brady asked curiously.

"Oh!" Alex frantically tried to think of a plausible excuse. "I, um—"

"There you are!"

Both Alex and Brady turned. James Maxwell strolled up to them, smile gleaming.

"I was worried you'd left," he said. "I meant what I said in there, by the way."

"That's great, James," Alex said quickly, "let's talk about this later—"

Unfortunately, James had noticed Brady. "Who are you?" he demanded. "I didn't see you inside."

Brady frowned. "Inside where?"

"Nowhere!" she yelped. "Look, Brady, I'll see you later—"

James stabbed a finger at Brady's chest. "There are rules, you know. You can't just barge in, man. Haven't you ever done speed-dating before?"

Brady raised an eyebrow. "Speed-dating?"

Alex clapped a hand to her mouth in horror. She couldn't imagine a moment more mortifying than this. She was never going to hear the end of this, never going to be able to face Brady again.

As James continued blathering on, Alex turned and fled.

Cross-Examination

fifteen

THE NEXT day, Alex could barely drag herself to work. Usually, she would march into the office, a whirlwind of energy waiting to tackle the thorny legal issue of the day. But today, all she could think about was how much she dreaded seeing Brady.

As it turned out, there really wasn't an opportunity to discuss the speed-dating incident. She and Brady had a settlement negotiation that day, and he raced into the meeting five minutes before it was scheduled to start.

Besides, there were more pressing matters to deal with. Alex was sitting in a conference room staring at a wall of suits—two very old, very rich men, a couple of lawyers, and Brady, who was duking it out with their opposing counsel. Brady, of course, was in his element. There was nothing like alternately berating, coaxing, and browbeating their adversary to bring out that very special afterglow that no woman could ever hope to give him.

Watching him now, Alex couldn't help but be impressed. Underneath all his foibles, Brady Jameson was a damn good lawyer. More than good—amazing, the wunderkind prodigy of the firm. He was like P. T. Barnum in the courtroom, winning over judge and jury alike with his innate showmanship and movie star–like charisma. Worse, he was an inveterate do-gooder with all his pro bono asylum work, a legal shark with a hero complex and a heart of gold, if there was such a thing. At the same time, he could turn on a dime, becoming a mercilessly ferocious and ruthless adversary.

"This is ludicrous," the other lawyer was sputtering. "Your client doesn't have a leg to stand on and you know it! The only reason we even agreed to entertain settlement discussions with you was because it was our understanding that your client was ready to make a good-faith effort to resolve this situation without incurring additional litigation costs on both sides."

"And we've made a more than generous offer," Brady responded. "One-point-two million should amply compensate your client for any losses he may have suffered."

"Your client embezzled almost ten million dollars from our company!" The opposing attorney was almost apoplectic with outrage. "He should be thanking his lucky stars that we're not going to prosecute him and have him thrown in jail!"

Seated beside Alex, their client, Ed Duncan, stiffened in alarm. Alex turned and gave him a reassuring look, but she was feeling a twinge of alarm as well. Brady was taking his hardball stance dangerously close to the edge. They both knew that their client had embezzled the ten million, and that they didn't have a snowball's chance in court. Their opposing counsel was right; offering one million under the circumstances was downright dangerous.

She tried to subtly nudge Brady under the table, but he shook her off impatiently.

"Our offer is final," he announced. "You either take it or we'll see you in court. We'll give you some time to think about it." He turned back to Alex and their client. "Let's get some coffee."

The minute they were out in the hallway and their client was safely out of hearing range, Alex confronted him. "Brady, what are you doing?" she demanded. "Why won't you up the offer?"

He shrugged. "I think they'll come around."

"But what if they don't?" she exclaimed. "You and I both know that we'll be crucified if we bring this case to trial. Why push this?"

"Because," Brady said calmly, "sometimes you have to roll the dice and see where the numbers take you."

Alex stared at him. She opened her mouth to tell Brady that

that was the most imbecilic thing she had ever heard when the door to the conference room opened behind them. Their opposing counsel trudged out wearily.

"We'll take the offer," he snapped, looking none too happy. "We'll leave the initial drafting duties to you."

"Our pleasure," Brady sang out as the man slammed the door shut behind him.

"See," he said, turning back to Alex, "sometimes you just have to take a risk."

Alex shook her head. There were times when she hated Brady's fearlessness, his ability to face down every adversary and obstacle without a flicker of doubt. Everything came so easily to him—it often seemed as if Brady floated on a cloud of invincibility. She hated how everyone from the janitor to the senior partner worshipped him and hung on his every word. More than anything, though, she hated how much she wished she could be like him—as unflinching in the soul as he was on the surface.

She suddenly realized that they were alone in the hallway—the first time they had been alone together that day. For a moment, they just stood there awkwardly. Alex waited for the inevitable jokes about speed-dating . . . but none came.

Finally, Brady cleared his throat. "So," he said, all business, "is the Rauchway meeting on for tomorrow?"

Alex nodded slowly. "Yes, it's at eleven."

"Okay, good," he said, reaching into his pocket for a cigarette, "this is what we need to get ready for tomorrow's meeting—"

As he continued on, Alex couldn't help but stare at him in disbelief.

LATER, WHEN Alex thought back to her encounter with Brady, she was still at a loss to explain the whole situation. After years of working with him, she knew him pretty well, and she knew what a consummate predator he was. Give him the slightest inkling of a weakness, and he would latch on to it and exploit it to its fullest

extent. It was what made him such a great litigator and such a formidable opponent in court. This would have been a prime opportunity for him to embarrass her to no end . . . and yet, he hadn't.

She was still thinking about that as she headed in the balmy
spring weather to a nice, quiet lunch with her girls. But the minute
she stepped into the restaurant and saw the conspiratorial whisper-
ing between M.J. and Lin, she knew she was in for trouble.

"Okay, so what did I miss?" Alex asked as she slid into a seat at
the Sweet-n-Tart Cafe. Unlike the typical, no-frills Chinatown
joint, the Sweet-n-Tart Cafe was bright and airy, outfitted in cheerful pastels that allowed one to dine on scrumptious turnip cakes in
an amusement park setting.

Across from Alex, M.J. and Lin were sporting suspicious
Cheshire cat grins.

"You won't believe who we saw today!" Lin blurted out.

"Who?" Alex asked, even though she had a sinking feeling she
didn't want to know.

"None other than Mr. Ryan Barstow himself!" M.J. said triumphantly.

Alex sighed. She should have known. She'd dated Ryan in law
school for several months, and he had been, without a doubt, the
most popular boyfriend she'd ever had. Her friends loved Ryan; to
them, he was the perfect guy, the man every girl should be so lucky
to meet. She couldn't deny that part. Ryan was perfect in so many
ways. He was handsome, gentle, and kind, and he treated Alex like
a princess—arranging elaborate dinners, romantic getaways, and
fairy-tale surprises. He treated her friends almost as well, charming
them with his attention and laid-back manner. On top of that, he
was also wealthy, athletic, and a neurosurgeon to boot.

There was only one drawback: Ryan was completely, utterly, in-
curably boring. Oh, Alex tried, she really did. She brought up every
subject under the sun with him, trying to find one topic that they
could share a passion for. But while Ryan was more than happy to
listen to her rant and rave about everything, he didn't really have
anything to contribute to the conversation. He was content to just

sit back, smile, and agree with everything she said. There was no joy in being victorious over Ryan for the very simple reason that he was happy to let her win every time.

Which was the death knell for Alex, who lived for excitement, the thrill of the battle, and the sweetness of conquest. It got so bad that Alex started picking fights with him just to see if she could provoke some kind of reaction. But that only resulted in Ryan looking at her with the shocked, hurt look of an innocent puppy who'd been reprimanded by its loving master, and that made Alex feel like crap. Which is why she had to break up with him—for his own good and for her well-being.

"So how's he doing?" Alex asked grudgingly.

"Great," Lin gushed. "He made assistant head of the neurology department at NYU, and he just bought a house on Long Island."

"I assume for his wife and 2.3 kids?" Alex said, taking a sip of her water.

"No, that's the best part." Lin's expression was gleeful. "Ryan's still single!"

"And he still has this thing for you," M.J. added. "When we saw him at the park, he couldn't stop asking about you."

"Let me guess," Alex interjected, "you told him about every single thing that's happened to me in the past three years, including the toothpaste I'm currently using."

"Oh, Alex," Lin said, "don't be silly. Ryan obviously still cares about you. Don't you think it's time you rethink this crazy idea you have about him being boring?"

"I have a better idea," Alex countered, "why don't you go out with him, Lin? Then you guys could be Mr. and Mrs. Trump and make lots of money together."

"Anyway," M.J. said, determined to ignore Alex, "we decided that it would only be polite to invite Ryan to our party Saturday night."

"You mean my birthday party?" Alex asked.

"Yep," Lin said excitedly, "it'll be so much fun!"

"Right," Alex sighed. "*Fun* is just the word for it."

. . .

AFTER BIDDING good-bye to her friends, Alex returned to her office. Hours later though, as she sat at her desk, she still couldn't get over what her friends had done.

It was going to be horrible. Alex knew it. Bad enough that she was turning thirty. Did she really have to deal with an ex-boyfriend as well?

Then again, what was so bad about having Ryan at her party? It would make the girls happy, and it wasn't like she was going to have a ton of other romantic prospects there anyway. Could it hurt to spend her birthday with a guy who thought she was the most amazing goddess to walk the earth?

Alex flashed back to Auntie Lee's words: "Open yourself to new possibilities." What if the new possibilities that Auntie Lee was talking about had to do with Ryan? Maybe she'd never really given him a real chance. Maybe all she needed was some time apart from him to really appreciate Ryan for the great guy he was. . . .

Shaking her head, Alex turned back to her desk and started checking her e-mail. And that was when she saw it.

> Dear Alex,
> This e-mail will probably come as a surprise after all these years, but I know a big day is coming up soon and I just wanted to wish you Happy Birthday. I hope everything is going great for you.
>
> Josh
> PS: I'm coming to New York in a few weeks. Maybe we can meet up.

Alex stared at the screen. No, she thought, it couldn't be. She hadn't seen Josh in ten years. What was he doing contacting her now? He'd made his choice back in college—why reopen this long-closed chapter in their lives?

Alex knew she should delete the e-mail, forget it ever existed, treat it like the insignificant thing that it was. And yet, as she sat there, staring, it was suddenly everything.

AT WORK the next day, Alex couldn't help being distracted. She couldn't concentrate on her brief, couldn't get her contract revisions done, couldn't focus on any one of the five hundred things she had on her task list. Which was why she kept returning to Josh's e-mail in some futile hope of finding an answer. . . .

"You're going to burn a hole in that computer if you keep staring at it like that."

Alex looked up to see Brady leaning against her doorway. She quickly closed the e-mail.

Sauntering in, he took a seat on her guest chair. "So, Allie, what's got you so preoccupied?"

"Nothing." She cleared her throat, deciding that she was definitely not telling Brady about Josh. "I . . . was just talking to my friends, and they have this obsession with my ex, Ryan. They think he's perfect and that I should get back together with him."

"Really?" He pondered this. "What made you break up with him in the first place?"

"Well," she said, "there was nothing really wrong with him. He was just a little . . . um . . ."

"Boring?" Brady offered.

Alex's eyes widened. "Exactly! How did you know?"

He shrugged. "There's nothing worse than the boring ones. Life is just way too short to spend it bored out of your mind."

"Yeah." She nodded slowly. "So I guess I'm not the only one that thinks that way."

"Look, don't get me wrong," he said. "I love a beautiful woman. But after all the fluff, you need to have someone with a brain and some personality to keep you interested. Me, I like a girl who can surprise me even when I think I know everything about her." He looked at the contract on Alex's desk. "Hmm, I wonder what kind of woman our new client Isabella is—"

"Shit!" Alex jumped up. "I was supposed to send Isabella the contract twenty minutes ago."

"Relax," Brady said, "I took care of it. She called. I said you were tied up and faxed over the contract."

"Oh." She sat back down again. "Thanks."

"No problem." He shrugged, walking off. "I'm here to clean up your messes after all, Lexicon."

Alex sighed. She hated it when he was being flip. It was times like these that she wished she could write him off, dismiss him as just another asshole. But then there would be those moments when he would act like a sincerely nice human being, when he seemed to actually care . . . and those were the moments when Alex couldn't help wondering if there was more to Brady Jameson than the looks and the charm and the Perry Mason derring-do.

sixteen

THAT EVENING, Alex decided to take a leisurely stroll to Orchid Lounge, a chic new Asian bar where she was meeting Lin and M.J. After being cooped up in the office all day, Alex couldn't think of anything she needed more than some fresh spring air and a nice glass of wine with her friends to help her relax . . . and forget about Josh's e-mail.

"—so what do you think?" Lin thrust the menus in Alex's face. "Dumplings or egg rolls? Which would you rather have?"

Alex sighed. "I don't care. Whatever you decide is good with me, Lin."

"Don't say that!" Lin playfully swatted her. "It's *your* birthday party!"

"I know," Alex replied, "but I doubt I'll be eating much anyway that night."

"Oh, because of Ryan, right?" M.J. said with a sly grin. "Well, don't worry, he'll love you no matter how much you weigh!"

Alex rolled her eyes. "Anyway, J, how are things going with you and Jagger?"

M.J. smiled softly. "Great, actually. It's so weird because he's nothing like the person I imagined myself with, but somehow he's perfect for me. I mean, I hate it when he pushes me and makes me face stuff I'd rather not deal with, but maybe that's what I need." She shot Lin a glance. "Even if Lin thinks he's not boyfriend material."

"Hey"—Lin put her hands up—"I never said that. He's just a little different, that's all."

Alex and M.J. grinned at each other. They both knew that was Lin-speak for saying that she would never date someone like Jagger in a million years.

At that moment, Lin's cell phone rang. As she walked off to answer the call, Alex turned to M.J.

"Don't worry about Lin," Alex said. "As long as he's good to you, it doesn't matter if he wears Billabong instead of Brooks Brothers."

M.J. chuckled. "The other day, I tried to get Lin to wear one of Jagger's T-shirts. You should have seen how hard she tried to not look disgusted. I almost busted out laughing."

Alex smiled. She studied her glass silently for a moment. "Do you regret seeing Kevin again?" she asked. "I mean, do you wish you hadn't run into him at MSG that day?"

M.J. pondered the question. "No—" She shook her head. "—even though it hurt to be rejected again. I think I needed to see him. For the closure, you know?"

Alex took a deep breath and nodded. "I know."

Lin appeared at the table suddenly. "Hey, guys, I got to go."

Alex and M.J. both looked up.

"The VP of the futures division asked me to swing by his apartment to discuss a new account." Finishing her drink, Lin grabbed her bag and quickly slung it over her shoulder.

"Is anyone else going to be there?" M.J. asked. She looked at Alex with concern.

Lin shook her head. "Nope. Just me. I better get going—"

"Lin." Alex caught her friend's arm. "You can't go."

"What do you mean?" she asked.

"I mean this guy is a big honcho at your company! He can fire you in two seconds if he feels like it."

Lin furrowed her eyebrows. "Why would he do that?"

"Guys do funny things when they don't get laid," M.J. remarked.

"Oh." Lin waved the comment aside. "That won't be a problem. He's really nice. He would never do something like that."

"That's what you think," Alex said. "Look, regardless, it's still completely inappropriate for you to be going over to your boss's apartment at night—I mean, why can't he discuss this account with you at work like a normal person?"

"Oh, Alex," Lin groaned, "stop acting like my mom. It's no big deal."

"Are you crazy?" Alex demanded. "Do you think this guy wants you to go over to his place for some fine conversation? Lin, stop being so naïve and grow up!" The minute the words left her lips, Alex regretted them.

Lin drew back, stung.

"Lin," Alex began, "I didn't mean that—"

"No, I think you did." Lin got up, sniffling a little. "I'm gonna go."

Jumping to her feet, Alex started to go after Lin, but M.J. grabbed her hand.

"Let her chill," she said. "Give her some space."

Alex sat down slowly. "Me and my big mouth," she groaned. "Why do I always do that? I wasn't trying to be mean. I just don't want to see her get hurt."

"I know," M.J. said soothingly, "but sometimes you have to let your friends make their own mistakes."

Alex looked up at her sadly.

THE NEXT morning, Alex's head was pounding like a Metallica concert during the third encore. She tried to tell herself that it was the wine, but she knew better. All night, she had called Lin repeatedly, only to be met by the irritating drone of her voice mail. Which left Alex with nothing to do but lie in her bed, toss and turn . . . and brood.

By the next day, she couldn't stand it anymore. She knew she had to talk to Lin—even if her friend didn't want to talk to her. She picked up the phone.

"Hey, Lin," Alex said tentatively, "how's it going?" Staring out the window of her office, she shifted her weight nervously from one foot to the other.

There was a long silence. "Hi," Lin said finally.

Alex took a deep breath. "Okay, so I know you don't want to talk to me, but I have to tell you how sorry I am. You know me, I have the biggest mouth in the world, and sometimes I just don't think—which is a really bad thing for a lawyer, I know—but there it is. What I said about you was totally, completely—"

"True," Lin finished.

Alex paused. "What?"

"Everything you said was completely true." Lin sighed. "I confronted him, and he admitted that he was expecting us to hook up."

Alex's jaw dropped. "So what did you do?"

"Well, I thanked him very nicely for wanting to work with me, but I told him that I had a conflict, and then I walked out. You were right, Alex. I was being naïve about the whole thing."

"No," Alex replied, "you're just sweet and trusting."

"Aka naïve," Lin said ruefully. "Look, what do you say we just drop the whole thing and pretend last night never happened?"

Alex broke into a smile. "Okay by me."

"Good," Lin sighed. "I've had an awful day. Aside from the whole VP thing, I have a million things to do, and my mother just called and demanded I go and buy moon cakes for her. As if I have time!"

Alex couldn't help smiling. There were some aspects of Kim that were omnipresent in all Chinese parents—like the expectation that centuries-old Chinese traditions would always be upheld and that one's child would drop everything to go and do something like buy moon cakes.

She chuckled. "Mama Kim strikes again!"

"I know," Lin laughed. "What about you? Are you going home for the moon cake festival?"

"Me?" Alex asked. "I don't even know what it is."

"Of course you do!" Lin chided. "It's when the Chinese people rebelled against the Mongolian invaders and they communicated with each other by putting notes inside the moon cakes—"

"I can't believe you remember that!" Alex exclaimed. "I'll have to send my kid to you for some Chinese culture classes."

"Oh, so now you've decided that you're going to have a kid?"

"Sure," Alex said dryly, "as soon as I can go to Asia, pull an Angelina Jolie, and bring home my own Mohawk baby."

Lin chuckled.

"But to answer your question, I already told my mother I couldn't go home. I've got a ton of work to do if I even want to make it to my own party this weekend." Alex sighed. "Unfortunately, our country hasn't quite caught up to all these Chinese holidays."

"I know," Lin said, "it's going to be a while before we get Chinese New Year off."

Alex snorted. "Please. I've tried to take off for the past six years. I'll be lucky if I don't have to work on my birthday." She frowned, suddenly realizing that her party—along with seeing Ryan again—was mere days away. And then there was the still unresolved matter of what to do about Josh's e-mail. . . .

"Are you okay?" Lin said after a moment. "Are you stressing out about your birthday?"

Alex took a deep breath. "Maybe. Anyway, I gotta go. I'll talk to you later."

AFTER ALEX hung up the phone, she tried to go back to her work but couldn't. She suddenly felt tired—tired of the same old story, tired of feeling mired in a rut, tired of not knowing how to change things. She'd thought that the fortune-teller had the right idea, but so far, her efforts to welcome new opportunities had failed spectacularly. What if this was all pointless? What if she was destined to live in this limbo forever? And how did Josh fit into this jigsaw puzzle?

When Alex felt weak, she had to talk to the one person who she had never seen be anything but strong. She grabbed the phone. "Hey, Ma?" she said.

Her mother picked up on her tone immediately. "What's wrong, Alex?"

"Nothing," she said, "I'm just . . . Mom, have you ever thought about doing something that you knew was wrong? Something you just had to do because if you didn't, you would drive yourself crazy thinking about it?"

Her mother was silent. Finally, she said, "No."

"Okay." Alex decided it was a lost cause. "I didn't think so. Well, anyway—"

"But," she interrupted, "sometimes, you need to finish things. When I was think to come to America, I know my parents angry with me for leaving Hong Kong. I just going to leave, but when I get to airport, I could not. I feel there something I had not done, something that keep me from doing what I must do. So I tell your father change the ticket to next flight, and I went home and see my parents."

"What happened?" Alex asked.

"They very upset," Margaret admitted. "They yell, cry, beg me to stay. But they accept it, and finally I went to airport." She paused. "Sometimes, you must face past to have the future."

Alex smiled. "Thanks, Mom. I know exactly what I need to do now."

Closing
Statement

seventeen

THE GIRLS had done a wonderful job.

"I can't believe you guys did all this!" Alex marveled. They had transformed her NoHo brownstone into a Shanghai Nights spectacle. Vivid red silk tents blanketed the apartment, framed by delicate, brocaded fans. Ornate paper lanterns hung from the rafters, casting an intimate, sensual glow, while the scent of jasmine perfumed the air.

"It was all Lin," M.J. said. "She's the one who picked out all this stuff. I just hung where she told me to hang."

"Oh, whatever." Lin waved it off. "J was the one who came up with the idea."

Alex laughed and put an arm around her friends. "You guys are amazing." Thinking back to all the times she'd lectured and scolded them, she let out a deep breath. "Okay, I have something to say."

"Uh-oh." M.J. grinned.

"Look, you guys both know that I can get . . . a little crazy sometimes. And sometimes, I get totally carried away, and I end up saying things I don't mean that hurt my friends." She looked the girls in the eye. "For all the times I've done that to you guys, I just wanted to say I'm sorry."

There was a moment of silence. Then M.J. reached over and

put a hand on Alex's shoulder. "Hey," she said, "it's cool. We all lose it a little sometimes. I mean, look at me—I've called Jagger every name in the book, and fortunately, he always forgives me."

"Yeah." Lin nodded. "You're coming from a good place, and that's what's important." She met Alex's gaze. "We may not like what you're saying, but we still need to hear the hard truth."

Alex smiled. "Thanks, guys." She felt some of the pent-up tension within her dissipate. Maybe what she needed all along was to let go, to worry less about her friends' lives and more about her own.

"Okay, enough of this." M.J. handed Alex a glass of wine. "It's time to get this party started. And you, my dear, look fabulous."

Alex did a mini-twirl in her chic, mandarin-inspired Shanghai Tang sheath and long, dangly, gold earrings. "Well, it helped that Lin was standing in my room handing me what to wear."

"Oh, but the outfit only works if the model knows how to wear it," Lin said as she floated about the room.

Alex snorted. "That's me—Alex Kwan, supermodel, complete with greasy, unwashed hair."

"Now, now," Lin said, "you know what our mothers would say." She struck her Kim pose, complete with pointing, reproving finger. "Alex-ah, it bad luck to wash hair on birthday."

"According to our grandmothers," Alex retorted. "We, on the other hand, live in the twenty-first century."

"So maybe it is all Chinese superstition." Lin shrugged. "But better safe than sorry. Personally, I'm still a little freaked out over that fortune."

Alex couldn't completely disagree, but instead she just said, "Fortunes, dirty hair? What next, Lin? Are you going to start casting spells?"

"Okay, okay," M.J. interrupted, "enough about hair washing and magic. Lin, I think it's time."

Alex frowned. "Time for what?"

"For your birthday surprise, of course," Lin announced as she handed each of the girls a glass of wine. They gathered together in a circle. M.J. raised her glass.

"To Alex," she said. "She can be tough, she can be stubborn, and she can be really, really bitchy—"

"This is a birthday toast?" Alex asked, laughing.

"But through it all," M.J. continued, "she's the best, most loyal friend a girl could ever have."

The girls cheered their agreement as they clinked glasses.

"And now," M.J. said, "it's time for the surprise."

Lin came forward, bearing an envelope which she reverently handed to her friend.

Alex took the envelope and looked at it curiously. "What is this?" she asked, shaking it.

"Open it," M.J. instructed, "and you'll see."

Alex looked at them both and then opened the envelope. She carefully pulled out two tickets.

"They're plane tickets," M.J. said helpfully, "to Vegas!"

"Vegas—" Alex laughed. "That's fabulous!"

"We've also made reservations for you," Lin declared, "at the Mandalay Bay!"

Alex gasped. "Guys, this is amazing. Thank you so much."

"Wait," M.J. said, "you haven't heard the catch yet."

"There's a catch?" Alex looked quizzically at her friends.

"Yep." M.J. grinned. "The catch is that you have to go with a guy."

Alex looked at her, then at Lin. "You're kidding me."

"Nope." M.J. shook her head. "We are sending you to Vegas to get some action!"

She and Lin hooted and cheered.

"You guys are crazy." Alex smiled. "Where am I going to find a man to go to Vegas with?"

At that moment, the doorbell rang.

"It's time," M.J. said. "Go find yourself a man."

AS ALEX made her way through the apartment, she suddenly felt jittery, the anticipation of the evening turning her legs into half-cooked spaghetti. Her mother had told her she needed to finish things, and Alex knew that meant e-mailing the guy who had broken her heart into a million little pieces. Even if it was out of the insane notion that there might still be something between them. And then there was the matter of Ryan—another reminder of her failures, of her self-destructive need to choose heartache over happiness. How was she going to deal with all of this?

Alex didn't know the answer. But she knew what she had to do. She couldn't keep living in limbo, drowning in a sea of what-ifs. She needed clarity, certainty, the ability to start off her thirties with a clean slate. More than anything, she needed to face her past if she was going to reclaim her life again.

IF THERE was one person Alex had always had clarity about, it was Ryan. Of course, he was the first person to show up at the party.

"Ryan!" Alex said with as much enthusiasm as she could muster. "It's so good to see you!"

She leaned forward to give him a perfunctory peck on the cheek, but instead, Ryan swept her up in his arms and swung her around like a rag doll.

"Alex!" he exclaimed. "You look wonderful!"

Alex smiled politely and somehow managed to free herself from his embrace. "Thanks, Ryan. You look pretty good yourself."

And he did. He still had a thick head of chestnut hair and a perfectly buff body sculpted by all that rock climbing and hiking that he was probably doing at his spread in Long Island. But then somehow Alex knew that he would look great. It was fate's way of mocking her by saying, *Hey look, he's perfect, what more could you want?*

"I brought you these." Ryan pulled out a huge bouquet of orange tea roses.

Behind her, Alex could hear the excited gasps of her none-too-discreet friends. Ignoring them, she smiled at Ryan and took the roses. "You remembered," she said.

"How could I not?" he asked, smiling at her in that way that always made her feel like the most ungrateful bitch in the world.

Alex wasn't sure what to say to that, so she settled for inviting him to come with her to get a drink and a vase. As she walked past her friends, both of whom greeted Ryan just a little too excitedly, she made a point of not looking at either of them.

"So," she said as she poured Ryan a glass of merlot, "how have you been?"

He shrugged. "Good. I just got a promotion at work."

"I heard," Alex said, handing him his drink. "Congratulations."

"And you?"

Alex poured herself some wine. "I'm good. Fine. The same. You know how it is with work."

"Yeah . . ." He fidgeted with his glass. "So what about everything else? Are you seeing anyone?"

"Um, no," she took a quick swig of her drink. "I'm still on my own."

"You're kidding me," Ryan said. "That can't be possible."

She looked up at him, hating the way his eyes had lit up with hope but hating herself even more for liking the way he looked at her. It had been a while since anyone had gotten this excited just at the prospect of her availability.

Suddenly, she heard the doorbell ring.

"I'll be right back," she told him.

Ryan raised his glass. "I'll be waiting."

Alex made her escape from the kitchen. As she strode into the living room, she ran straight into Lin.

"Well?" she demanded. "How's it going with Ryan? Doesn't he look amazing?"

"Yeah." Alex suppressed a sigh. "He looks scrumptious. Now, Lin, can you be a sweetheart and go into the kitchen and keep him busy while I greet everyone?"

Lin started to protest, but Alex gave her a quick, hard shove toward the kitchen. That done, Alex zipped toward the living room.

Someone had apparently gotten the door because the apartment was filling up with new guests. Alex wandered around the living room, saying hello to friends and accepting birthday wishes and presents on the way.

After a bit, Alex relaxed a little. She finished off her glass of wine and snared another. So far, no disaster yet. Maybe this party was going to be fun after all.

Somewhere, she heard the phone ring, but she ignored it. A moment later, though, Lin appeared again—this time with the phone.

"Who is it?" Alex asked.

"It's your Peking Duck House blind date, Grant," she responded. "He said he'll be here in ten minutes."

Alex froze and stared at Lin.

After a second, she relented and burst into giggles. "I'm just kidding. It's something about work."

Alex shot her friend the evil eye as she took the phone. "Hello?"

"Hey, Al." Brady's voice came through loudly. "It's Brady."

She sighed. "Yes, Brady, what can I do for you?"

"I was wondering whether you knew where the Rosenbaum file was."

"Exactly where you left it," she replied, "in the file room under *R*."

"Ah," Brady said, "that could be a possibility."

Alex sighed. "Good-bye, Brady—"

"Wait!" he called out. "What are you doing right now?"

"Well, if you must know—" She took a sip of her drink. "—I'm in the middle of a birthday party."

"Really?" Brady asked. "Whose birthday?"

She paused. "My thirtieth."

"No way!" he exclaimed. "You mean the big three-oh? That's pretty intense. You're no spring chicken anymore, sweetheart!"

"Thanks," Alex said through gritted teeth. "Now is there anything else I can do for you?"

"Well, yeah," he remarked, "I have to say, Lexie, I'm a little offended that you didn't invite me to your birthday party—"

"Oops, I gotta go greet some more guests! Talk to you later, Brady!" Alex cut him off and hung up the phone.

Grinning, she put the phone down. Damn, that felt good. Euphoric, she strolled through the living room, pausing to welcome new guests as she encountered them. Her friends of course were doing a bang-up job of overseeing the party. M.J. was busy spinning some rocking tunes on the CD player, while Lin was generously topping off everyone's wineglass. All in all, the party was in full swing.

Satisfied that everyone seemed to be having a good time, Alex slipped outside to get some air. Leaning against the banister, she took a long sip of her wine and pulled her BlackBerry out from her pocket. Looking down at it, she stared at Josh's e-mail.

Alex shook her head. Enough, she decided. She was going to do it. She was going to ignore the naysayers, the cautious part of her heart that kept telling her to forget about him.

"Should you really be looking at your BlackBerry on your birthday?"

Alex looked up. Brady stood at the foot of the steps. Startled, she almost dropped the device.

"Brady?" She tucked the BlackBerry behind her back. "What are you doing here? Weren't you just on the phone with me?"

He ambled up the steps. "Well, once I heard it was your birthday, I had to come over and help you celebrate." He lifted up a bottle of wine.

Alex rolled her eyes. "I'm sure."

"You don't believe me?" he asked, walking up next to her.

"Yeah," she snorted. "I'm sure my birthday is first on your list of priorities."

Brady chuckled. Alex started to say something then stopped, suddenly noticing his intent gaze. It was strange how she never noticed until now how very blue his eyes were—clear, azure, almost cerulean . . .

"You look beautiful," he said suddenly.

Of all the things Alex had ever expected Brady to say to her, this was most definitely not one of them. She stared at him, for once at a complete and utter loss for words.

For a long moment, they just stood there. Alex was suddenly aware of everything around them—the traffic on the street, the activity in the house, the very movement of the air. But for some reason, she couldn't seem to think, her brain somehow short-circuited, her tongue suddenly numb.

After what seemed like an eternity, she finally stepped back. "Uh, thanks," she mumbled, looking away from Brady.

Brady blinked. "So," he coughed, "you got any Jack in this place?"

Alex gestured behind her. "The bar's inside."

He nodded and strode past her into the house.

What was that? Alex wondered as she stared after him. A thought teased at the edge of her mind, but she pushed it away.

At that moment, Ryan walked out. "Hey." He smiled at her. "I was wondering where you were."

"Oh, right," Alex stammered, forcing a smile. "Sorry, I was just . . . getting some air."

"That's okay," he said softly. "Actually . . . I was wondering—do you want to grab dinner sometime?"

Biting her lip, Alex glanced down the street, back at the house—anywhere that might provide a distraction from this moment. But no luck.

"Ryan," she began then stopped, not sure how to continue.

As it turned out, she didn't need to—because Ryan saw the answer etched on her face. His expression fell. "Never mind," he mumbled. "I think I better be going." He gave her a curt nod and walked quickly down the steps.

Alex felt a twinge of guilt. "Ryan!" She caught up with him at the bottom of the stoop.

He turned around, and there it was again—the wounded cocker spaniel look.

She swallowed. "Ryan, I'm sorry. I wasn't trying to hurt you, honest."

For a moment, he didn't say anything. Standing there, Alex

could hear the steady beat of music in the background. Finally, he nodded slowly. "I know."

"You're a wonderful guy, Ryan." Alex ran a hand through her hair. "It's just that . . ."

"I'm not who you're looking for," Ryan finished for her.

She looked up at him, opened her mouth to deny it, and then stopped. What could she really say? When it came right down to it, Ryan wasn't Josh and never would be.

Ryan nodded slowly, as if he had known all along.

"Bye, Alex," he said quietly. "I hope you find what you're looking for."

He started to turn away, but Alex caught him by the arm. She leaned forward and kissed him gently on the cheek. "Bye, Ryan," she whispered. "I hope you find a girl who deserves you."

He smiled briefly, squeezed her hand, then headed down the stairs. Alex stood there for a moment, watching him go, wondering if she had done the right thing, and knowing that there was really no other course open to her. She wanted to love him, wanted to make it work so that she could have the fairy-tale ending that all women dreamed of. But in the end, it was nothing more than a little story she told herself, with no more chance of becoming reality than Alex had at becoming the perfect little Asian wife.

Turning around, Alex trudged back into the house, and walked past Brady, who was chatting up Lin. She needed some more wine, a shot of courage before going back outside and responding to Josh. As she poured herself some Chianti, Mara Benson, her lab partner in college, came over to her.

"Alex," Mara said, "I just came over to wish you happy birthday." Dressed in a plain blue sweater and black Mary Janes, she looked exactly as Alex remembered her.

Alex smiled. "Thanks, Mara. It was very sweet of you to come."

"I wouldn't miss it for the world. Gosh, doesn't it seem like just yesterday that we were at school?"

Alex nodded wearily. "Yeah, I know what you mean."

"I still remember it, even after ten years. Old Campus, Wright

Hall. You were always hanging out on the steps with that cutie Josh."

Alex chuckled. "I guess I was."

"He was such a nice guy," Mara remarked. "I was really happy to hear that he just got married. Did you go to his wedding?"

Alex blinked at her, the words not quite registering. Josh— married? Yes, she supposed that was a possibility. But he'd con- tacted her after all these years . . . that had to mean something. After all, what would be the point of seeing her, if not to rewrite the past? Feeling her throat close up, she turned and walked away. Behind her, she heard Mara blather on obliviously. "I heard they're going to Venice for their honeymoon. . . ."

ALEX SAT on her front stoop, a bottle of bourbon in hand. She stared blindly out into the street, feeling nothing but the too-loud pounding of her heart.

It was strange, really, she thought. Strange how the heart could cloud even the most obvious signs. How could she have been so clueless? It was just an e-mail, just some offhand comment about meeting up. Did she really think that he'd still be carrying a torch for her after all these years?

She knew better, of course. It wasn't as if she'd exactly pulled a Miss Havisham herself the past decade. No, she'd long reconciled herself to the fact that she and Josh were never meant to be. After all, whatever feelings he might have ever had for her, they hadn't been enough back in college—why would things be any different now?

Alex dropped her head, squeezing her eyes shut. She knew all this, and yet she had let Josh haunt her, let him cast a pall on all her future prospects. Sitting on the very steps where she'd broken Ryan's heart for the second time, she suddenly realized that she had settled for Ryan as Josh had for Christine. And like Josh, she ended up hurting someone else—all because she'd been too cowardly to take a chance on true happiness.

But no more, she thought. She was tired of riding this merry-go-round, tired of living in fear of heartache. Her mother had said she needed to see things through, and Alex had thought that meant meeting up with the man who'd robbed her of her nerve all those years ago. But now, staring out into the empty street, Alex finally knew what she had to do.

She fingered the track wheel until the message came up: DELETE?

She pressed the wheel. And just like that—it was gone. Josh, the e-mail, the ghost from her past . . .

Alex closed her eyes. She suddenly felt empty, drained. It wasn't until this moment—when she'd come face-to-face with the prospect of letting Josh into her life again—that she realized his effect on her. But maybe that was what she needed—to come dangerously close to the edge to feel alive again.

Taking a deep breath, she got up and headed back into the brownstone, and this time, Alex didn't look back. She was done with Josh and done with the past. Auntie Lee had said she would only find happiness when she was open to new opportunities, but until this very moment, Alex hadn't understood what she meant. It was only now that she could turn the page and begin her thirties on a clean slate, with all the possibilities of the world open to her.

eighteen

"HAPPY BIRTHDAY to you!"

Alex leaned down and blew out her candles. Everyone applauded exuberantly as she cut the first slice of cake.

"Thank you." Alex smiled. "I really appreciate you guys helping me celebrate. You've all made it really special. Now go party!"

Everyone cheered as M.J. cranked up the stereo. Soon the party was in full swing again.

Lin handed Alex the first slice of cake. She nodded her thanks and dipped her finger into the icing. She licked the chocolate slowly.

"How's it going, girl?" M.J. came over and slung an arm around her friend's shoulders.

Alex smiled ruefully. "It's amazing how chocolate can make things better."

M.J. laughed. "It's the all-purpose cure-all," she said. Then her expression became serious. "So I saw Ryan leave."

Alex nodded. "He did."

"You all right?" M.J. wrinkled her brow.

"Yeah." Alex sighed. "Believe it or not, I actually am."

M.J. smiled. "I knew you would be. You're strong."

"Everything okay?" Lin stood before them, looking worried. Despite herself, Alex broke into a smile. Her friends—what would she do without them?

"Guys," she said, "I appreciate the concern, I really do. But I'm fine—in fact, I think I'm going to be better than fine." She took a deep breath. "Hey, we're supposed to get smarter as we get older, right? Maybe I shot up a couple of IQ points tonight."

The girls looked at her. Then Lin stepped forward to give Alex a huge hug. A moment later, M.J. joined in.

"There's nothing I like more than seeing girl-on-girl-on-girl action," Brady remarked as he strolled by.

Alex gave him the finger without looking up from the embrace.

"BYE, GUYS," Alex said. "Thanks again for everything!"

She waved good-bye to M.J. and Lin as they got into a cab. Once she was sure they were gone, she leaned back against the step and took a long swig of her beer. She closed her eyes, suddenly feeling very old.

And stupid. There, she'd admitted it. More than anything else, more than the sadness and the disappointment, Alex felt like a fool.

Because she hadn't just given Josh her heart back when they were in college—she'd given him the past ten years of her life. She had been so determined not to hurt like that again that she'd shut herself off—from life, love, new possibilities . . .

As she stood there thinking now about all those years that she'd lost, the bottle slipped from her grasp. The glass shattered, scattering like a hailstorm of miniature marbles across the stairs. A shard ricocheted against her open palm.

Dropping to her knees, Alex clutched her hand, suddenly unable to breathe, feeling the blood rush through her ears like a freight train running late.

"Hey, now, what's going on here?" Brady's familiar voice echoed behind her.

Alex squeezed her eyes shut, hating the moment even more than she could have thought possible. She felt Brady hunker down beside her silently. A moment passed. Neither spoke. Then, she felt him touch her briefly on the shoulder and get up.

"Let's get this cleaned up," he said quietly.

She heard, rather than saw, him bustle around her, putting down his bottle of bourbon on the top stoop, picking up the broom beside the trash can and sweeping up the broken glass with efficiency. When he was done, he knelt down in front of her and pried her hand out from its hiding place.

"Hmm," he mused, "it doesn't look like you got any glass in there. Just a little cut." Pulling out his handkerchief, he neatly wrapped it around her hand. She stared down at the neat, starched band of white before her.

"There," he said, "as good as new."

Alex looked up slowly at Brady. He smiled, sat down beside her, and lit a cigarette. For a long moment, neither of them said anything.

Finally, Alex took a deep breath. "So, I thought you were going after my friend—you know, the one who's a size two."

Brady shrugged. "Yeah, I thought I'd take a breather."

Alex shook her head. "You're such an ass."

"Yeah," he said, blowing a puff of smoke in the air, "so what's your point?"

Alex laughed. It was quiet out there on the street, save for the occasional passing car. Everything seemed to be moving at half pace, the nearby windows were dim, and the flicker of the traffic lights and the swirls of steam from the street vents all conspired to make the city seem smaller, cozier, more intimate.

"No point," she said, "I'm the last person to be making any points tonight."

"Yeah?" Brady asked, his tone perfectly neutral. "How's thirty treating you so far?"

"Not so good," Alex admitted. She sighed and stared out into the twilight. "I used to be fearless, you know. Back when I was a kid, I was the crazy little Asian girl who did all the things no one expected me to do." She hugged her knees to her chest. "I was the one who was never afraid to take a chance, to do something crazy and damn the consequences."

Brady glanced up at her. "And now?"

"And now . . . ," she trailed, "I don't feel quite so fearless. I don't know how it happened, but somewhere along the way, I got stuck."

"Well, if that's the problem," Brady remarked, "all you need to do is unstick yourself."

She swiveled toward him. "And how exactly do I do that?"

Brady studied his cigarette. "I don't know. Maybe open yourself up, do something crazy, damn the consequences?"

Alex grinned, thinking how Brady sounded just like Auntie Lee. "You know what I hate about you, Jameson?"

Brady looked at her, curiosity flickering across his face. "What?"

"That you're never afraid," Alex confessed. "It doesn't matter how big of an asshole you're facing or how high the stakes are—you never let any of it stop you."

There was a moment of silence. Then Brady reached up toward the top stoop and gently pulled down his bottle of bourbon.

"Just because I don't let any of it stop me doesn't mean I'm not afraid," he said quietly. "And it doesn't mean I haven't been knocked down before. It just means that I have to pick myself up when that happens. That's what we all have to do, Alex."

Brady smiled at her slightly, and for a minute, he suddenly appeared younger, less cocky, just a touch vulnerable.

They sat there for a long moment. Finally, Brady turned away and took a healthy gulp of the bourbon. "Ah," he said, "that sure gets the old motor running, if you know what I mean."

Alex snagged the bourbon from him and took a long swig. Then she put the bottle down and looked at Brady.

"So," she said, "you ever been to Vegas?"

lin

Hot Stocks

What's moving the Cho Show

Stocks to Watch	Forecast
Mah-jong (The Inspiration) The game that initiated Lin into risky business	Speculative
Drew Black (The Broker) He may be a stockbroker's dream, but is he Lin Cho's?	High-Risk
Kim Cho (The Mother) A Trial and a Treasure	Blue Chip
Foreign Markets (The Catalyst) Uncharted waters: an opportunity to crash—or to start anew	Growth
Alex Kwan & M. J. Wyn (The Girls) The gals who are always there to catch Lin when she falls and celebrate when she soars	Priceless

Opening
Bell

nineteen

WALL STREET. Lin loved everything about it. The Bull and the Bear. The Dow Jones and the NASDAQ. The five-to-one male-to-female ratio at Merrill Lynch.

Every morning, five days a week, Lin Cho strolled into her downtown office with a cup of chai tea and a herd of male colleagues trailing behind her. This Friday, it was her boss Rob Stein, the senior vice president of sales, and client assistant Mike O'Rourke—members of Lin's Synergy Group team.

"Mike, I need you to make appointments with these prospects as soon as you get a moment, please." As she passed by reception, Lin took a sip of her tea, then flipped through the mail her secretary handed her. Smoothing down the lines of her Valentino shirtdress, she nodded absently as Rob rambled on about their latest customer targets. Fortunately, Mike's insistent questions on what gifts to send to which clients drew Rob's attention away from Lin. She quickly seized the opportunity to escape.

Striding into her office, Lin slipped on her headset to prepare for a long day of schmoozing. She had five clients to call and that was only before noon. Just as she was about to punch in the numbers, Lin suddenly heard a knock on the door. Looking up from her computer, she saw Drew Black, a recent recruit to the firm and her soon-to-be client management partner. Dressed in a dapper gray Armani suit with a pink silk shirt, he smiled at Lin.

"So, you must be the famous Lin Cho." Drew strolled in and gave her a none-too-subtle once-over. "We haven't been properly introduced. I'm Drew," he said, holding out his hand. "I've heard a lot about you."

Lin was taken aback but smiled, intrigued despite herself. With his gleaming white teeth, wavy dark hair, and killer tan, Drew Black was, without a doubt, one of the most beautiful men she'd ever met.

"Hi, it's a pleasure to meet you," Lin said, grasping his hand in what she hoped was a professional handshake. "Welcome to our team. The boss has talked a lot about you."

"Oh, yeah?" Drew grinned. "Good things, I hope."

"Well . . . Rob kind of led me to believe that you were some fifty-year-old guy with a potbelly," Lin said, laughing. "Not to mention bald."

Drew chuckled. "Really? You'll learn that I'm full of surprises. Like the fact that I'm a preferred Frédéric Fekkai customer."

"That's funny," Lin replied, tossing her head.

Drew shot her a crooked smile. "I'll fill you in on the rest of my beauty secrets sometime. Right now, I have to get ready for the meeting at noon. I hear Rob wants to talk to us about some potential new clients. Word is we're looking to cash in on a guy named Henry Rutman."

"Really? Rutman's a surgeon at Bellevue with a lot of money to spare," Lin said eagerly. "It's like going to an all-you-can-eat buffet."

The two looked at each other and laughed. Lin blushed at the obvious connection between them. Maybe this was the surprise man Auntie Lee had told her about, she thought as Drew headed for the door.

"By the way," he said, turning back to Lin, "since we're going to be partners, we should get better acquainted. Some buddies of mine are having a happy hour get-together at Sutton Place, and I thought I'd extend the offer to you."

Lin smiled. "Thanks for the invite. I'll try to make it." She picked up a file folder, trying to look cool and collected even though her heart was beating double time. "I should get back to work. I've got some sucking up to do with the Mariucci family about why we lost them two mil."

Drew winced. "Good luck."

Lin nodded, trying not to be too obvious as she watched Drew stroll out of her office. Contrary to her words, she wasn't actually that worried—sure, two million was a lot, but she was used to betting all her chips on one pony. As a stockbroker, Lin was used to living on the edge—in fact, she thrived on it. How else was she supposed to score in the biggest high-stakes game in the world?

WHILE LIN could never resist a gamble, she sometimes wondered whether she was able to take risks because she always knew that she had a safe haven to retreat to. No matter what happened at work, no matter how crazy her mother might be making her, no matter what disaster with a guy befell her—Lin knew that she could count on her girls to be there for her.

"Oh, I'm gonna need some bubble tea pronto." M.J. groaned as she collapsed onto a chair at Saint's Alp Teahouse.

It was late Saturday afternoon, and the girls had spent a warm, sunny day shopping at Shanghai Tang's sample sale. Now, laden with bags, they had decided a rest stop was needed—and what better pick-me-up than some coconut butter toast and bubble tea?

"Mmm—" Lin sipped her drink happily. "—this tastes sooo good."

"Yeah," Alex agreed, "there's nothing like a little condensed milk to soothe the soul." She swirled the black tapioca balls around with her straw. "White people don't know what they're missing."

"Tell me about it," Lin said. "None of my white friends like it."

"Probably because all this shit has a thousand calories in it." M.J. took a long sip of her drink. "Thank God for our Asian metabolisms!"

The girls all laughed. Lin smiled at how they always seemed to understand each other. She didn't know if it was being Asian or having known each other forever or just their innately complementary personalities, but somehow they fit together just right—like a perfectly interlocking puzzle.

Just then, M.J.'s cell phone beeped. Alex and Lin chewed on their toast as they watched their friend smile at the text message on the screen.

"Let me guess," Alex teased, "that must be Sewing Boy."

M.J. blushed and swatted her, as she and Lin giggled knowingly. "Very funny. I'll have to come up with a nickname for your lover-boy, Alex."

"Go ahead," she grinned. "There isn't anything you can call him that I haven't already said myself."

"Oh, yeah?" M.J. asked. "How about . . . Alex's Slavemaster?"

"Very funny." Her friend made a face at her. "More like Alex's Slave."

As they continued to spar, Lin felt a small pang of jealousy. It was stupid, she knew. She had dated a number of boyfriends, probably more than M.J. and Alex combined. What was novel was Lin being the only one without a guy . . . and as she sipped her tea, she realized that she really didn't like that feeling.

EVEN THOUGH Lin didn't have a man in her life, she certainly didn't lack for male attention. In the world of finance, money was not the only important asset around the office—good looks and feminine wiles could also do wonders. As one of the few female brokers at Merrill Lynch, Lin knew this all too well. Eating lunch in the firm's cafeteria on Tuesday, she found herself sitting in her new Versace wrap dress with her tossed salad, a bottle of Evian, and a table of six salivating male colleagues around her.

"So, Lin, hot outfit today," Tom remarked. "Really shows off . . . your collarbone. You should come out to Bliss Bar with me and my buddies tonight and show it off."

Tom Wexler was known as the sleaziest trader on the company floor. A former football player from Notre Dame with tousled, light brown hair, green eyes, and a sly smile, he possessed no subtlety whatsoever in his efforts to seduce every woman he met. Lin avoided him like the avian flu.

"Lin isn't interested in drinking Bud Lights at some frat-boy bar," Mark called out. "Wouldn't you rather try that new restaurant in Chinatown with me tonight, Lin?"

Mark Shin, the assistant branch manager and a graduate of Harvard Business School, had been smitten with Lin since the moment she first stepped through the Merrill Lynch doors. Tall and lean, with thin gold spectacles and a prominent Adam's apple, the Taiwanese native used to flood her office with My Melody headsets, Hello Kitty dolls, and other assorted Sanrio trinkets. Flattered by the attention, Lin decided to give him a chance and took him up on his offer of an "Asian" night.

The plan had been for Mark to woo Lin by cooking her a Chinese feast in his luxurious, Park Avenue pad. And a feast it was— lychee martinis, fried rice, and a three-jeweled seafood dish of jumbo shrimp, thin-sliced squid, and tender abalone. But as the two sat down to eat, Mark couldn't loosen the lid of a small oyster sauce jar. He refused Lin's offer to help, and turned crimson and sweaty as he struggled to open the jar for the next ten minutes. When Lin finally couldn't stand it anymore, she grabbed the jar from him and twisted it open with a flick of her wrist. Thinking that she could now dig into her fried rice, she was surprised to see Mark giving her a disgusted look. He then sat mutely through dinner despite all her efforts to get a lighthearted conversation going. Although Lin knew that Mark was embarrassed and probably feeling emasculated, she couldn't have cared less. How could she be with a man who insisted on refusing her help?

In some fantasy world, they might have made a perfect couple, with lots of money, cute babies, and her mother's wholehearted blessing. But Lin could tell that, in the long run, Mark's Asian gender stereotypes would only drive them farther apart.

Yet, despite all this, here he was, asking her to go to dinner with him.

"I can't," Lin lied. "My dad wants me to attend this Asian heritage dinner with him. Guess that means I can't go to Bliss Bar either, Tom."

Tom shrugged. While Mark raised a skeptical brow, he said nothing, no doubt appeased by the fact that Lin had refused Tom as well. She knew that Mark, like most Asian guys, hated it when she flirted with white men.

Ironically, Drew strolled over with his tray at that very moment. "Hey, Lin." Drew waved. "Is there a seat for me?"

"Sure," she said, trying not to look too excited, "let me introduce you. Guys, this is Drew. Drew, this is Tom, Joey, Krishan, Mark, and Carl."

The guys looked up and nodded their greetings.

"Drew's from Prudential. He was one of the partners there who helped the Speidman group rack up seventeen million dollars in revenue last year."

"Welcome." Krishan extended his hand. "Good to have you on our team."

Lin smiled at Krishan. Her golf team captain from college, he was not only hip and stylish, but also her best friend in the office.

As Drew stood there chatting with everyone, five of the floor's scatterbrained admin clan walked over for their daily flirt session with the guys. Of course, they noticed Drew immediately.

"Hey, everyone." Lana, a statuesque brunette with a perfect 10 figure and very long legs, flashed a smile at Drew. "And who might you be?"

"Drew." He held out his hand. "It's a pleasure to meet you."

"Where are you from?" Lana fluttered her eyelashes as she slowly shook Drew's hand.

"I just joined Lin's team in mutual funds," he explained, returning her grip.

"Excellent," she cooed. "I'll see you around then."

The guys burst out laughing the minute Lana had turned the corner. Drew flashed the crew a crooked smile.

"I think Lana likes you," Carl said, admiration in his eyes.

"It certainly looks like you are quite the ladies' man," Lin teased. "We'll have to get Mike to screen your phone calls soon."

Drew laughed as all the other guys joined in the half-laudatory, half-envious ribbing. Watching him, Lin smiled. Drew had been at work for only half a day, but he'd already managed to establish himself as the alpha male of the group. Not bad for a newbie, considering the amount of testosterone swirling around in a place like Merrill Lynch.

Glancing down at her watch, Lin realized that she was about to be late for an asset management meeting. "Got to run, guys." She quickly gathered up her lunch. "Work calls."

Drew flashed her a swoonworthy smile. "I'll see you later, Lin."

Lin blushed and returned the smile shyly. Arrogant, charming, and successful, Drew was definitely a classic boiler room guy. Lin had met his type before—guys who reeked of self-assurance, guys who were used to getting everything, whether it was the hottest girl or the biggest deal. And yet there was something different about Drew, something that set him apart from the other guys at work. And there were a lot of guys at Merrill Lynch.

If there was one thing that Lin disliked more than anything about her job—and it wasn't the long hours or the grueling process of making her clients happy—it was dealing with the male egos. Like M.J., Lin was in a field predominantly filled with men. And like her friend, she sometimes wished that there was a more balanced mix of men and women, if only so she could have another girl to chat with during the day. Even though Lin loved the attention she got from the guys at work, there were times when the lack of estrogen around really got to her.

If it weren't for her passion for the job and the thrill of competition, Lin would have hung up her headset a long time ago. But even when she was eight, Monopoly had been Lin's favorite game; she remembered jumping up and down after blanketing Boardwalk and Park Place with hotels. Unlike other kids, Lin's favorite holiday wasn't Christmas or Easter—it was Chinese New Year, when she would receive a stack of red envelopes filled with pocket money. But nothing could beat mah-jong.

The first time Lin watched her family play mah-jong, she was hooked. She couldn't get enough of it—the thrilling, victorious

shouts of *pung* or *sic woo* that were accompanied by the triumphant crash of unveiled tiles. She loved the strategizing, the
risk-taking, the rush of adrenaline that came with the simple flip of
a smooth stone tablet.

There was one night in particular—the Qing Dynasty Christmas party of 1995 at her Uncle Bill's house. Wearing a red cheongsam, her straight black hair pinned back with chopsticks to
perfectly frame her heart-shaped face and almond-shaped eyes,
Lin slipped into the empty seat at the mah-jong table as her
mother went to check on dinner in the kitchen. A quick fib to her
aunts about her mom asking her to take her place, and the game
was under way. It was the West wind, and Lin had a mah-jong
hand made up of four triples, a run of three, and a red dragon.
Across from her was her aunt Helen, who flaunted nine tiles of a
clean sweep wheel suit. Lin's heart pounded when her turn came
around and she fished a wheel tile. With sweaty palms, she pondered the possibilities. If she threw out the tile, she was risking a
three-hundred-dollar loss, but if she didn't, she'd forfeit any
chance of winning.

Taking a deep breath, she decided to go for it. As she tossed the
tile, her aunt turned and looked at her with a smirk that made Lin's
heart sink. But then her aunt chuckled and said to her in Chinese,
"Nay ho wun!" Translation: "You have good luck."

Lin exhaled deeply. She would live to see another turn. Two
rounds later, it was her aunt who threw out a red dragon. Lin
gasped and quickly laid out her tiles, screaming, *"Sic!"* And with
that risky, heart-pulsing move, she'd won four hundred dollars.

From that moment on, Lin knew she was an unrepentant
daredevil. She often took risks that she shouldn't have. While most
of the men at Merrill quaked and pulled the trigger prematurely,
Lin would ride the wave until the very last minute and wait for the
perfect moment to sell some dead-end-looking stock and make the
big score. The trick was knowing when to sell and when to hold
fast. That was how she'd been able to hold her own in the boiler
room all these years. But there was never really any doubt that Lin

had nerves of steel; the only question was whether she would push her luck too far one day.

twenty

EVERY TWO weeks, Lin went back home to Long Island to visit her family, especially her beloved *gung gung*, her grandfather, in Syosset. As she was boarding the train at Penn Station after work on Friday, Lin felt her BlackBerry vibrating. She reached into her purse and found a message from her sister on the screen: "Lin, so glad that you're coming home. Mom has gone off the deep end. She was talking to her auntie Grace in Hong Kong yesterday, who wants to set you up with her friend's nephew. He's on his way to the house now! His name is Larry Wong. He's twenty-seven and is coming to America to start a business—Sarah."

Lin's eyes widened as she read the e-mail. Another setup date! She couldn't believe it. Her mom had been nagging her about finding a nice Asian boy ever since she'd broken up with Stephen Xiang two years ago, and especially since the fortune-teller's dire prediction. Stephen was everything an Asian mother could want in a son-in-law. He was a cardiologist and a graduate from Princeton. Most important, he knew three different Chinese dialects and treated Lin's family like gold. Every Saturday afternoon, Stephen would go over to her parents' home and take Lin's *gung gung* to Chinatown for a roasted pork bun and Hong Kong–style coffee made with evaporated milk. He would always bring Kim an order of her favorite roast suckling pig and complement that by cooking up his specialty dish, ginger and scallion snapper. Or he would pretend he was Bob Vila around the house and help with every conceivable chore that Kim could dream up. Handsome, tall, and smart, Stephen was an incomparable boyfriend—his only fault being his irritating perfection.

In the end, Lin realized that they were doomed. Stephen was a traditionalist. She knew he would expect her to stay home with the kids while he went to work every day. He couldn't see that she was made for grander things, that she had hopes and dreams of Europe and conquering a financial world that went far beyond the role of a quiet little housewife. While Lin loved Stephen, she needed more—someone who was truly compatible with her, someone more sophisticated and exciting.

Lin didn't know who was more devastated when she broke up with him, Stephen—or her mother. Kim clung to the old Chinese belief that the firstborn needed to be married first. She herself had been married by the time she was sixteen, and concluded that a woman who wasn't married by age eighteen was verging on old maid status. Which made Lin, at the ripe old age of twenty-seven, the queen of the old maids. Add to this the fact that her younger sister Amy had had a boyfriend for years who was champing at the bit to get married, and it was no wonder that their mom was obsessed with marrying Lin off. That was no doubt why Mama Kim had started threatening to make Lin go to China with her, to pick a husband for her daughter if she hadn't found anyone by age thirty.

When Lin got off the train, her mother was already waiting for her on the platform. A devout Buddhist, she wore a palette of jade jewelry and red silk. The jade was there for health, luck, and protection. As for the red, Mama Kim never went a day without wearing something that color, whether it was a red blouse or a red barrette in her short, tightly permed hair.

Today, she awaited Lin with a wooden box filled with bamboo steamed rice, duck liver sausage, and slivers of taro, which she thrust into her daughter's hands with the instructions to eat up right away. As they walked in the waning sunlight to her Lexus 450, Kim immediately started clucking over Lin's BCBG tank dress and babbling about how her auntie Grace had found someone for her.

Lin sighed. "But Ma, I don't need to be set up," she whined, feeling like she was ten again.

"Of course you do," Kim said briskly. "You almost thirty and not married. When I was your age—"

"I know, I know," Lin said. "You were married, you had two children already—I've heard it all before."

"You listen to me." Kim wagged her finger at Lin. "I am your mother. You think you know everything just because you young and make lot of money? I was like you when I your age. I could have been rich, too—but I marry your father and had you girls instead."

Lin sighed. Ever since she could remember, Kim had been telling her and her sisters what she could have been had she not gotten married and become pregnant. Lin knew it was a typical Chinese mother guilt trip, but she still hated hearing it. Somehow, it never failed to make her feel like the roadblock to her mother's fabled prospects for fame and fortune.

"I just don't think I'm going to have a lot in common with some guy from China," she said finally.

"Don't argue with me," Kim said. "He good for you. Maybe you give me grandkids soon. You work so hard, you never meet anybody. Larry flew in from the airport today. He doesn't know anybody, and I told him to come over."

Lin jerked back. Grandkids? Spending millions on high-risk stocks didn't give her a heart attack the way the word *grandkids* did. It wasn't that she didn't want to have kids; she absolutely did—one day. There was just no way she was having them any time soon, when she still had so many hills to climb, so many millions to make. And she certainly wasn't having them with someone she didn't even know and who probably couldn't speak English.

Just thinking about it gave Lin the chills as she got out of the car and followed her mother into the house. As she settled down on the living room couch, she couldn't help but imagine the scene. . . .

"POW! POW! *Pow!*"

Without warning, a spiky-haired, three-year-old baby boy darted out of the house, screaming and bombarding Lin with his water gun.

"Stop it, son!" Lin, feeling haggard, tired, and like a complete stranger to any beauty product whatsoever, screamed from the door, wiping her hands on her apron. "Come over here and eat one of these wontons I made for you."

"No!" the devil boy howled as he sprinted into the house.

Lin sighed wearily. As she headed back into the kitchen, Larry, her skinny, fresh-off-the-boat, bespectacled, Canton husband stomped in with a briefcase. He threw the briefcase down onto the dining room table, dropped onto the sofa, and plopped his feet on top of the ottoman.

"Sic fon may uh?" Larry demanded. Or in English, "Where's dinner?"

"EARTH TO Lin!"

Lin blinked, suddenly realizing that she had fallen asleep on the couch. Sarah was snapping her fingers in front of Lin's face.

Lin's youngest sister was nineteen and the snoop of the family. Any tidbit of gossip would inevitably be unearthed by Sarah. A petite size four, she had a heart-shaped face like Lin's.

"Hey!" Lin shook herself. "I just had the most horrendous dream."

"I can tell," Sarah laughed.

"Where's this Larry character?" Lin asked, looking around the living room frantically. She saw all her aunts, her uncles, and her cousins there . . . but no horrendous blind date.

"Don't worry, he's not here," Sarah assured her. "He got on the wrong train, so he's not coming anymore. You lucked out. He's going to Boston to visit his grandmother instead."

Lin exhaled in relief. Still, even though she'd dodged this bullet, she knew that it was only a matter of time before her mother would be back with another matchmaking scheme.

"Ugh," Lin groaned, "when will Mom ever get over her delusions?"

.   .   .

IN HER day, Lin's mother Kim had been quite the heralded beauty. The moment she turned sixteen, her family had suitors from all the neighboring villages doing their best to bid for her hand in courtship. They brought gifts by the armful—cured meats, sugary confections, all the gold trinkets they could scrape up. It reached a point where jealous whispers started circulating among the neighbors, and Kim's family had to start distributing the wealth just to appease them.

Not that any of it mattered. In her red silk bower, Kim turned up her nose at all the would-be wooers. She had no use for any of them—nor for the life of a farmer's wife. She had higher goals, dreams of celluloid stardom in the Hong Kong cinema. As soon as she could, she would be on the first boat to Kowloon and away from the banality of village life.

Of course, nothing turned out the way Kim had planned. When she turned seventeen, her parents betrothed her to a small merchant in a neighboring village. All the tears in the world couldn't change her parents' minds; times were hard, and a beautiful daughter was a valuable commodity—there simply was no other way.

The night before her wedding, Kim had one last chance to escape. Her friend May's brother was going to Kowloon; all she had to do was steal out of her house under the cover of night and join him. So she packed her bags, wrote her note, and got ready. And yet, when the time came, she couldn't do it. All of a sudden, faced with the prospect of an uncertain future, Kim did what she swore she would never do—she chose the safe and steady road over the unknown.

The years that followed the wedding were hard ones. Financially, times were tough. Kim's new husband soon lost his business, and they had to scrape around doing odd tasks to make ends meet. But that was nothing compared to the mental toll; married to a man she barely knew and haunted by what could have been, Kim grew bitter and sullen. Years later, even after they had immigrated to America and had attained a level of middle-class prosperity, she still harbored these resentments. She eventually grew to care for her husband, but there was no mistaking what her first love was.

Lin knew all this. Kim didn't believe in hiding things. She told her daughter everything in the hopes of teaching her important life lessons: that she must have ambition, drive, and financial independence to do whatever she wanted if she planned to have a better life. Lin was a quick student, but there was one lesson she took to heart that Kim never counted on: to throw caution to the wind and forsake the safe path, lest she spend the rest of her life caged by regrets.

IF THERE was one thing that Drew Black most definitely was not, it was safe. Then again, none of the guys Lin worked with were.

"So then this guy Mike at work was telling a group of guys at the table how he 'didn't see daylight' with some blonde in the Hamptons," Lin recounted to M.J. and Alex as they nursed drinks at the Oriental Palace Restaurant in Koreatown. It was Monday night, and after a down day at the stock market, a vent session with her girls was just what Lin needed.

"I told you that brokers were pigs," Alex said. "I don't know how you deal with all these jackasses every day. No wonder you want to move to the London office."

Lin smiled wistfully. While it would be nice to get away from some of the jerks in her office, that wasn't her driving force for wanting to move to London. Like New York, London was a major player in the world of big-time finance. It was inevitable that she would want to try her hand, to see if she was up for the challenge. But London was no easy proposition; aside from the difficulty of getting a job there, Lin was also well aware of what she'd be giving up. She had a good life in New York: friends, family, a job where she was respected and well-liked. London was a crapshoot, and she wasn't sure if she was ready for it.

"Yeah, well," Lin shrugged, "who knows when I'd be able to get to London. In the meantime, I'll just have to deal with the guys at work as best as I can."

"That blows," M.J. said. "I know it's hard to work with a lot of men, but for them to be discussing that shit at work is bogus."

"Well, one good thing happened at work last week," Lin said, changing the topic. "This new guy Drew started, and he's great. Cute, charming." She carefully tucked a stray strand of hair back into her immaculately styled upsweep. "Did I mention cute?"

"Ahh." M.J. nodded slowly. "So you want to jump him or what?"

"He's very sexy," Lin conceded, her expression dreamy as she thought of Drew's hypnotic green eyes. "But he's not ready to settle down, that's for sure. I'm totally on to him." She took a sip of her Malibu pineapple and muttered under her breath, "I'm definitely on to him."

"Forget about Drew for now." M.J. leaned forward. "How about doing something fun tonight?"

"What did you have in mind?" Alex asked.

"Karaoke!"

Karaoke had been one of M.J.'s favorite activities to do with the girls when they were teenagers and had sneaked a few drinks on a Saturday night out in the city. Their favorite pastime was sneaking into other people's private rooms at the famous Jeung Color OK Karaoke house and pretending they were part of the party group—all the easier to make fun of the "singers."

"Uhh . . . singing?" Lin wrinkled her nose. "I don't think so, J. Go with Jagger and you two can sing your hearts out."

Alex burst out laughing as M.J. adopted a mock-offended look. "Well, I know M.J. thinks she's the next American Idol and all, but maybe it could be fun. We never do crazy stuff like that anymore." She rubbed her chin. "Lin, what do you say?"

"I can't believe you two are serious! Alex—I think I liked it more when you weren't so into crazy stuff!" Lin exclaimed. "But okay, fine. Just don't expect me to get up on stage!"

M.J. didn't need any further prodding. After she hailed the waiter, they paid the check and departed from the Oriental Palace. Ten minutes later, they were sailing through the doors of the Jeung Color OK Karaoke house, a dimly lit lounge with disco lights and vinyl booths. To pacify Lin, M.J. requested a private room for the three of them so that no one else would witness Lin singing.

"I'm feeling a bit tipsy," M.J. said, weaving as she walked. "I'm going to sing some Celine Dion and really belt it out."

Alex and Lin both rolled their eyes.

"And, as usual, we'll laugh at you." Alex grinned. "Hey, speaking of Ms. Dion, I think I hear someone singing 'A New Day' right now in the main room."

"I do, too," Lin agreed. "Let's go watch."

As the three girls walked into the main singing room, they all caught a glimpse of the performer on stage and had the same reaction—sheer and utter shock.

"Oh my God!" Alex grabbed M.J.'s wrist. "Is that—?"

"Stephen!" M.J. screamed.

Sure enough, on stage for all the world to see, was Lin's ex-boyfriend Stephen. And he wasn't just on stage. He was swaying and shaking his hips and belting out the lyrics to Celine Dion's hit song—"Hush, now I see the light in the sky . . ."

Alex and M.J. both turned to look at Lin, who had been stunned into silence.

This couldn't be right, Lin thought. This wasn't the Stephen she knew—the uptight doctor whose craziest maneuver consisted of wearing stripes with solids. He didn't know anything about singers, and he certainly didn't know anything about singing.

"You okay, Lin?" M.J. grinned.

"I am . . . I mean . . . ," Lin stammered. "I just can't believe that he's up there—and singing to Celine Dion!"

"I know!" M.J. said gleefully. "And you dated him!"

"Yeah," Alex chuckled. "Who would believe that was Lin Cho's boyfriend?"

As her friends laughed and high-fived each other, Lin could only cover her face and cringe. Sure, Stephen was free to do as he pleased, and if he wanted to sing karaoke, what say did she have in it? Yet, Lin couldn't help wondering what people would think if they knew that was her ex-boyfriend up on stage. . . .

Just then, Stephen finished his song. He turned, caught sight of the girls, did a double take—and headed straight toward them.

"Lin?" Stephen broke into a grin. Lin, who'd been trying to nudge M.J. and Alex away, froze.

"Uh, Stephen?" She forced a smile. "Hi, how are you?"

"I'm good." He paused, looking a little confused. "What are you doing here? I never figured you for the karaoke type."

"Well . . . J here wanted to sing," Lin said quickly. "It's kind of a girls' night out."

"Very nice." He nodded at her friends. "Hi, Alex. M.J., it's good to see you again."

M.J. grinned. "Same here."

"Hey, why don't you guys come and join us at our table?" He smiled at Alex and M.J. "I don't know if you heard, but I just belted out a tune."

M.J. grinned from ear to ear as Alex flashed him a thumbs-up.

"Oh, was that you singing Celine Dion? I almost didn't recognize you up there," Lin said.

Stephen chuckled. "I guess I've been trying a lot of crazy things ever since I turned thirty. I've always wanted to sing karaoke, so I figured I'd give it a shot." He clasped his hands. "And you know what? I actually had a blast up there, just me and the microphone."

Alex and M.J. looked at each other and grinned. As for Lin, all she could do was stare at him in disbelief. Her friends were right—how could an ex-boyfriend of hers enjoy singing karaoke?

"Right," she said, deciding to humor him. "Well, I'm glad you enjoyed yourself. We actually have to go because we reserved a private room. But good running into you!"

"You, too." He smiled. "It was really nice seeing you. And remember," he winked, "a new day will come and you'll be touched by an angel."

M.J. yelped and high-fived Stephen as Alex guffawed.

"Well, we better get going," Lin said loudly, ushering her friends away. "See you later, Stephen!"

As they headed toward their private karaoke room, Lin shook

her head. She couldn't believe she'd dated someone so dorky. And Celine Dion? What had she been thinking?

THE NEXT morning, Lin still didn't know the answer. But there was one thing she was sure of: Drew would never have looked so uncool. Sitting in her office, Lin decided that she would stick to the stock market and Drew from now on. Just as she had that thought though, Lin glanced down at her computer screen and gasped.

"Aaarggh!" she screamed. Drew rushed in.

"What's wrong?" he asked.

"Tyco just went down three points in the last four hours! George Levin—our biggest client—is going to flip. I told him we'd be okay last week."

"That's not good." Drew rubbed his temples. "He's not exactly a happy camper. In fact, he's pretty much the greediest old man I know."

"Just like everybody else," Lin said. "Everyone wants to be rich by the time they're old."

"Well, the man's got a point," he replied. "Money does make a man . . . or a woman."

Lin shook her head. "There are a lot of people in this world who are smarter than us, but who make less money." Lin thought about her mother, who was, without a doubt, one of the most enterprising people she had ever known. Having come to the United States with absolutely nothing, Kim had worked three jobs, shopped at Goodwill, and scraped together every cent so she could give her daughters a better life. Even though Lin now made several times what her mother had made at the height of her earning power, she wished she had even an ounce of the shrewdness that Kim had.

"That's true, but with money comes power." Drew pointed to Lin's pocketbook on her desk. "Look at you with your Louis Vuitton bag. Or me in my Armani suit. People are drawn to anything that exudes wealth."

Lin shrugged as she focused on her computer monitor. There was no way Drew could understand. He'd never had to wear hand-me-downs; he'd never known what it was like to be in a foreign country where he didn't speak the language; he probably didn't even know what Spam tasted like.

"Well, then, what are you doing here if not for the money?" Drew persisted.

"I happen to like what I do. Not for the payout itself, but for the . . . pursuit of it. I like helping my clients . . . make money." She cleared her throat.

It was a strange contradiction, to say the least. While Drew didn't understand that Lin's family didn't have the luxury of wealth, he wasn't completely wrong about Lin's infatuation with it. After all, how could she not be obsessed? Growing up, Lin had seen her family evolve from barely eking out a living as immigrants to being firmly entrenched in the American middle class. This progression would never have happened if the Chos weren't preoccupied with money; it was only by counting every last cent that they had gotten to where they were now. So what if they talked incessantly about incomes and vacations? So what if they were constantly comparing cars and houses and TVs? Her family had worked hard to get to where they were, and Lin didn't think there was anything wrong with their being a little materialistic if they wanted to be.

"Wow, that was touching," Drew said. "It sort of turns me on."

"Be quiet." Lin crinkled her nose. "Do you always have to act like a chauvinistic male?"

Drew grinned. "Only when I can get a reaction like that out of you. You're pretty opinionated for an Asian chick."

She glared at him as her phone rang. It was their boss, Rob.

"Lin, I need you guys to get the fiscal report from Mike on my desk by eight A.M. Monday morning. Just so you know, I'll be out of the office the rest of the week."

"You got it, Rob," Lin said. She hurriedly hung up the phone.

"So I heard the boss is going to Martha's Vineyard for the

Memorial weekend." Drew came over and sat on the edge of her desk. "What about you? Any plans?"

"Not much. I'm meeting with my parents for dinner at Shun Lee, then I'll probably just go out with my girls," she replied. "What about you?"

"Well, I'm volunteering tomorrow at the Y, but after that I'm actually moving into my new place. I have my very own bachelor pad now. You should come check it out sometime," Drew said, winking at Lin.

Lin started to smile then paused, struck by Drew's words. "You volunteer?" she asked.

"Yeah, I've been tutoring these fifth graders in math for the past two years."

"Wow," she said slowly, "I'm . . . speechless."

"I bet that doesn't happen very often," Drew said lightly. "So you think you can stop by this weekend?"

It was moments like these that always got Lin in trouble—when she would somehow get sucked in by a guy like Drew even though the whole situation reeked of trouble.

"Well—" She smiled flirtatiously. "—we'll see."

EVEN THOUGH there was a part of Lin that was tempted by the prospect of seeing Drew, she had more pressing weekend plans—like taking her mother and father to dinner. One of the perks of making a good salary was that Lin could afford to take her parents out to the nicest restaurants in New York City. Like Shun Lee, an exquisite, ultra-expensive, haute-Chinese restaurant on the Upper East Side. The emerald shrimp dumplings were a particular favorite of the Cho family. Unfortunately, this time, the appetizers came with an extra item.

"Lin?" Drew suddenly appeared at their table. "How are you? What are you doing?"

"Drew?" Lin gasped. "I should be asking you the same question."

"I just had dinner with my aunt and uncle," he said. "A friend of mine thinks this is a great place for a family dinner."

She shot him a look, but he beamed innocently. As she fidgeted with the linen napkin on her lap, her mother gave him a frown of disapproval. Lin knew her mother wasn't going to be happy about her socializing with Drew.

"Hey, Drew," Lin said nervously, "this is my mom, Kim, and my dad, Harry."

Drew flashed them one of his trademark smiles. "Hi, Mr. and Mrs. Cho. It's nice to meet you."

Kim forced a smile. Harry managed a pleasant "Hi, how are you?"

"Drew works with me," Lin said brightly. "He's actually one of the partners from our team."

"Partners?" her mom asked skeptically.

"Yes," Lin explained, "we work together on several mutual funds projects. He's one of the best traders in the business."

Kim ignored Lin. "So are you married?"

Lin couldn't believe her ears. What was her mother up to?

"No, I'm not married," Drew said, "but I'm still young and looking for the right woman." He looked pointedly at Lin, who flushed and stared down at her plate.

"Are you interested in my daughter?" Kim asked.

Lin almost passed out from embarrassment. She knew that her mother was old-fashioned and pretty much crazy when it came to Lin and guys, but this was too much. "Um, Mom," she interrupted, "you're so funny. Drew works with me, Mom. *Works with me!*"

Of course, Drew Black was no dummy.

"No, Mrs. Cho," he said very seriously. "Lin is a lovely lady, but we're nothing but friends. We work together. That wouldn't be right."

"I see." Kim nodded. "Good."

"Mom." Lin gritted her teeth. "Would you like another Tsingtao beer?"

"I like five right now," Kim said coldly.

"I'll get the waiter right away. Drew, it was good seeing you. Have a lovely evening."

He took the hint. "Have a pleasant dinner, Mr. and Mrs. Cho. It was very nice to meet you both. Take care."

The minute Drew was out of earshot, Lin confronted her mother. "Mom, how could you do that to me?" Her voice rose. "You can't embarrass me like that in front of my friends."

"He is white," Kim lectured. "I want you to find someone like Stephen again and stop fooling around with these playboys. They only want one thing. The fortune-teller warned you."

"Ugh!" Lin groaned as she turned to her food. Would she ever get through an entire meal without her mother criticizing and second-guessing her?

As soon as dinner was over, Lin's parents dropped her off at her apartment on the Upper West Side. She immediately whipped out her cell phone to call Drew.

"I'm so sorry about what happened at the restaurant," Lin apologized as she walked into her living room.

"No worries, Lin." He laughed. "Believe me, I understand. I have a Jewish mother. She's pulled shit like that before."

"Thanks." Lin broke into a smile. Not only was Drew gorgeous, but he was understanding as well! The fortune-teller had it half right—she was lucky. "She has some crazy idea that I'm going to go back to China with her and marry some farmer from Canton."

"That's funny." Drew chuckled. "Who would ever imagine Lin Cho with a farmer from China. . . . By the way," he added, "will you be at the office party on Friday?"

"Nowhere else."

"Good! I'll have to keep my eye on you. Everyone adores you."

Lin dropped down on a chair, kicked off her Jimmy Choos, and wriggled her toes. "Everyone?"

twenty-one

COMPANY PARTIES at Merrill Lynch were a lot like the Oscars. Leggy, beautiful women, sleazy old men, young dashing bucks, and a lot of free-flowing booze. At Lin's office Friday night, the branch's annual party was in full swing. The gunners were schmoozing, the ladies were glowing, and the air was thick with money. There couldn't be more fertile grounds for an office romance if one tried.

Dressed in a dazzling red spaghetti tube dress with sparkling bling all over, Lin ordered herself another glass of Cristal.

"Do you know how many of these guys have come up to me to tell me that I'm the luckiest man in the world because I work with the hottest woman in the office?" Drew walked over and whispered into Lin's ear.

Lin laughed. "Well, thank you. I must say you're not looking bad yourself."

Ding! Ding! Ding! Everyone turned toward the president of the branch, Henry Greenberg, who was poised to give a toast.

"If I could have your attention please." Greenberg raised his glass. "I'd just like to thank each and every one here for your hard work and dedication. With such determination and talent, our branch has managed to increase its revenue by thirty percent this year. Congratulations!"

The room roared as everyone applauded and turned back to the bar. At that moment, Rob walked over to Drew and Lin.

"I just want to say a few words to my team over here," Rob said as he raised his whiskey, obviously a bit tipsy.

Drew and Lin looked at each other and tried to suppress smiles.

"Mr. Black, with your addition, I have no doubt that our team will do even better this year. And Ms. Cho, without you, there wouldn't even be a team. You two kids are doing a tremendous job and have put an old guy like me to shame," Rob slurred.

Drew flashed a smile at Lin, a striking figure in his black Versace suit, midnight blue shirt, and silver tie. Lin had to resist the temptation to stare.

"Thank you for your kind words, Rob. I just want to say that I've never worked with such a good group before. Rob, with your guidance and wisdom, and . . . and with Lin's talent and intelligence, I feel privileged to be a part of this team. Thank you. Cheers!" Drew winked at Lin as they clinked glasses.

"God bless you two," Rob mumbled. "Hopefully, there will be many more years of success to come. Now if you'll excuse me, I think I'm going to grab some nuts."

Lin and Drew both laughed as Rob stumbled off.

"I was touched by your speech," Lin remarked. "Here's to you sucking up."

Drew smiled. "Oh, is that what you thought I was doing?"

"Most definitely," Lin said, taking a sip of her Cristal. "You're the kind of guy who always knows just what to say."

"Well, they don't call me Badass Drew for nothing." Drew snagged another glass of champagne from a passing waiter.

"Who's 'they'?" Lin chuckled.

"My boys from college," he said, taking a swig of his drink. "That was my name because I charmed all the girls."

"Oh, really?" Lin smirked. "Does that charm still work?"

"You tell me," Drew said as he turned toward her, his expression suddenly turning serious. "You know, I have a confession to make. I've been trying to think of an excuse to get you alone since the first time I laid eyes on you. But I didn't think I had a chance."

"Why not?" Lin looked into his eyes and felt her heart leap.

"Because you're so amazingly beautiful. And smart and a damn good broker. I figured you were out of my league." He leaned forward. "But maybe my confidence has grown because I think I have a chance."

"With who?" Lin looked innocently around the room.

But Drew was not to be sidetracked. He gazed at Lin very seriously. "I lied to your mom that time we met," he confessed. "I think you're absolutely breathtaking, and my interest in you is definitely not platonic. What do you say we go back to my place and have a few drinks?"

At that moment, Lin's radar kicked up. What was she doing? Yes, she loved flirting with men, but this was more than just flirting. Drew was sexy and charming and she liked him despite his ego. The only problem was that they worked together. But then again, taking risks was part of her everyday job.

"I think I'm going to head home," she said. "It's getting late, and I've already had way too many drinks."

"Are you sure?" he asked, his intent gaze making Lin feel light-headed. "Do you want me to take you home?"

Lin suddenly felt paralyzed, presented with such an oh-so-tantalizing prospect. There was a part of her that was doing somersaults, exulting that the wonderful Drew Black wanted her. Then there was the part of her that whispered that this was a terrible idea, that she was getting herself into a mess she might never be able to extricate herself from, that she was opening herself up to heartbreak.

"I'm afraid," Lin said slowly, "that if you take me home, you'll try to take advantage of me."

Drew pretended to look offended. "I would never do something like that, Lin. Come on, what do you say? We'll have a few drinks and I'll show you my new pad." He gave her his most seductive smile.

In the end, there was really no other choice for Lin. She wasn't her mother Kim. She wasn't going to settle for safe and steady. She wouldn't spend her life obsessed with what-ifs. And she would never stop reaching for the brass ring.

So she succumbed to the inevitable. "All right, all right. But I can't stay long."

IN LIN'S world, the stock market was a never-ending roller coaster. People could feel like king of the world one day or like shit the next. It could be a high on Monday, exhilaration Tuesday, and complete misery the rest of the week.

Lin was having one of those exhilarating days. It was the morning after the company party, and there was an extra skip in her step as she basked in the sunlight on her way to the Rickshaw Dumpling Bar. Was it because Nabisco had risen a few points or was it because she had finally merged assets with Drew Black?

"Hi, girls!" Lin beamed as she got in line behind M.J. and Alex. "How are you this morning? Isn't this place great?"

M.J. and Alex gave each other looks.

"What up?" M.J. said. "You certainly seem happy today."

"Oh, nothing." Lin looked up at the menu. "Isn't today just a beautiful day? I think I'll get the Peking duck dumplings and maybe the chocolate soup dumplings for dessert."

"That's it?" M.J. asked. "I heard the owner here has forty dumplings at a time. I'm going to have the chicken thai basil, szechuan chicken, shrimp, and classic pork and chive. Ten each for me!" she announced.

Lin stared at M.J., wondering how her friend wasn't eight hundred pounds. "Does Jagger know you eat like this?"

"Trust me," M.J. assured her, "Jagger would be getting forty dumplings himself if he were here."

"Fine," Alex said, "I'll order for us and make sure they know that the forty dumplings are for the oinker in the Adidas warm-ups."

"Thanks, Alex." M.J. shot her a pretend-outraged look as she and Lin laid claim to an empty table.

The minute Alex walked away, Lin turned to M.J. and relayed her big news. "Okay, you know I don't normally say these things, but he was so good in bed," Lin gushed.

"Shut up! You never say shit like that," M.J. exclaimed. "Was he even better than the guy you interned with years ago at Paine Webber?"

"Oh, him." Lin laughed. "But, um . . . yeah, I would have to say so. He's such a great kisser. He has such soft lips, and he definitely knows what he's doing."

Lin smiled. She was glad that she told J first. Not only was she more sympathetic to matters of the heart these days with her new-found coupledom, but she was also less likely to be judgmental than Alex.

M.J. saluted her with her fork. "I'm excited for you, Lin. I want to meet him!"

"I want you and Alex both to meet him." Lin twirled her wooden chopsticks. "He's great. And it's not just the sex. He treats me like a goddess. He just makes me feel . . . so special."

She tore her chopsticks apart gleefully. At that moment, Alex walked back over with their orders. M.J. quickly got up to help.

"So, what's all the commotion about? What did I miss?" Alex asked as she set the food down on the table.

"You missed a lot. Our girl Lin here just had the hottest night in her life with Drew Black," M.J. said, passing out their drinks.

"Drew Black?" Alex dropped down onto the chair across from Lin. "You mean the guy you work with?"

"Yes, that Drew. We went back to his place after the company party last night and it just sort of happened. We were up all night talking, and then one thing led to another . . . the next thing you know, all of our clothes were on the floor." Lin smiled at the memory as she took a bite out of her dumpling.

Alex's chopsticks clattered to the ground. "Lin!" she exclaimed. "What are you thinking? This isn't just some guy you met on a setup date. Haven't you heard all the warnings about dipping your pen in the company inkwell?"

Lin raised an eyebrow at Alex. "And you're completely immune to office romances, I assume?"

"All I'm saying is that these things have a way of ending up ugly," Alex responded. "You've got to be sure this isn't going to affect you at work."

Lin stared down at her tea. If there was one thing about her world that she would toss right out the window, it would be the rules. Without them, she would be able to make all the trades that she wanted and be a millionaire by age thirty. Who made up the rules anyway?

"Alex, I'll be fine," Lin said. "I'm a big girl."

.   .   .

DESPITE HER blasé attitude, Lin was more bothered by Alex's reaction than she let on. Alex just didn't seem to get it that she was happy because of Drew. Okay, so part of it was her fault, considering the way she'd first described him to her friends. But since then, things had changed. The two weeks following the company party had been pure bliss for Lin; they had spent almost every waking moment—and nonwaking moment—together. Drew was everything she had hoped for: romantic, fun, and surprisingly tender. He surprised her with long-stemmed roses and intimate weekend getaways to the Hamptons. And when they went out, he always managed to get them into the poshest restaurants and the most exclusive clubs. Above all, he treated her like a princess, constantly telling her how she was the most beautiful woman he knew. Drew could have had any woman he wanted, but he'd chosen her . . . it was almost enough to make her believe she was as wonderful as he said she was.

Now that Lin had gotten to know the real Drew, she wanted her friends to get to know him, too. So she invited Alex out to drinks on Thursday night at Le Colonial, a sleek, sultry French colonial restaurant and lounge where the clientele mingled under palm fronds. Lin knew she had been neglecting the girls the past two weeks, and this seemed like a perfect way to kill two birds with one stone: be with Drew and hang out with Alex all at once. The prospect of showing Alex, her biggest skeptic and closest pseudo–family member, that Drew was someone special was an added bonus. This could even be a test run for his official meeting with Lin's family at their house.

"Alex, I'm so glad you came tonight," Lin gushed as the girls sipped bamboo martinis in the upstairs lounge.

"Not as glad as I am to be out of work." Alex sighed happily as she leaned back in her chair. "But I should probably be grateful I don't have to travel—I bet M.J.'s bored out of her mind in Detroit."

"I know." Lin shook her head. "Poor J. When is she supposed to get back?"

"Tomorrow night, I think." Alex sipped her martini and glanced around the room. "So this is where the brokers hang out, huh?"

"Yes," Lin said distractedly, checking her phone. "I wonder what's keeping Drew."

"Is that him over there?" Alex asked.

Lin looked up in the direction that Alex was pointing. That was when she saw Drew and the rest of the guys from work at the bar chatting with Lana and the admin girls.

"Oh, yeah," Lin exclaimed, "there he is!"

"He looks awfully chummy with those women."

For a moment, Lin felt a stab of concern. But she brushed the thought aside, determined not to give in to her insecurities. "Oh," she waved it off, "those are just some of the secretaries." She got up and waved to Drew. "Drew! Over here!"

Drew looked up and nodded toward Lin. He ambled over to the girls. "Well, hey there." Drew grinned at Alex. "You must be Alex."

Alex smiled. "That would be me."

"You're everything Lin said you were." Drew winked at Lin, who giggled.

"Thanks," Alex said slowly.

"So—" Drew dropped down beside Lin. "—Lin says you're a lawyer."

Alex nodded. "That I am."

"Well, I'm glad to finally meet you," Drew said. "Before, when Lin said she had a friend who was a lawyer, I was picturing some ugly old broad, not a looker like you. Then again, I should have known that Lin's friends would be beautiful."

He leaned over and nudged Lin. She laughed a little and looked at Alex. Her face was expressionless—not a good sign.

"So," Drew continued, "did Lin tell you about our big score to-day?"

"No." Alex's eyes narrowed. "But I'm sure you're going to tell me about it."

"Oh, yeah." He turned to order a drink from a passing waiter.

"See, there's this rich asshole named Jankowski who we've been trying to land for a while. He's got a billion-dollar portfolio, and we've been trying to steal him from Smith Barney for a year. Anyway, we finally got him into the office today, but he was totally stonewalling us and even started to walk out. Which is when our lovely Lin came to the rescue!"

Lin's eyes widened. "Um, honey, I don't think Alex would be interested in hearing about this."

"Are you kidding me?" Drew exclaimed. "This is a great story." He turned eagerly to Alex. "I told Lin to put on the shortest skirt she had in the office, then drop her pen in front of Jankowski and lean over to pick it up. You should have seen the look on Jankowski's face! We signed him five minutes later!"

Lin bit her lip and stole a glance at her friend. Alex's eyes were steely.

"Isn't that great?" Drew said gleefully. "I'd like to see those bastards at Smith Barney try to match that!"

"Ingenious," Alex said coolly.

"You know," he continued, "you should try what Lin did. I bet you'd win more cases!"

"I'll have to keep that in mind," Alex said, looking utterly disgusted. She downed the rest of her drink and got up. "If you'll excuse me now, I forgot to send something out at work. I guess I'll have to take a raincheck on tonight."

"Oh, okay," Drew said. "It was nice meeting you, Alex."

Alex didn't even respond as she turned on her heel and stalked off. Lin jumped up out of her seat. "I'm just going to walk Alex out," she told Drew as she ran after her friend. Lin caught up with her on the sidewalk outside of Le Colonial.

"Alex, wait!" she called.

Alex turned around, hands on her hips.

"Look, Alex," Lin began, "I know what you're thinking—"

"I hope not," she snapped, "because then you would know what an asshole I think Drew is. Lin, you could do so much better than this! I expected a lot more from you."

"You don't understand," Lin pleaded. "I know Drew can come off as a jerk at first, but deep down, he's a good guy. Besides, you, of all people, should know what it's like to date a coworker."

"Lin!" Alex yelled. "That's completely different. First of all, Brady and I are just hanging out. Second, I would castrate him if he even suggested I do something like that. This guy Drew has you flashing your underwear to land an account! This from the woman who was the top moneymaker at Merrill Lynch last year. Don't you think there's something wrong with that?"

There was a part of Lin that knew Alex was right, that this behavior with Drew was wrong in about a million ways. But then there was the other part of Lin—the stubborn part—that didn't want to think about the ramifications of her relationship with Drew.

Lin's eyes welled up. "Look," she said, "you don't understand. You don't know what it's like between us. When it's just him and me, he's different. We're different. And I think I might be falling for him."

Lin wiped away her tears and glanced up at Alex. She knew her friend didn't understand. All her life, Alex had everything come easily to her. She went to the best schools, became a big-time lawyer, earned several times what her peers were making. While Lin herself earned a decent living, she didn't come close to Alex in terms of credentials. Most important, Alex had parents who adored her and believed she could do no wrong. She didn't have a mother like Kim, who never hesitated to tell Lin all the ways she had erred.

Her friend looked away as a long pause stretched between them. Then Alex glanced back toward Lin. "I'm sorry," Alex said finally. "You're right. I don't know what it's like between you two." She took a deep breath. "Just don't change yourself for this guy. You have to . . . be careful, okay?"

Lin nodded slowly. Alex leaned over and gave her a brief hug. Then she walked off as Lin silently watched her go.

Closing
Bell

twenty-two

LIKE EVERYTHING else in life, the market was a gamble. Some people refused to sell their shares when they rose. Instead, they got greedy and invested more and more—until they hit the wall. In Lin's world, love and stocks paralleled each other perfectly.

Continuing to see Drew raised a glaring red flag in Lin's mind, but like those investors, she wanted to push the limits to see how far she could get. She saw the warning signs and the roadblocks, but she was determined to keep stepping on the pedal. She had come this far, and there was no turning back.

Dressed in a sharp navy blue power suit, Drew sauntered into Lin's office on Tuesday morning. He closed the door behind him, locking it afterward. Lin's face lit up. It had been several weeks since the company party, but her stomach still did a somersault every time she saw him.

"Hey, gorgeous." He smiled as he leaned in to kiss her. "How's my favorite girl?"

Lin blushed as they moved onto her couch. Drew always had a way of making her feel like the most beautiful woman in the world.

He was unbuttoning her blouse when her phone rang.

"Let's not get that," Lin whispered in Drew's ear as she continued to kiss him.

"You have to get that," he whispered back. "It could be important."

"Okay, okay." She got up and straightened her skirt. "Hello, Lin Cho."

"Hi, Lin," Lana said, "I have a package for you up by the front desk."

"Thanks, Lana." Lin fumbled to hang up the phone.

"Where were we?" she whispered to Drew as she threw his tie on the floor.

"Right here." Drew smiled as he nuzzled her neck. "You know, Lin," he said huskily. "I think we have the best business meetings in the world."

Lin smiled. "Oh really?"

"And you haven't seen the best yet," Drew said as he pulled her down onto the couch.

As they made love in Lin's corner office, someone knocked.

"Lin?" Rob called from the other side of the door.

Drew and Lin stared at each other in horror. Jumping up from the couch, they rushed frantically to get dressed and straighten themselves out. Lin helped fix Drew's tie, while Drew zipped up Lin's skirt. As Drew made his way over to the windowsill, Lin smoothed down her blouse. Her heart was pounding like a jackhammer, and she suddenly felt on the verge of hyperventilating. How could she have let this happen? This was her worst nightmare come true—her boss and mentor discovering the two of them *in flagrante delicto* in her office. She had to put a stop to this. She just prayed that she wasn't going to lose her job.

Silently cursing herself for being so stupid, she slowly unlocked the door. "Come in," Lin chirped in an overly bright tone.

"Hey, kids," Rob said upon entering. "Private meeting?"

Lin flushed and looked away. Fortunately, Rob didn't seem to notice.

"Drew, I've been looking all over for you. We need to sit down and talk. I got word from our headquarters that we'll be making some changes with management here. That means a couple of things, but most importantly, it affects our team. There'll be some different strategies and plans to discuss. How about we meet on Thursday?"

"Great!" Drew and Lin said in unison. Rob gave the two of them a curious look.

"Since when did you two begin sharing a brain?" he demanded. "But you know what—I like it! Just means that our team is in sync. Go team, go! Gotta run, but let's talk Thursday."

Rob closed the door behind him as Drew and Lin both exhaled.

"Boy, was that a close one!" Drew shook his head.

"Tell me about it," Lin said. "This is so wrong. I've never had sex in the office before." And she'd never do it again. She just hoped she'd have the resolve if or when that time came to say no. "Look," she began, "Drew, I think this wasn't such a good idea—omigosh!" she screamed, seeing the shattered remains of her bamboo plant on the floor.

"Oops." He spared a glance over as he fiddled with his tie. "I guess that must have gotten knocked over during our . . . activities." He snickered a little.

Lin was not amused. "This isn't funny," she snapped. "You've messed up all the feng shui in my office."

Drew frowned. "What do you mean?"

"I had someone come and take a look at my office when I moved in." Lin grabbed a small dustpan from her drawer and carefully swept up the mess. "I had to make sure the feng shui was good, and that included having a bamboo plant here."

"I see," Drew said, though he clearly did not, "is that why you have that weird thing hanging up there?" He gestured toward a concave mirror attached to one of the top corners of the window behind her.

"Uh, yeah." She reddened a little. "There's a church across the street, which is supposed to be bad luck. The mirror is supposed to combat that."

He nodded slowly. "Well, that's really cute, your little Chinese superstitions."

Lin frowned. "It's not supposed to be cute," she said a little testily.

"Sure, sure, whatever you say." He smiled as he slipped his arms around her. Despite herself, Lin felt her resolve weaken.

"Pick me up at eight tonight," she whispered as she kissed him lightly on the lips. "Now go! I have work to do."

The moment he left her office, Lin collapsed into her chair. That had been close—too close. She hid her face in her hands. She would never have done something so reckless when she was with Stephen. What was it about Drew that made her lose all control of her senses?

She knew exactly what it was: He was dangerous, but he was also exciting. Just being around him was intoxicating, an addictive mixture of thrills and the forbidden. When she was with him, Lin felt invincible as well. Which was why, despite her misgivings, she couldn't help but fall under his spell again.

BY THE end of the day, the close call with Rob had become a distant, distinctly less alarming memory. Lin couldn't stop smiling as she strolled down the hallway after her afternoon Starbucks run. She'd had a number of good flings in her life but never like this. Who said that you couldn't mix business with pleasure?

"Lin, how are you?" Krishan called out from the copy machine as she walked down the hall toward her office.

Lin broke into a grin and strolled over to him. "How's the market doing today?"

"It's doing great," he replied. "Green on my screen."

"Excellent!" she applauded.

"What's with the cheeriness?" he asked. "Looks like you're having a good day."

"I am." Lin smiled. "Things are great."

"Really?" Krishan asked. "New man?"

"Sort of," she giggled.

"Details, I need details. You can't leave your captain hanging like that."

"Carry on," Lin said as she walked away. "So long, Krishan."

He called after her. "Hey, how can you sell out on a fellow alum like that?"

Lin chuckled. Krishan always knew what to say and he always seemed to know what was going on—which was why she had to steer clear of him. At least for now. Just as that thought crossed her mind, she almost tripped on the carpet outside her office. Quickly composing herself, she turned around to see Krishan looking at her curiously.

"Later!" she said with fake cheer before she quickly closed the door.

FORTUNATELY, THE rest of the week didn't bring any further threats of discovery. By the time Lin met up with Alex and M.J. that weekend at the Chelsea Wine Vault, she had all but forgotten her near-brush with disaster.

"This is so exciting," Lin exclaimed. "I've always wanted to do a wine tasting!"

"Me, too," M.J. said, looking around the spacious red-brick winery. "I might not know the difference between a ten-dollar bottle and one of these expensive wines, but I still like to drink it!"

"Well, then it's time to start your education," Alex said. "Here, try this."

"Mmm," M.J. took a sip of the white wine Alex handed her, "tastes like apricots—what's it called? Fal-and-geena?" She frowned at the label of the bottle.

"Falanghina," Alex corrected her. "It's an ancient Italian grape. This wine is made by the Ocones in Campania, and it's really excellent. Soft, dry, no oak and just a touch of vanilla."

"I couldn't have said it better," M.J. said, downing the rest of the glass. "I was just going to say it's delicious! You chose a great place, Alex."

"M.J.'s right," Lin agreed. "We've talked about this for years. Thanks for finally organizing."

Alex waved it off. "It was easy. They do a wine tasting every month."

"Well, I think this is great," Lin said. "In fact, I'm going to bring Drew here! He's a big wine guy, so he'll be really impressed."

M.J. and Alex exchanged knowing glances.

"I think Lin might be in love," M.J. teased. "She's stuck in happy world."

"Hush, guys." Lin took a sip of her Syrah. "What's wrong with being happy? Drew treats me like a princess. Last night, he cooked me dinner, and we watched *Casablanca*. Then we had amazing sex."

"Hmm," Alex said noncommittally, "so what else is new with Drew?"

Lin giggled, feeling her face flush as she did. "Actually, we made love in the office the other day—"

"You're kidding me!" Alex said, appalled. "Weren't there other people there?"

"It was in my office; we locked the door, of course. Our boss walked in right after that, but we were fine," Lin said, refusing to admit how scared she'd been at the time. "It was sort of kinky."

"Ohmigosh!" M.J. covered her mouth. "You're that girl in the office. You're that boiler room girl people talk about!"

"Lin," Alex said, "this behavior is really crazy. You better be careful. News gets out quickly."

Lin swallowed. She knew Alex would have this reaction. And even though she'd been having the same thoughts herself, she wasn't willing to sit and hear her friend voice them.

"Look, Alex, I know you don't like Drew. But it's all great, really. He and I both promised we would never say anything." Lin looked at her watch. "Actually, I have to go now."

Her friends stared at her.

"You're leaving?" M.J. asked, mid-sip. "But . . . we're not done here."

"Yeah, we've only tasted two wines," Alex pointed out. "We've got five more to go."

"I know," Lin said. "I'm sorry. But I told Drew I would meet him at four. We're going shopping for something nice to wear to Auntie Betty's barbecue at the end of the month."

"Your aunt Betty's? Doesn't that mean your parents are going to be there?" M.J. asked. "They hate him."

"I know, but they have to accept the fact that Stephen and I are over and that Drew is in my life now." Lin put down her glass. "Look, I'll talk to you guys later, okay?"

As Lin sailed out of the winery, Alex looked after her with a frown. "I can't believe she just left. This is the fourth time she's bailed because of Drew."

"She's in love," M.J. said weakly.

"Yeah," Alex scowled, "in love with a jerk. Stop making excuses for her, J. Lin knows better than to ditch her girlfriends."

LIN DIDN'T think about ditching her girlfriends. The truth was, she didn't think about her friends, period. Her thoughts were completely occupied with Drew, and there was no room for anyone or anything else.

The last straw came several weeks later on the night that they were supposed to celebrate M.J.'s long-awaited interview with the legendary Michael Jordan. Caught up in sunbathing with Drew on his roof deck, Lin didn't remember the dinner until the last second. By the time she arrived, the girls were already finishing up their meals.

"I'm so sorry," Lin apologized as she ran into the restaurant. "I know I'm really late."

"Let me guess," Alex said tartly, "you were too busy having sex with Drew to remember?"

Lin blanched, taken aback by the anger in Alex's voice. M.J. bit her lip.

"Look," Lin retorted, "I know you're angry, Alex, but it's not Drew's fault."

"Why not?" Alex demanded. "You never ditched your friends

until you met him. You never acted like this when you were with Stephen."

M.J. stepped in. "Let's just simmer down for a second, girls."

Lin swallowed, feeling a sudden pressure in her chest. "That's not fair, Alex," she protested. "Drew is the best thing that's happened to me in a long time, and I would think that my friends would understand."

"Understand what?" Alex snapped. "This is a huge night for M.J. Remember M.J., your best friend? You know she's been waiting all her life for this interview, and she finally got it. You're telling me that you can't drag yourself away from this guy for one evening to help her celebrate?"

"Alex, it's okay, really—," M.J. said quickly.

"No, it's not okay," Alex interrupted, "and don't try to let her off, M.J. Lin, do you know how upset J was because you weren't here? And it's not just tonight. It's pretty much every single time we're supposed to go out nowadays. Either you're going out with Drew, or Drew needs you to do something for him, or it's something else having to do with Drew. If this guy is as great as you think he is, he can deal with you hanging out with your friends once in a while. He should want what's best for you." Alex looked Lin in the eye. "Then again, if he's hooking up with you in the office, maybe he's got his own interests in mind."

For a moment, there was nothing but silence. Then Lin whirled around toward M.J. "Is that what you think, too, J?"

M.J. dropped her gaze. After a moment, she nodded reluctantly.

Lin's face crumpled as she drew back from her friends. "You're wrong about Drew—both of you. He's sweet and romantic and supports me like no other guy ever has. He doesn't treat me like an idiot or tell me about the ten million things that are wrong with me. He makes me feel beautiful. Special. He could have any girl in the world—but he wants me. Don't you guys know what that means to me?" she cried. "Why can't you just be happy for me?"

And without waiting for a response, she turned around and fled the restaurant.

twenty-three

LIN FELT awful after her fight with the girls. So awful that she sent a much-too-expensive, overly extravagant, congratulatory bouquet of roses to M.J.'s office the next morning. And yet, she still couldn't bring herself to pick up the phone, call them, and admit that she was wrong. Because that was what this boiled down to essentially. It didn't matter that her friends were looking out for her or that they spoke with the best of intentions. All she knew was that she didn't want to believe that they could be right about Drew. She'd staked her reputation and her pride on him, and she was determined to back this pony to the finish line.

So a week passed and Lin still didn't call her friends. Even when she was aching to pick up the phone and tell them how sorry she was, she resisted the impulse. Instead, she focused her energies on Drew and occupied herself with planning his momentous introduction to her family at Aunt Betty's barbecue potluck on Thursday night.

Auntie Betty was Lin's favorite relative. She threw the best parties and made the greatest sticky rice with chicken wrapped in bamboo leaf. And for dessert, Lin could eat bowls of her famous tofu-fa, pudding made out of tofu topped with sugar cane syrup, followed by helpings of red bean with sweet lotus seed tong shui. Lin couldn't wait to introduce Drew to the sugary concoctions.

More than anything, though, Lin couldn't wait to introduce her family to Drew. A few months ago, she would never have imagined this, but now that she and Drew were a real, honest-to-goodness couple, she was finally ready to be an adult. Which is how they ended up at her aunt's doorstep on Thursday—he dashing in his Ralph Lauren jacket and she resplendent in her Pucci halter dress.

"Auntie Betty!" Lin hugged her aunt at the door. "So good to see you."

Auntie Betty was one of the most gorgeous Asian women Lin had ever known. She was fifty-three, hip, sassy, and "in" with the program. Formerly a fashion designer in Hong Kong who used to dress celebrities like Jet Li and Michelle Yeoh before they made it big, she'd quit the business when her *low-gung*, her husband, died in a car accident. These days, she depended on her mah-jong pals to keep herself occupied.

"Lin—" Her aunt embraced her. "—you get more beautiful every day."

"Thanks, Auntie." Lin beamed. "I have someone I want you to meet."

Drew walked up from behind. "Hi, I'm Drew. It's nice to meet you."

Auntie Betty hesitated for a moment then smiled. "Hello. Welcome."

As the three of them walked inside the house together, Aunt Betty pulled Lin aside and whispered, "He's very good-looking, but your mother is going to have a heart attack."

Lin smiled nervously. "You think so? I mean, I know Ma is never satisfied with anything I do, but I think she would like Drew if she got to know him. At any rate," she took a deep breath, "I guess it's time that I grow up and face the drama."

"Your ma will be okay," Auntie Betty reassured her. "She just wants to make sure you're happy and that you receive the love you deserve. Maybe she thinks you can find that with an Asian man. She's just looking out for you, you know."

"I know." Lin sighed. "It's just that I can look out for myself now."

"Understandable." Her aunt nodded and wrapped her arm around Lin. "Now let's go in and have some barbecue!"

Meanwhile, Drew was standing in the middle of the living

room, surrounded by Lin's relatives, who were all giving him death glares of disapproval. Lin caught up with him. "My parents are in the kitchen," she warned. "Just be cool, and things will be okay."

"Things will be fine, sweetie." He smiled. "Just relax and go grab yourself a burger."

Lin kissed him lightly on the lips—then froze as a tall, familiar figure strolled toward them. "Stephen!" Lin squeaked. "Wha . . . what are you doing here?"

"Hi, Lin," Stephen greeted her with a warm smile. "I was visiting my folks and ran into Aunt Betty. She mentioned you were coming home, so I thought I'd drop by. It's been a while since karaoke."

Lin turned and shot Aunt Betty an accusing look. Her aunt had the grace to appear sheepish, but she still seemed to find the whole thing more amusing than anything else.

"You guys were at karaoke?" Drew asked.

Lin blushed. "Oh, the girls and I went the other night and ran into Stephen," she said quickly.

He stuck his hand out. "I'm Stephen."

"Oh," Lin said hastily, "this is Drew, my—" She stopped, not knowing how to proceed, given the awkwardness of the situation.

Stephen shook Drew's hand. "Nice to meet you."

"So," Drew said slowly, "you're Stephen. I've heard about you."

Lin groaned. Drew was doing that thing she hated— deliberately saying something to assert his supremacy. It was one thing to do this in the workplace, but to pull this kind of thing here . . .

Fortunately, Stephen seemed unfazed. "So," he said cheerfully, "have you sampled Lin's grandmother's fried dumplings yet—"

Lin exhaled inwardly. Thank goodness for Stephen. She could always count on him to bail her out of tough situations. Certainly, considering how much Lin's family adored him, Stephen could have made an already awkward situation infinitely worse. Instead, he was actually smoothing things over for all of them. Maybe this wouldn't be a complete disaster. . . . Then Kim walked into the room with a skinny Asian man Lin didn't recognize, who was wearing a bow tie, horn-rimmed glasses, and pants that were much too short for him. Behind Kim, she could see her sister Sarah gesturing wildly at her, but Lin had no idea what she was trying to convey.

"Lin!" her mother said excitedly when she caught sight of her daughter. "Guess who made it to dinner tonight? This is Larry—"

Larry? Her supposed setup from a few months ago? Of all the ridiculous coincidences! Not to mention horrendous timing. How could she deal with Stephen, Drew, and her fresh-off-the-boat blind date all at the same time? Lin gaped at her would-be suitor. He seemed nice enough, but he wasn't Lin's type at all. Certainly, he could not have been more different from Drew, if he tried. Or Stephen . . .

Meanwhile, Kim had finally caught sight of Drew. Stopping abruptly, her animated smile immediately flattened out into a thin line. She planted her fists on her hips. "What is going on?" she demanded.

"Nothing, Mom." Lin smiled cheerily. "Are you enjoying Aunt Betty's fried fish balls?"

"Yes, I am." Kim pointed at Drew, undeterred. "But what is going on with you and him?"

"Hi, Mrs. Cho." Drew came over and gave her his sweetest, most sincere smile. "How are you? Good to see you again."

Kim frowned. "So you two dating?"

Lin and Drew looked at each other. This was the moment of truth.

"Mom," Lin began, "I know how you feel about me dating someone who's not Chinese, but I really like Drew and he really likes me, so yes, we're dating."

Kim looked stunned. Poor Larry had a what-have-I-gotten-myself-into expression on his face. Suddenly, Lin had a flashback to when her mother had taken her and her friends to the fortune-teller. Kim had been so worried that Lin would end up with a "white devil"—apparently, her fears had come true.

Meanwhile, in the background was Lin's great-grandmother Ling. Once she caught sight of Drew, she dropped her porcelain spoon and immediately started screaming in Chinese, *"Ah-Yah . . . bok gwai ah!"*

Stephen hurried over to Lin's grandmother to try to calm her down. Drew looked around like he had just walked into some alternate dimension. Lin turned to Aunt Betty, pleading with her to make Ling stop screaming "Oh my goodness, there's a white man!" At the same time, Sarah hastened over to help Stephen, while Larry stood off to one side, looking like he wished he could disappear. In short, it was chaos.

Meanwhile, the rest of the relatives burst into excited Cantonese chatter.

"Who is the white devil?"

"Why did Lin bring him home? What was she thinking?"

"She is a bad daughter. How could she do this to Kim?"

"Is he her boyfriend?"

"Of course not. He is a white devil. He can't be her boyfriend."

"White devils only want one thing—to corrupt good Chinese girls."

Fortunately, Drew didn't understand what they were saying. Unfortunately for Lin, she understood every word. How could her relatives say such awful things? She felt like screaming, lashing out, telling them that they were wrong. But she couldn't. Once again, she had shown herself to be a disappointment, yet another example of how she would never live up to her mother's expectations. . . .

Kim turned to frown at Lin. "Look at the mess you made."

Lin's eyes began to well up.

"I'm sorry to disrupt your family," Drew said. "If you want me to go, I'll go."

"Stop it," Lin cried. "You're not going anywhere. It's about time that my family learns to deal with reality. I'm not going to let them tell me how to live my life. You're with me, and I want everyone to know it."

Unfortunately, Kim did not share her daughter's views. Turning Lin toward her, she snapped, "How could you, Lin? You bring white guy home and scare your *pau pau*."

"Mom!" Lin screamed. "Look, the last thing I want to do is to come here and cause trouble, but you all have to understand that I really like Drew. Just because he's not Asian doesn't mean that he's evil."

"Lin," Drew interrupted, "I'm going to go. I shouldn't be here. I'll call you later. You need to straighten things out with your family."

He gave her a quick kiss on the forehead and left. Lin watched him leave as tears rolled down her cheeks.

AFTER THE fiasco with her family, Lin dreaded seeing Drew. She was sure that he was horrified by the whole scene, convinced that she came from a family of lunatics. He would probably tell her he never wanted to see her again, while she would burst into an embarrassing display of tears.

As it turned out, she didn't have to worry. Because she didn't see Drew the next day or the day after that. Apparently, their office was a lot larger than she realized because he was nowhere to be found. And he didn't even e-mail or call or leave a voice mail.

Finally, he showed up on her doorstep Sunday night. He smiled at her, and when he took her into his arms, Lin couldn't bring herself to say anything about the "incident." They never did speak about it. And while a part of Lin was relieved, the other part of her wondered why.

She was still wondering hours later, as they were lying in her bed in silence. Why couldn't they talk about the episode with her family? With Stephen, her family had been an ever-present topic; if anything, it was Lin who had tried to deflect the conversation away from them, tried to create space between them and the overpowering presence of Kim.

She looked across the pillow at Drew, and for the first time, she noticed that they never really had anything to say to each other in moments like these. It was as if they had both expended all the conversation they had in them to get to this moment, and once they did, there was nothing left.

It didn't matter, Lin decided. He was with her, and that was good enough. Now she just had to get her parents to speak to her again.

A WEEK later, Lin finally had a talk with her parents about Drew over dim sum at the Gum Fung restaurant in Flushing. Taking a deep breath, she calmly sat down with them and told her parents they needed to accept that she was making decisions for her own life.

"I knew that Drew man would be trouble first time I saw him!" Kim declared. "He has shifty look in his eyes—"

"Mom!" Lin threw up her hands. "Have you heard a word I said? I know you don't approve of Drew, but it's my life, and I want to be with him!"

Her parents stared at her, momentarily silenced by her outburst.

"I just love you," Kim said, lowering her voice, "don't want to see my daughter hurt. You know white men like to divorce. . . . I don't want you to go through that."

"I know, Mom," Lin said, "but I can look out for myself. I know you want me to be with someone like Stephen, but I'm an adult now and you have to let me make my own decisions."

Lin's dad, Harry, had always been the quiet father, who no doubt developed this self-defense mechanism after years of marriage to Kim. Although he never said much, Lin always thought of him as the voice of reason in their family.

"Forget it," Harry spoke up. "Just eat some more turnip cakes and finish this dish of chicken feet."

"You're the best, dad." Lin hugged him. "I'm glad that everything is okay."

Lin glanced over at her mother, but Kim was mute.

. . .

"HENRY, IT'S been a rough few weeks," Lin said on the phone to her client, a surgeon at Bellevue. It was the day after dim sum with her parents, and Lin was having one of those no-time-for-coffee kind of mornings. "The market should be fine in the next couple of days. No worries, okay?"

As Lin hung up the phone, Rob knocked on her door.

"Hey, Rob, come on in," she said. "Have a seat. What can I do for you?"

"Not much," he said as he closed the door. "Have a few minutes? I want to talk to you about a couple of things."

"Sure," she said slowly, "something wrong?"

"Well, I guess I should tell you this before we meet with Drew later on," Rob began.

"Okay." Lin nodded uncertainly.

"Lin, I know that since you first started here, you've always expressed an interest in the international development of our company. Well, one of the changes that we're making is that we're trying to give some traders here the chance to work overseas. So I'm offering you a position in London for six months at the headquarters there. It would be a great opportunity for you," he explained.

Lin's mouth dropped open. "Wow, thank you so much for the offer. I don't know what to say. I'm honored, but I don't think I can give you an answer just yet. I mean, this is so sudden."

And yet, even as she babbled on, Lin felt the excitement bubble up inside her. All her life, she'd dreamt of two things: being a millionaire by the time she was thirty—and living in London. She'd always loved London. The tradition, the history, the unique old-world charm so different from the strip malls that she grew up with. She was sixteen when she first visited, and it was still the most exhilarating experience of her life. Besides that, this was her chance to finally see how she measured up against the competition.

"You don't have to decide anything immediately. The offer is there, and I've told my colleagues all about you. When you feel you're ready, please give them a call," Rob said, handing her a piece of paper. "By the way, I'm not going to mention anything to Drew because this should be something that's between us until you make your decision."

"Agreed." She nodded. "Thank you so much, Rob. I'm really grateful about this . . ." She trailed off as she noticed Drew chatting with Lana, the admin girl, outside her office.

Noticing Lin's preoccupation, Rob glanced behind him and chuckled. "He's quite the charmer, that Drew."

Her face froze. "Oh, really?" she asked.

"You must have noticed," Rob remarked. "You two spend a lot of time together."

"Actually, I didn't notice . . . ," she began when Drew entered her office.

"I hope I'm not interrupting this party," he said blithely, oblivious to Lin's frown. "How is everyone today?"

"Great, Drew. I was just saying how popular you've been lately." Rob looked pointedly at Lana outside the office.

Drew chuckled. "Well, I guess I'm just a popular guy. Right, Lin?"

Lin blinked. What kind of a line was that?

"Let me know how it goes." Rob shot Drew a wink. "Anyway, catch you all later and thanks again, Lin."

"Thank you," she responded automatically.

Drew closed the door behind Rob. "Hey, cutie," he said, reaching for her hand. "What's going on?"

"Nothing." She pulled her hand away. "Why don't you go talk to Lana out there?"

"What? What are you talking about?" Drew opened his eyes wide.

"I'm not invisible, you know. I was right here when you practically gloated to Rob about being Mr. Popularity with the ladies."

"Look, I can't help what other people think. You and I are together, but no one can know. You know that. I have to play it as cool as possible." Drew leaned forward. "Look, guys check you out all the time, but I don't give a shit because I know in the end, I have you."

On any other day, Lin might have let the comment slide by. But she couldn't get Rob's words out of her head. "Have me? Am I some kind of prize?" she demanded, her voice rising.

Drew jerked away. He was used to the flirty Lin, the sweet Lin—not this angry woman finding fault with him.

"Where is this coming from, Lin? I don't need this from you first thing in the morning." He scowled. "I'll see you later."

Lin watched miserably as he stormed out of her office.

THE REST of the day was unmitigated torture. Lin tried to focus on her work, but it was a futile task. The thought that she might have lost Drew—she didn't even want to contemplate the possibility. All her life, she'd wanted someone like him—handsome, successful, and most of all, confident. Drew believed he was better than anyone else—and when Lin was with him, she felt like she was better than anyone else, too. Not like she felt when she was with her mother, who never failed to point out how she was lacking in one respect or another.

The worst part, though, was she had absolutely no one to talk to about this—after all, she wasn't exactly on the top of M.J. or Alex's favorites list at the moment.

Still, after a sleepless night tossing and turning, Lin picked up the phone and called the person most likely to forgive her. "J?" she said tentatively. "It's Lin."

There was a pause. "Hey, Lin! What's up?"

Lin exhaled as she heard M.J.'s cheerful voice. Fortunately, M.J. was much more willing than Alex to let bygones be bygones. After a few awkward moments, they were talking like old times, and Lin had poured out the whole story about Drew.

"I don't think I'm a jealous person," Lin said to M.J. as she stared out her window at the city skyline.

"You're not, chickie," M.J. said soothingly. "He just overreacted and didn't know what to do. Men avoid confrontation. You need to talk to him."

"You're right." Lin sighed. "I do. I just think I'm used to talking everything out like I did with Stephen. Deep down, I feel like I don't know how things stand anymore. I think I want a commitment from Drew, but I'm trying to talk myself out of one because I don't want to deal with anything."

"Of course you feel that way, honey. You just got into a fight with a guy you really care about, and you don't want to get hurt."

"Well, it's not just that." Lin hesitated. "I just feel . . . an emptiness in my life right now. I mean, I know I have a good job, and I have a really good life, but still . . ." She took a deep breath. "J, you know how I used to dream about working overseas?"

"How could I not? That was all you could ever talk about for a while. I was going to smack you over the head and buy you a plane ticket to Europe myself." M.J. laughed.

"Well," Lin paused, "I've been offered a job in London, but I haven't made my decision yet."

"Are you serious?" M.J. gasped. "That's amazing! Congratulations! What's holding you back? Drew?"

"No. Well, yes and no. I mean, all of that stuff about Europe was just talk. Now that it's finally happening, I'm not sure what to do . . . I love New York. I love my friends. I love my job. I love my family. And now I have Drew. How can I just leave him without giving him a chance . . . without seeing if we have something together?"

"I understand." M.J.'s tone was sympathetic. "Look, whatever you decide, I know you'll make the right decision."

"Thanks, hon." Lin sighed. "I'm sorry I haven't been in touch. I know you and Alex are annoyed with me."

"It's okay," M.J. replied. "And Alex will be fine. We're just worried about you. Even though we'd really miss you if you went to London, we'll support you one hundred percent, no matter what you decide to do."

Lin smiled. "I know. You're the best friend a girl could have. And I promise I'll make more of an effort to see you guys." She took a deep breath. "I think I'm going to tell Drew about the job offer tonight. I haven't spoken to him all day, and I've been ignoring his phone calls."

"Just talk to him," M.J. urged her. "Everything needs to be out in the open. That's what a real relationship is—well, that's what I'm learning it's all about anyway."

"You're right. Normally, I wouldn't hesitate, but we work together so it makes things a bit tricky. . . ."

LIN ALWAYS thought that the worst thing about a fight with a boyfriend was the waiting. Was there going to be another screaming match? Was it over? Or would there be kissing and making up? As she sat in her office Wednesday morning, she couldn't help wondering. Then there was no more time to ponder as she heard a knock on her door.

"Come in," Lin called as she typed in a trade.

"Hi." Drew appeared in the doorway.

She looked up. "Hi."

Drew closed the door behind him. He walked over to Lin and handed her a rose, which she accepted slowly. "Lin, I acted like an ass, and I'm sorry."

She bit her lip. "You're sorry, huh?"

"Yes." Drew gave her a remorseful look. "I shouldn't have blown up at you like that the other day . . . but you do have to admit that you were acting pretty jealous."

"Well, I have the right to be when my boyfriend is flirting with other women in front of my face," Lin shot back.

"Okay, okay." Drew held up his hands in surrender as he leaned over to give her a light kiss on the lips. "How about we go out for some drinks with people here tonight, then go back to my place and make up?"

"Hmm . . . sounds like a plan, but what's with tonight's gig?" Lin wrinkled her forehead.

"Everyone's going to grab some drinks at Victor's Café for Rick's going-away party. I want you to be there," Drew said.

"I'm swamped, but I'll stop by, I promise." She licked her lips. "I also want to talk to you about something important tonight. It's about my meeting with Rob."

"Okay, no problem. Speaking of which, I have to talk to him now, too." He headed for the door. "I'll catch you later."

As Lin watched him walk out of her office, she relaxed into a smile. That was definitely better than she'd expected it to be. As she smelled her red rose, someone knocked on her door again. A moment later, Krishan poked his head in.

"Hey, Krishan." She smiled. "What's up?"

"Just wanted to let you know that you have a package outside by reception." He nodded toward the flower. "Nice rose, by the way. Did you steal that from Mary Klein's office? Her husband sent her a dozen roses for their anniversary, and she's missing a few."

Lin looked momentarily confused. "Um, no, someone gave this to me."

"Ahhhh . . ." Krishan smiled. "The boyfriend, huh? Very nice. Very nice." He waved good-bye. "All right, I'll catch you later."

AFTER KRISHAN left, Lin sat at her desk for a long while. It was strange, this feeling she had. She should have been thrilled, ecstatic, basking in happiness because all was well with Drew again. Instead, all she felt was a quiet unease. . . .

Stop it! Lin told herself sternly. *Stop looking for trouble, Lin.* She took a deep breath, determined to combat this bout of insecurity. After all, didn't Auntie Lee say she would find love? Well, she definitely loved Drew, and he clearly loved her since he still wanted to be with her after the fiasco with her family and her little meltdown.

Resolve strengthened, she called M.J. to gush about the positive turn of events.

"Well, that's cool," M.J. said, "it's great that you guys patched things up."

"I think I just blew the whole thing out of proportion," Lin sighed. "I was overwhelmed and tired and I just lost it. It's not his fault that all these women flirt with him. Considering how crazy I acted, he was really very understanding. And he was so sweet when we made up!"

"Mm-hmm," M.J. said.

Lin paused. "What's wrong?"

"What do you mean?" her friend asked.

"Because you sound like Alex."

"It's nothing," M.J. said quickly. "It just . . . sounds like you're making excuses for him."

Lin frowned. "Don't be ridiculous. I'm just being supportive. J, you should know that's a huge part of every relationship."

"Right," M.J. said neutrally.

"Look, Drew is a great guy, despite what everyone says. You'll see." And she would do whatever it took to make things work, Lin vowed to herself. Including not going to London.

"SO, DREW, where's Lin and Rob?" Krishan took a sip of his Belvedere on the rocks.

"Rob isn't going to make it, and I think Lin's coming in a little while. Nice tie, by the way." Drew flipped over Krishan's tie to check out the brand.

Krishan swatted his hand away. "Excellent. How is her new boyfriend, by the way?"

Drew jerked to attention as he looked at Krishan strangely. "New boyfriend? What are you talking about?"

"Don't play dumb with me, Mr. Charming. It's not a secret anymore. I know all about it. Lin and I went to college together, and she hasn't been this happy in years. You should have seen her the other day when she came out of her office. She was glowing," Krishan smiled. "By the way, every guy in this office is so envious of you. You get to spend every moment with her."

Drew was stunned but played it cool. How could she have told Krishan? Now the entire office knew. He drained his beer in a single gulp. "How long have you known?" he asked calmly.

"For a few weeks." Krishan frowned as he quickly caught on to Drew's reaction. "What's wrong? You look like you're about to kill a small country."

Drew asked the bartender for two shots of tequila and downed them both. Then he ordered a couple more shots.

"I say we call Lin now," he shouted to all the boys after his fifth shot.

"You don't have to," Krishan said, "she's right here."

"Hey, guys!" Lin smiled as she walked in and gave them all a hug.

As she turned to hug Drew, he pushed her away roughly. Lin was confused but she just turned and ordered herself a drink without saying anything.

"What's wrong with you?" Lin asked him quietly a few minutes later. "Is everything okay?"

"Oh, everything is just dandy." Drew downed his sixth shot. "Actually, I was just telling the boys here how good you were in bed."

Her eyes widened. "What?"

Krishan and all the guys started laughing, thinking that Drew was clearly wasted.

"I don't know what he's talking about," she joked. "How many shots has Mr. Black had here?"

"Stop playing dumb!" he hollered. "How dare you tell everyone in the office about us!"

As his voice rose, conversation around them came to an immediate standstill.

Lin stared at him. She had no idea what had possessed Drew, why he seemed hell-bent on ruining everything. All she knew was that she had to get out of there—immediately.

"Listen, I don't know what kind of stunt you're trying to pull, but I'm leaving," she announced, turning toward the door.

"Hold it!" Drew said. "Before you go, I just want to let you know that no one does a 'meeting' like you do."

Lin froze. She couldn't believe her ears. Fighting back tears, she forced herself to turn around and face Drew as her whole office watched them.

"You know what, asshole?" she yelled. "I don't know what you've been drinking, but I never, and I repeat, never, told anyone about us. You, on the other hand, obviously can't keep your big mouth shut."

"Oh yeah? Then can you explain to me why Krishan knows about your new boyfriend?"

"He knows because I told him I had a new boyfriend, but I never told him that it was you. I'm not the one who's a moron," she said, silent tears rolling down her cheeks.

Drew stared at her, stunned. Unable to stand the whispers and glances around them anymore, Lin turned and fled.

Krishan walked up to Drew. "Man, you're a sack of shit. She never told me her new guy was you. And it was *you* who stole Mary Klein's roses, wasn't it?"

Drew's mouth opened but no words came out.

twenty-four

LIN COULDN'T breathe.

Somehow, she'd gotten herself home, slammed the door behind her, and collapsed in a heap on the floor. How could she have let this happen? How could she have been so wrong? Lin clutched her head in her hands and started rocking back and forth, her breath coming in short, ragged sobs.

"Oh my God," she whispered, "what have I done?"

She knew the answer, of course. She'd taken her wonderful life, her super-successful career, her supportive family and friends—and trashed them all for an obnoxious jerk.

There was only one thing to do. Lin reached into her bag and yanked out her cell phone.

"OPEN UP!" M.J. banged on the door. "I know you're in there!"

Lin opened the door in tears. "Leave me alone. I want to curl up and die right now."

"No, you don't." M.J. followed her into her apartment. "The Lin Cho I know is not going to let some asshole get her down."

"How could he humiliate me like that in front of everyone from work? And after all I've gone through to get my parents to accept him," she sobbed. "I will never understand."

At that moment, the doorbell rang. M.J. opened the door—it was Alex. Lin bit her lip. It had been weeks since they last spoke. . . .

Alex stepped in. "Oh, Lin," she said as she gave her friend a big hug. Lin's face cleared as she relaxed in her friend's embrace.

"Do you want me to kick his ass for you?" M.J. asked.

Lin smiled through her tears. "Oh, guys . . . I feel like such an idiot."

"Don't say that," Alex said. "You know that's not true."

"I have to," Lin cried. "You guys warned me—but did I listen? No—even though I knew what kind of guy Drew was." She wiped a tear from her eye. "I knew he was bad news. I knew—I knew he could be a jerk," she sniffled. "I saw all the signs, but I just . . . I guess I just didn't think he could be a jerk to me."

"Honey, honey." M.J. stroked her hair. "You were in love. We've all been there."

Lin shook her head. "This is different," she cried. "I took him home. I even ditched you guys for him!"

Alex put an arm around Lin. "Forget about that. It's in the past now. Look, what can we do to help?"

Lin looked up at her friends gratefully. After all she'd done, she wouldn't have blamed them for turning a deaf ear, and yet, here they were. That set her up for a new round of tears.

"I just want all of this to go away," Lin sobbed. "I don't want to be part of that world anymore."

"Then make a fresh start," M.J. said. "Take that job in London!"

"You got a job offer in London?" Alex exclaimed. "That's so awesome. You better take it before I do."

"Yeah, it's—it's a six-month gig. It would be amazing, but—"

"But what?" M.J. persisted. "But you can stay here and look at that asshole every day and have the whole office know about your sex life? You should go, explore the world, and see what's out there."

"Do you really think so?" Lin asked, her eyes moist.

"We both do," Alex said firmly. "Maybe something good can come out of all this."

"Maybe." Lin bit her lip. "I feel really awful about how I've been acting lately." She swallowed hard. "I know," she sniffled, "I know I've been a terrible friend. You guys were so patient with me, and I—I treated your friendship like it was nothing." She hung her head. "I'm so sorry," she whispered, "I just hope you guys can forgive me."

Her friends were silent. Lin stared down at the carpet, afraid to look up. She didn't blame her friends if they didn't want to have anything to do with her, but she was also terrified of losing them. She'd failed everyone: her friends, her family, but most of all herself. With that track record, she'd be lucky if they'd ever want her back.

Finally, after what seemed like an eternity, she looked up at them. All she saw was kindness.

"Don't cry—of course we forgive you." M.J. threw her arms around Lin and hugged her tightly.

"M.J.'s right." Alex put her arms around them both. "We'll always be here for you—no matter what."

Lin smiled. "Thanks, guys," she said tearfully. "What am I going to do without you in London?"

"You're going to have a great time," Alex said firmly. "And you're going to dazzle everyone over there with how great a stockbroker you are."

"That's right," M.J. added. "You've always got us, but this is a once-in-a-lifetime opportunity."

For the first time that day, Lin's face lit up. "Wow, me and London?" she mused. "It really could be something."

AS LIN set foot into the office two days later, she couldn't help but think of the times in college when she got really drunk, woke up in some guy's bed, and then had to face his roommates in the morning. At this very moment, Lin felt the same way about facing everyone at work and worst of all—Drew.

"Good morning, Lana." Lin forced a smile as she walked by reception.

"Good morning," Lana sneered, narrowing her eyes. "You don't look so good. Bad night?"

"I'm fine." Lin walked away quickly—and right smack into Tom Wexler.

"Hey, Lin." Tom leered. "I had no idea you were such a naughty girl."

"Shove it, Tom," she snapped as she strode off.

Behind her, she could feel his eyes boring into her back. Tom had always been a sleaze, but previously his innuendo had always been tinged with respect. The way he'd looked at her today, though . . . she could still feel him mentally undressing her without even the slight hint of pretense.

Get a grip, Lin thought as she made her way to her office. *Don't let them get to you.*

But no sooner did she have that thought than she turned the corner—and saw Mark Shin. He was busy looking at a sheaf of papers in his hand, but just as Lin started to tiptoe past him, he looked up and saw her.

She stopped, caught. "Uh, hi, Mark," she mumbled.

For a moment, he just stared at her, no doubt thinking how she had disgraced the Asian race by her affair with the "white devil." Then, without saying a word, he walked off.

It was strange, Lin thought. All that time when Mark was chasing after her, she had wanted nothing more than to be rid of him. But now . . . seeing him look at her as if she were last night's trash, Lin felt herself yearning for anything—a glance, an understanding smile—from him.

Still, that was nothing compared with her meeting with Rob. For the first five minutes she was in his office, he didn't even acknowledge her as he chatted on the phone and pounded out e-mails. Finally, after an eternity, he put the phone down.

"Rob—," Lin began. She'd practiced this speech ever since she'd called Rich Benjamin to accept the offer the day before, and yet, now that the time had come, the words died in her throat. What could she really say to make this better? They both knew this world they lived and worked in remained a male-dominated vat of misogyny. It wasn't enough for a woman to be successful and hardworking; the women who survived the boiler room knew that they had to be twice as tough, twice as good as their male counterparts. There was no room for error, no cushion for slipups—Lin knew this, and she'd always prided herself on being able to ride the top echelons with the boys. Rob had seen her ability, had rolled the dice on throwing his support behind a twenty-something Asian woman—and now, Lin had crushed both their hopes. With one slip of judgment, she had gone from top-flight, universally respected power broker to just another trader's floozy.

"I'm sorry, Rob," she said finally.

Rob didn't look at her as he shuffled the papers on his desk. "Rich Benjamin is one of my closest friends, and a really good guy. He'll take care of you there."

Lin nodded. She tried to think of something to say, anything to alleviate the awkward tension. . . .

"Thank you, Rob."

He looked up at last, and in his eyes, Lin saw disappointment and sadness. Rob held out his hand. "Have a safe flight, Lin."

Somehow, Lin managed to step forward and shake his hand limply. She escaped to the door and shut it gently behind her.

Standing there in the hallway, Lin felt herself start to tear up. She was hunched over sniveling when footsteps sounded behind her.

"Lin?"

She turned. Thankfully, it was Krishan.

Upon seeing her face, he quickly steered her into an empty office nearby. "Come on, Lin." He gave her a fierce hug. "Don't let those bastards get the best of you."

Lin sniffled. "I'm trying, but it's so hard, Krishan. It's bad enough that I have Lana looking at me like I'm trailer trash, and

Mark acting like he never knew me, but Rob—Krishan, you don't know what it was like with Rob. He could barely even look me in the eye!"

Krishan looked at her gently. "This whole thing sucks. It's not your fault that Drew can't keep his mouth shut."

"I can't even think about him," Lin cried. "Hopefully, I can leave this place without seeing him."

Krishan laid a hand on her shoulder. "Listen to me, Lin Cho. You are stronger than Drew Black. You are stronger than those jackasses out there. You are stronger than this whole office."

Lin wiped her eyes. "I don't know . . . this is the only job I've ever known. I'm not going to know anyone in London. It'll be like starting all over again."

"And you're going to love it," he declared. "You're going to show those Brits how it's done by the big boys. Or girls. And that's an order from your captain."

That finally got a smile out of Lin. "Thanks, Krishan."

GIVEN THE miserable day that she'd already had, Lin had only one wish: to get out of the office without seeing Drew.

After saying good-bye to Krishan, Lin headed to her office and closed the door behind her. Krishan had already packed up most of her stuff the day before after she told him she'd accepted the London offer, so she just had to make a quick check to be sure she wasn't leaving anything behind.

She found the note and the bouquet of roses on her chair. It read: "Dear Lin, I feel like such an asshole. I am so sorry for everything and hope that we can still talk things over. I miss you, Drew."

Lin suddenly felt tearful again. She took a deep breath and looked outside her window. She had to keep telling herself that she would be in London in no time. Then her heart started racing when she heard a knock on the door.

"Hi." Drew entered tentatively. "How are you?"

Lin forced a bright smile. "I'm doing great. Going to London."

"I know. I heard. Big decision, huh?"

Lin nodded wordlessly. There was an awkward moment of silence.

Then Drew closed the door. "Lin, I'm so sorry. I really am. I'm the biggest jerk in the world." He looked into her eyes. "I'm going to miss you so much. We really had something special."

"Look, Drew," she managed to say, "nobody is sadder than me about what happened. But we had nothing. You love the idea of me. You loved that everyone at work was jealous of you when you were with me. But you don't really care about me, because you never would have said such horrible things and embarrassed me the way that you did."

Drew swallowed. "Come on, Lin. That's not true. I had to have you the moment I saw you. It was love at first sight."

"No, Drew, it was lust at first sight. You had to have me, and once you did, there was nothing left." She blinked away the tears in her eyes. "I'm sorry, but I have to leave. I mean, do you honestly think that I could work here with all these people knowing about us?"

"Lin." Drew actually looked sorry. "How can I make you change your mind?"

Lin stared at him. Once upon a time, this would have been all she ever wanted: Drew willing to do anything to be with her. But as she looked at his handsome, familiar features, all she could hear were the words he'd said to her the night before—words so hurtful that just remembering them made her physically cringe.

"You can't," she whispered. "Good-bye, Drew."

She grabbed her purse and the box on her desk, then jetted out of her office without a backward glance.

SEEING DREW had been hard, just as Lin knew it would be. But it was even tougher telling her parents the next night.

"What?" Kim gasped. "You going to London?"

Lin took a deep breath. "I know this is a shock, but it's a big step up for me. Only a couple people get this opportunity. I can't turn it down."

"But you going to be alone in London!" Kim exclaimed.

"I'll be fine," Lin reassured her. "The company's found me a fantastic apartment, and I've already started researching all the London neighborhoods. You'll be happy—there's supposed to be a great supermarket right around the corner from my apartment."

Kim frowned. "That not enough."

"Look, I know you guys don't want me to go," Lin sighed, "but I wish you wouldn't make this more difficult for me. I have to go—I really have to go."

There was a long pause, then her dad spoke up. "Go, Lin," he said. "This wonderful honor. You accept it."

Lin smiled at her father gratefully. Somehow, he always came through for her. Which was why he wasn't the one who worried her. She turned to look at her mother. "Mom?"

Kim sat down heavily on a chair, suddenly looking old and tired. "London far away. Who take care of you there?"

Lin looked at her mother, and suddenly, it was like a veil had been lifted. For the past fifteen years, all Lin could see and hear were the lectures, the reprimands, the ceaseless murmuring. Now, for the first time, she realized her mother was scared—scared about what would happen to Lin and scared of losing her.

She reached down and hugged her mother tightly. "I'll be okay, Mom. I promise."

WHILE SAYING good-bye to her parents was hard, it was nothing compared with saying good-bye to her girls.

The evening before Lin's departure, M.J. and Alex took Lin out for a glamorous night on the town. They went to her favorite restaurant, Tao, and ended the evening with cocktails at Lotus.

For most of the evening, they gossiped and chattered away about anything and everything. Alex talked about some big case she and Brady were working on, M.J. told them about Jagger's clothing line being launched in some stores in the West Village. Even Ming dropped by to say good-bye.

"Just remember," he instructed before he left. "Stick with the fish and stay away from the Chinese food."

Lin smiled at him. Even though Ming had been M.J.'s friend first, he'd become like a surrogate brother to all of them over the years. "Aren't you going to tell me that this is what comes from being with white guys?"

Ming just hugged her. "You'll have a great time."

Later, as the evening drew on, and things started to come to their inevitable close, Lin felt increasingly tearful. "Oh, guys," she sighed, "maybe I shouldn't do this!"

Her friends stared at her.

"What are you talking about, Lin?" Alex touched her hand. "You have to do this!"

"You'll be living in a fabulous city," M.J. added. "You're going to have so much fun there!"

"But I won't be having fun with you guys," she said. "It won't be the same."

"Of course it will," Alex assured her. "We'll e-mail and talk on the phone all the time."

"Yeah," M.J. chimed in, "you can tell us about all your exploits and make us crazy with envy!"

Lin laughed despite herself. She knew that her friends were trying hard to make her feel better. And even though she had no doubt that they would write and call all the time, she also knew it wouldn't be the same. If she had a bad day, she wouldn't be able to complain to her friends over a drink. She couldn't count on getting the latest, up-to-the-minute scoop on whatever was going on in their lives. She wouldn't be able to join their dinners, late-night cocktails, their Saturday morning brunches. Lin felt as if a part of her was being severed, cut off forever.

"You're going to love London," M.J. declared. "You've always wanted to go there."

"Yeah, but there's a difference between wanting to do something and actually having to do it," Lin said sadly.

LIN KNEW it wasn't going to be easy.

As the moment of her departure drew near, she became increasingly conscious of how much she depended on her friends, her family, her mom. Even when she went to college, she could count on having M.J. there. Certainly, she'd relied on all of them now to get her through this ordeal—helping her pack, sublet her apartment, and take care of the myriad details that she would never have been able to handle in such a short time period. But now, there was going to be an entire span of ocean between her entire support network . . . and her.

The farewells at the airport were the hardest part. Lin's father patted her awkwardly then stood silently by her side as Kim alternated between lecturing, scolding, and crying. As for Alex and M.J., they managed to keep up a cheerful chatter until it was time for Lin to leave—at which point, they both looked suspiciously shiny-eyed as they hugged her good-bye at the security checkpoint. Standing there in her friends' embrace, all Lin could think about was how she'd be able to weather the next year without them.

Still, Lin felt a sense of relief as her plane lifted off and away from New York that night. She loved her city, but at that moment, it had Drew's imprint all over it—the restaurants where they'd shared candlelight dinners, the park trails they'd jogged, the stores where they'd spent huge chunks of their salaries. Leaving all that for a completely foreign city was exactly what she needed.

Seven hours later, the jet landed at Heathrow. Carrying a messenger bag and sporting a black blazer, jeans, and sneakers, Lin exited the plane and walked through customs. She smiled as she heard the accents in the airport, saw the policemen in their bobby hats, and experienced the familiar-yet-unfamiliar feel of London.

Once she was in the baggage claim, though, her smile faded. A mass of unfamiliar faces confronted her, smiling, calling out greetings, holding out welcome banners—but not for Lin.

"Are you Lin Cho?"

She looked up. A handsome, ruddy, reddish-blond-haired man was smiling at her.

"Um, yeah," she said. "And you are—?"

"Ned Stone." He held out a hand. "Your new colleague and current welcoming committee."

Lin smiled and shook his hand. "It's nice to meet you. Actually, it's really nice to meet you. I was just wondering how I was going to get myself to the apartment."

"Well, wonder no more. Rich Benjamin sent me to make sure we got you to corporate housing safe and sound. So, to that end . . . let's get your bags."

"Sounds good to me!" Lin followed Ned toward the baggage claim area.

"And once we get you to your place, we'll go lift a pint at this pub I know nearby and get to know each other," he added.

Lin hesitated. "Look, Ned," she said slowly, "I just want you to know right off the bat that I'm not really looking for any kind of involvement. . . ."

Ned looked at her, his brow furrowed. Then his forehead cleared. "Oh, wait," he chuckled, "you got it all wrong." He held up his left hand and wiggled the ring finger—where a bright gold band gleamed.

Lin covered her mouth. "Omigosh," she gasped, "I am so sorry. I am such an idiot—"

Ned laughed and put an arm around her. "Don't worry about it. In fact, you'll meet my wife at the pub. She's a broker, too, so you guys will have a lot in common."

Lin smiled. "I would really like that."

twenty-five

LIN LOVED London.

She loved that she could walk to work along the Thames in the mid-August haze. She loved that she could watch *Romeo and Juliet* on the floor of the Globe by moonlight. She loved that she could spend an entire Saturday exploring Harrods and never manage to see everything. More than anything, she loved that there was an entire ocean between her and Drew Black.

It wasn't until now that Lin realized how much he'd influenced her everyday life. Working with him and dating him at the same time had imposed an omnipresent strain on her that she hadn't noticed until it was gone. Not only did Lin have to deal with the pressures of work, but she was also constantly on edge about their romance being discovered. Not to mention her worries about keeping Drew interested and away from other girls.

In comparison, being in the London office was a relief. The only thing anyone there knew about her was her reputation as a stockbroker. Lin was able to walk the halls freely and not have to worry about whispers following her. Her new boss and colleagues accepted her readily, while e-mails from Alex and M.J. provided a welcome touchstone any time Lin felt a touch of uncertainty or self-doubt.

Now that the pressure was gone, Lin was amazed at how relaxed she felt, how clearly she was able to think without the specter of Drew around every corner.

"OKAY, I'LL take that in pink," Lin pointed to the cotton-candy-colored Kate Spade straw purse in the window. "And if you have the wallet that goes along with it, I'll take that, too."

It was Saturday, and Lin was spending it in her favorite way imaginable: shopping at Harrods. There was something comforting about the brightly lit display cases, the endless stream of chattering tourists, the confectionery-like array of consumer goods before her. It was exactly the kind of sensory overload Lin liked—the kind that distracted her enough so that she wouldn't have to think.

Because Lin had a lot of time to think in London. She had time to think as she trudged home alone after a tough day at work. She had time to think as she ate takeout fish and chips in her empty apartment. And she had time to think while having a cup of tea by herself in the corner café as she watched a group of girlfriends gossip together at the next table.

Mainly, she thought about how she'd gotten to this point: how she'd decided to pursue a romance that everyone in her life—her family, her best friends—had warned her about. She didn't know why Drew had been so irresistible—or why someone like Stephen had been so repulsive. Now that she was a million miles away from him, Lin found herself thinking about Stephen quite a bit. She thought about how he treated her like gold, better than she ever deserved. She thought about how he was always there when she needed him, whether it was to cater to some whim that Kim had or to pick up her laundry because she was stuck at work. More than anything, she thought about how she never had to worry whether she was good enough for him.

"Here you go." The sales clerk handed Lin a giant shopping bag.

Lin shifted her other two bags onto her left arm as she tried to juggle her latest purchase with the unwieldy hatbox at her right elbow. Even though her shopping habits weren't any less exorbitant back home, she always had one of her friends with her to help. M.J. might shy away from all the haute couture, but she was always willing to offer a hand with Lin's bags.

"Ma'am, is everything okay?" The salesclerk peered at her from behind the counter. "Will you be able to carry all of that by yourself?"

Lin steadied the box and bags in her arms. She took a deep breath and straightened herself. "Yeah," she said, "I've got to."

As she staggered her way to the exit, Lin flashed back to her visit to the fortune-teller. Auntie Lee might have been wrong about her finding love, but she'd been right about Lin being lucky. She was lucky that London had fallen in her lap and that Rob had still been willing to let her go. Lucky that her family was still talking to her even if they disapproved of some of her choices. And lucky that her friends were still willing to take her back even after she'd abandoned them. Lin knew that there weren't that many second chances in life, and she was determined to make the most of this one.

. . .

"HEY, LIN, want another Guinness?"

Lin glanced up. It had been three weeks since she arrived in London, and her new colleagues had convened for a little after-work get-together at the pub around the corner. Ned was at the bar, calling out to her and nodding toward the empty mug in his hand. Lin shook her head with a smile and pointed to her own half-full mug. She was glad to have met Ned. He was kind, sweet, and absolutely in love with his wife, who, by the way, was pretty great in her own right.

"Okay," Ned slid into the seat beside her, "I know you're on a hiatus from guys, but I think the bartender has a soft spot for you. You sure you couldn't chat him up for a few free pints?"

Lin just looked at him. "Ned."

He nodded. "I know, I know. And can I tell you again how impressed I am with how you've handled this whole situation?"

She blushed. "I was really worried you wouldn't respect me anymore after you found out what happened."

"Are you kidding me?" he demanded. "This job is hard enough. I'm just glad I'm not a woman who has to deal with the wankers of this profession—"

Before he could finish his sentence, Lin heard a noise. They both looked up to see a Burberry-clad blond Prince William looka-like smiling down at them.

"Ned, who's your lovely friend here?"

"Oh, Ian. Uh, Lin, Ian works in the funds department. Ian, Lin came over from New York—"

"I know who Lin is." Ian leaned down and took her hand in his. "I've had my eye on her since the first day she walked through our doors."

From the corner of her eye, Lin saw Ned looking at her, but all she did was smile politely at Ian. "It's nice to meet you."

"Not as nice as it is for me to meet you." Ian flashed her a charming smile. "So, tell me, what can I do to convince you to get out of here and go somewhere quiet with me?"

Lin raised an eyebrow. Next to her, Ned sighed.

"That's very flattering," she said, slowly withdrawing her hand, "but I'm actually about to head home soon."

Ian shrugged. "Okay, your loss."

As he strolled away, Lin turned to see Ned smiling at her.

"What?" she said, as she pulled on her coat.

"Nothing." Ned shook his head. "I just find it hard to believe you ever had a designer suit addiction."

Lin chuckled as she got up. "Good night, Ned." And with that, she headed home.

SUNDAYS WERE the loneliest.

Even though she'd sworn to make the most of this chance at redemption, it was still hard being by herself. Lin didn't realize until now how much she missed the Sunday schedule: dim sum with her friends and dinner with her parents. She was so used to it that she had come to take the whole tradition for granted. It had always been yet another burden imposed by Chinese tradition and the expectations of her family.

Once in London, though, Lin found herself yearning for those Chinese Sundays. She missed the easy comfort that came from being around her family—listening to her sister's chatter, her grandmother's stories, Kim's lecture of the day. She missed the expectation that she was supposed to be somewhere, and the knowledge that her absence would be felt and the topic of much discussion and concern. More than anything, she missed knowing that her Sunday would be filled with noise and activity and her family's unconditional love.

"Hi, Mom," Lin said into the receiver.

"Lin!" Kim's voice reverberated over the phone. "What going on with you? Why haven't you called this week?"

"I'm sorry," Lin apologized. "I've been really busy with work and settling in and figuring out where everything was—"

"No excuse," Kim interrupted her. "Are you eating? Are you getting enough sleep? Are you taking your vitamins? Those people in England have bad teeth. I see pictures. You make sure you drinking milk and eating your fruits and vegetables—"

As Kim's voice droned on, Lin leaned back against the wall and smiled.

Date: Thursday, November 15
To: M.J.; Alex
From: Lin

Hey girls!
London has been amazing. I can't believe it's been almost five months already! I wish you were sitting here with me in my office right now. The Tower of London is right across the river from me—can you believe it? It's the most breathtaking sight. The people here have been really nice, and I've made some good friends. My new coworkers are great (we go out to the pub all the time!), and my boss here, Rich Benjamin, has been a real mentor to me. Mostly though, I've been spending a lot of time on my own—sightseeing, going to the theater, taking walks along the Thames. It's actually kind of nice. Been thinking a lot about life and what I really want . . . mostly just trying to be happy with myself first. Until I do that, I don't think I'll be ready to be with someone else . . .

After doing a quick scan of the message, Lin took a deep breath and pressed SEND. Writing an e-mail wasn't even remotely close to satisfying, but until she could see her friends in person, this would have to do.

"Lin!" Ned knocked on the door. "You coming out with us to the pub tonight?"

"Not tonight," she replied, typing rapidly. "But have a pint for me."

"Okay," he said as he strolled off, "see you tomorrow."

As Lin shut down her computer, she looked outside and watched the lights turn on in the Tower of London. She smiled, a real smile from the inside. There would be no pub-crawling for her. She had a special visitor to see tonight.

.   .   .

AFTER RIDING the tube for half an hour, Lin was finally standing in Heathrow, craning her neck at the stream of disembarking passengers. Just as she was checking her watch, a familiar voice rang out above the crowd.

"Lin!"

Lin whirled around and saw a sight that brought a smile to her lips: her mother Kim making her way through the crowd, dragging three suitcases that probably weighed more than she did.

"Mom!" Lin ran over to give her a kiss and to help with her bags.

"Look at you—face pale, so skinny, hair like bird's nest. Good thing I bring you some ginseng tea. I need some myself—that was terrible flight," Kim complained. "Food bad, people noisy—"

As she launched into one of her patented rants about the plane and the terrible things she'd been forced to endure, Lin felt a sudden surge of affection for her mother. Kim would never be June Cleaver, but looking at her now, Lin realized just how much she'd missed having her mother fuss over her.

Leaning forward to hug Kim, she whispered, "I'm glad you're here, Mom."

"SO YOU like London?" Kim asked.

It was Friday night, and Lin and Kim were sitting in a little café near Piccadilly Circus, fresh from spending the evening at the theater. Even though they hadn't had time to order any food, her mother had already managed to cover her feelings about the chilly weather and the exorbitant London prices in the short time since they were seated.

Lin sipped her water. "London is good. It's been really nice living here. But don't worry, Mom, I'm not planning on moving here permanently."

"Did I say anything?" she asked. "I just want you happy."

"I know." Lin studied her glass. "Mom, I have to tell you something. You were right about Drew. He was bad news. I just didn't want to see it."

As the words left her lips, she lowered her eyes and waited for her mother to launch into her triumphant I-told-you-so speech. To her shock, it never came.

"Lin." Kim gazed at her sadly. "I'm sad what happened with Drew. I don't like him, but you did. I didn't want you hurt. Do you understand?"

Lin nodded slowly. "I do now. I was just so determined to prove you wrong about him."

"Why?" Kim frowned.

"Because . . . because . . ." Lin couldn't quite bring herself to say it.

"Because what?" Kim asked.

Lin bit her lip. "Because, Mom, you tell me every minute of my life how I'm doing everything wrong."

Her mother stared at her for a moment. Then she did exactly what Lin knew she would do—she completely poohed-poohed the entire notion. "Don't be ridiculous." Kim waved the idea off. "I don't do that. I just look out for you."

"Yes," Lin said patiently, "you look out for me by telling me how I'm always doing something wrong."

Kim leaned forward. "When?" She squinted at Lin. "When do I do that?"

"All the time! Like with guys. Maybe if you weren't always pushing Stephen on me, I wouldn't have been so quick to get together with Drew."

"What's wrong with Stephen?" Her mother shook her head. "I never understand you, Lin. Stephen is a nice boy with good job and good manners. What's so wrong with that?"

Lin opened her mouth to argue and closed it. What indeed was wrong with that? Once upon a time, a nice boy with a good job and good manners was the last thing Lin wanted. She wanted excitement, a challenge, someone who wasn't tailor-made for her mother. But now, sitting here in London almost half a year after the whole Drew chapter of her life, Lin suddenly began to find the idea of a nice, normal boy pretty appealing.

"I don't know," she mumbled, staring down at her tea.

"Lin—" Her mother reached out to tip her chin up. "—did you not like Stephen because of me?"

Lin knew the answer, of course, had known it all her life. Because, like Rome, all roads led back to Kim. "Yes," she conceded finally.

"But why?" Kim looked genuinely confused. "Is so bad if I like him?"

Lin shook her head. "No, Mom, it's not. It's just that . . . I don't want to be you."

The moment the words left her lips, Lin winced. That had come out sounding terrible, all wrong, not at all the way it had sounded in her head.

Indeed, Kim was looking at her with a hurt that Lin had never seen in her before. "So," she said, "you don't want to be like me."

"No, that's not what I meant," Lin groaned. "I mean, it is, but . . ." She started again. "Mom, you've always told me the truth. You told me how when you were growing up, you wanted nothing more than to be a movie star in Hong Kong. But then you got married, even though you didn't want to do it."

Kim frowned. "And?"

Lin took a deep breath. "And you regretted it for the rest of your life."

There was a long moment of silence.

"This is why you get involved with that Drew?" Kim asked.

Lin hesitated then nodded slowly. "A little. I mean, I liked him for who he was, too, but maybe part of it was that he wasn't someone you would have chosen for me. Mom, I see how you get when you talk about what you could have been. I don't want to be like that. I don't want to look back years from now and wish I had lived my life differently."

"Stop!" Kim said. "Stop that. Who said I want my life to be different? I have good life, good daughters. Nothing wrong with that."

Lin rolled her eyes. "Oh, come on, Mom. You and I both know that if you could live your life over, you wouldn't have chosen this life. You wouldn't have chosen us."

And there it was—she'd said it. The thought that had haunted her all these years, that had informed her every decision, that had ruled how she lived her life . . .

After what seemed like an eternity, Lin looked up. "I'm sorry, Mom—"

"No, I sorry." Kim's gaze was filled with sadness. "I sorry because I failed you."

Lin creased her forehead. "What are you talking about—?"

"If I was a good mother," she said slowly, "you wouldn't think this."

This couldn't be her mom talking, Lin thought. She couldn't ever recall a time when Kim had admitted to being wrong.

"Maybe when I was girl, I wanted to be actress, but that was a long time ago. When you get older, you learn more—you see things differently," she explained. "I know what is important in life now. Not being a movie star. What important is my daughters—nothing else."

Lin looked at her mother, and suddenly saw herself. For so long, she'd felt like the prodigal child, convinced that she would never be good enough, would never be able to compensate for Kim's lost ambitions. It had never occurred to her that Kim had been young and naïve once, too, consumed with girlish fantasies. Like her, Lin, too, had learned what was important in life. It had taken a broken heart, a near-career-ending disaster, and a move across the Atlantic, but she could finally see what was real—and what was a mirage. Suddenly tearful, she reached over and hugged her mother.

Kim held her tightly. Then, suddenly she pulled back, cupped Lin's chin in her hand, and gazed at her intently. "You good, smart girl, Lin. I'm proud of you. Why you don't see that?"

Lin smiled through her tears. "I guess I just didn't want to be a failure," she admitted. "I didn't want to be another one of your disappointments."

Kim shook her head. "You could never be disappointment, Lin. That stuff about Hong Kong—your auntie Betty always say I talk too much nonsense. Yes, before, I wish I went to Hong Kong. But now I look at you and your sisters, and I know I did the right thing."

Lin glanced up, and for the first time she could remember, she suddenly felt free, light, as if a tremendous weight had been lifted off her shoulders.

EVEN THOUGH there were times when her stay in London seemed like an eternity, Lin found the end came sooner than she thought. After six months, her rotation was up, and it was time to return to the States. Her last week in London was consumed with furious, last-minute shopping for gifts at Harrods, one more show at the theater, and a visit to Wimbledon. Her coworkers threw her a going-away party her last night in London, and unlike that night at Victor's Café with Drew, this evening was filled only with happiness. As she stood there in the pub, hoisting one last pint with Ned and his wife, Lin suddenly realized that she really was going to miss London.

Saying good-bye was the hardest. Standing at Heathrow again with Ned, Lin couldn't help but shed a tear. "Thanks for everything, Ned," Lin said sincerely. "I was so nervous about being here by myself, but you and your wife really made me feel at home."

"It was our pleasure," Ned said warmly. "Come back and visit, okay?"

Lin smiled. "That's a promise."

As she boarded the plane, Lin thought about her time in London. Professionally, the experience had been invaluable. Not only was she now well-versed in foreign markets, but she was also on a first-name basis with countless London CEOs. Plus, she'd fulfilled her lifelong dream of matching wits with her English counterparts—and found that she measured up pretty well. But most important, she'd had time to evaluate her life, ponder her decisions, and figure out what exactly it was she wanted. It was only now that she felt healed, whole, and strong enough to face New York again.

. . .

WORKING AT the New York Stock Exchange and living in TriBeCa, Lin strolled down the street with a different attitude. It had been a month since she'd moved back to New York. Knowing that she could never go back to Merrill Lynch, she'd accepted an offer from the Exchange once her London rotation was up. Now, back in the same town that had once caused her so much heartbreak, she truly felt like she was living a whole new life. In a way, coming back to New York City was like living in a new city in Europe. In the end, Lin wasn't sure if the city itself was all that different—maybe it was just the way she saw it these days.

As she walked up Fifth Avenue and into Central Park to meet her girls for a little ice-skating, she hummed to herself, drinking in the snow-covered trees, the crisp, winter air, the laughing children building snowmen on the Great Lawn. Life was good.

That was when she saw an attractive, familiar-looking man standing near the entrance to Wollman Rink.

"Lin!" Drew beamed as he came up to her. "You're a hard woman to track down. I had to do a lot of calling around before I found out where you were."

Looking at him, Lin was flooded with a sudden torrent of emotion. All the old feelings came back in a rush. "Drew—" Lin's heart beat wildly. "I'm doing great. How are you? Oh my gosh, it's been over half a year."

"I know. You still look great, like you always did. What have you been up to?"

"I work at the Stock Exchange now," Lin said. "What are you doing?"

"That sounds awesome. I'm still at Merrill Lynch. But I'm assistant vice president at the branch now."

"Wow, good for you." Lin smiled. "You must be psyched."

"I am, I am . . . I can't believe it's really you. You know, I sent you a few e-mails when you were in London, but you never wrote me back," Drew said hesitantly.

Lin shrugged. "Well, you know how it is."

Drew's face fell. He stared at her, clearly stunned that Lin was not falling at his feet.

"Well," she said quickly, "it was really nice running into you. Take care of yourself, okay?"

"Lin, wait." Drew stared at her, still waiting for the inevitable invitation. "Don't . . . don't you think this is weird?"

"Weird?" she asked.

Drew sighed, his shoulders slumped. "Lin, don't you think it means anything that I went to all this trouble to find you?"

For a minute, Lin didn't know what to say. So she'd finally gotten him to cave first—but now what? He still looked wonderful—if anything, the passage of time had only served to make him more handsome, more sophisticated and mature. And there was still that old chemistry between them—even now, Lin couldn't deny the attraction. Part of her wanted to throw her arms around him, to throw caution to the wind. But then there was the rest of her telling her to stay strong, reminding her about that awful night at the bar, and forbidding her to undo all the hard work she'd done to get her life back on track. In the end, she did the only thing she could do.

"Look, Drew, I'm not going to lie to you. I still think about you a lot." She paused. "But our time together . . . our time together has passed."

Drew looked stunned. "Lin, I told you that I was truly sorry for everything. I don't know what else I can do."

"There isn't anything to do, Drew. Things are just different now. I'm different now. So are you. Maybe we just can't be different together anymore." Adjusting her bag on her shoulder, Lin took one last look into his eyes. "Take care of yourself, Drew."

And with that, Lin walked away from Drew and from her past. In the end, it turned out that the fortune-teller was wrong. She hadn't ended up with Drew. But she *was* lucky—lucky to have her friends and her self back.

Her girls were waiting for her at the rink.

Alex could tell immediately that something was up. "What?" she demanded. "What happened?"

Lin laughed. "I guess I really am an open book." She took a deep breath. "I just ran into Drew on the way over here."

Her friends both gasped. M.J. put a hand on Lin's arm. "You all right?" she asked, concern etched on her face.

Lin smiled at her friends. "Yeah," she said, "I really am."

And she was. Drew would always possess a small part of her heart, but she was ready for bigger and better things. She was ready for the rest of her life.

lunar new year

Gun Hai Pat Choi

Come one, come all!
You're cordially invited to the annual
Lunar New Year Festival on February 18th
at the Cho residence located on
88 Pond Lane, Syosset, New York 11030

As usual, festivities begin at noon so bring your ly sees
(red envelopes), you married ones, and for all those single
kids out there, wear something red with lots of pockets
to collect all your pocket money!

Don't forget to bring your appetites
and your recipes!

Please RSVP Pau Pau or Gung Gung
as soon as possible! See you all there!

Epilogue

FOR EVERY time her grandmother made Lin cringe or wince or wish that she could shrivel up and die, there was a time when she felt blessed to have her dictating her every move. There was a certain comfort in being able to relinquish control of her seesaw life and retreat to the security of being a child in her *pau pau*'s eyes. Sitting in her family's kitchen, Lin couldn't help but feel content as she struggled to knead the perfect crescent for her grandmother's legendary shrimp and pork dumplings. She only wished she could keep up with the staccato commands of the elderly—but no less dominating—matriarch.

"*Bawk dee! Bawk dee!* Thinner! Thinner!" Ling exhorted her to attain that impossibly delicate, paper-thin shell for the savory meat mixture she was stirring in a nearby pot.

Lin wiped her brow and sneaked a peek at the clock above the kitchen sink. Thankfully, it was almost noon. She'd been at her grandmother's beck and call since six that morning. While she'd always loved being in her family's cluttered, warmly lit house—always so full of delicious delicacies and mah-jong thrills—she was starting to feel the effects of too much cooking and too little caffeine. Fortunately, her mother was slated to relieve her at noon. Lin's stomach growled as she took in the aroma of the last batch of piping hot dumplings—her favorite New Year delicacy—that her *pau pau* had set out on the counter to cool. Deciding that she'd earned herself a treat, Lin reached out to grab one.

"*Mai sic!* Don't eat!" Her grandmother swatted her and whisked the dumplings away.

Lin sighed, eyeing the heaping dishes of food around her wistfully—the fragrant black bean jai vegetarian dish, the succulent garlic and scallion lobster, the tantalizing red bean paste puffs. There was nothing worse than cooking on an empty stomach.

As Lin contemplated the feast before her, Kim came in and started smoothing Lin's hair. "The guests will arrive any minute. Put on something pretty for once!"

Lin made a face and tried to pull away, just as she did when she was five. Of course, Kim only took this as further incentive to start criticizing Lin's hair, shoes, the very tint of her lip gloss. Fortunately, at that moment, the doorbell rang. Lin was out of her chair like a shot.

"I'll get it!" she sang out as she sprinted to the door.

The first set of visitors to arrive was her father and her aunt Betty. Lin hugged them then quickly composed herself to impart the traditional New Year's greeting.

"*Gung hai fat choi,*" she said. "Happy New Year," she repeated in English. "Where are my red envelopes?"

"*Gung hai fat choi,*" her aunt responded as she pushed the requisite red envelopes into Lin's hand, "but you forgot '*Sun ty geen hong.*' Have good health."

Lin nodded dutifully and fingered the envelopes just as she'd always done as a kid. It was crazy how excited she still got about the twenty bucks, especially given her current salary. But there was nothing like the feel of the red paper and the telltale bulge within to get her as giddy as she'd been when she was a child.

"Lin!"

Lin turned around and broke into a smile when she saw M.J. and her mother, Esther, at the door, with Ming and his fiancée, May, just behind. Lin hurried over to give them hugs.

"*Gung hai fat choi!*" she greeted them.

"Yeah, yeah, Happy New Year," M.J. said as she sailed in, while Ming and May opted for more traditional New Year greetings. Esther took Lin's face in one hand while she pressed a red envelope into her palm.

"You being a good girl, Lin? Still making a lot of money?"

Lin nodded. Satisfied, Esther clucked something at M.J. before taking off to find Lin's mother and grandmother. Lin shot M.J. an apologetic look, but her friend brushed it off with a shake of her head.

"So where's your dad?" Lin asked as she took everyone's coats.

"Oh, he'll be by later," M.J. replied. "He had a crazy morning."

Lin raised an eyebrow. "How so?"

"M.J. brought the white guy home." Ming wiggled his eyebrows. "I think her dad is still recovering from the whole thing right now. Her mom only came with us so she could tell your mother all about it, Lin."

M.J. smacked his arm. "That's not what happened, Ming." She turned to Lin. "Jagger did meet my folks, but they were actually semi-okay with it. Basically, if I stay off 'Page Six,' they'll be willing to put up with everything else." She rubbed her chin. "In a strange way, he's the perfect person to deal with them because it doesn't matter what they say or do—nothing offends him. It's water off his back."

"You say that now," Ming said, "but wait until your mom gets you alone. Then you'll get it."

M.J. rolled her eyes.

May gave Ming a warning nudge. "Now, Ming," she said, "you promised to behave."

"That's right." M.J. jumped at the possibility of reinforcements. "That's the only reason I agreed to let you meet Jagger—because you swore to keep an open mind about him."

"Yeah, yeah," Ming said airily, "so where's the white boy anyway?"

"He'll be here in a bit." M.J. chewed her lower lip. "He said he had to go home and get his Jet Li T-shirt."

Ming's eyes widened. "That is exactly the kind of thing I'm talking about," he exclaimed. "The white man raping and pillaging the Asian culture—" Fortunately, May dragged Ming away to the dining room before he could say any more.

M.J. shook her head and turned back to Lin. "I hope introducing Drew to your family wasn't as bad as that."

Lin sighed. "Pretty much everything involving Drew was bad."

"Aw, Lin." M.J. slipped her arm around her friend. "You're so much better off without him, ya know. I mean, look at Kevin—Auntie Lee was totally right about him."

Lin nodded emphatically. "I know." Still, she couldn't help wondering when she'd meet her own Jagger.

"I know just what you need," M.J. declared, "a good, old-fashioned pigging-out. And we can start right now, with some of your grandmother's delicious red bean puffs." She reached out to grab one of the delicacies—and upended the entire plate. The bean puffs crashed and scattered onto the floor. M.J. and Lin both winced.

"Uh-oh," M.J. said, "I better grab the broom before your grandmother comes in—"

"No!" Lin gasped. "No brooms! It's Chinese New Year—brooms are bad luck, remember? My grandmother will say we're sweeping our good luck away!" And if there was one thing the fortune-teller had been right about, it was Lin's luck.

M.J. gazed at the mess. "I hope you're not suggesting that I eat what's on the floor."

"Don't be ridiculous." Lin knelt down and started picking up the pastry pieces with a napkin. "See, we don't need a broom—"

At that moment, the doorbell rang again. M.J. seized the opportunity to leave Lin to clean up and went to answer the door. This time, it was Alex and her folks. Lin finished disposing of the food and quickly got up, smiling. Her friend looked great—there was a glow to her cheeks, a certain lightness in her walk that had appeared in the past couple months. Lin was sure it had something to do with Brady, but of course, Alex would never admit to it.

"Alex!" M.J. and Lin both shouted.

Alex exhaled as her parents quickly went to join their friends. "Thank God!" She shook her head. "We just went to my aunt's house to wish her happy New Year, and she started telling me about these Asian 'love boats' where singles go on this cruise ship to meet a wife or husband—like the ones for college kids but older. As if I would ever go on one of these things! But you know what the worst thing was? My parents were totally in on it. The minute my aunt started talking, they were mysteriously nowhere to be found!"

Lin and M.J. chuckled.

"I told you," Lin said. "Your parents may be afraid to say anything to your face, but they are no different from any other Chinese parents."

Alex sighed. "I'm just grateful they haven't met the guy I'm actually involved with. Who knows what they would say then?"

"Well," Lin slyly slung an arm around M.J., "our girl J just did that this very morning. And now she's bringing him to his first family gathering—here, tonight, in this very house!"

M.J. blushed.

Alex stared at her incredulously. "You invited Jagger here?" she said. "Are you insane?"

"Well," M.J. shifted uncomfortably, "I—"

"This is going to be great!" Alex exclaimed. "I can't wait to sit back and watch the show. M.J., you have more guts than I ever gave you credit for—"

She was abruptly interrupted by the familiar ring of the doorbell. M.J. bit her lip. Shooting her a quick smile, Lin went to answer the door . . . and found herself face-to-face with a compact Billy Joe Armstrong look-alike in a Jet Li silk-screened T-shirt and bright red Skechers. Jagger.

"Lin, right?" he said. "I think we met a long time ago at Serafina's."

Behind Lin, Alex snorted. "You don't sound sure," she called over Lin's shoulder. "I guess we Asians all look alike."

Jagger chuckled. "Nice to see you again, too, Alex." He turned to Lin. "She's wrong, you know. I remember you. Besides, I would never confuse you with Alex—M.J. said you were the nice one."

"Hey!" Alex managed to look both offended and pleased at the comment.

Jagger laughed as he winked at M.J. "Hey, babe."

Alex turned away with a dismissive wave. "Better take care of your guest, Lin."

"That's 'guests,'" a voice behind Jagger rang out.

Jagger turned and they all peered around him to see—Brady. Studying the dapper newcomer closely, Lin couldn't help thinking that this was the unexpected man Auntie Lee had told Alex about.

Brady smiled rakishly at the girls and then at Alex. "Hey, Alexa."

"Brady?" Alex staggered back. "What—what are you doing here?"

"Oh, I called your parents' house earlier today, and they told me that you guys would all be here this afternoon, so I figured I'd come over and wish my favorite litigator a happy New Year."

Alex shook her head. "I can't believe it," she muttered. "First the love boat, and now my parents have sold me out to my partner."

Brady strolled over and slung an arm around her neck. "Alex, it's okay—you don't need to play hard to get anymore."

Alex made a face, but she didn't push him away. Lin observed all this with an interested eye, thinking that her friend was protesting just a little too much.

"So," Jagger said after giving M.J. a very boyfriendly kiss, "you're Alex's dude, huh?"

Brady turned toward him. "Yeah, I guess you could say that."

For a moment, the two of them just studied each other, Jagger in his tattered jeans and Brady in his crisply tailored blazer.

Finally, Brady held out his hand. "I'm Brady."

Jagger shook it. "Jagger."

Lin exhaled, not realizing until that moment that she'd been holding her breath. Alex and M.J. looked at each other and wiped their brows in mock relief.

"Well," Lin said gaily, "come on in—you guys are all welcome. Just leave your shoes by the door—"

"What? Now there's two of them?"

They all turned. Ming stood there, hands on his waist.

"All right, Ming," M.J. stepped forward, "before you get on your high horse—"

"Ming? Is that you?" Jagger asked.

Ming blinked. The girls stared as Jagger and Ming stepped forward—and embraced.

"Ming, man!" Jagger high-fived Ming exuberantly. "I haven't seen you since we got snowed in at the T-wolves game two years ago!"

"Don't remind me!" Ming chuckled. "We were stuck in that god-awful city for three whole days before we could get a flight out."

"Hey, you still have that cheesehead hat?"

"Somewhere probably. What about you?"

"Sitting in my office as we speak." Jagger turned to M.J. "This guy and I spent a lot of time in the Mall of America during those three days, and there was the coolest store that only sold cheeseheads—I guess because it's so close to Wisconsin."

M.J. stared at them, befuddled. "So you guys—know each other?"

"Oh, we go way back," Jagger assured her, "before you and I ever met, M.J." He turned back to Ming. "Hey, Ming, I want you to meet Brady. Brady, this is Ming Chan."

Ming shook Brady's hand. "Nice to meet you."

M.J. couldn't believe it. Who was this stranger? And what had he done to Ming?

"I read your column every day," Brady said.

Ming beamed. "Oh, yeah? What did you think of yesterday's?"

"It was right on. I've been saying for years that Floyd Greene is overrated—the Magic should just trade him while they can get someone decent."

"Thanks, man," Ming said. "Hey, why don't we go into the kitchen and grab a few beers? My fiancée's helping set the table right now, so there'll be plenty to eat soon."

Jagger clapped Ming on the shoulder. "You're a good man, Ming." And with that, all three guys strolled off toward the kitchen.

"Okay." M.J. rubbed her eyes. "Did I just hallucinate all of that or did we manage to get through the intros without any blood-shed?"

"Nope," Lin confirmed, "a miracle has happened."

"Well, I'm just glad that I won't be the only one introducing a white boy to her parents." M.J. slyly elbowed Alex.

Alex scowled. "My parents are in such big trouble."

"But I thought you said nothing happened in Vegas," Lin said innocently.

Alex looked heavenward. "Nothing did!"

"Well, I don't know about you," M.J. commented, "but my Ve-gas flings don't usually show up out of the blue at my Chinese New Year parties."

"That's true," Alex acknowledged. "Your fling just turns out to be Ming's long-lost Minneapolis buddy!"

Lin chuckled. "And here I thought Ming hated white guys."

The girls all burst into giggles.

"Yeah, all we need now is for Drew Black to show up," M.J. said slyly.

Lin shuddered. "Please, let's not ruin the New Year already. What do you say we go and do some toasting of our own?"

Alex grinned. "Sounds like a plan."

They headed for the kitchen, where they ran smack into Ming, Jagger, and Brady.

"Hey, girls," Jagger called out.

"Well, aren't you three a cozy trio," Alex remarked. "I guess this is what they call male bonding. What are you going to do now— watch hoops together?"

The guys exchanged looks. Then as one, they all headed toward the living room. M.J. and Alex glanced at each other—and hurried after them.

Watching them, Lin smiled as she pondered how Auntie Lee's

prophecies had come true for her friends. It was too bad hers had somehow gone awry, she thought as she went to check the refrigerator for any alcoholic beverage she could find.

"Lin?"

Lin glanced up and almost banged her head into the refrigerator door. Stephen?

"Lin," Stephen stepped forward, "it's so great to see you again."

"Same here," she managed as she hugged him, feeling a surprising flutter in her chest. "I have to admit—you caught me off guard."

"You mean you weren't expecting to see me in your kitchen?" Stephen joked. "Believe me, I'm really not stalking you. I ran into your grandmother yesterday when I was in Chinatown, and she invited me over."

Lin blushed. "I would never think you were stalking me, Stephen. I'm just . . . a little startled."

"So hey, we didn't really get a chance to talk at your aunt's house. How's your job?" Stephen asked. "Still raking in the money?"

Lin stared at him. Since when did Stephen become interested in her career?

"Yeah, work's good," she said casually. "How have you been?"

"Good," he responded. "I've actually been on a sabbatical of sorts—I spent three months traveling around Asia and Australia."

Lin clapped a hand to her mouth. "Omigosh! That sounds amazing! I've always wanted to spend some time over there."

"It was pretty cool." He nodded. "The best was when I was in Tibet—"

As Stephen went on to describe his travels, Lin took the opportunity to study him surreptitiously. Now that she wasn't so distracted by the karaoke, she noticed he looked surprisingly lean and wiry in his Diesel jeans and black Che Guevara T-shirt.

"—so anyway, some of the pictures I took are actually being shown at a gallery downtown," Stephen continued. "Maybe we can go see them sometime."

Lin smiled. "I would really like that."

Stephen looked a little taken aback, but then he smiled as well. He nodded at the refrigerator. "What are you looking for in there?"

"I was hoping to find a Sapporo at least," she whispered, taking a furtive glance around, "but it looks like we might be out."

"Hmm." Stephen gazed toward the living room. "What do you say we sneak out for a beer run in a little bit? I think your grandmother's getting ready to play mah-jong."

Lin stared at him. Who was this stranger with the cool, relaxed air, so willing to break the rules? Was Stephen always like this? Or was she looking at him with new eyes? Thinking back to her conversation with Kim in London, Lin thought that perhaps, for the first time, she was seeing Stephen for who he truly was—and not who she imagined him to be through her family-colored lenses. After all, what was wrong with a little stability? Having spent the past year on a roller coaster of emotions, Lin realized that she liked being on solid ground.

"Okay." She smiled. "That sounds like a fantastic idea."

Stephen beamed at her. "Great. I'll go do some reconnaissance and come back to get you." He started to walk out then stopped. Turning back to Lin, he leaned over and gently kissed her on the cheek. "It's good to see you again," he said softly. And then he was gone.

Lin exhaled. Of all the crazy, bizarre things that had happened so far that day, this had to take the cake. But then . . . could Auntie Lee have been right after all?

"Is that who I think it is?" Lin turned around to see M.J. and Alex staring at her from the kitchen doorway.

"Yes," she blushed, "that was Stephen."

Alex gave Lin a funny look. "Have you been talking to him all this time? When we saw him at karaoke, you didn't want to have anything to do with him!"

"Yeah," M.J. teased. "You two looked pretty cozy to me. . . ."

"Guys, guys." Lin shook her head. "We were just getting reacquainted. Nothing wrong with that."

"Uh-huh." M.J. raised an eyebrow. "At this moment, I think Jagger is giving Stephen orders for the kind of beer he wants."

"What?" Lin gasped as she headed toward the living room. The other girls followed on her heels.

Sure enough, Stephen was there chatting it up with Jagger, Brady, and Ming as they watched a Knicks game playing on TV.

"Did I just walk into an episode of *The Twilight Zone?*" Alex rubbed her eyes. "They look like they're all actually getting along."

"I figured Jagger would last all of two minutes in here," M.J. remarked. "Or that he and Ming would be embroiled in some celebrity death match by now."

She had no sooner uttered the words before they were interrupted by a crash in the corner. The girls turned to see the guys hurrying over to pick up some pillows and Ling's Buddhist lamp.

"Ohmigosh, is Jagger teaching Stephen how to shoot a jump shot with my grandmother's pillow?" Lin clutched her head. "She better not walk in right now."

Alex grabbed her arm. "I know what will make you feel better." She walked over to the kitchen and picked up a bottle of wine from the counter. "Let's have a drink."

"That's a great idea," M.J. said quickly.

As Lin whisked out the glasses, Alex carefully poured each of the girls some wine. Looking at them, Lin felt a sudden rush of love for her friends. It had been a long, tough year for all of them. But the fortune-teller had been right. Alex had experienced a life-changing event with Brady! And J had gotten what she wanted—both a chance with Kevin and a shot at her sportscaster dreams—and found that maybe those things weren't so important after all. And as for Lin, well, she did have luck. And as for love—well, who knew? After all, Stephen was the last person she expected to see today. . . .

They paused as M.J. gave the toast.

"To the New Year," M.J. announced, "may we have new adventures."

"I'll drink to that," Alex said, raising her glass.

"That reminds me," Lin interrupted. "I have a surprise for us. Guess where we're going tomorrow?"

"I CAN'T believe we're here again," M.J. said.

"I can't believe a whole year has passed already," Alex added.

"Well, believe it," Lin replied, "we said we would come back, so here we are."

The girls all gazed around at the familiar red incense-filled room of Auntie Lee's parlor. It looked exactly as it had a year ago—as if time itself stood still there.

"What do you think she'll tell us this time?" Alex wondered.

"Well, I gotta say she ended up being pretty right about me last year," M.J. said.

Lin fiddled with her diamond hoop earrings. "I just hope this year turns out to be smoother than last—"

"You've returned."

They looked up as Auntie Lee toddled into the room. Like her parlor, she looked exactly as she did the last time they saw her—tiny and inscrutable.

"Hello, Auntie Lee," Lin began. "We came—"

"I know why you come," the fortune-teller interrupted. "You wish to know your fates for the New Year. Let me look at your faces, children, and I will tell you all. . . ."

The girls just grinned at each other as they drew closer to Auntie Lee.